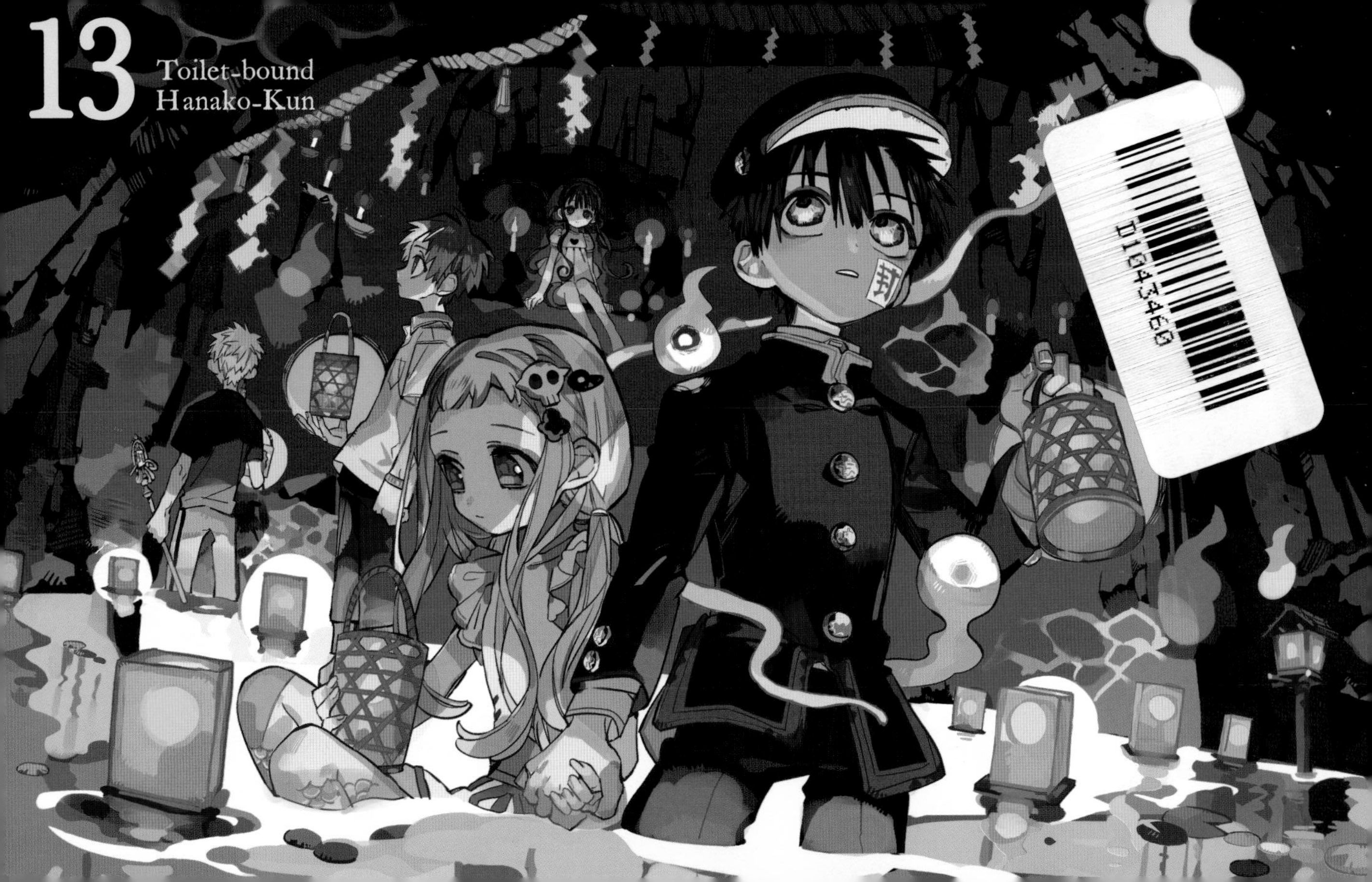
13
Toilet-bound
Hanako-Kun

Contents

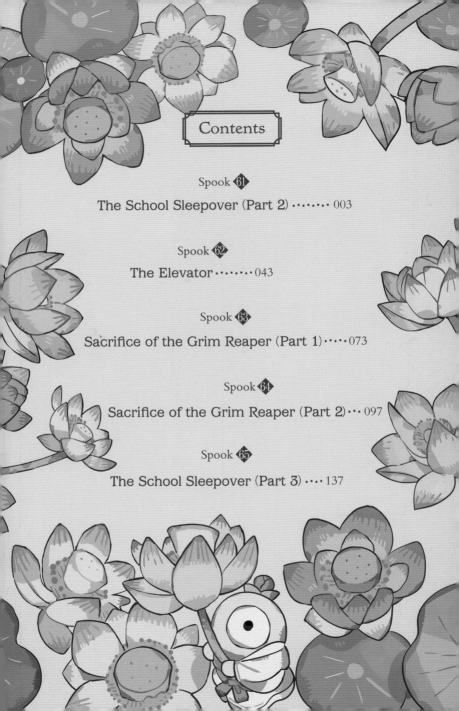

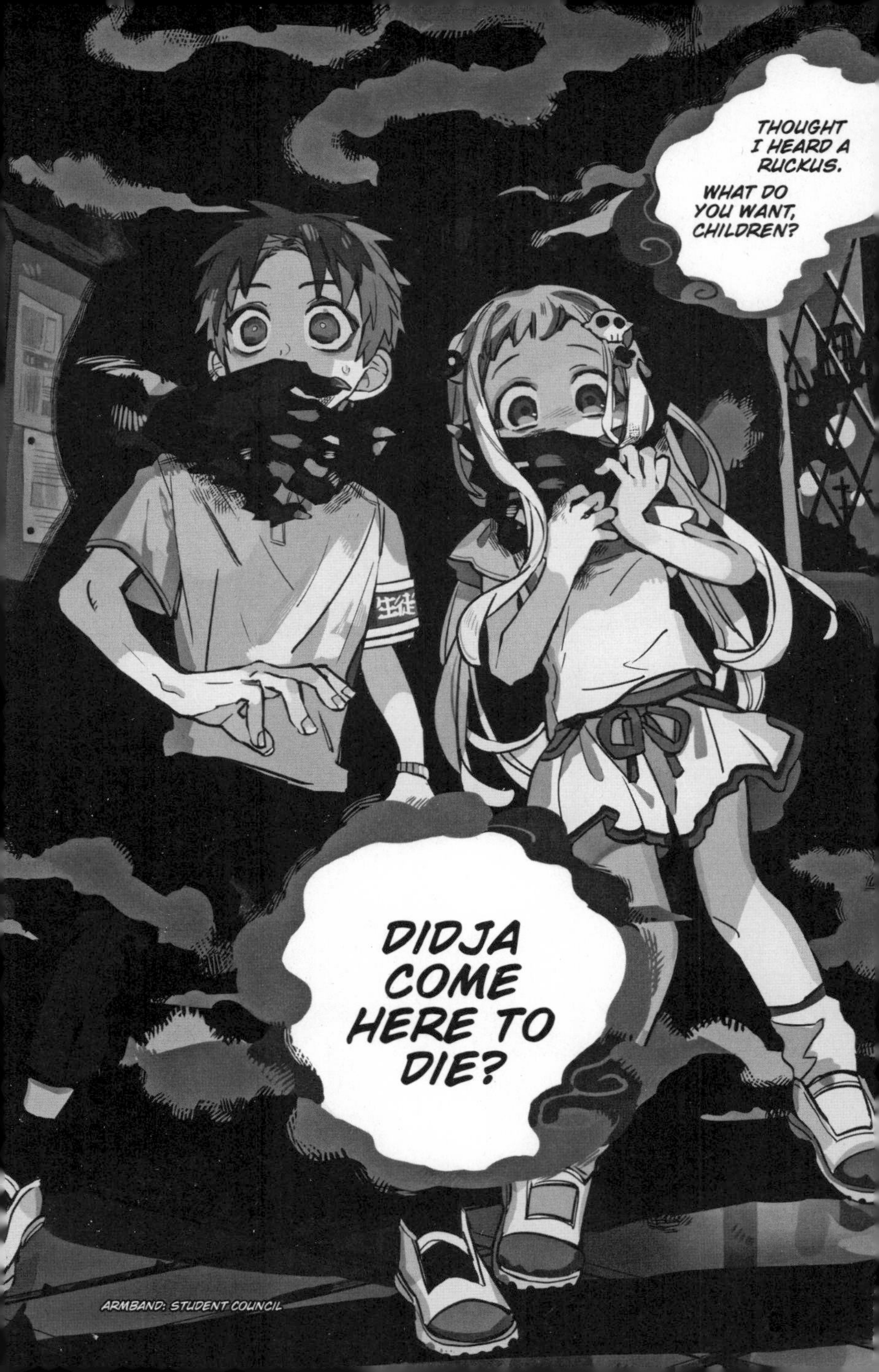
THOUGHT I HEARD A RUCKUS.
WHAT DO YOU WANT, CHILDREN?
DIDJA COME HERE TO DIE?
ARMBAND: STUDENT COUNCIL

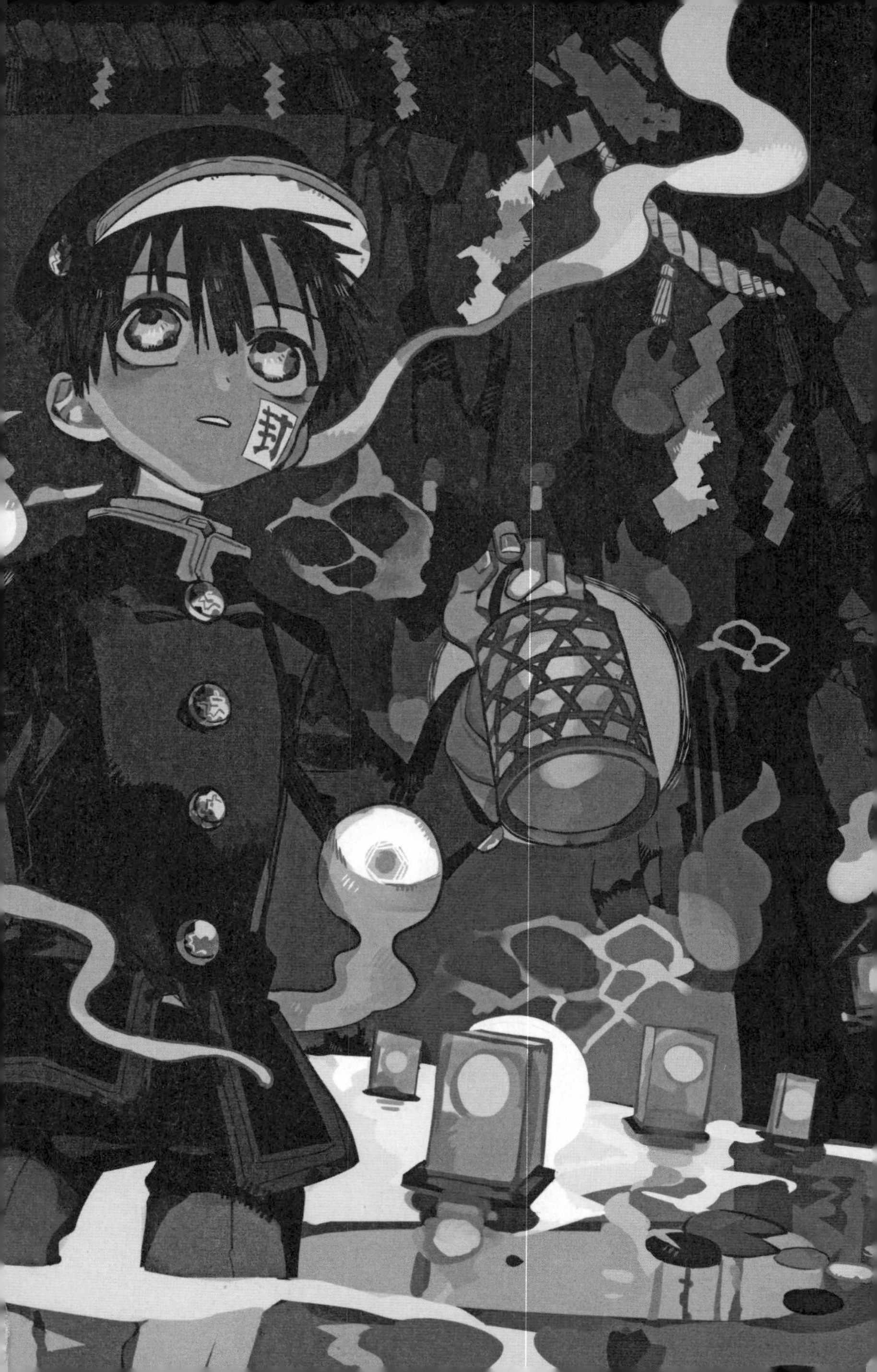
封

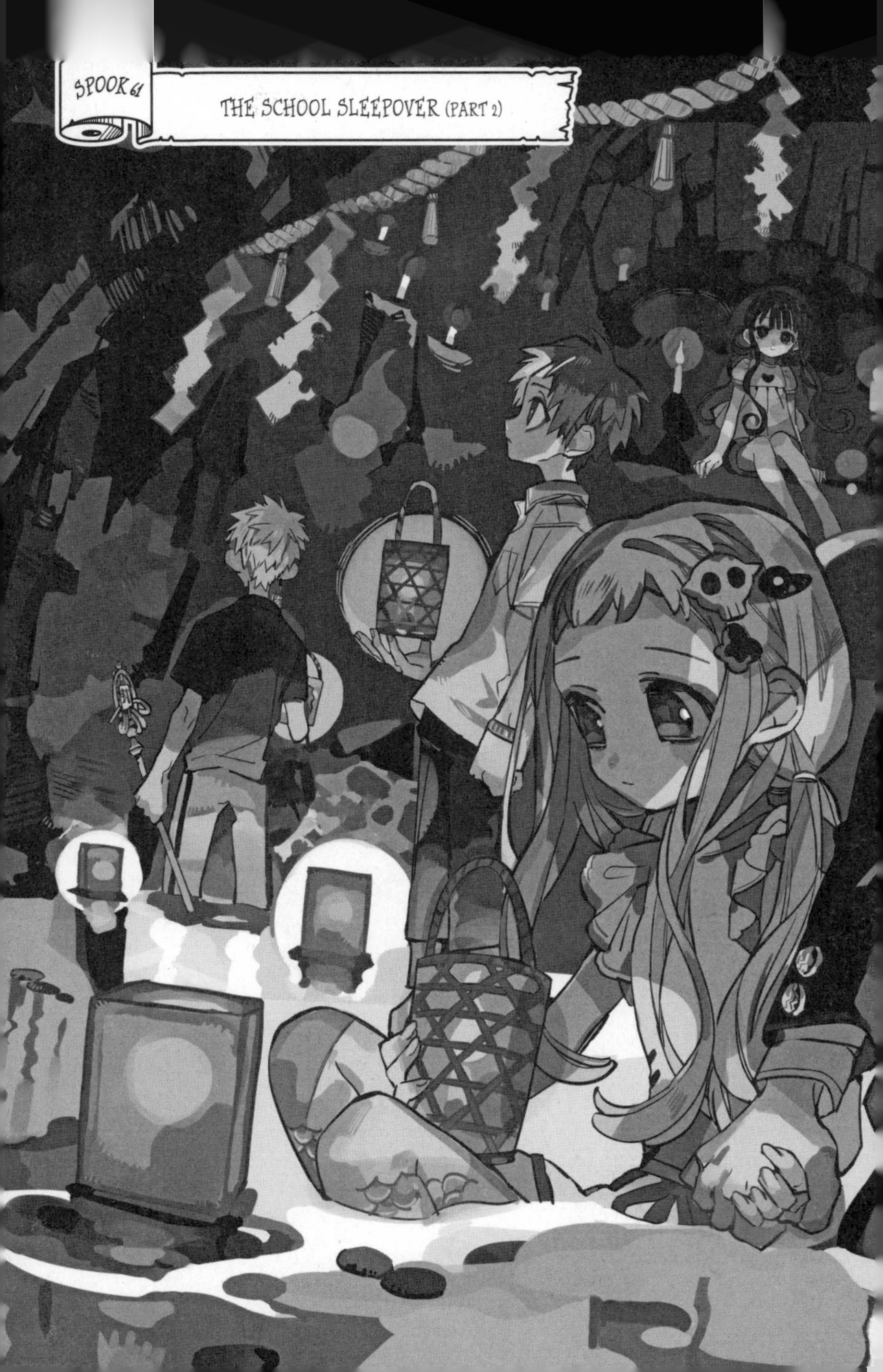
SPOOK 61
THE SCHOOL SLEEPOVER (PART 2)

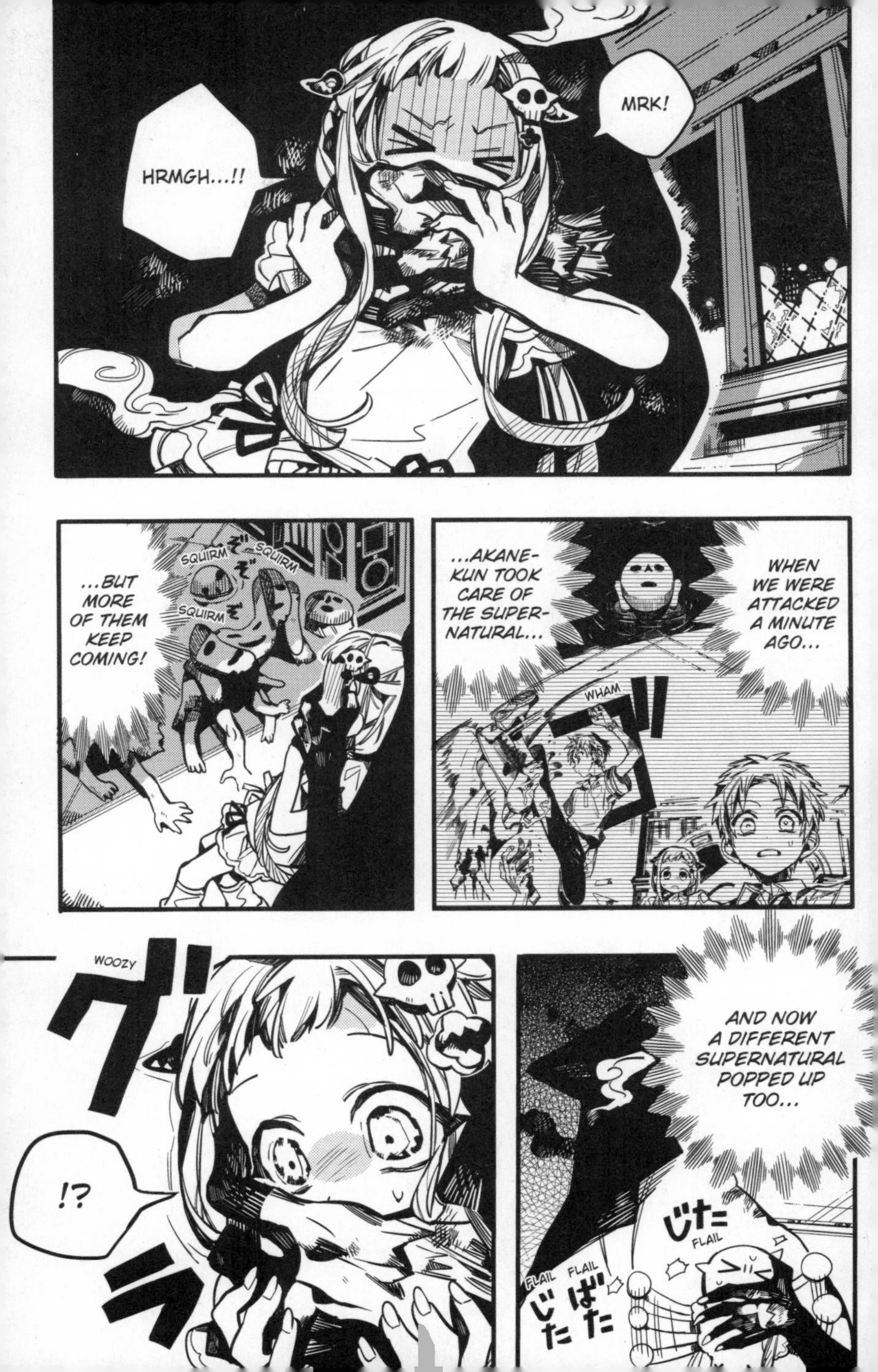

MRK!
HRMGH...!!
WHEN WE WERE ATTACKED A MINUTE AGO...
...AKANE-KUN TOOK CARE OF THE SUPER-NATURAL...
WHAM
SQUIRM
SQUIRM
SQUIRM
...BUT MORE OF THEM KEEP COMING!
AND NOW A DIFFERENT SUPERNATURAL POPPED UP TOO...
じた
FLAIL
FLAIL
ばた
FLAIL
じた
WOOZY
グラ
!?

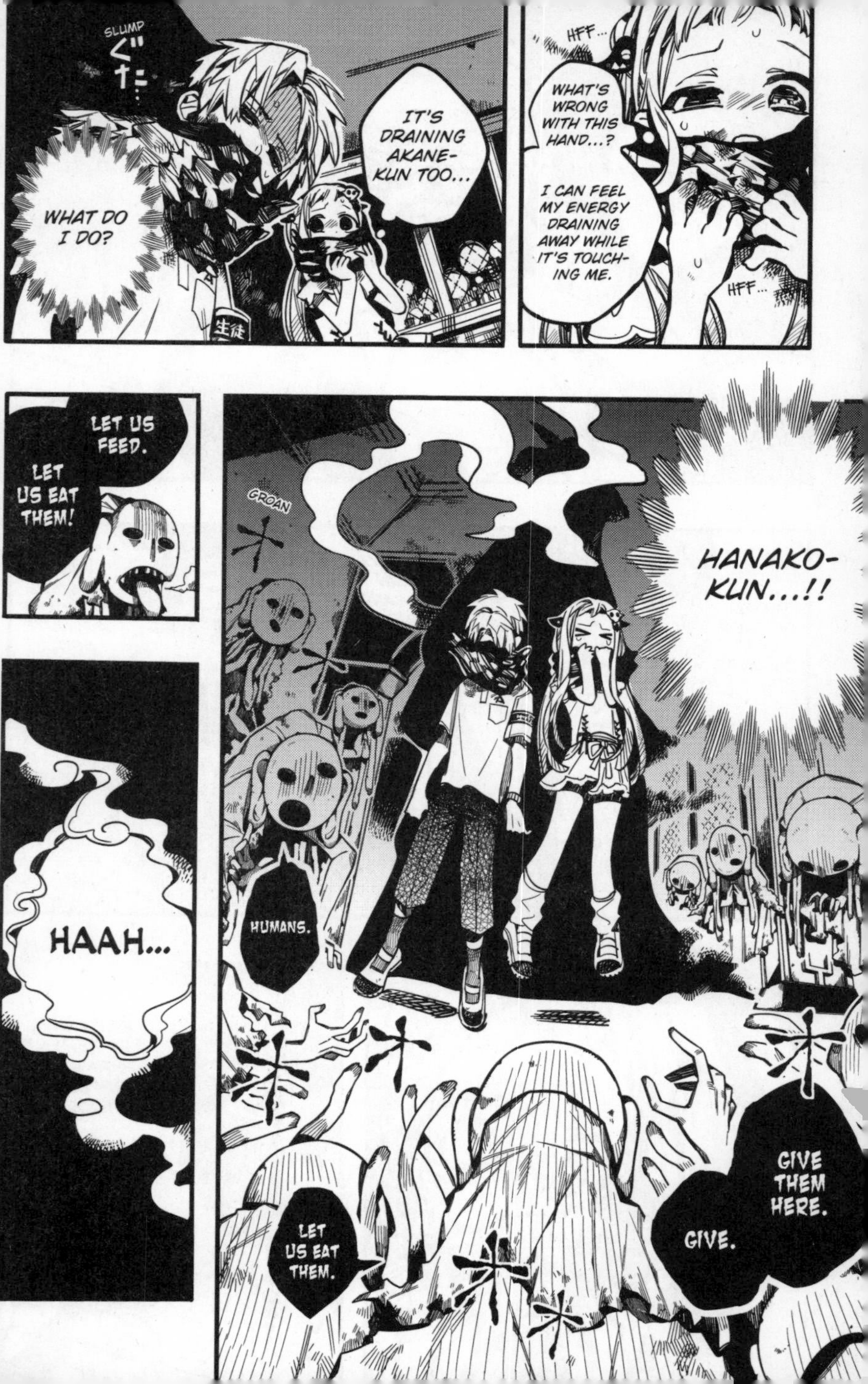
HFF...
WHAT'S WRONG WITH THIS HAND...?
I CAN FEEL MY ENERGY DRAINING AWAY WHILE IT'S TOUCHING ME.
HFF...
IT'S DRAINING AKANE-KUN TOO...
SLUMP
WHAT DO I DO?
HANAKO-KUN...!!
GROAN
HUMANS.
GIVE THEM HERE.
GIVE.
LET US EAT THEM.
LET US FEED.
LET US EAT THEM!
HAAH...

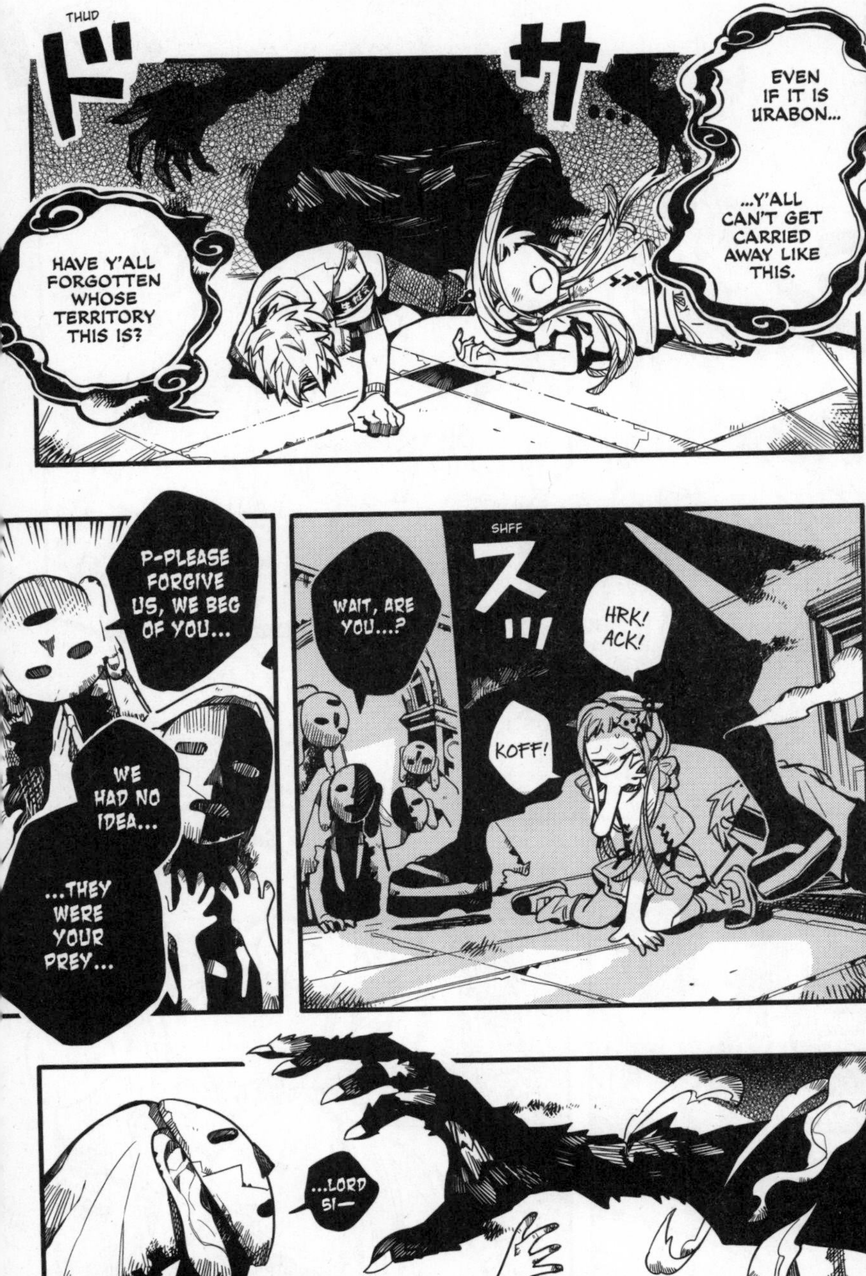
THUD
EVEN IF IT IS URABON...
...Y'ALL CAN'T GET CARRIED AWAY LIKE THIS.
HAVE Y'ALL FORGOTTEN WHOSE TERRITORY THIS IS?
SHFF
HRK! ACK!
KOFF!
WAIT, ARE YOU...?
P-PLEASE FORGIVE US, WE BEG OF YOU...
WE HAD NO IDEA...
...THEY WERE YOUR PREY...
...LORD SI—

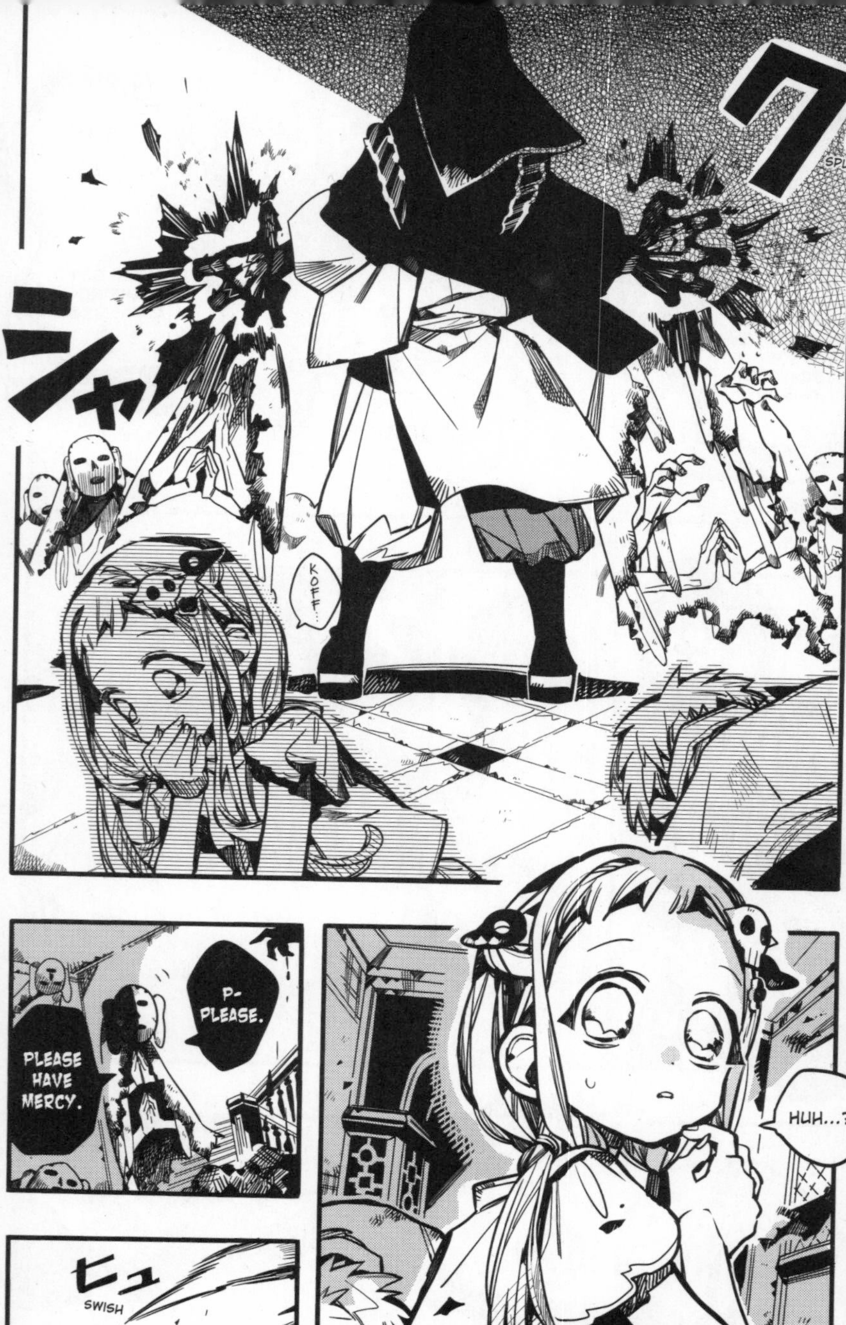
ワ
SPLURCH
シャ
KOFF...
HUH...?
P-PLEASE.
PLEASE HAVE MERCY.
ヒュ
SWISH

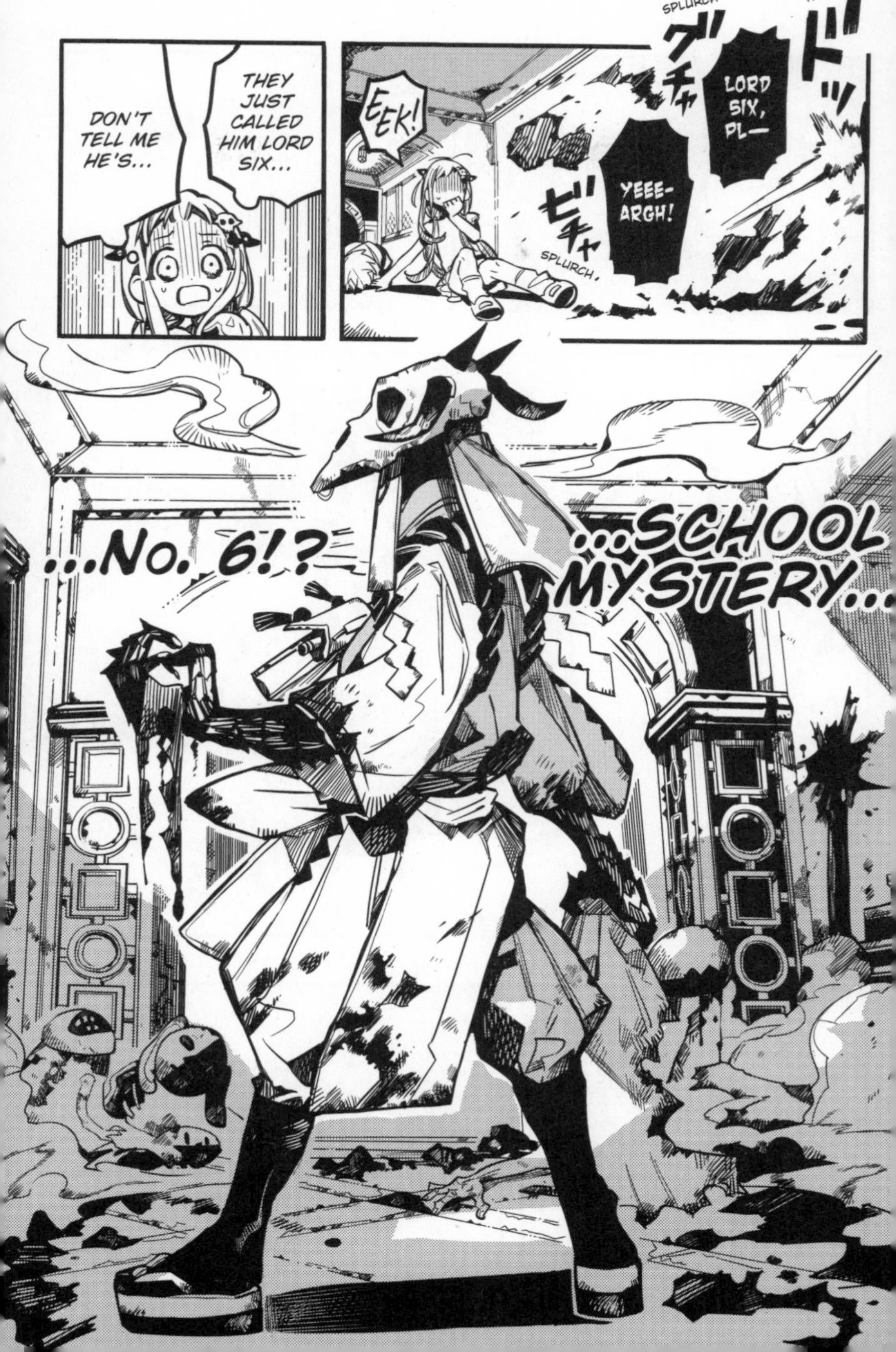

THUMP
ドッ
SPLURCH
グチャ
LORD SIX, PL—
YEEE-ARGH!
ビチャ
SPLURCH
EEK!
THEY JUST CALLED HIM LORD SIX...
DON'T TELL ME HE'S...
...SCHOOL MYSTERY...
...No. 6!?

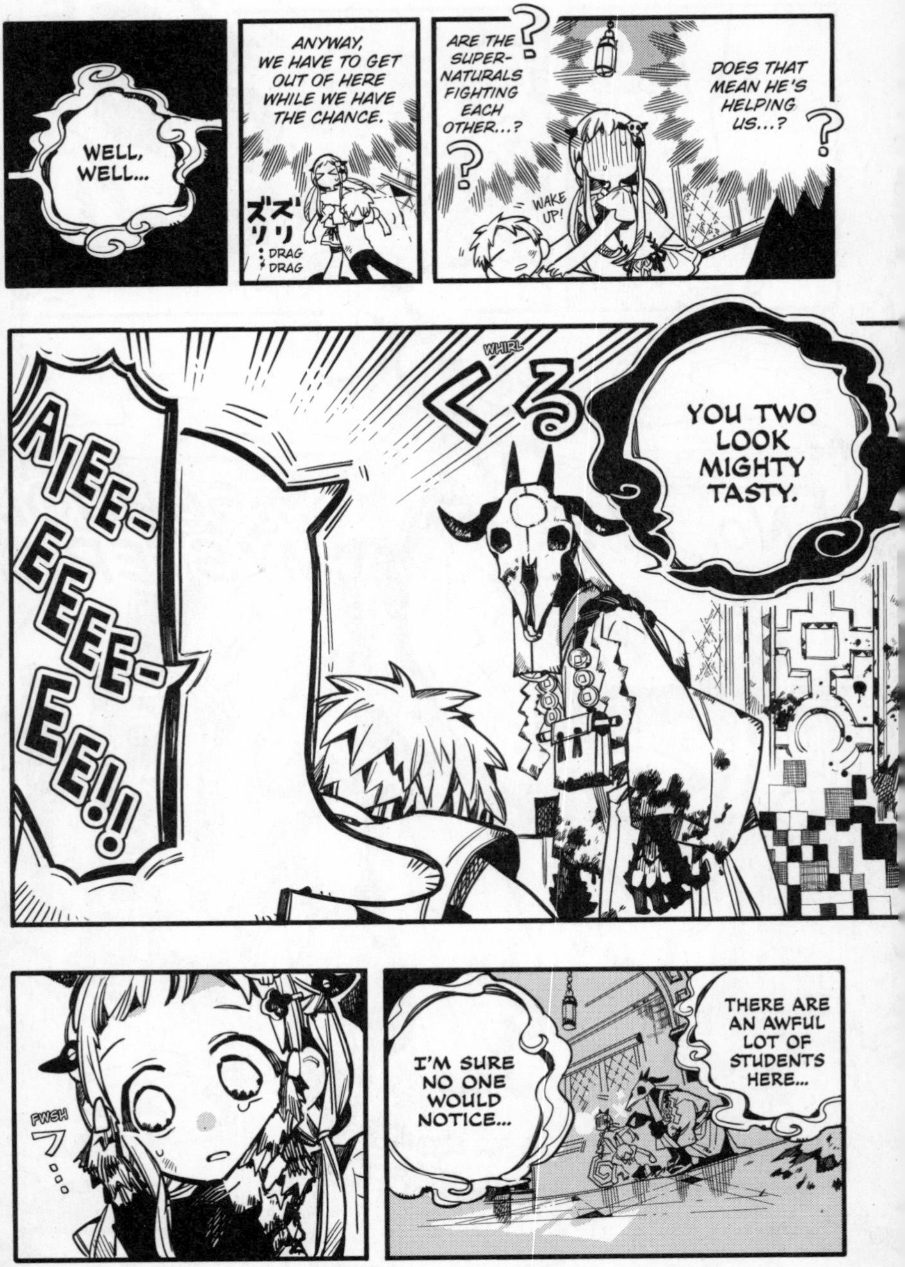
DOES THAT MEAN HE'S HELPING US...?
ARE THE SUPER-NATURALS FIGHTING EACH OTHER...?
WAKE UP!
ANYWAY, WE HAVE TO GET OUT OF HERE WHILE WE HAVE THE CHANCE.
ズリズリ
DRAG DRAG
WELL, WELL...
YOU TWO LOOK MIGHTY TASTY.
くる
WHIRL
AIEEE-EEEE-EE!!
THERE ARE AN AWFUL LOT OF STUDENTS HERE...
I'M SURE NO ONE WOULD NOTICE...
FWSH
フ

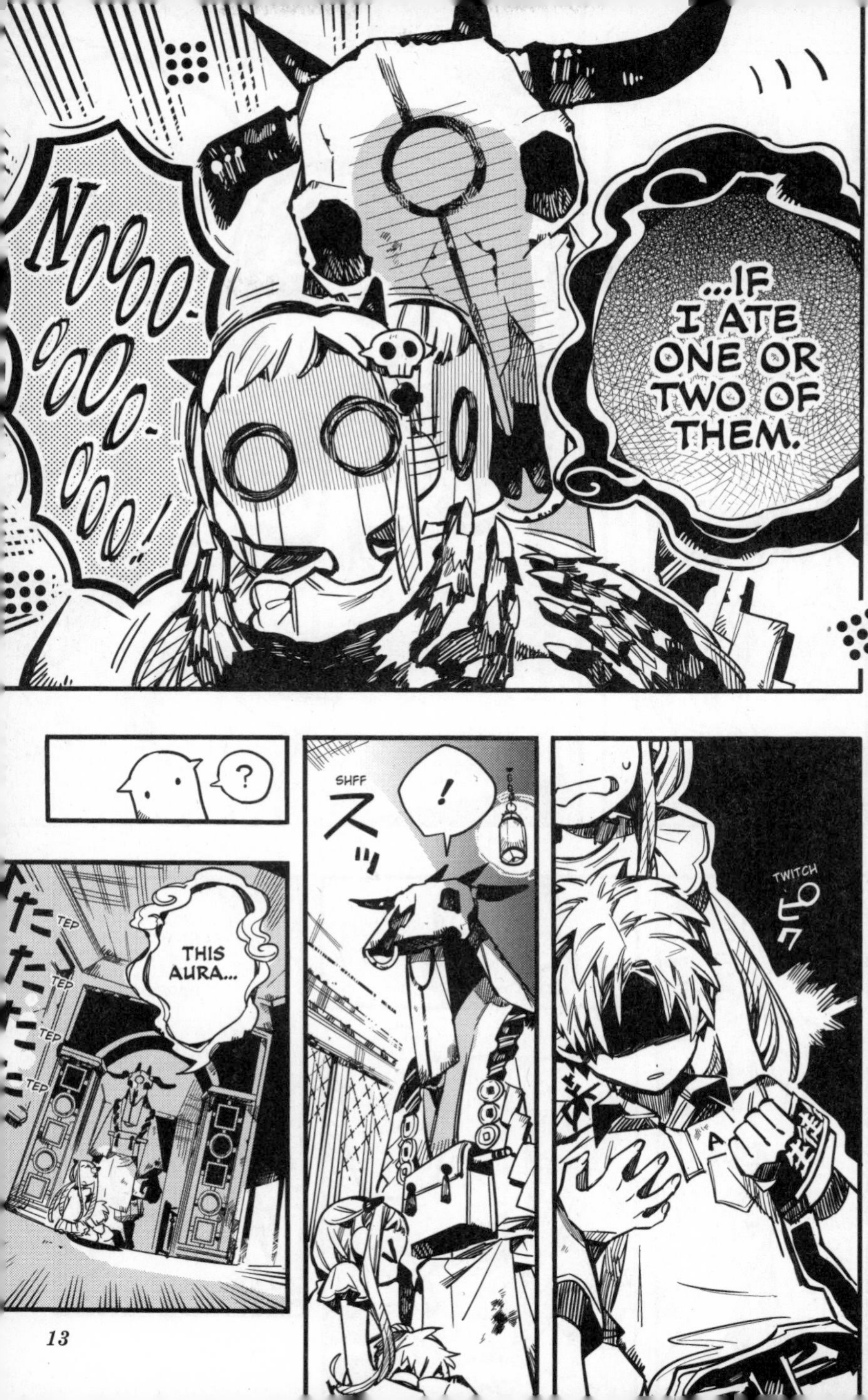

...IF I ATE ONE OR TWO OF THEM.
NOOOO-OOOO-OOOO-OOOO..!
TWITCH
SHFF
!
?
TEP
TEP
TEP
TEP
THIS AURA...

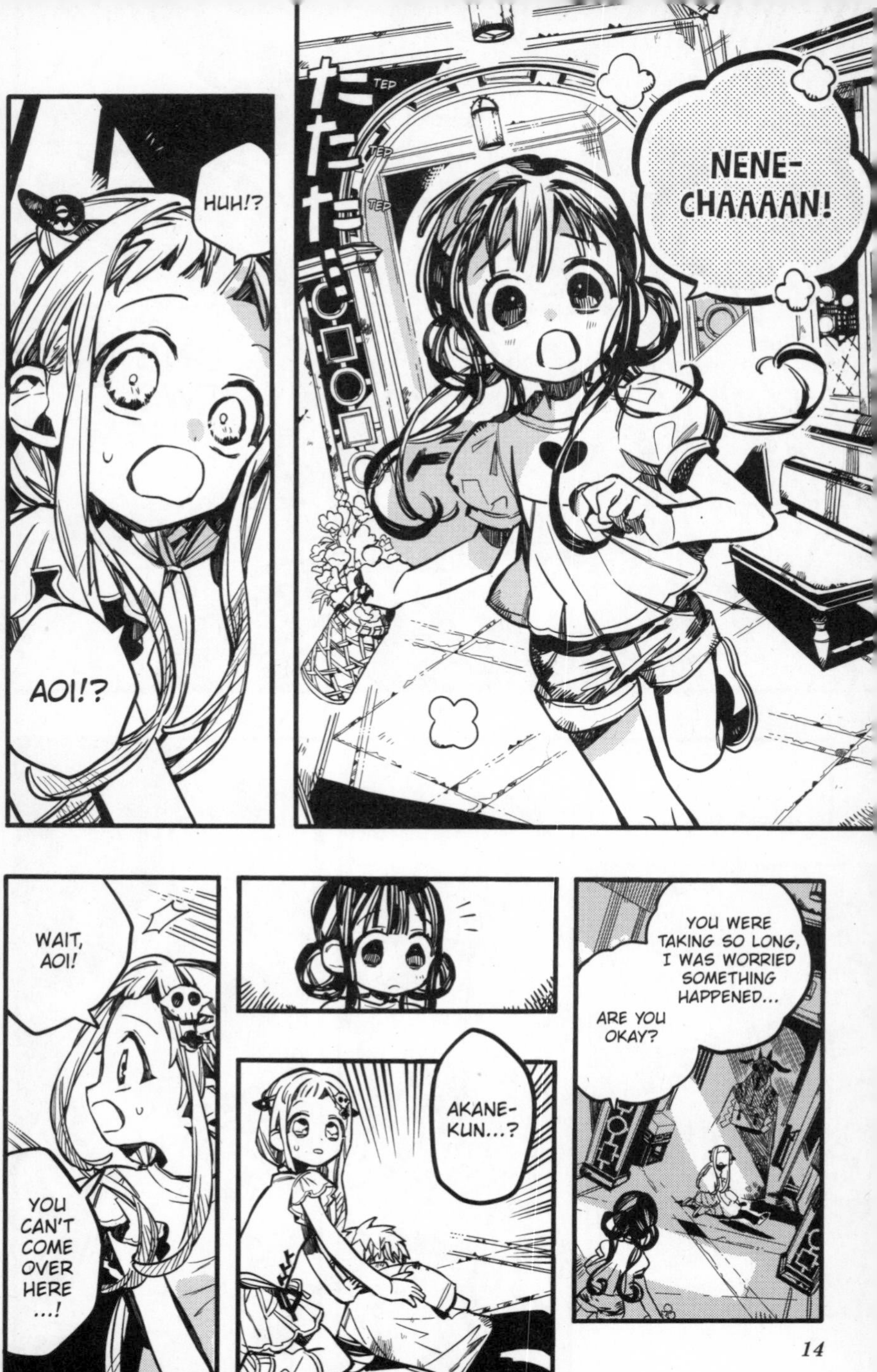
たたた
TEP
TEP
TEP
NENE-CHAAAAN!
HUH!?
AOI!?
YOU WERE TAKING SO LONG, I WAS WORRIED SOMETHING HAPPENED...
ARE YOU OKAY?
AKANE-KUN...?
WAIT, AOI!
YOU CAN'T COME OVER HERE...!

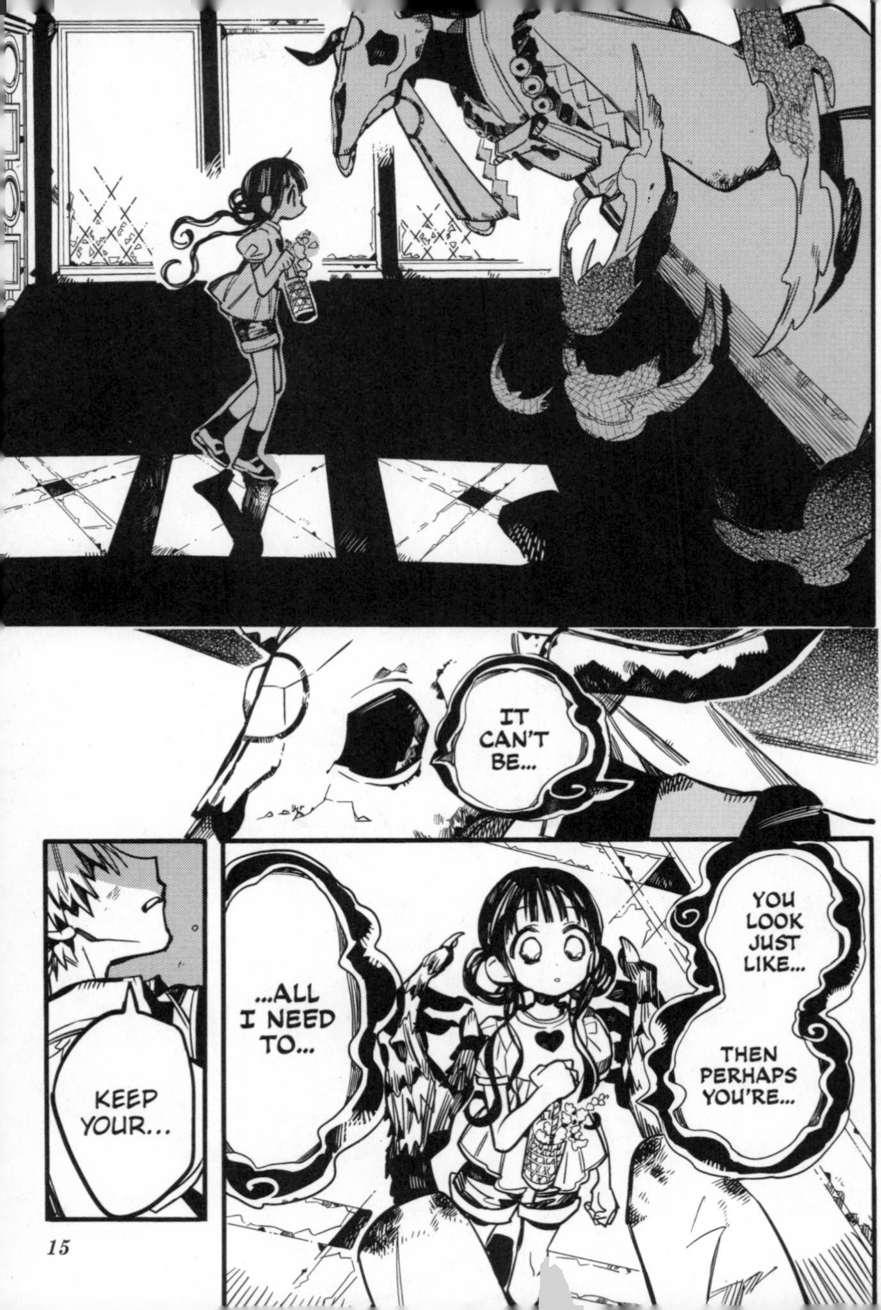
IT CAN'T BE...
YOU LOOK JUST LIKE...
THEN PERHAPS YOU'RE...
...ALL I NEED TO...
KEEP YOUR…

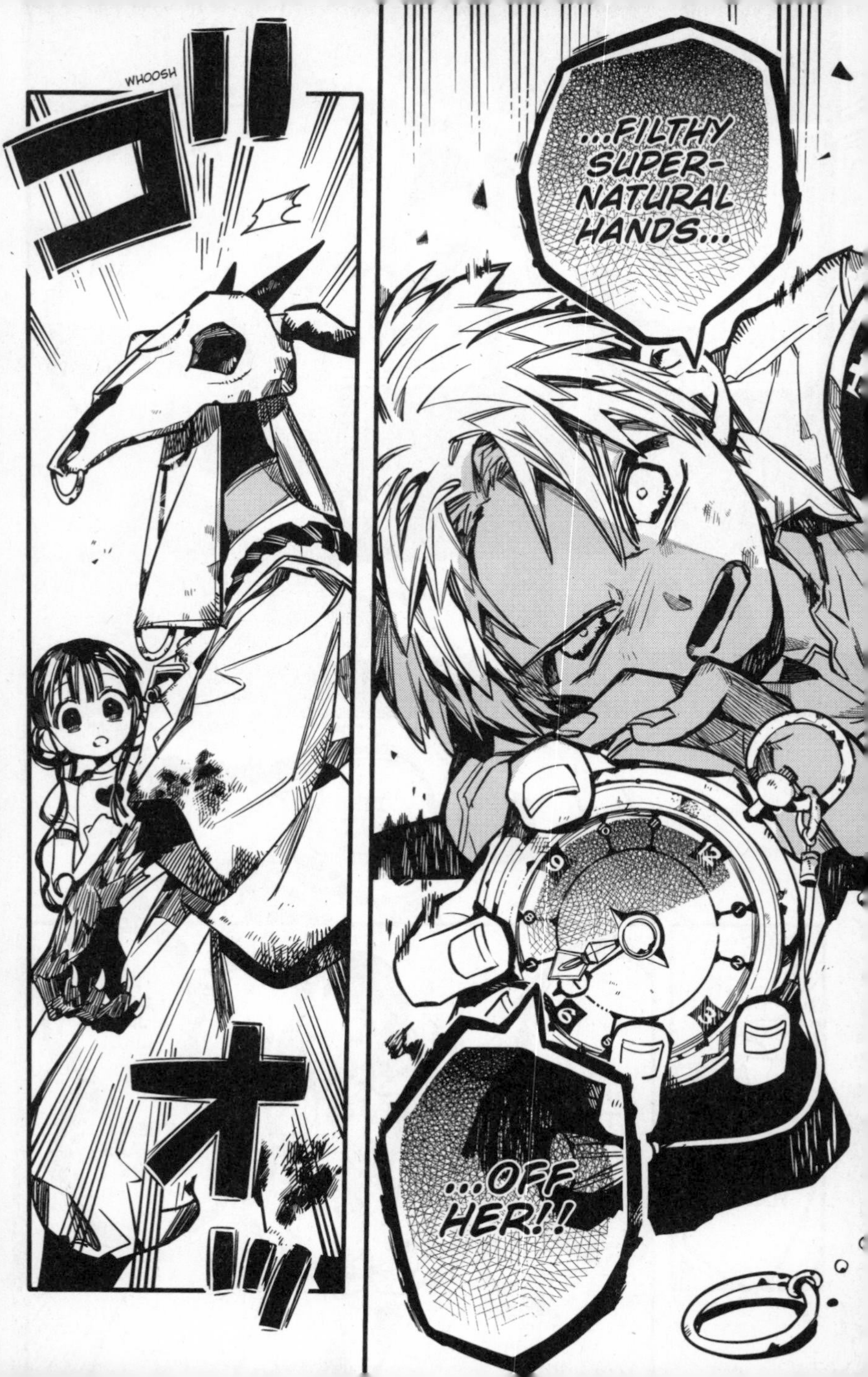
...FILTHY SUPER-NATURAL HANDS...
...OFF HER!!
WHOOSH

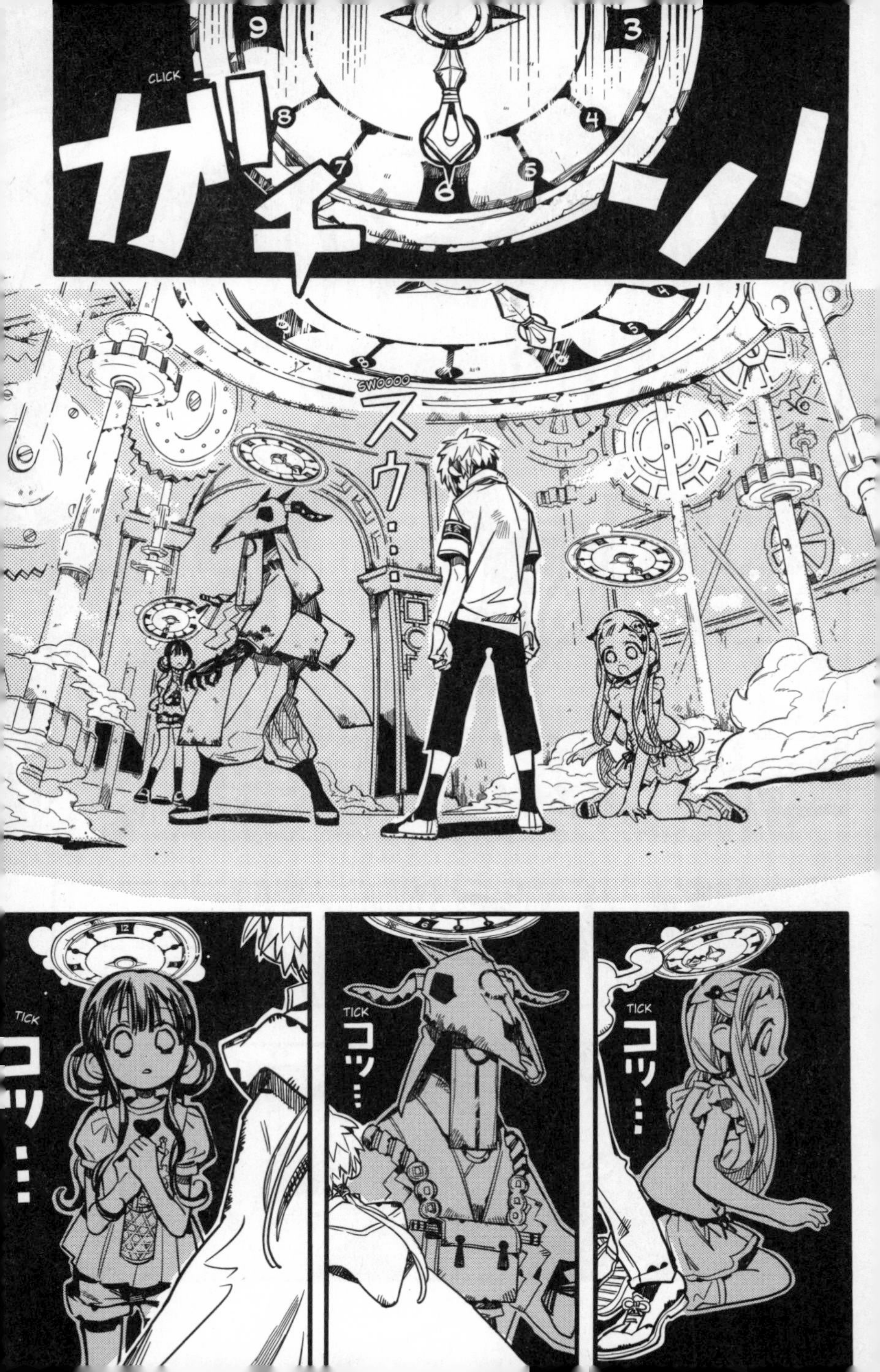
CLICK
ガキーン!
SWOOOO
スゥ…
TICK
コツ…
TICK
コツ…
TICK
コツ…

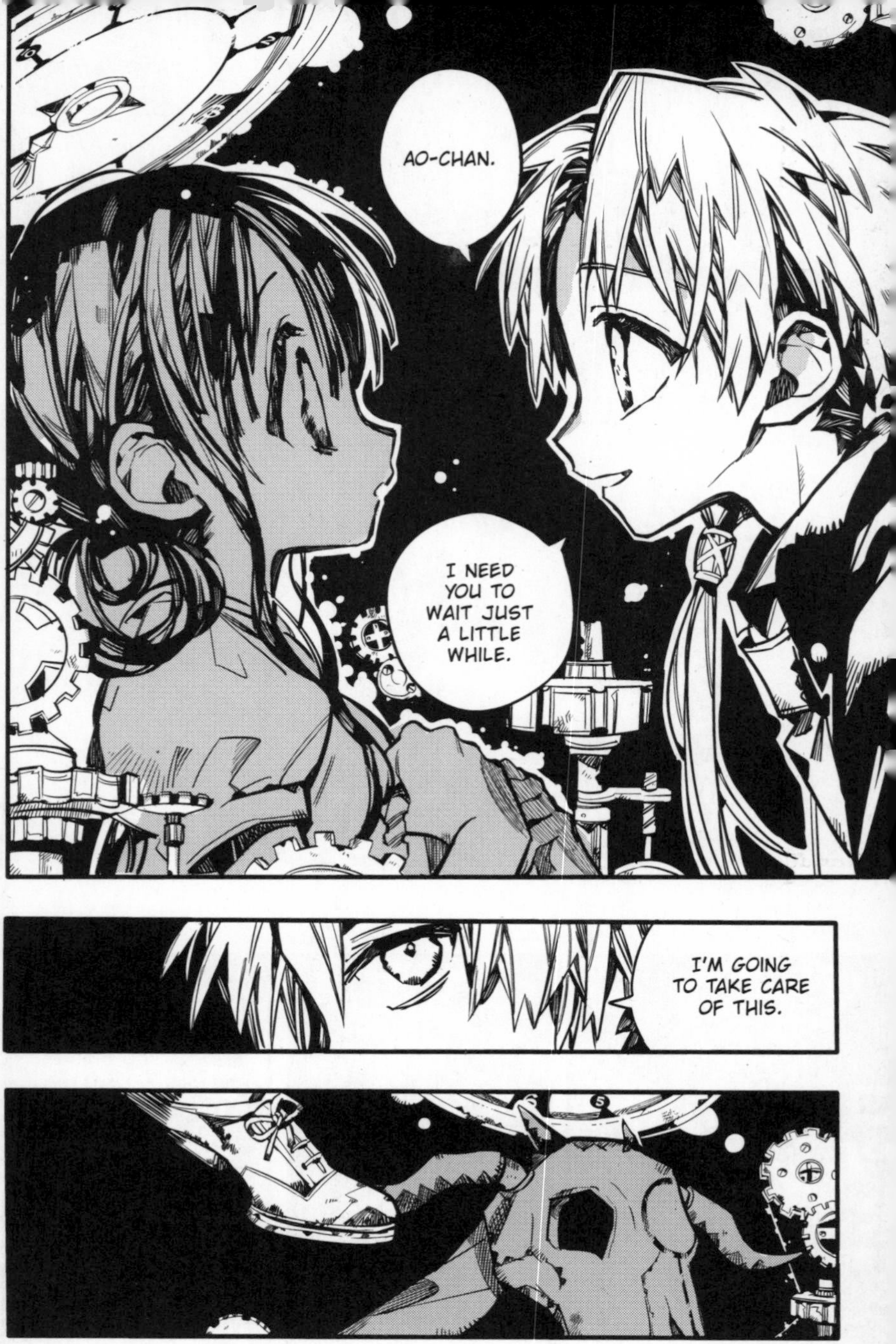
AO-CHAN.
I NEED YOU TO WAIT JUST A LITTLE WHILE.
I'M GOING TO TAKE CARE OF THIS.

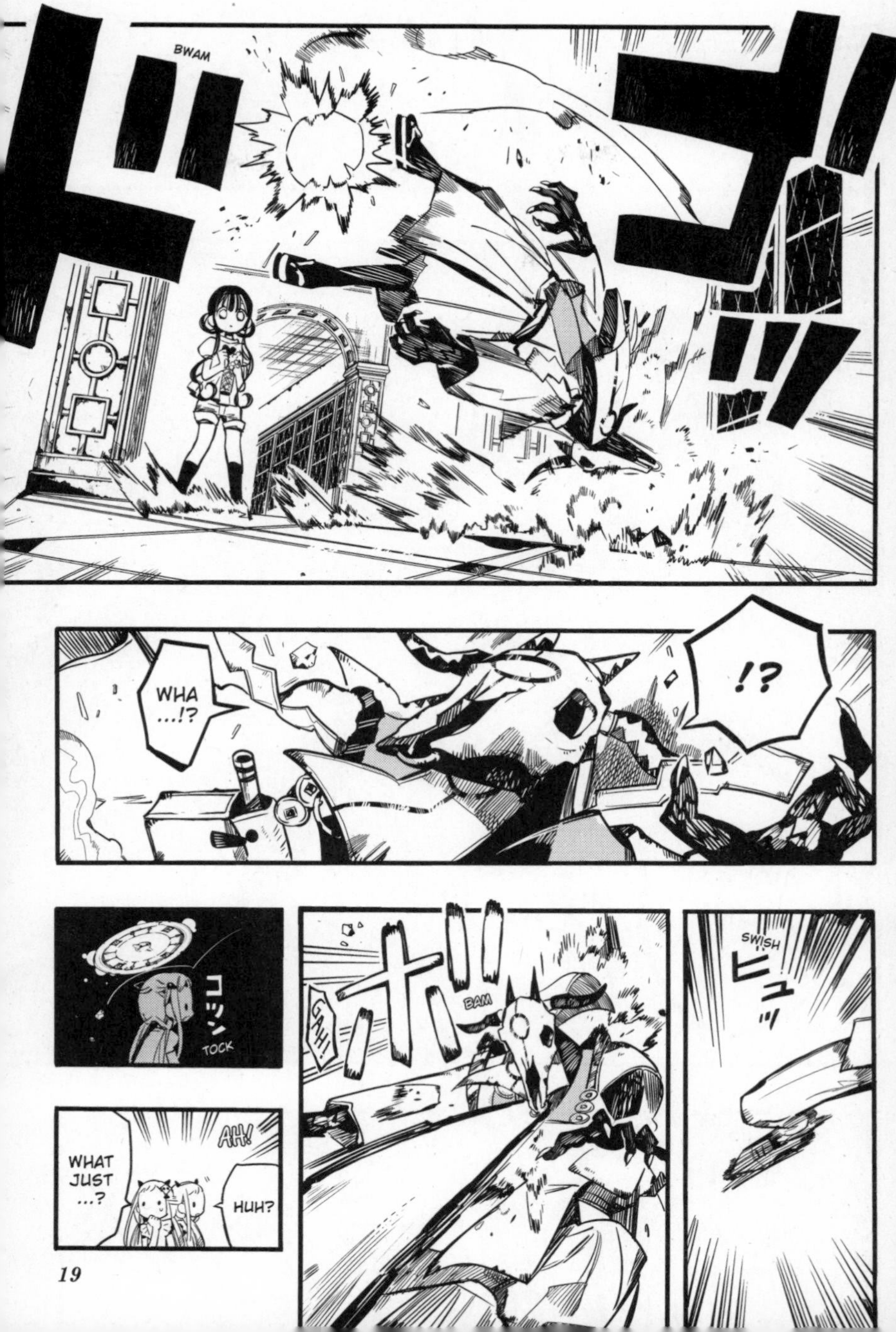
BWAM
!?
WHA ...!?
SWISH
ビュッ
BAM
GAH!
コツン
TOCK
AH!
HUH?
WHAT JUST ...?

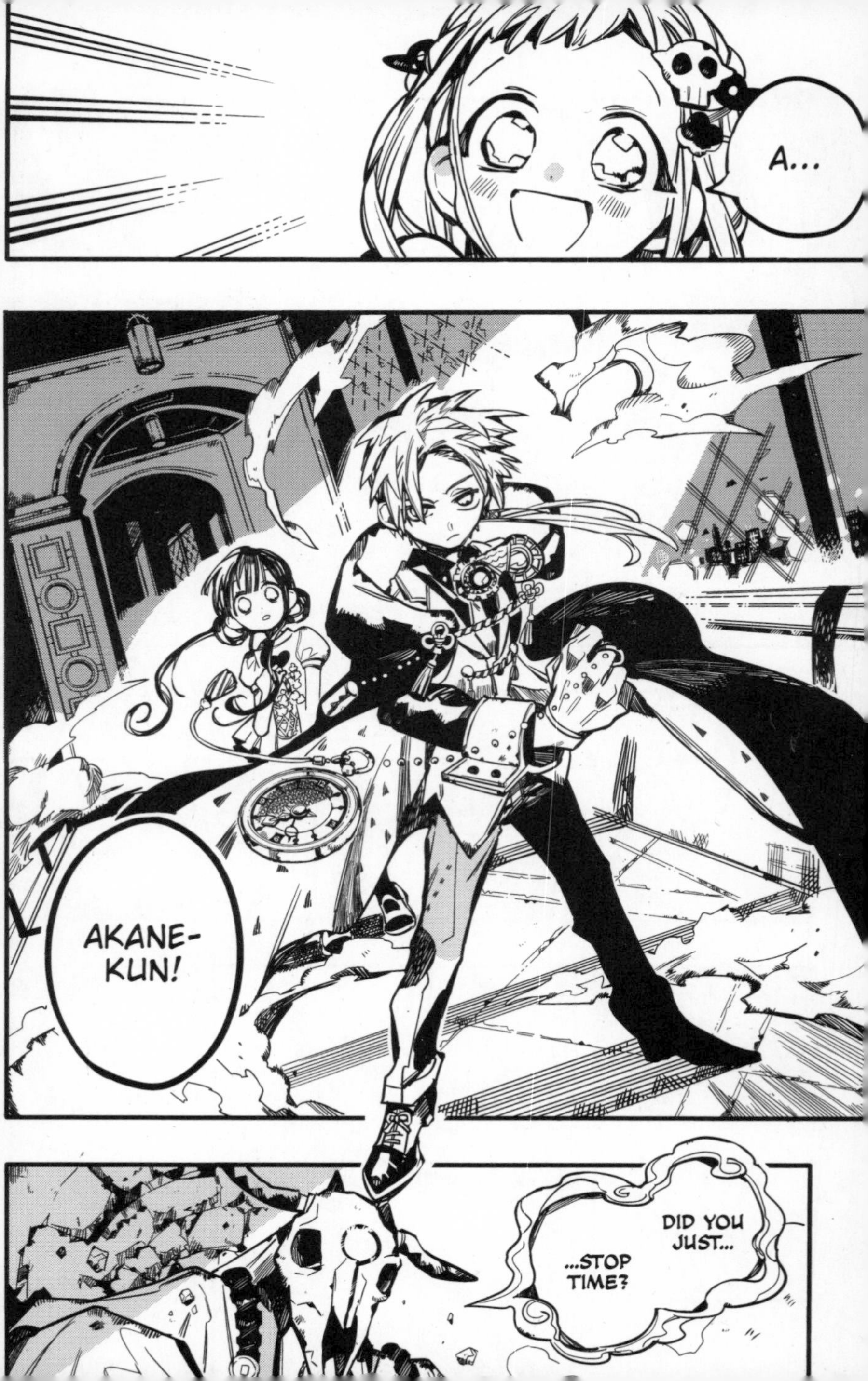
A...
AKANE-KUN!
DID YOU JUST...
...STOP TIME?

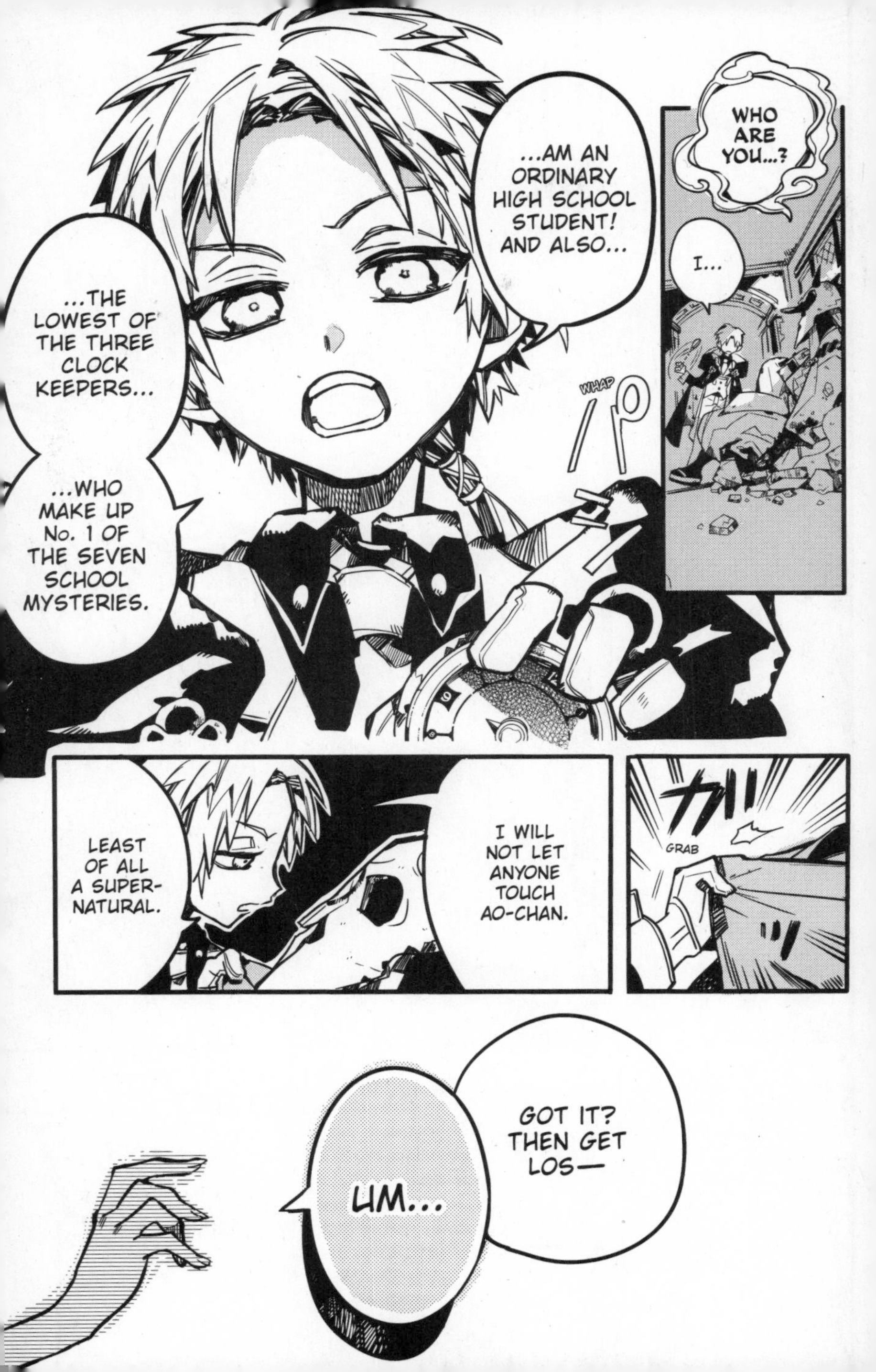
WHO ARE YOU...?
I...
...AM AN ORDINARY HIGH SCHOOL STUDENT! AND ALSO...
WHAP
...THE LOWEST OF THE THREE CLOCK KEEPERS...
...WHO MAKE UP No. 1 OF THE SEVEN SCHOOL MYSTERIES.
GRAB
I WILL NOT LET ANYONE TOUCH AO-CHAN.
LEAST OF ALL A SUPER-NATURAL.
GOT IT? THEN GET LOS—
UM...

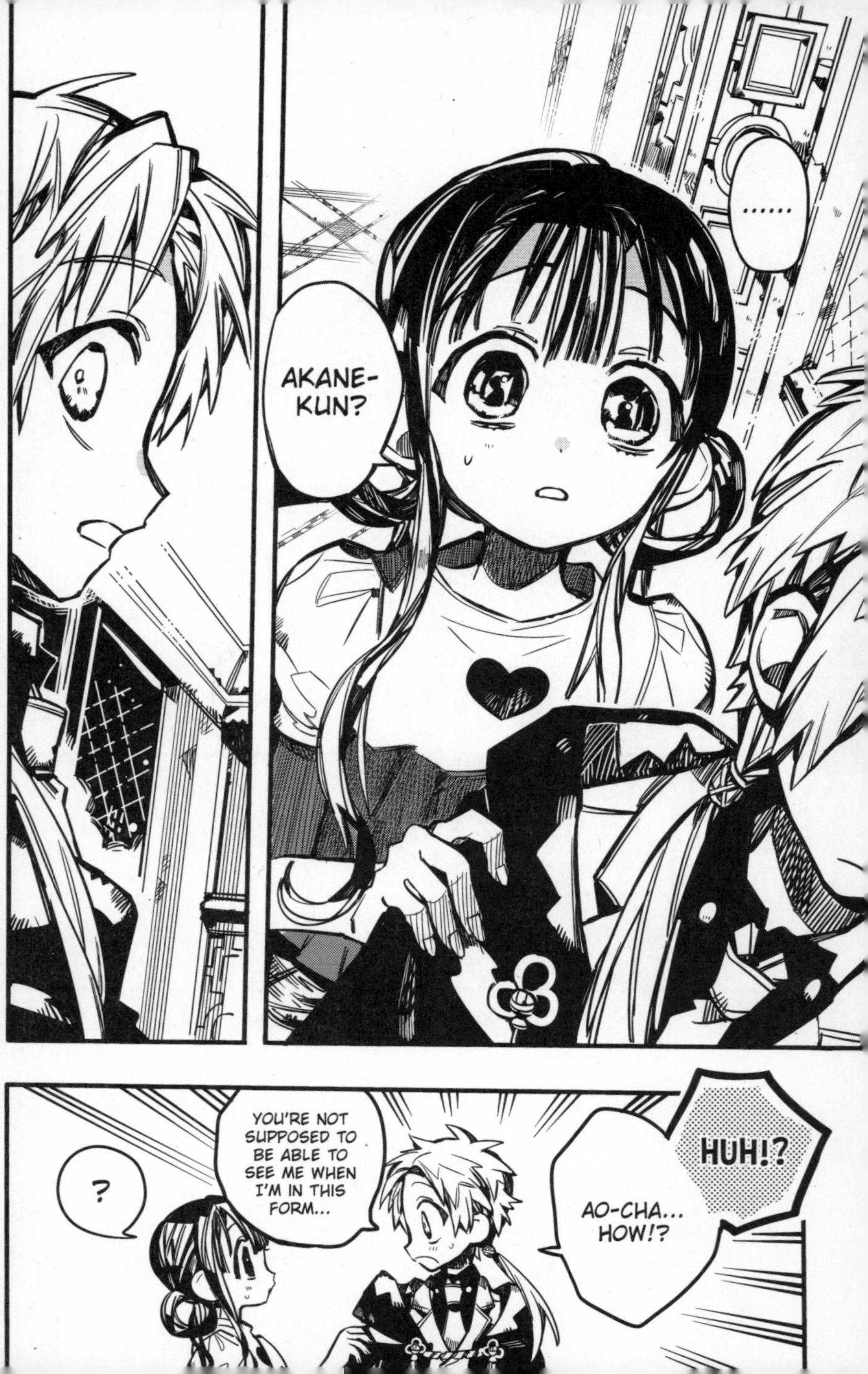
......
AKANE-KUN?
HUH!?
AO-CHA... HOW!?
YOU'RE NOT SUPPOSED TO BE ABLE TO SEE ME WHEN I'M IN THIS FORM...
?

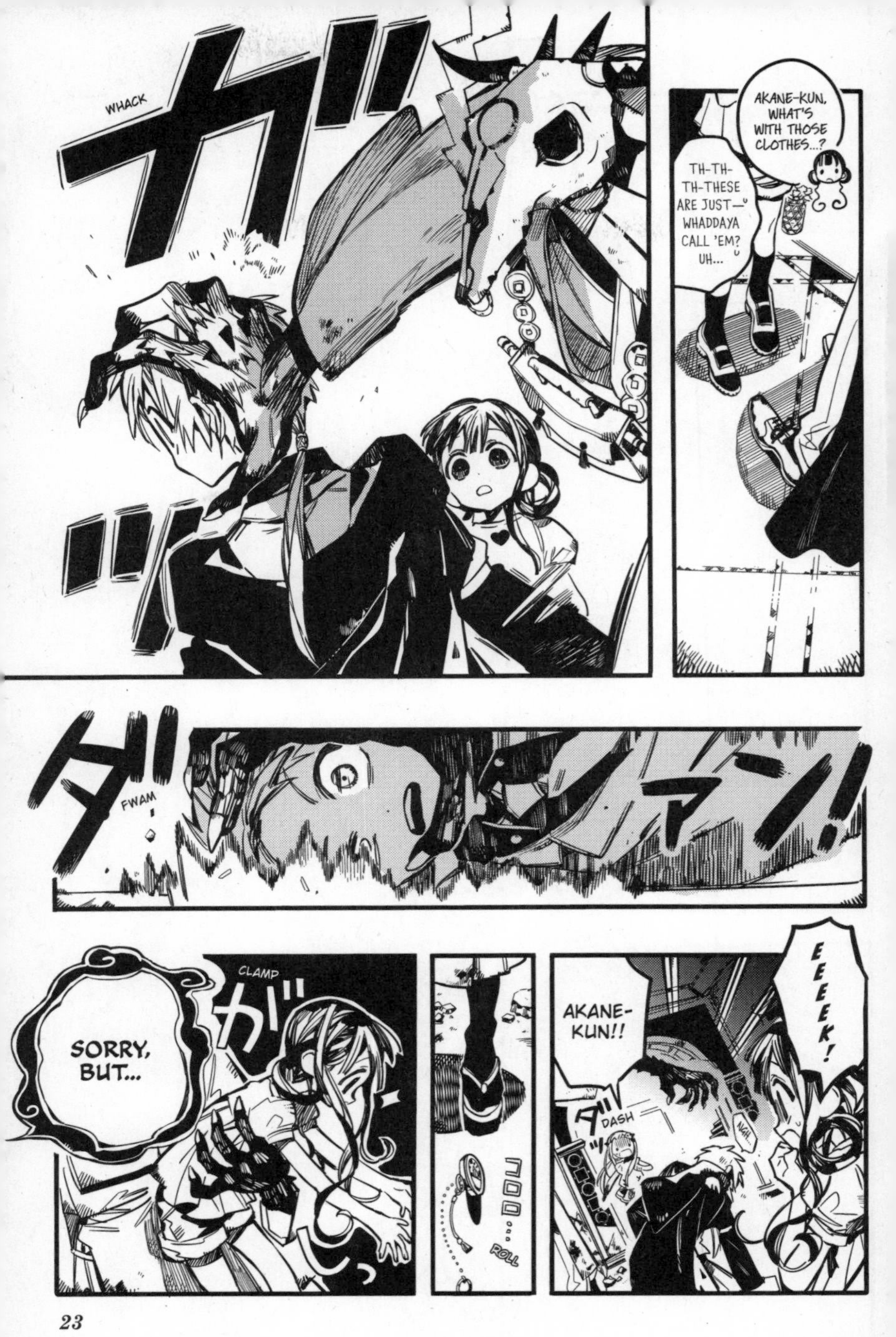

AKANE-KUN, WHAT'S WITH THOSE CLOTHES...?
TH-TH-TH-THESE ARE JUST— WHADDAYA CALL 'EM? UH...
WHACK
FWAM
EEEEK!
AKANE-KUN!!
DASH
NGH
ROLL
CLAMP
SORRY, BUT...

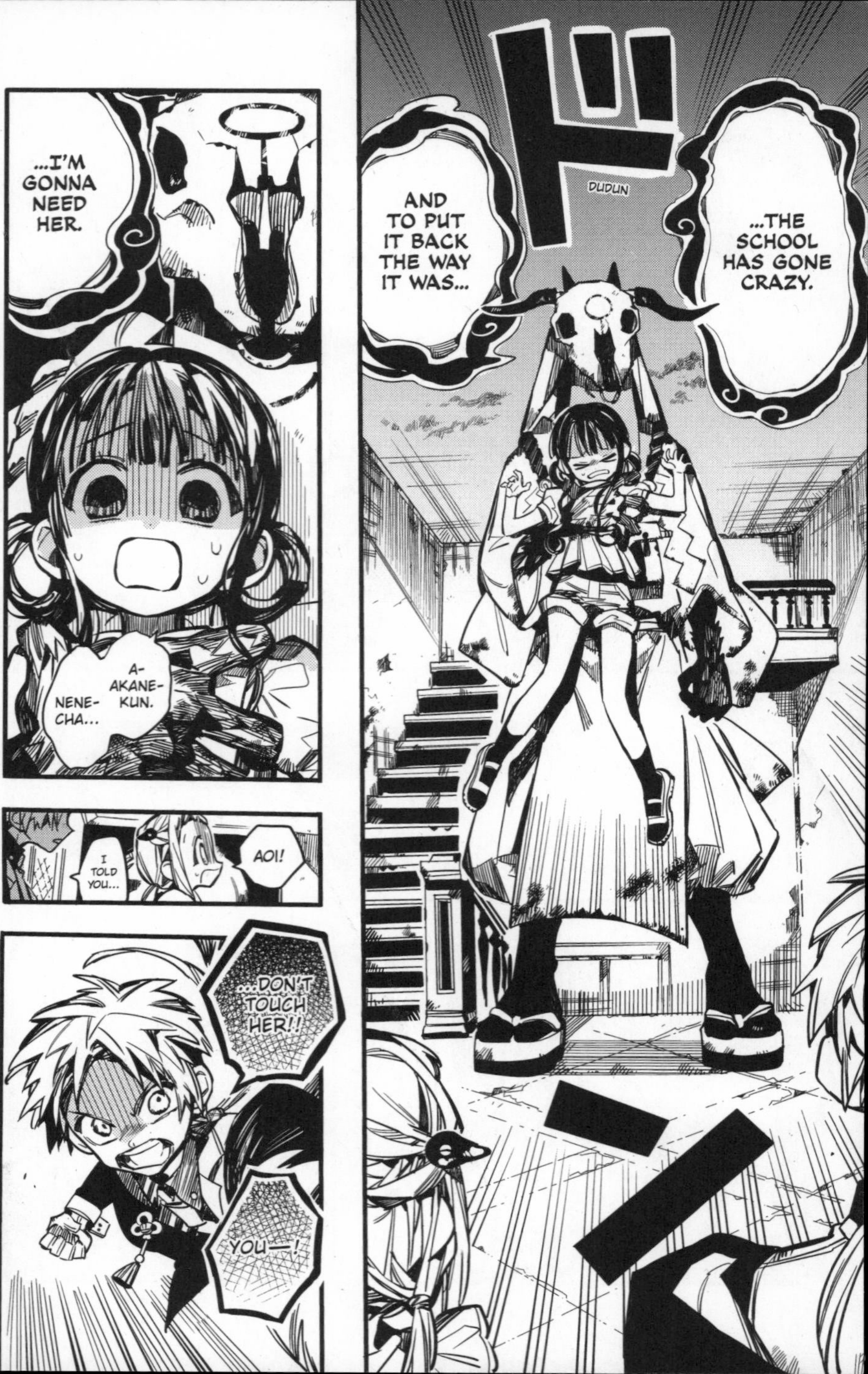
...THE SCHOOL HAS GONE CRAZY.
DUDUN
AND TO PUT IT BACK THE WAY IT WAS...
...I'M GONNA NEED HER.
A-AKANE-KUN.
NENE-CHA...
AOI!
I TOLD YOU...
...DON'T TOUCH HER!!
YOU—!

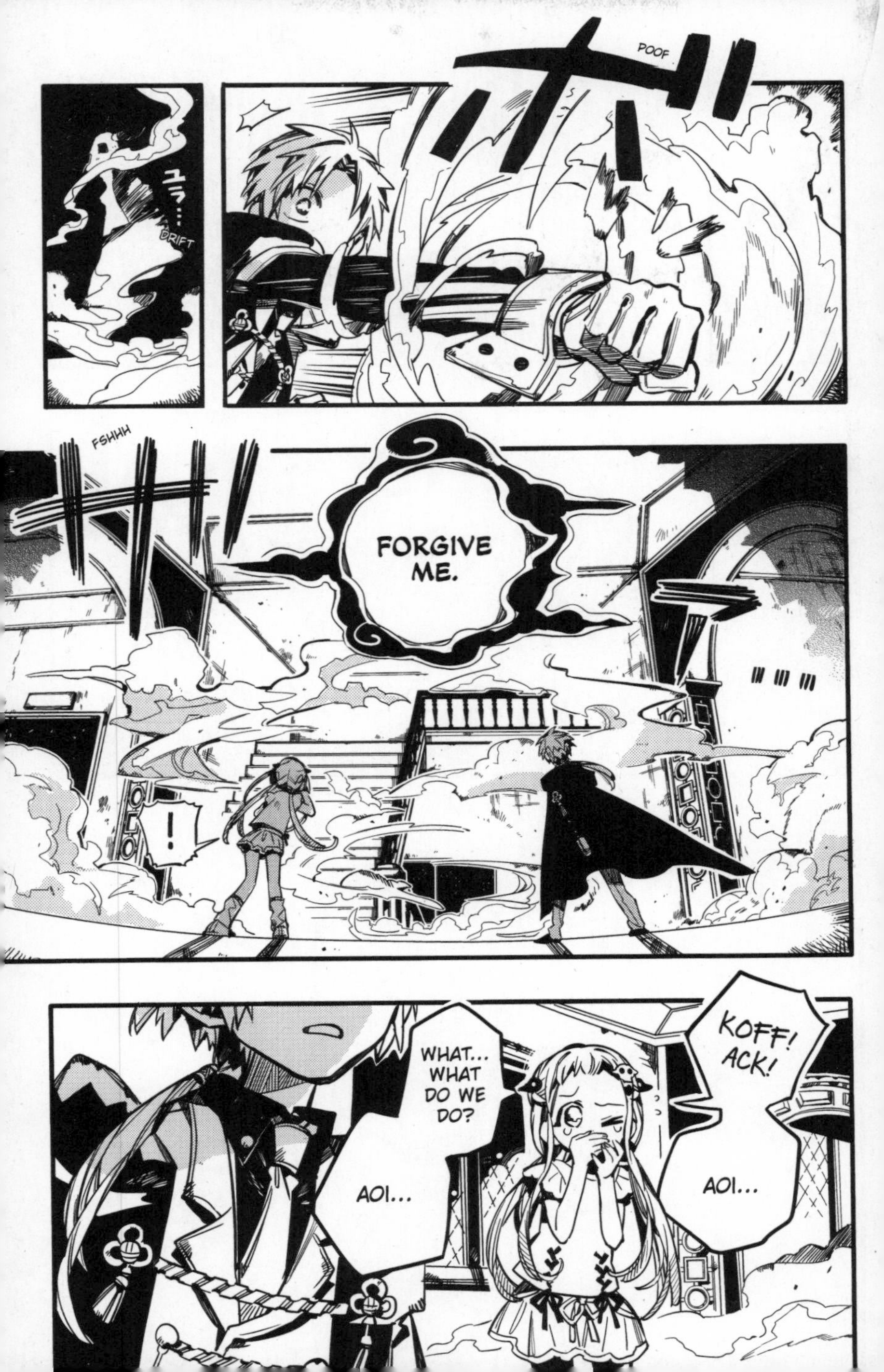
POOF
ユラ…
DRIFT
FSHHH
FORGIVE ME.
!
KOFF! ACK!
WHAT... WHAT DO WE DO?
AOI...
AOI...

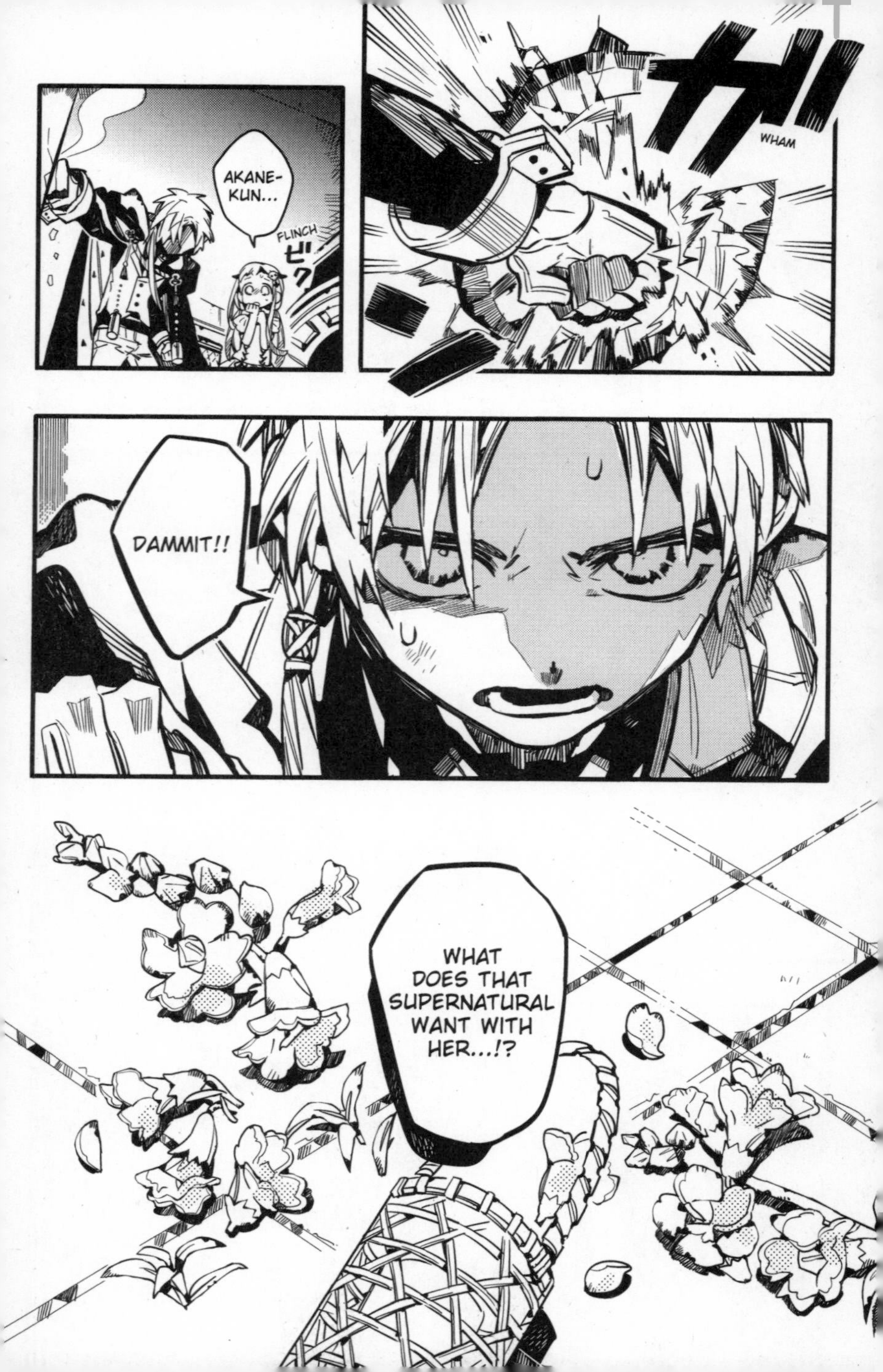
WHAM
AKANE-KUN...
FLINCH
DAMMIT!!
WHAT DOES THAT SUPERNATURAL WANT WITH HER...!?

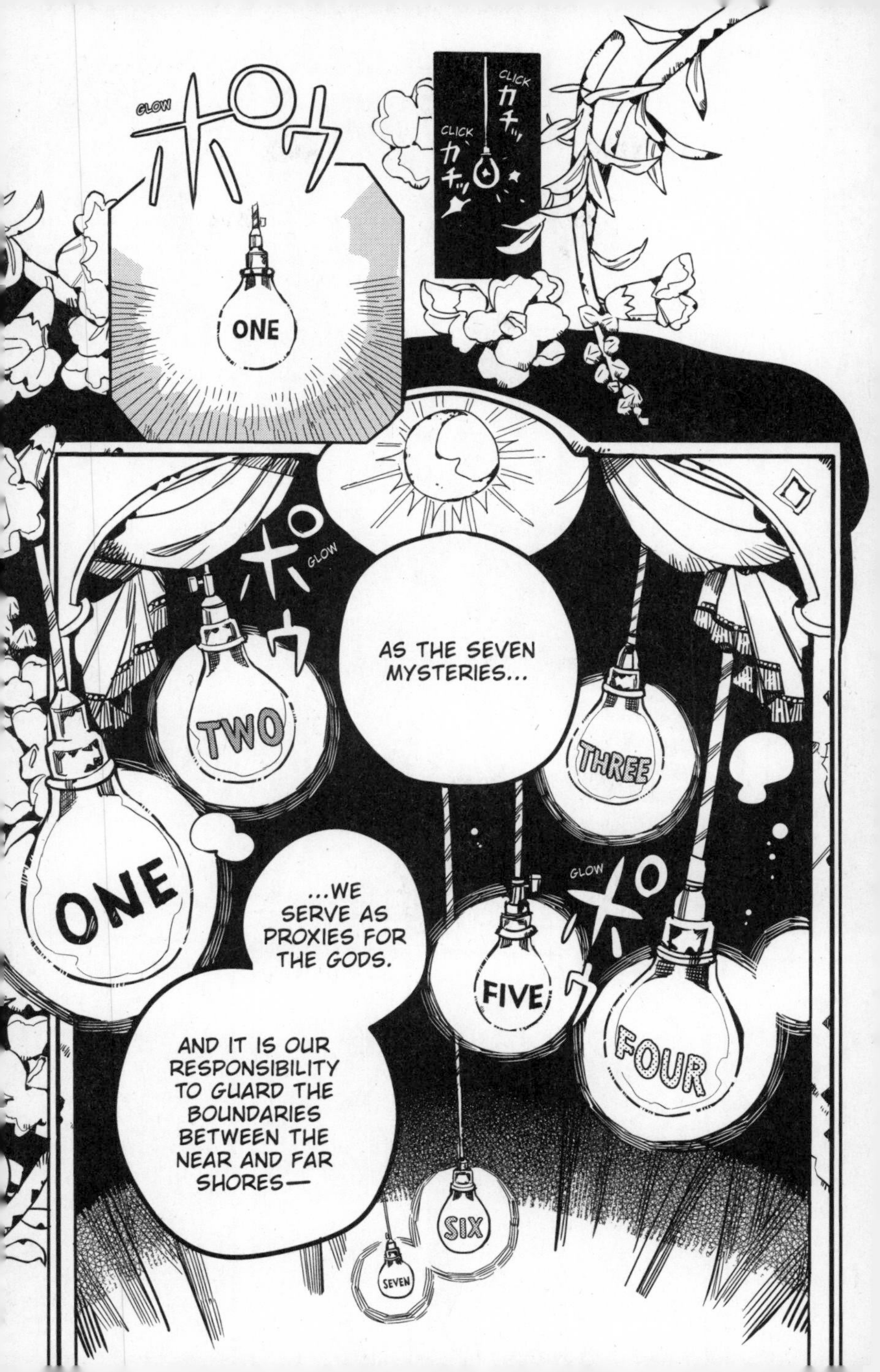
CLICK
カチッ
CLICK
カチッ
GLOW
ホウ
ONE
AS THE SEVEN MYSTERIES...
GLOW
ホウ
THREE
TWO
ONE
GLOW
ホウ
...WE SERVE AS PROXIES FOR THE GODS.
FIVE
FOUR
AND IT IS OUR RESPONSIBILITY TO GUARD THE BOUNDARIES BETWEEN THE NEAR AND FAR SHORES—
SIX
SEVEN

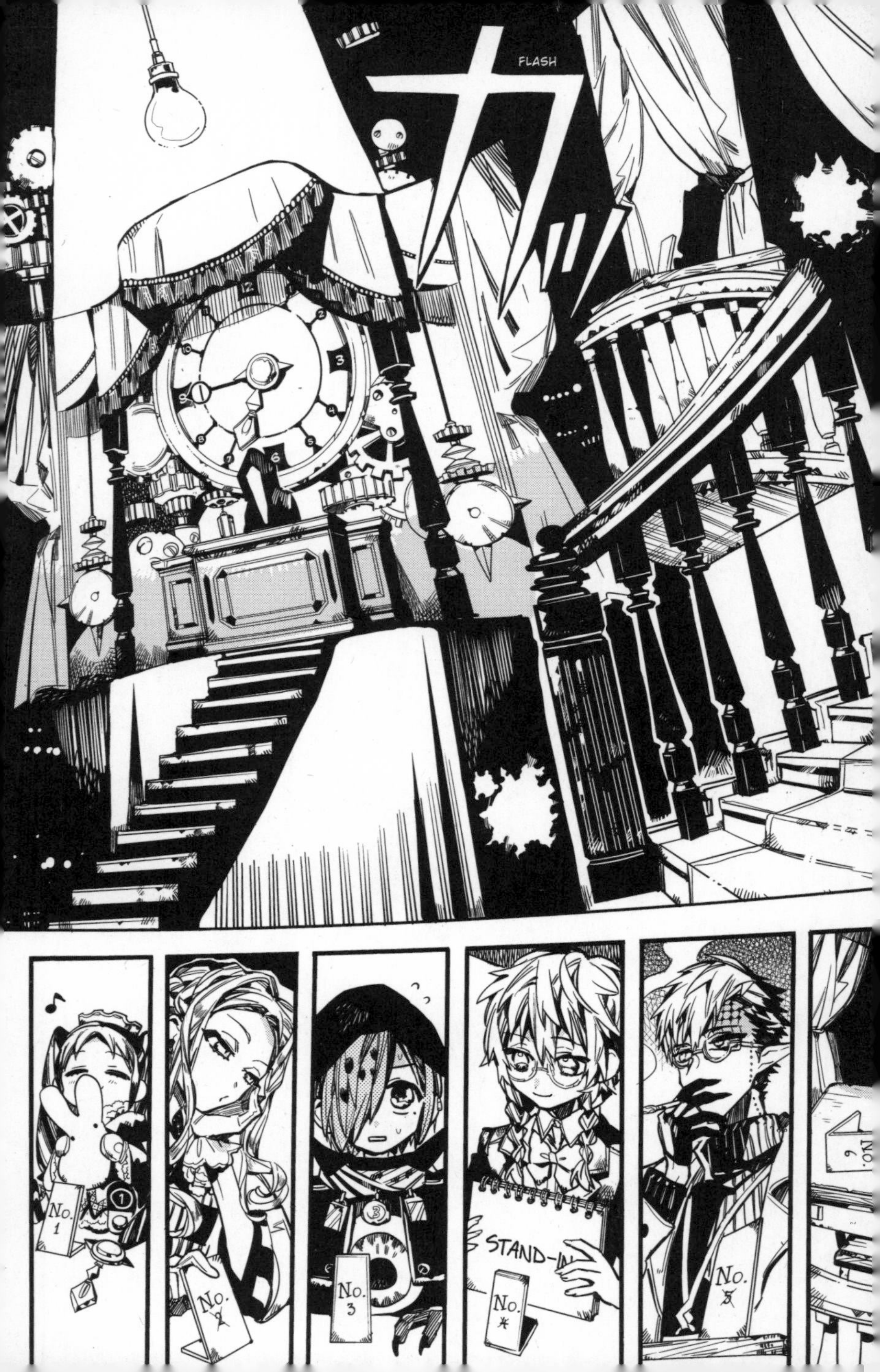
カッ
FLASH
No. 6
No. 5
STAND-IN
No. 4
No. 3
No. 2
No. 1

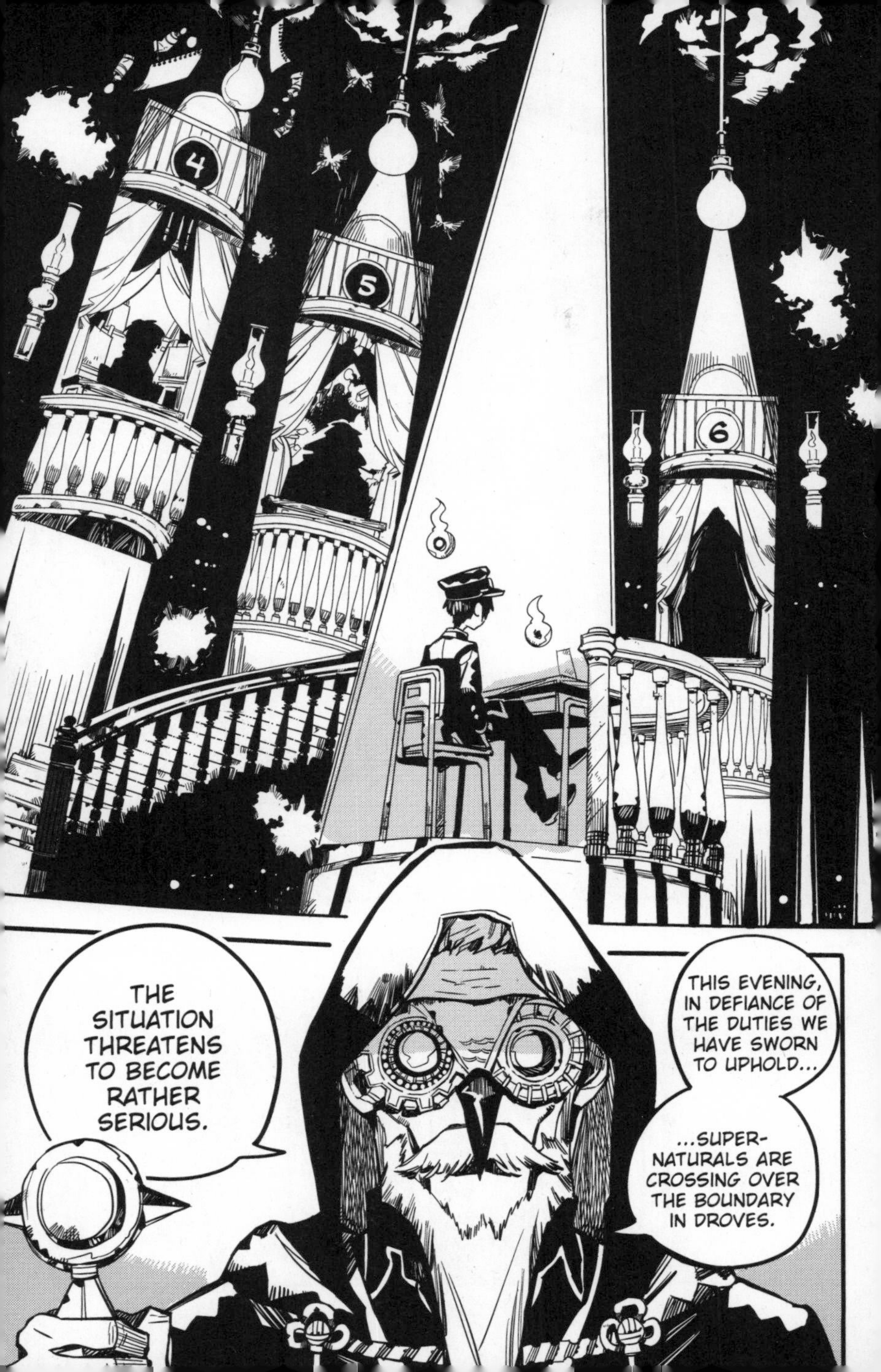
THIS EVENING, IN DEFIANCE OF THE DUTIES WE HAVE SWORN TO UPHOLD...
...SUPER-NATURALS ARE CROSSING OVER THE BOUNDARY IN DROVES.
THE SITUATION THREATENS TO BECOME RATHER SERIOUS.

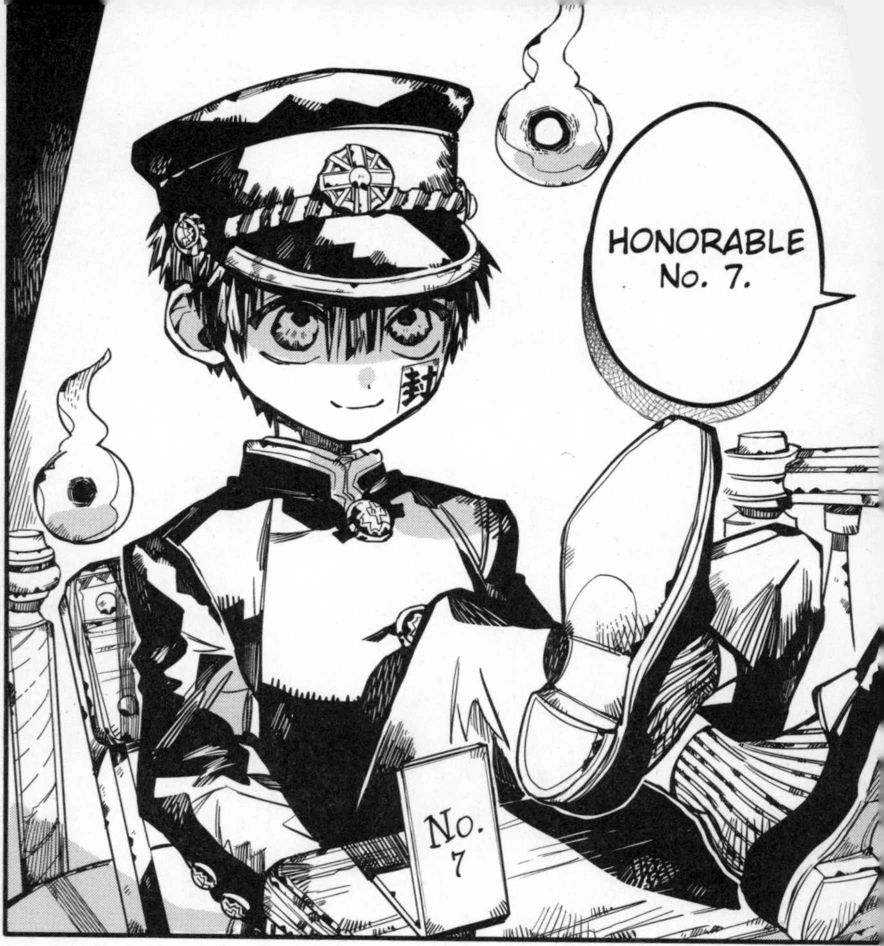
HONORABLE No. 7.
No. 7
PATCH: SEAL

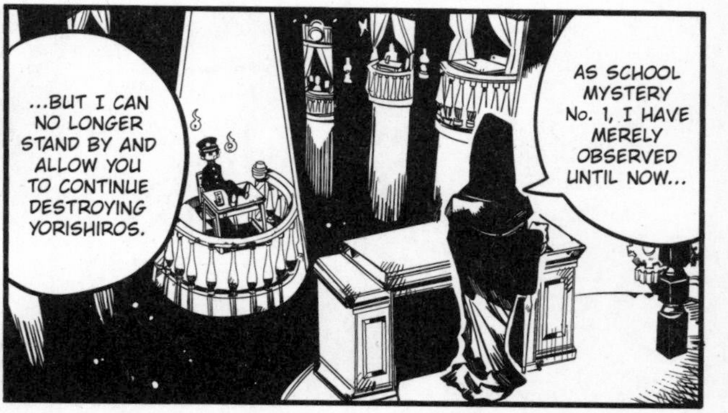
AS SCHOOL MYSTERY No. 1, I HAVE MERELY OBSERVED UNTIL NOW...
...BUT I CAN NO LONGER STAND BY AND ALLOW YOU TO CONTINUE DESTROYING YORISHIROS.

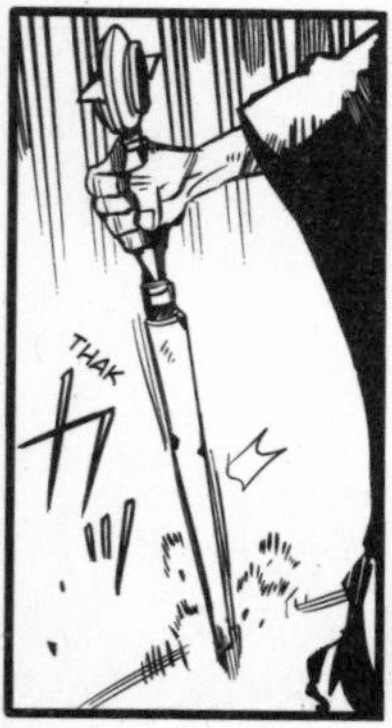
THAK

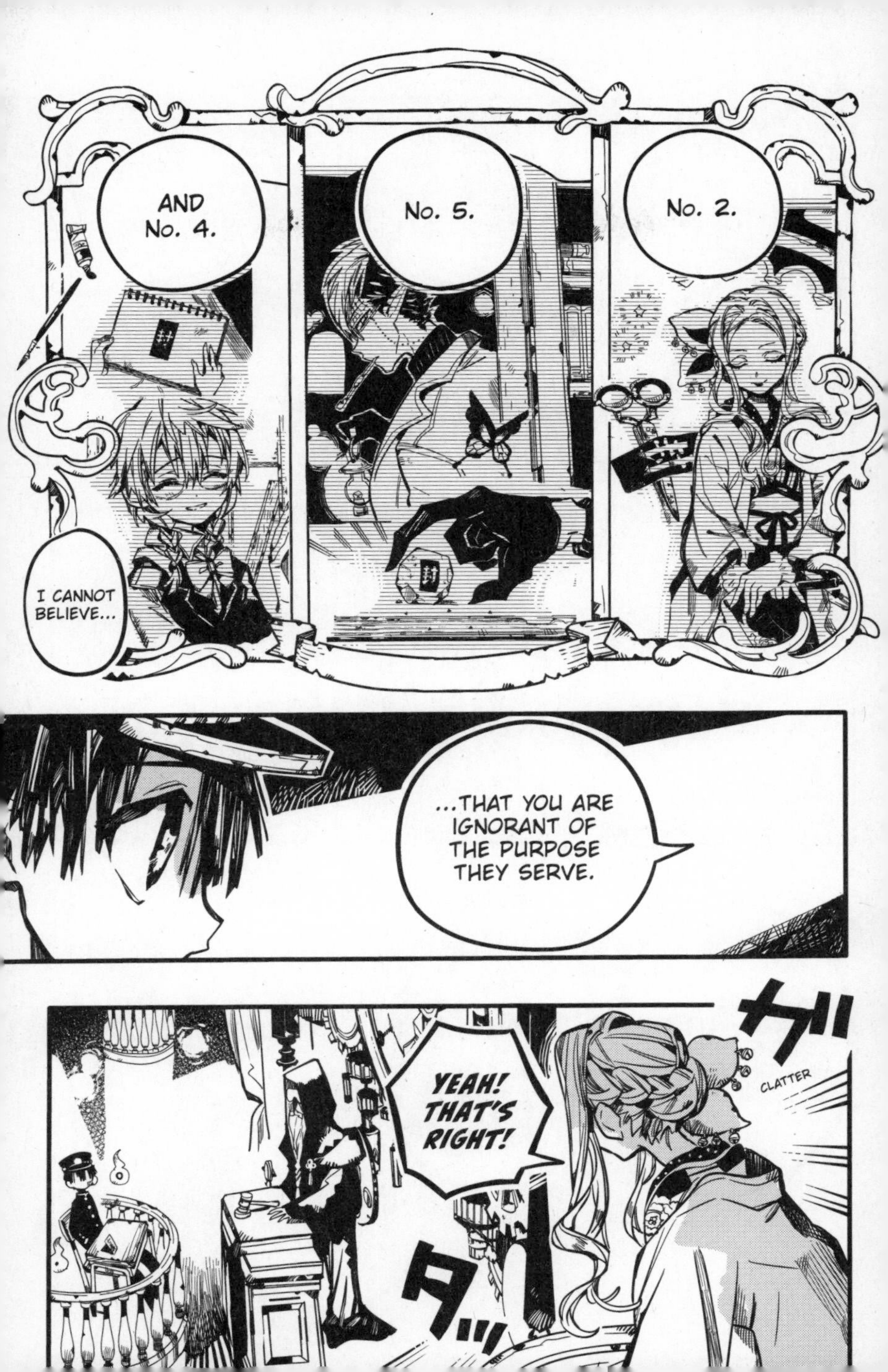
No. 2.
No. 5.
AND No. 4.
I CANNOT BELIEVE...
...THAT YOU ARE IGNORANT OF THE PURPOSE THEY SERVE.
CLATTER
YEAH! THAT'S RIGHT!
タッ

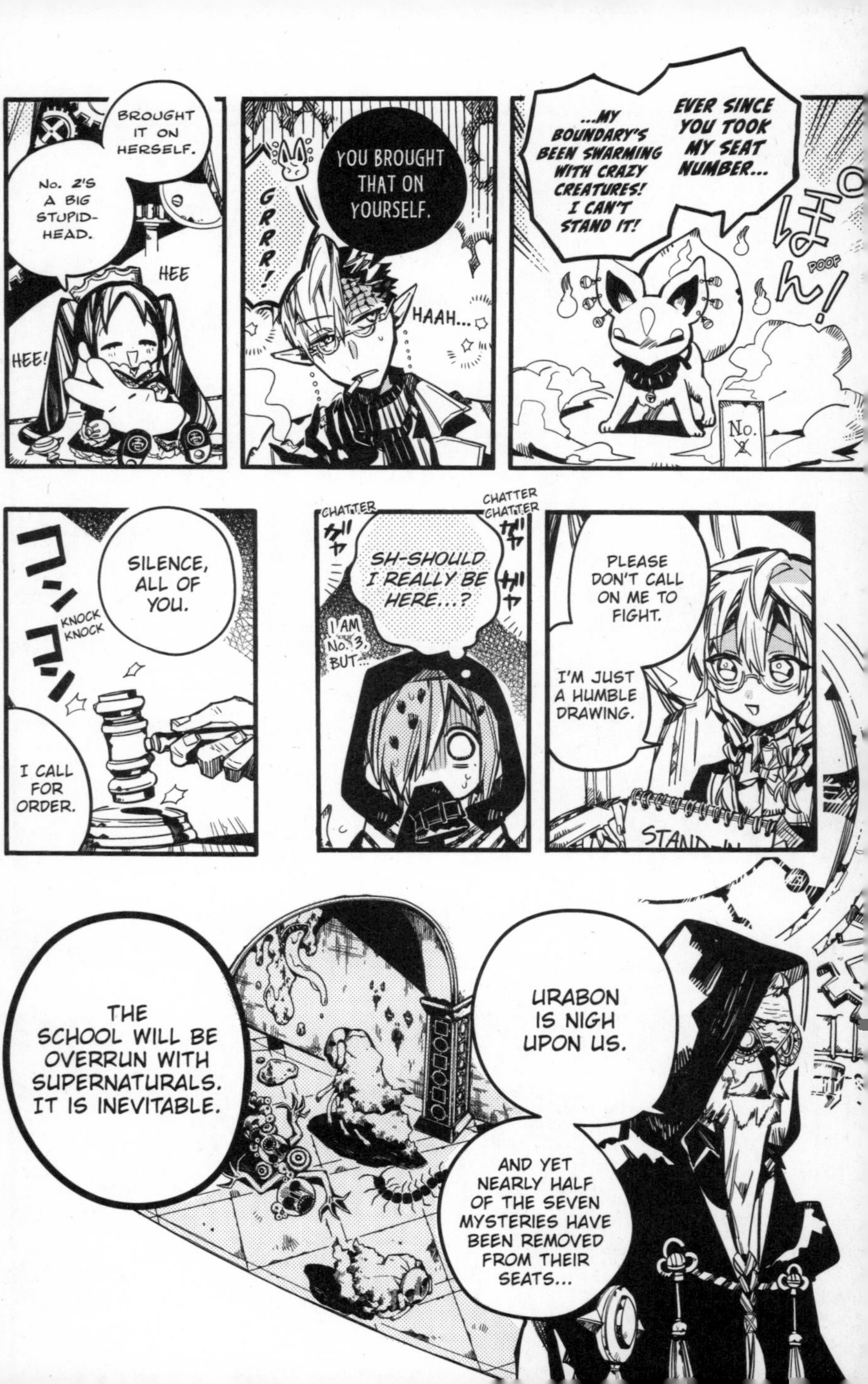
EVER SINCE YOU TOOK MY SEAT NUMBER...
...MY BOUNDARY'S BEEN SWARMING WITH CRAZY CREATURES! I CAN'T STAND IT!
ぽん!
POOF
No.
GRRR!
YOU BROUGHT THAT ON YOURSELF.
HAAH...
BROUGHT IT ON HERSELF.
No. 2'S A BIG STUPID-HEAD.
HEE
HEE!
PLEASE DON'T CALL ON ME TO FIGHT.
I'M JUST A HUMBLE DRAWING.
CHATTER CHATTER
SH-SHOULD I REALLY BE HERE...?
I AM No. 3, BUT...
CHATTER
SILENCE, ALL OF YOU.
KNOCK KNOCK
I CALL FOR ORDER.
URABON IS NIGH UPON US.
AND YET NEARLY HALF OF THE SEVEN MYSTERIES HAVE BEEN REMOVED FROM THEIR SEATS...
THE SCHOOL WILL BE OVERRUN WITH SUPERNATURALS. IT IS INEVITABLE.

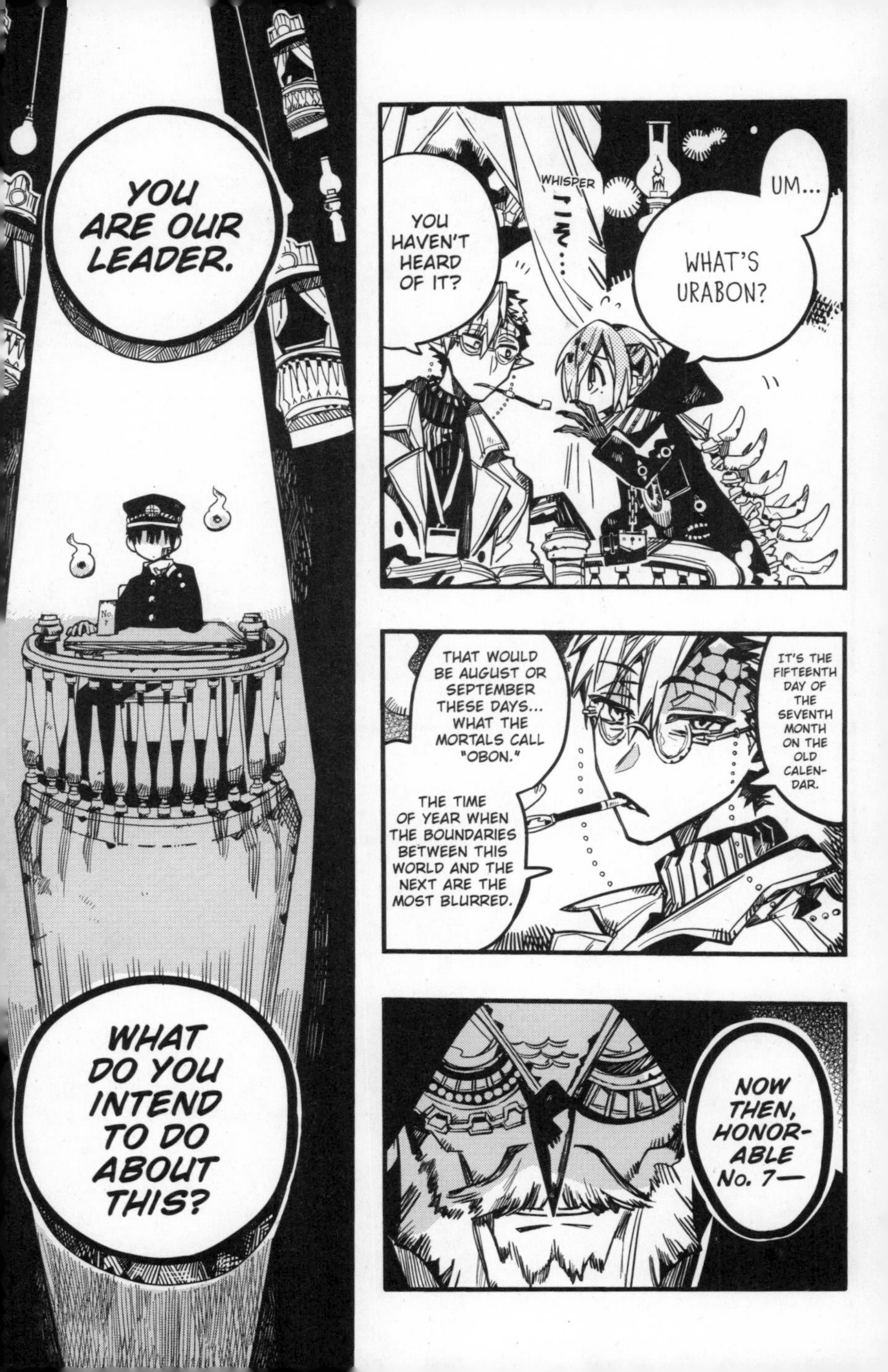
UM...
WHAT'S URABON?
WHISPER
YOU HAVEN'T HEARD OF IT?
IT'S THE FIFTEENTH DAY OF THE SEVENTH MONTH ON THE OLD CALENDAR.
THAT WOULD BE AUGUST OR SEPTEMBER THESE DAYS... WHAT THE MORTALS CALL "OBON."
THE TIME OF YEAR WHEN THE BOUNDARIES BETWEEN THIS WORLD AND THE NEXT ARE THE MOST BLURRED.
NOW THEN, HONORABLE No. 7—
YOU ARE OUR LEADER.
WHAT DO YOU INTEND TO DO ABOUT THIS?

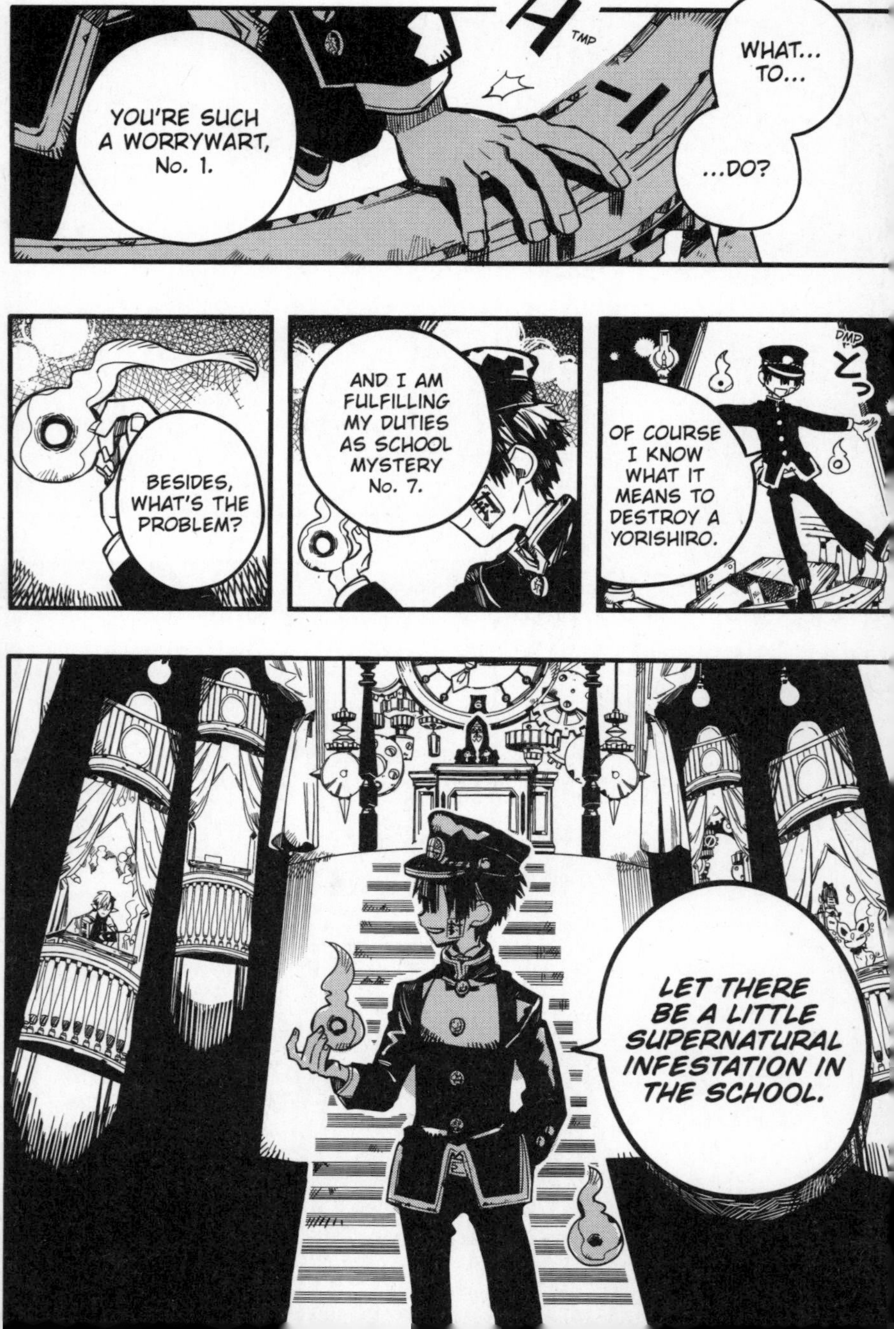
WHAT... TO... ...DO?
TMP
YOU'RE SUCH A WORRYWART, No. 1.
DMP
OF COURSE I KNOW WHAT IT MEANS TO DESTROY A YORISHIRO.
AND I AM FULFILLING MY DUTIES AS SCHOOL MYSTERY No. 7.
BESIDES, WHAT'S THE PROBLEM?
LET THERE BE A LITTLE SUPERNATURAL INFESTATION IN THE SCHOOL.

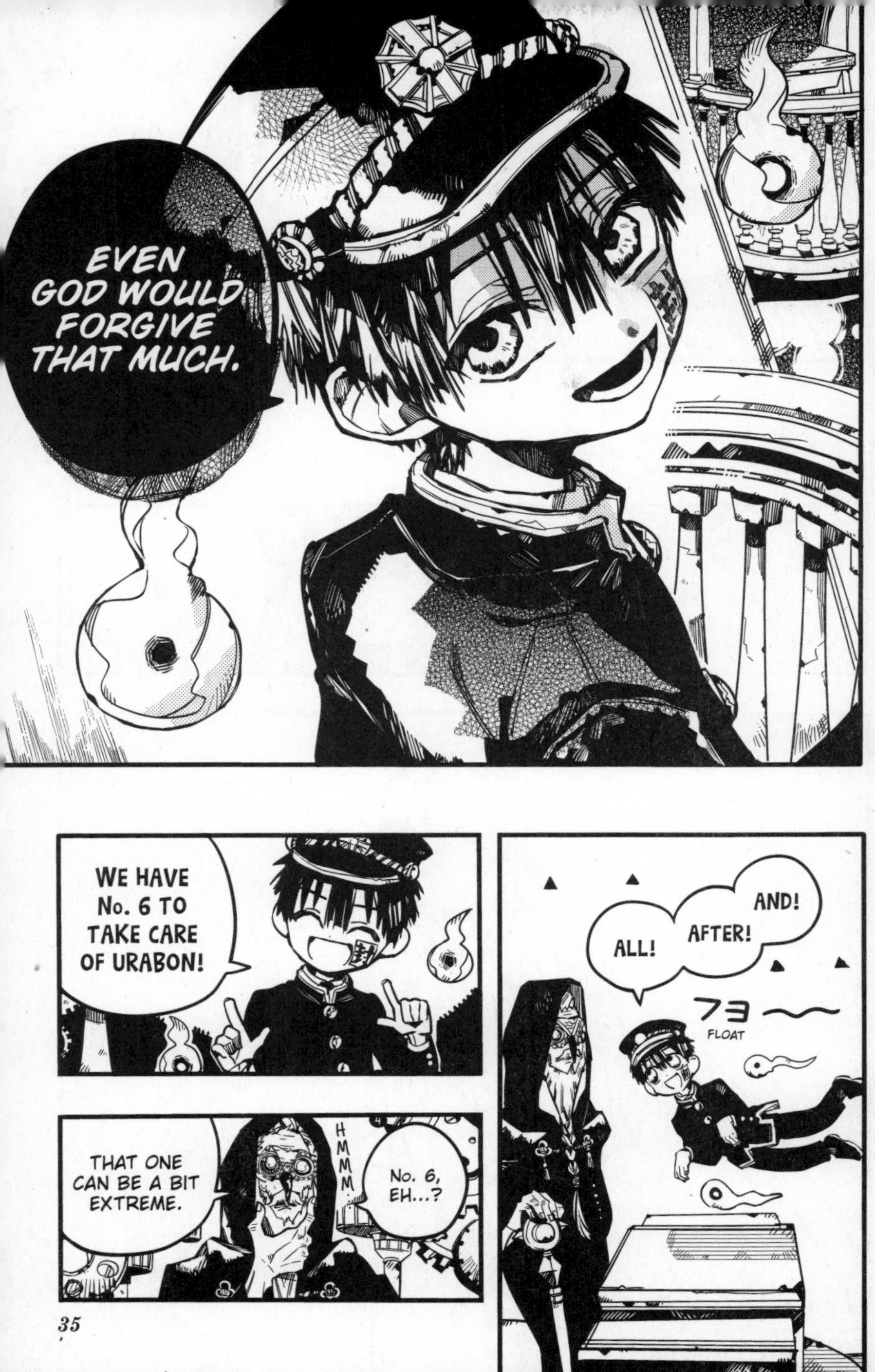

EVEN GOD WOULD FORGIVE THAT MUCH.
AND!
AFTER!
ALL!
フヨ〜〜
FLOAT
WE HAVE No. 6 TO TAKE CARE OF URABON!
No. 6, EH...?
HMMM...
THAT ONE CAN BE A BIT EXTREME.

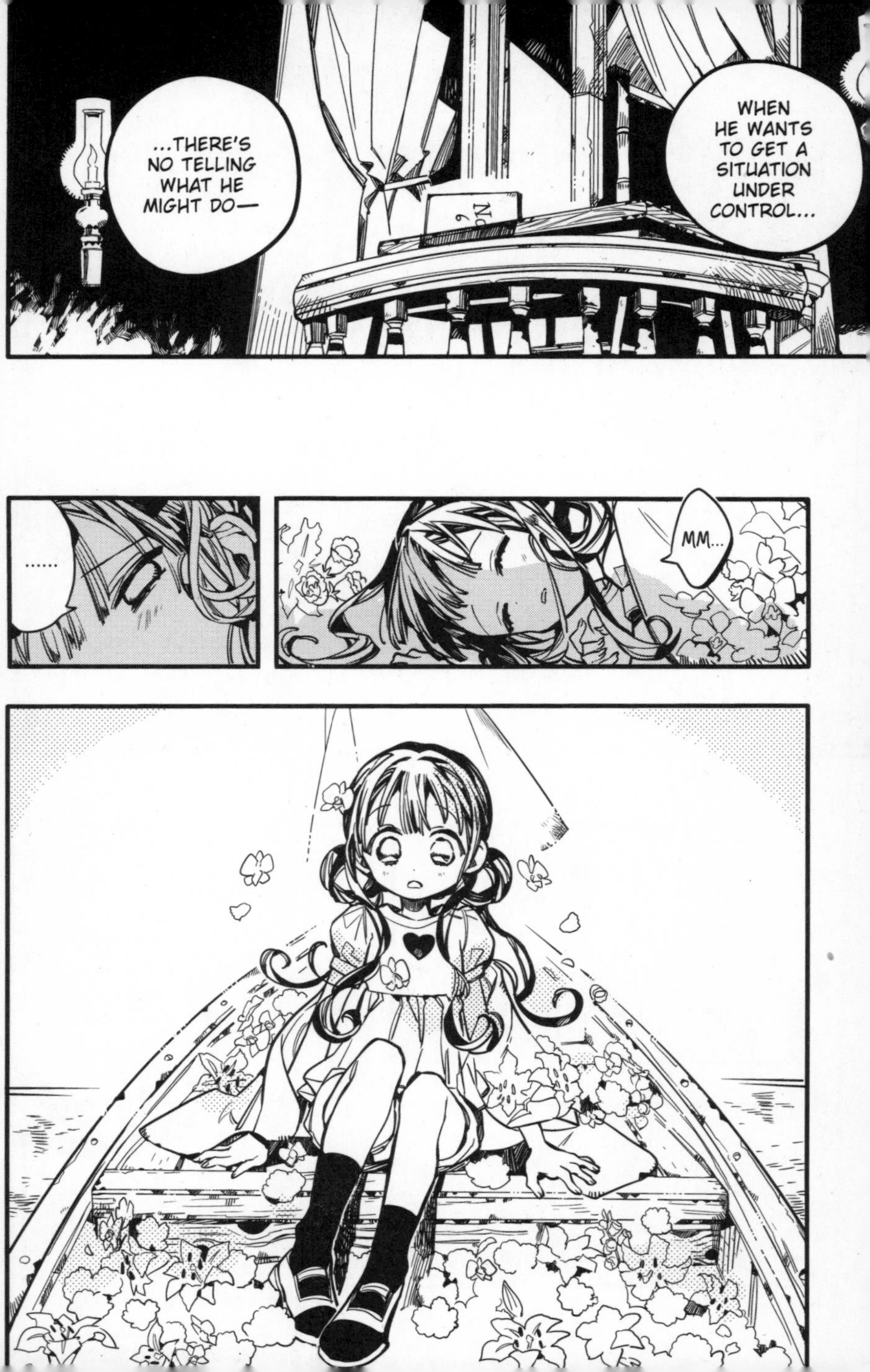
WHEN HE WANTS TO GET A SITUATION UNDER CONTROL...
...THERE'S NO TELLING WHAT HE MIGHT DO—
MM...
......

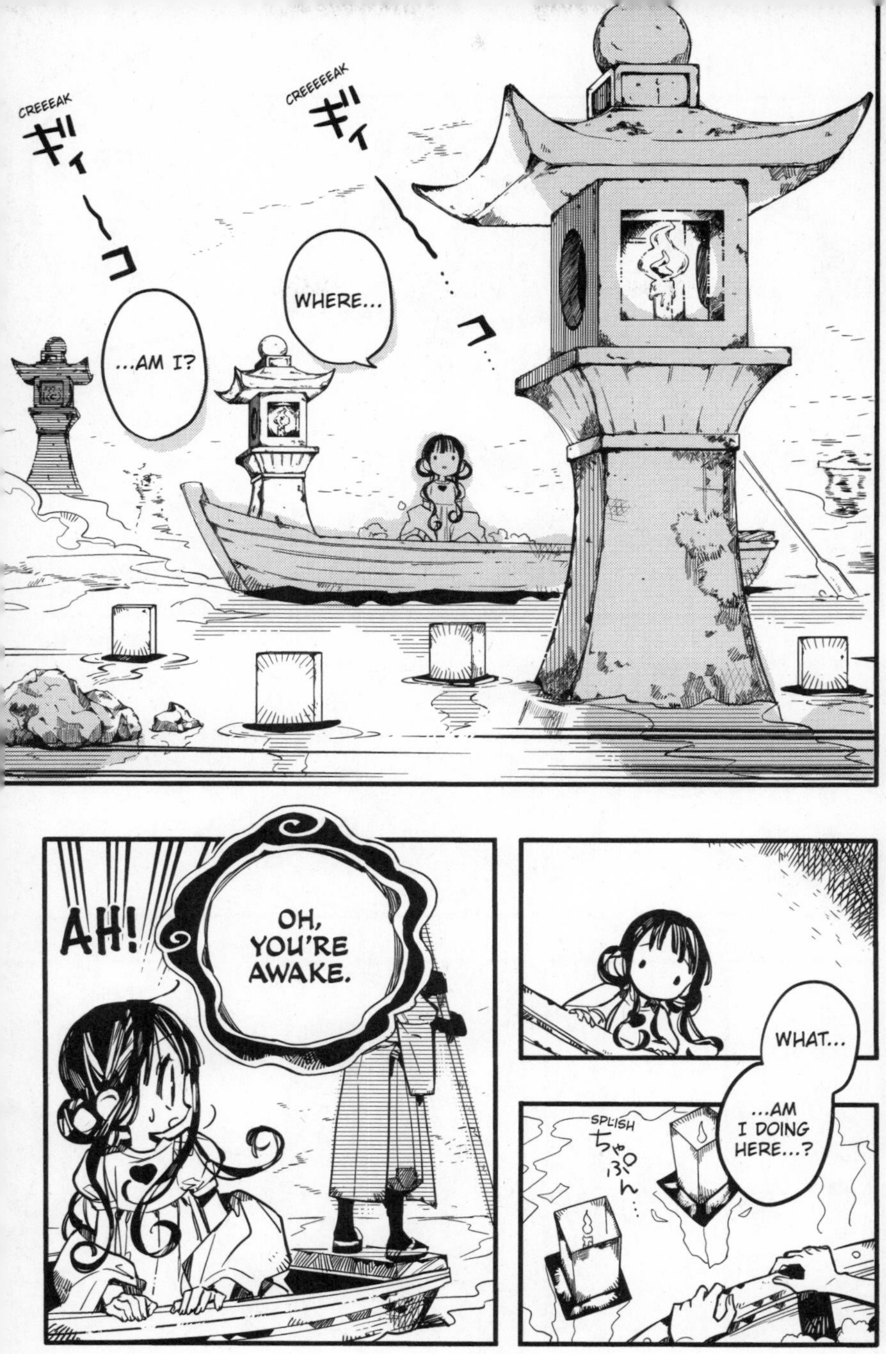
CREEEEEAK
ギィ〜…コ…
WHERE...
CREEEAK
ギィ〜コ
...AM I?
WHAT...
SPLISH
ちゃぷん…
...AM I DOING HERE...?
AH!
OH, YOU'RE AWAKE.

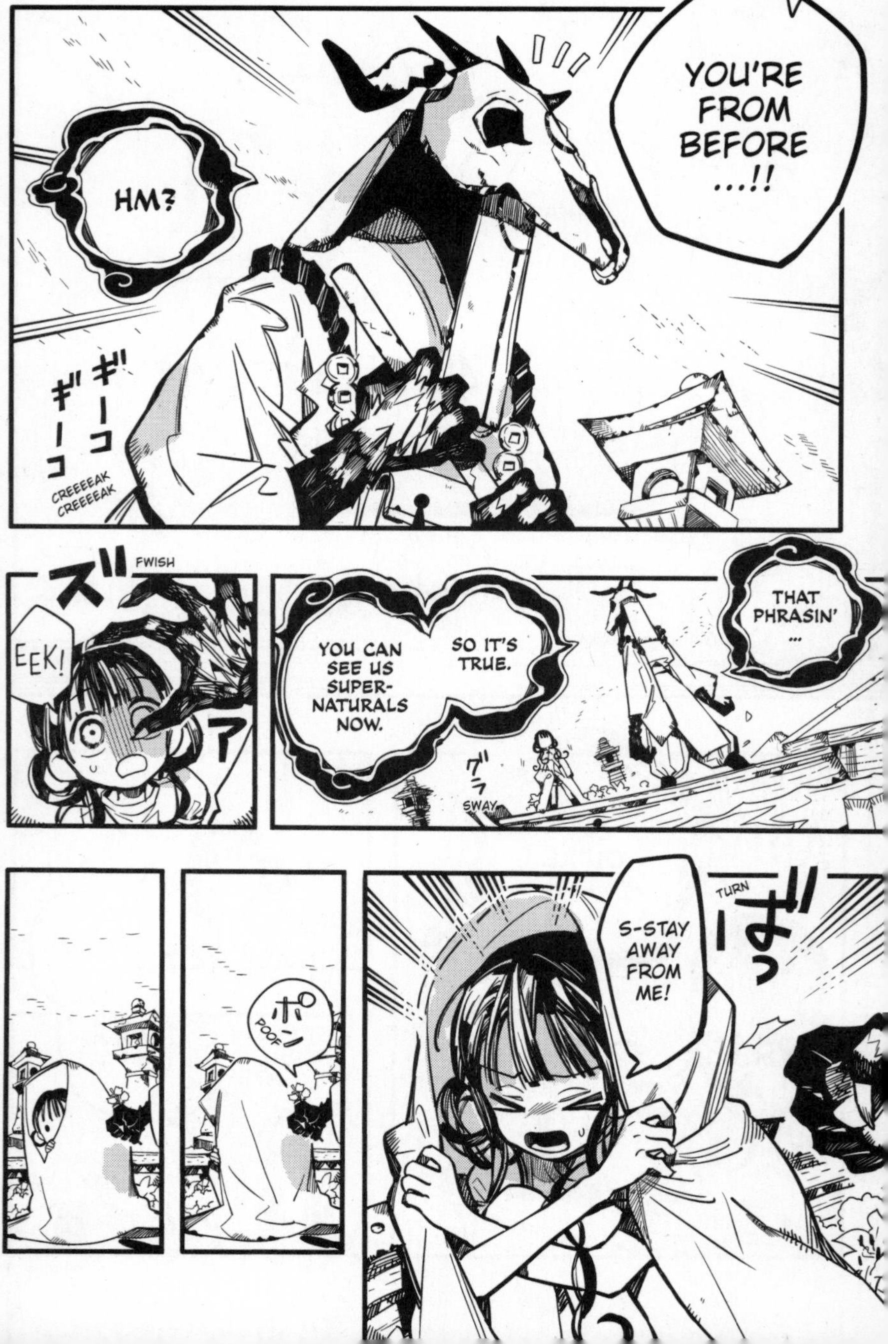
YOU'RE FROM BEFORE ...!!
HM?
ギーコ ギーコ
CREEEEAK CREEEEAK
THAT PHRASIN' ...
SO IT'S TRUE.
YOU CAN SEE US SUPER-NATURALS NOW.
グラ
SWAY
ズ
FWISH
EEK!
ア
ばっ
TURN
S-STAY AWAY FROM ME!
ポン
POOF

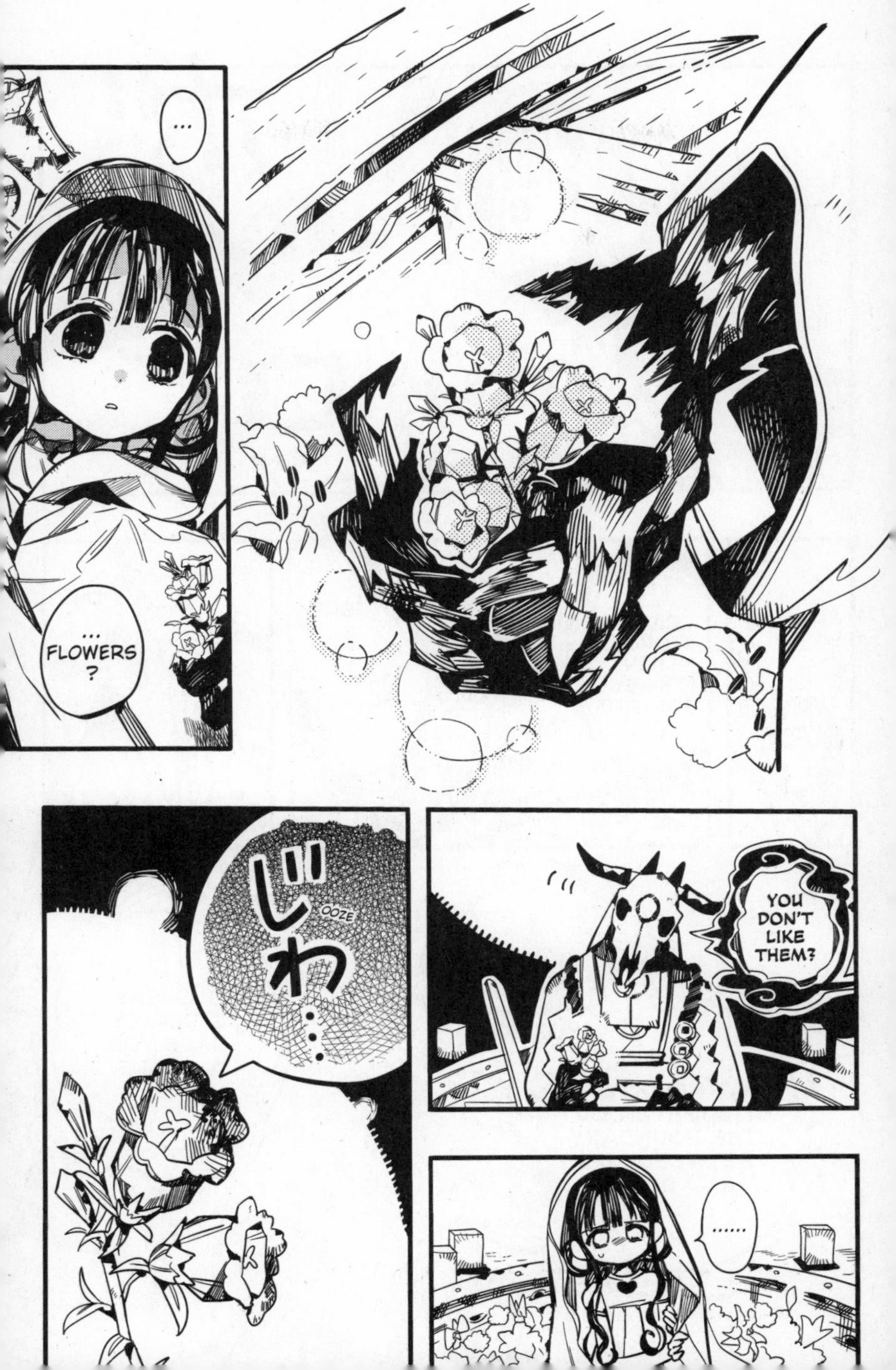
...
...FLOWERS?
YOU DON'T LIKE THEM?
......
じわ...
OOZE

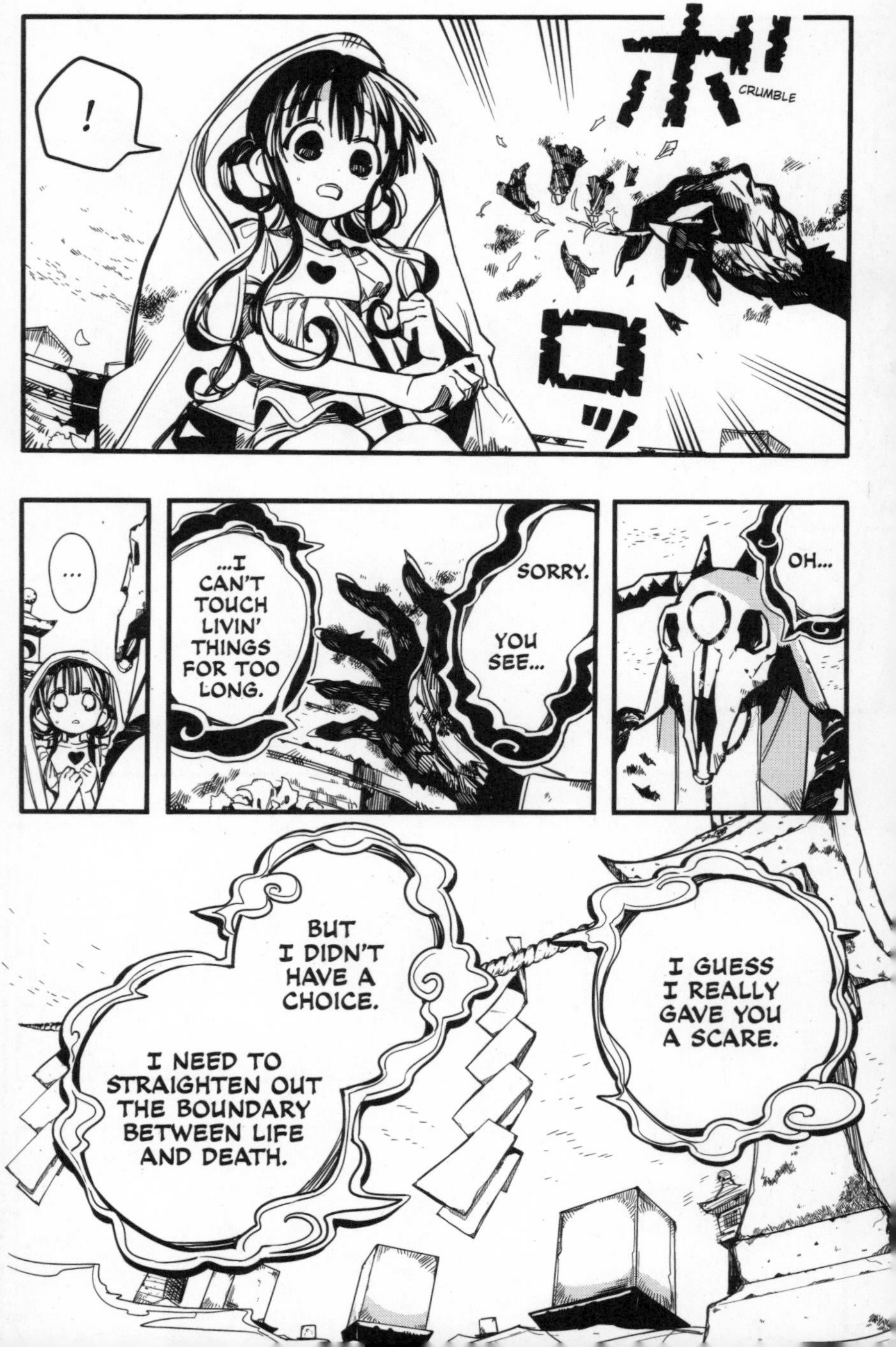
ボロッ
CRUMBLE
!
OH...
SORRY.
YOU SEE...
...I CAN'T TOUCH LIVIN' THINGS FOR TOO LONG.
...
I GUESS I REALLY GAVE YOU A SCARE.
BUT I DIDN'T HAVE A CHOICE.
I NEED TO STRAIGHTEN OUT THE BOUNDARY BETWEEN LIFE AND DEATH.

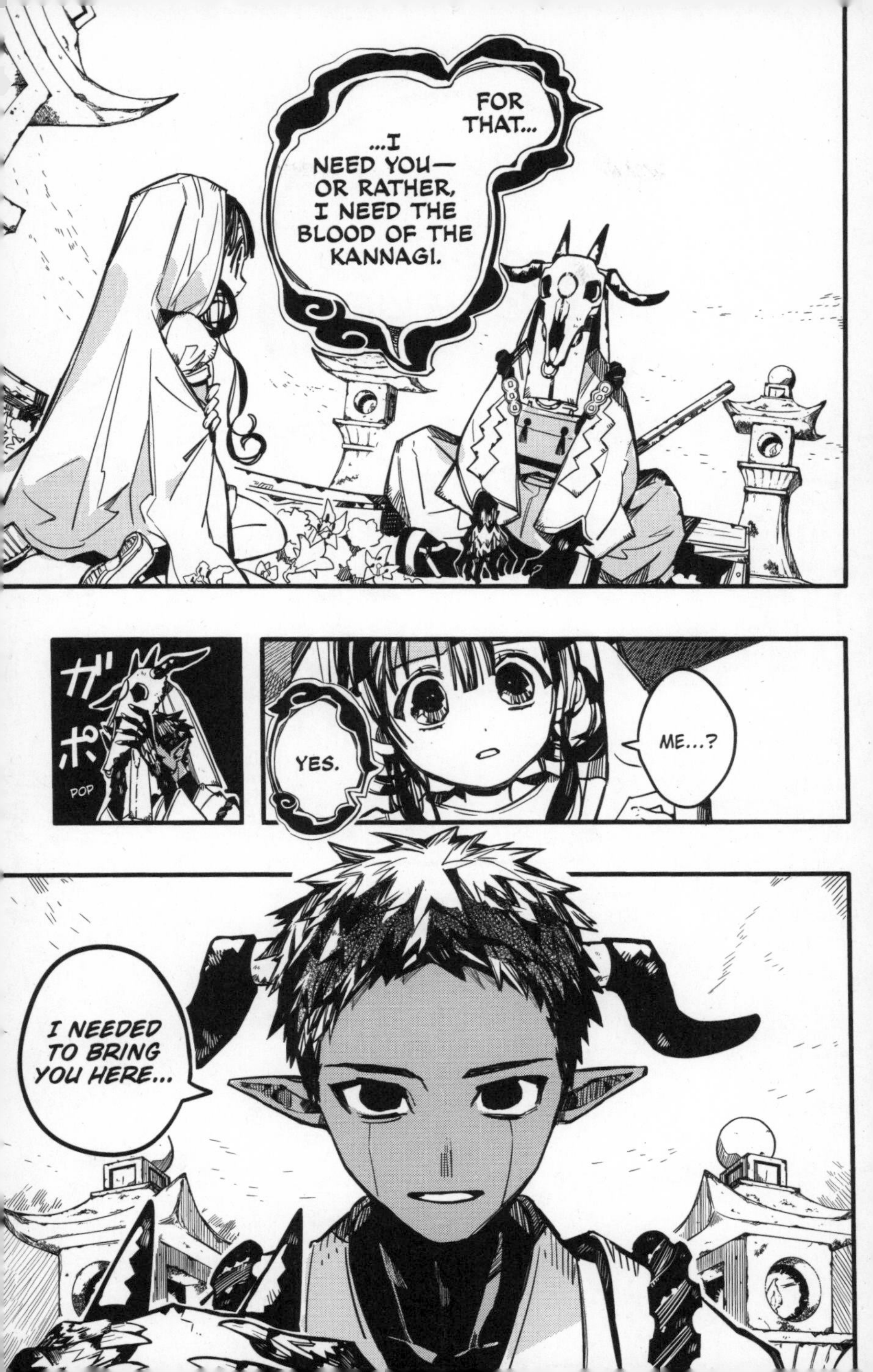
FOR THAT...
...I NEED YOU—OR RATHER, I NEED THE BLOOD OF THE KANNAGI.
ME...?
YES.
ガポ
POP
I NEEDED TO BRING YOU HERE...

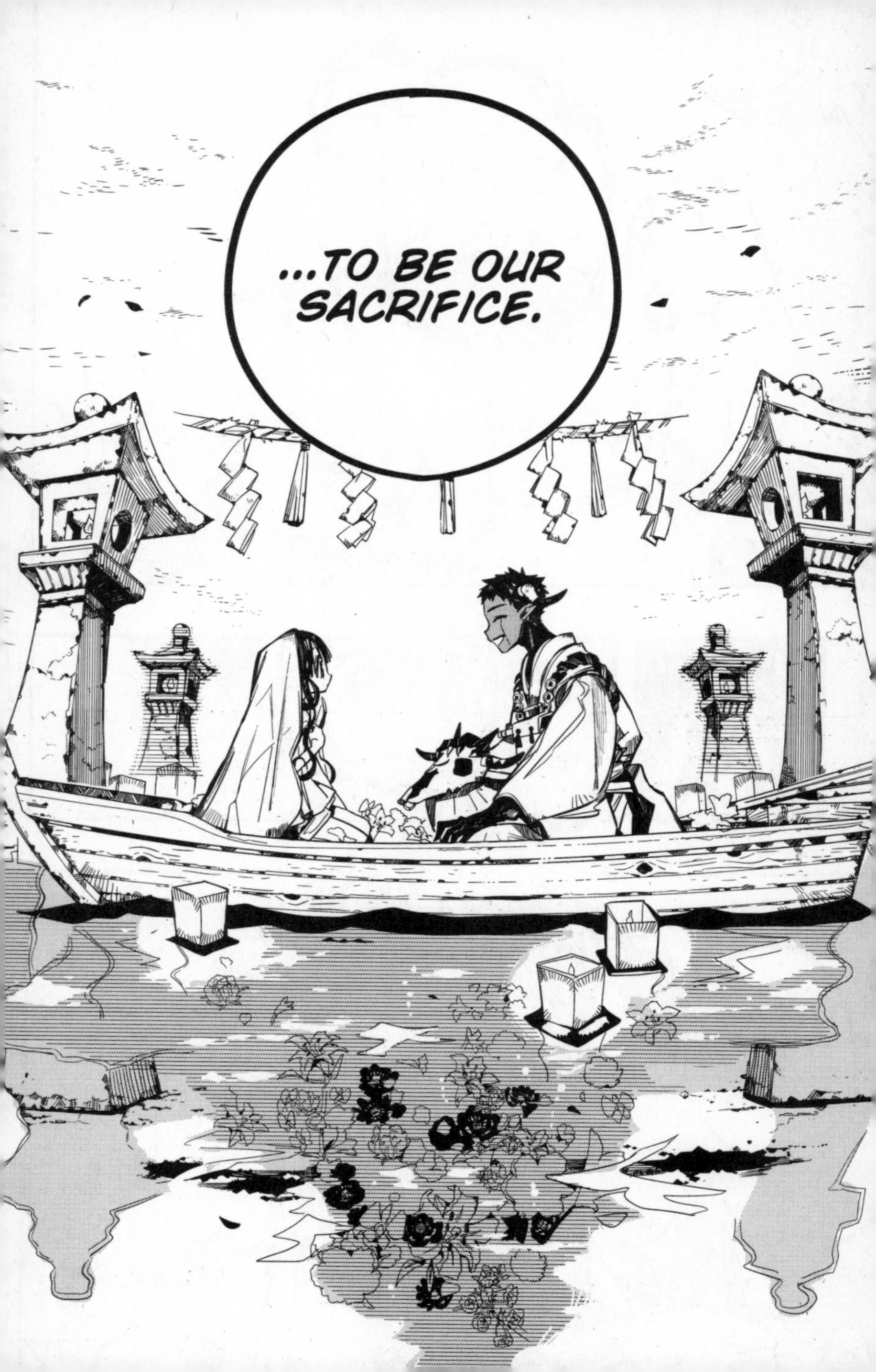
...TO BE OUR SACRIFICE.

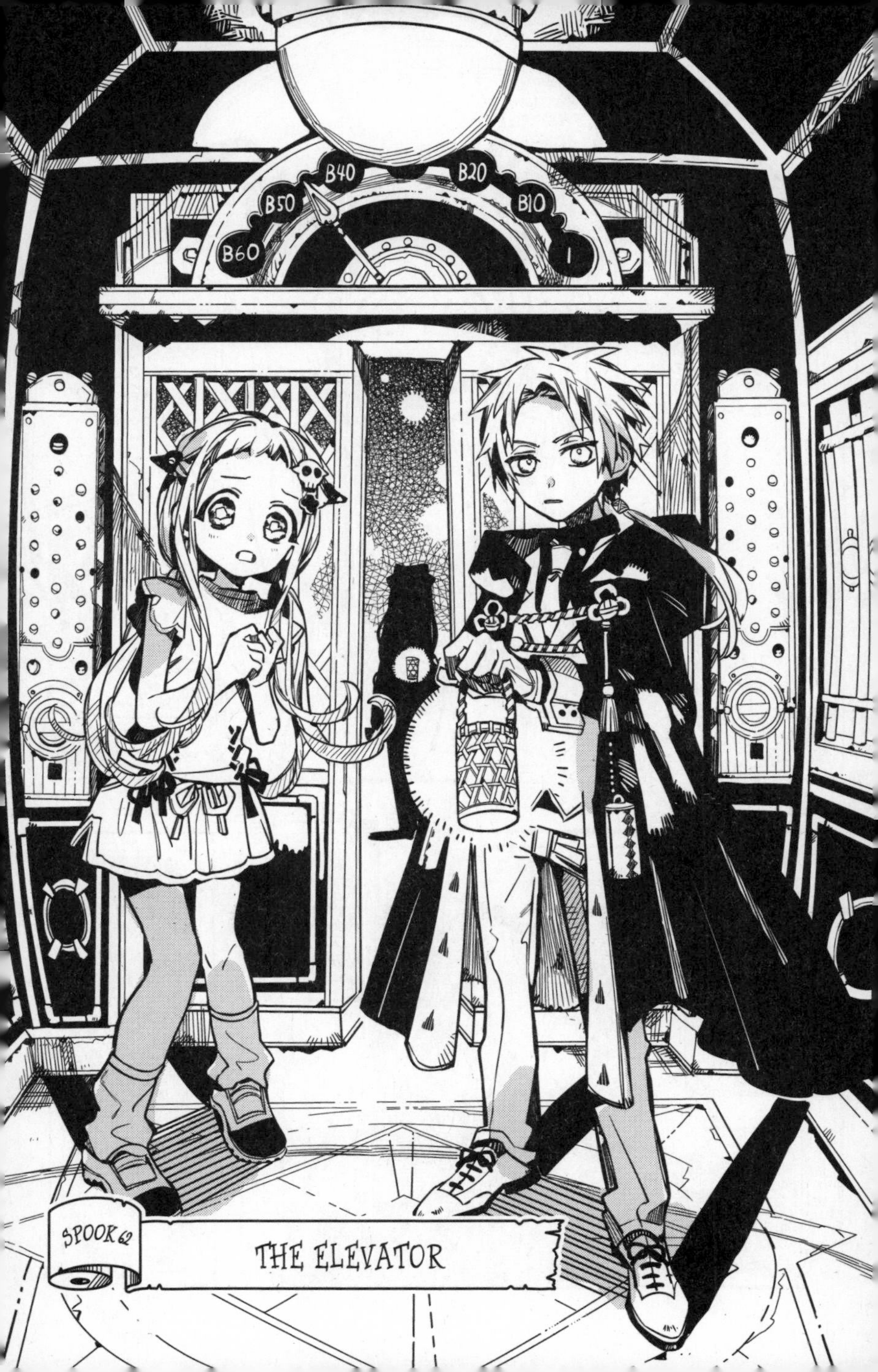
B60
B50
B40
B20
B10
1
SPOOK 62
THE ELEVATOR

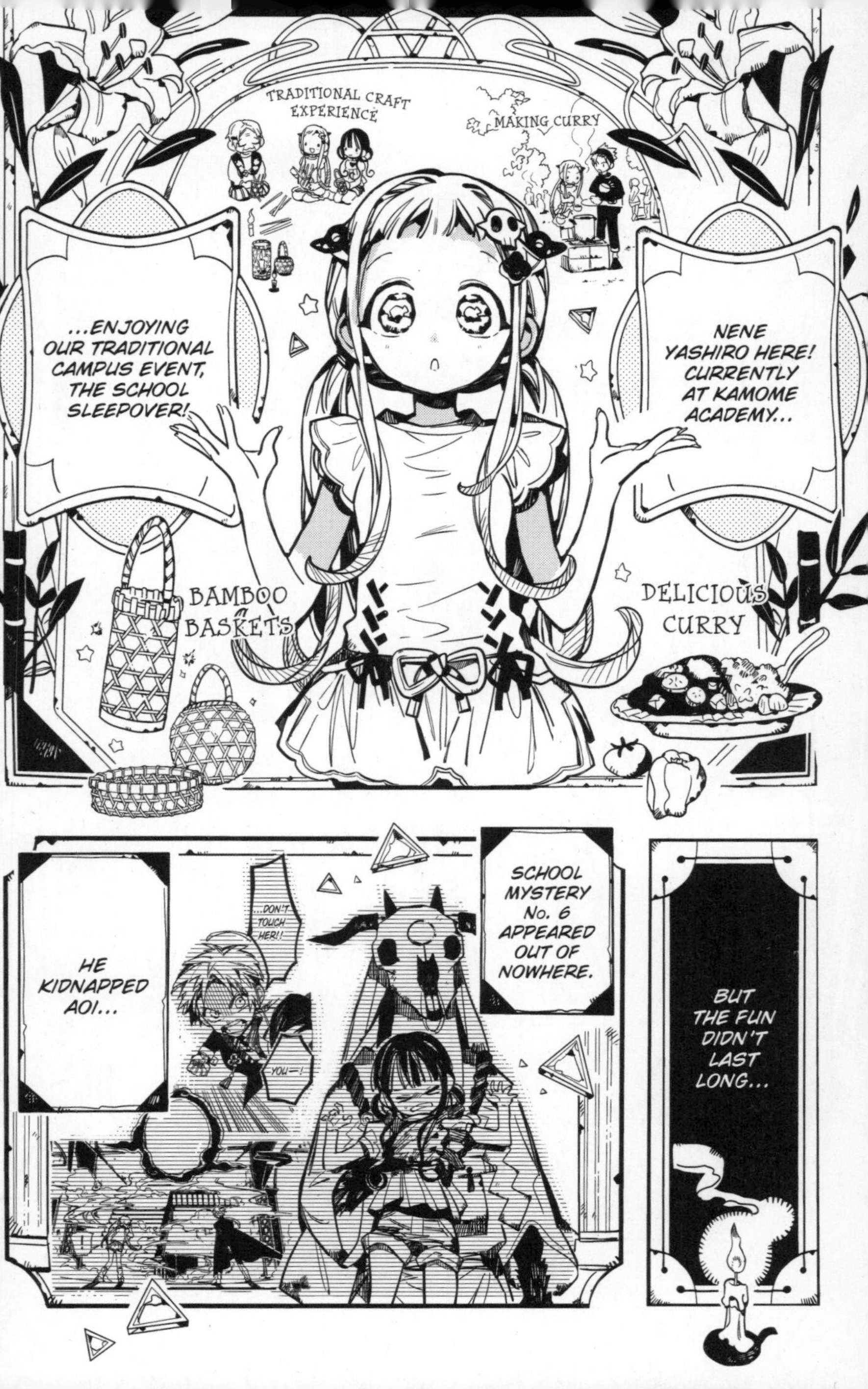
MAKING CURRY
TRADITIONAL CRAFT EXPERIENCE
NENE YASHIRO HERE! CURRENTLY AT KAMOME ACADEMY...
...ENJOYING OUR TRADITIONAL CAMPUS EVENT, THE SCHOOL SLEEPOVER!
DELICIOUS CURRY
BAMBOO BASKETS
BUT THE FUN DIDN'T LAST LONG...
SCHOOL MYSTERY No. 6 APPEARED OUT OF NOWHERE.
...DON'T TOUCH HER!!
HE KIDNAPPED AOI...
YOU—!

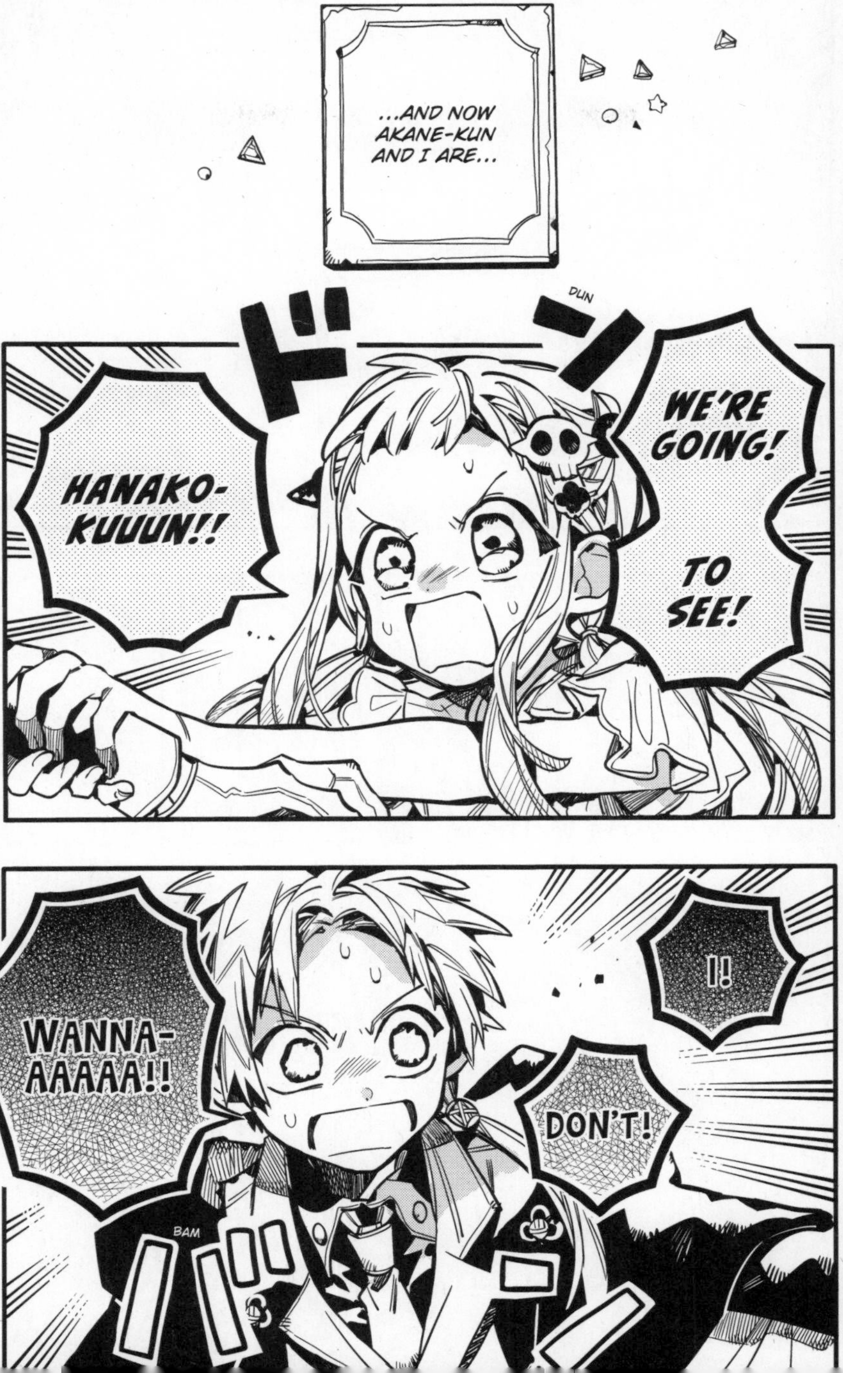

...AND NOW AKANE-KUN AND I ARE...
DUN
WE'RE GOING!
TO SEE!
HANAKO-KUUUN!!
I!
DON'T!
WANNA-AAAAA!!
BAM

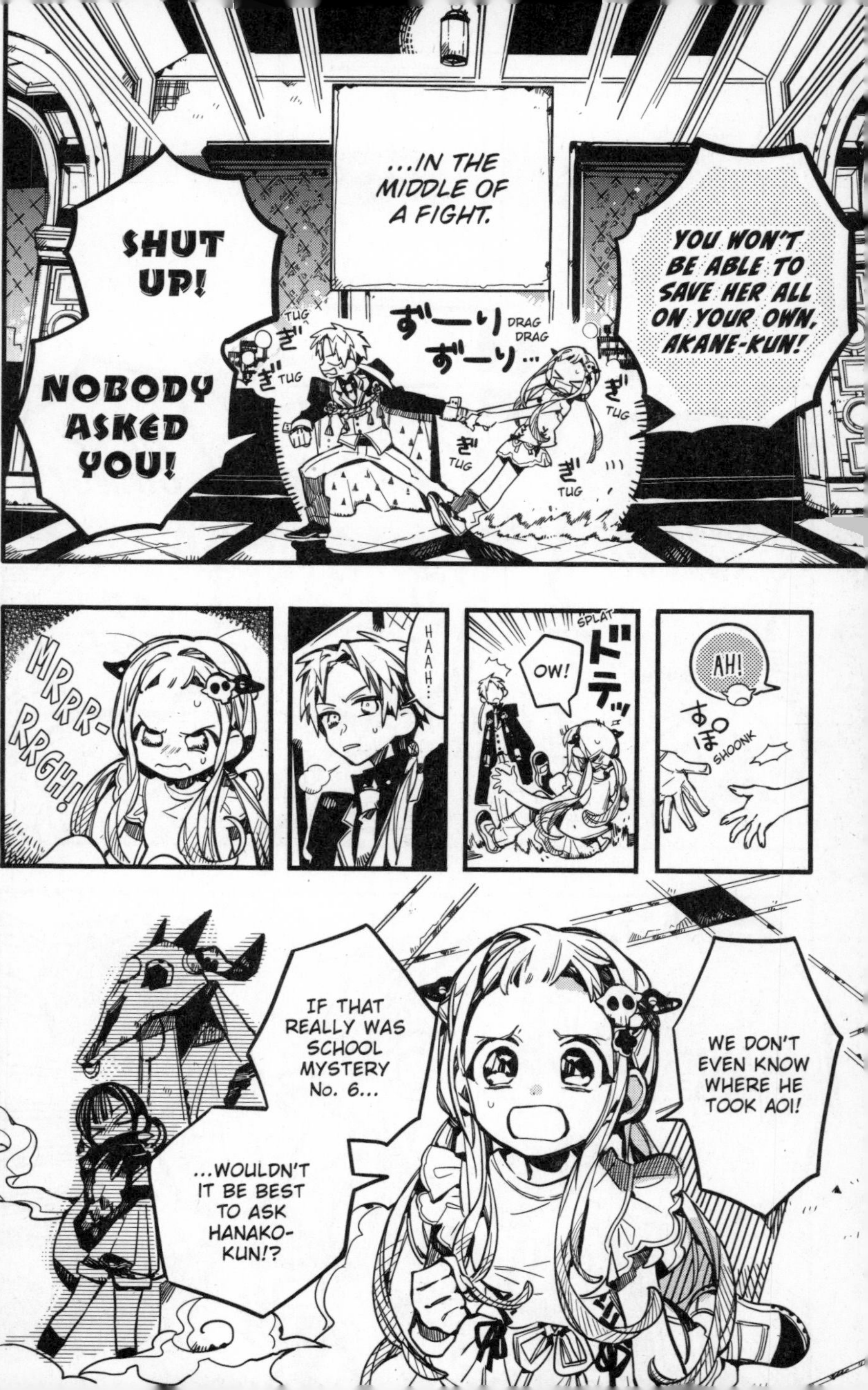
...IN THE MIDDLE OF A FIGHT.
YOU WON'T BE ABLE TO SAVE HER ALL ON YOUR OWN, AKANE-KUN!
ぎ TUG
ずーり DRAG
ずーり… DRAG
ぎ TUG
ぎ TUG
ぎ TUG
ぎ TUG
ぎ TUG
SHUT UP!
NOBODY ASKED YOU!
AH!
すぽ SHOONK
ドテッ SPLAT
OW!
HAAAH...
MRRR-RRGH!
WE DON'T EVEN KNOW WHERE HE TOOK AOI!
IF THAT REALLY WAS SCHOOL MYSTERY No. 6...
...WOULDN'T IT BE BEST TO ASK HANAKO-KUN!?

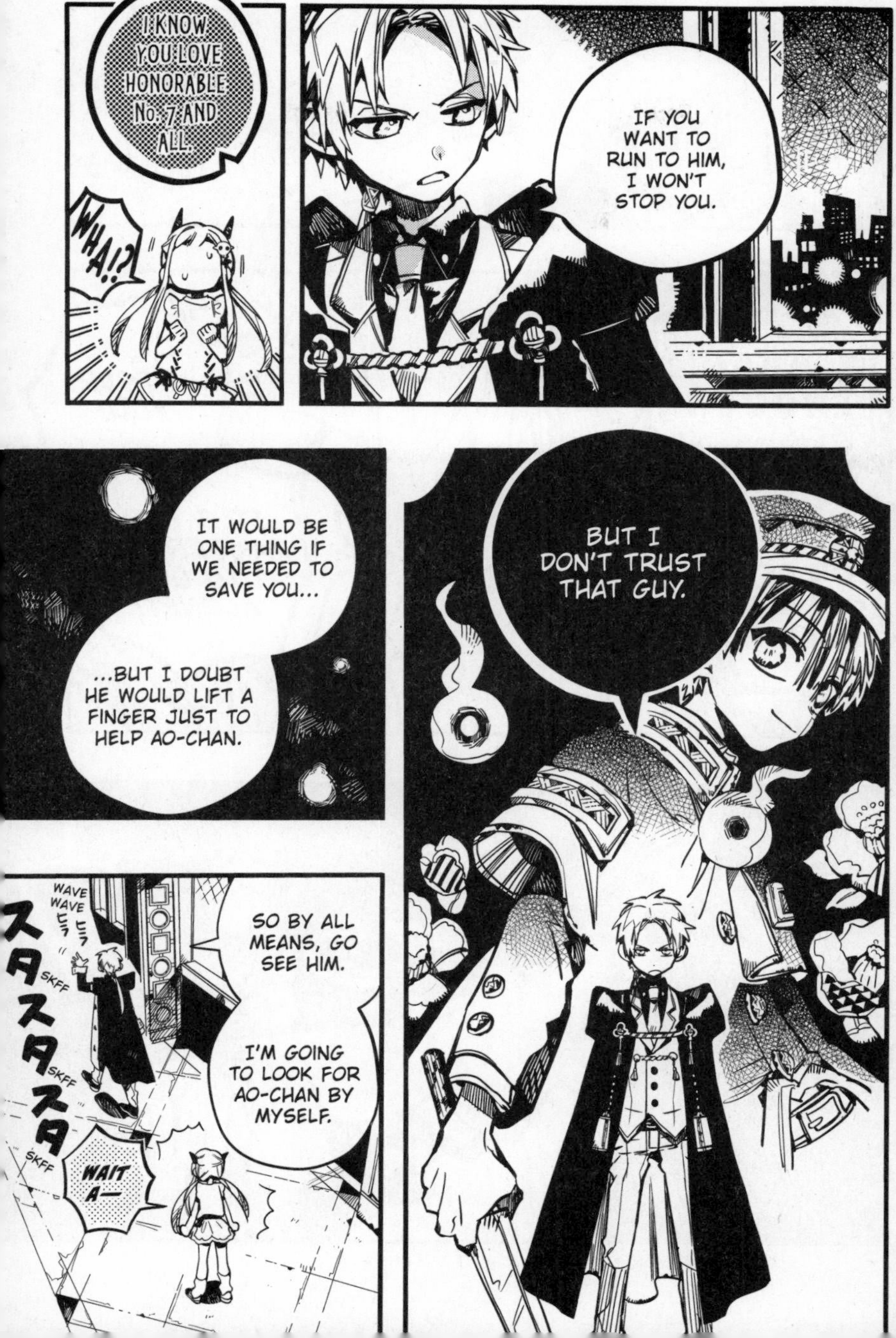
IF YOU WANT TO RUN TO HIM, I WON'T STOP YOU.
I KNOW YOU LOVE HONORABLE No. 7 AND ALL.
WHA!?
BUT I DON'T TRUST THAT GUY.
IT WOULD BE ONE THING IF WE NEEDED TO SAVE YOU...
...BUT I DOUBT HE WOULD LIFT A FINGER JUST TO HELP AO-CHAN.
SO BY ALL MEANS, GO SEE HIM.
I'M GOING TO LOOK FOR AO-CHAN BY MYSELF.
WAVE WAVE
ヒラ ヒラ
スタ SKFF
スタ SKFF
スタ SKFF
WAIT A—

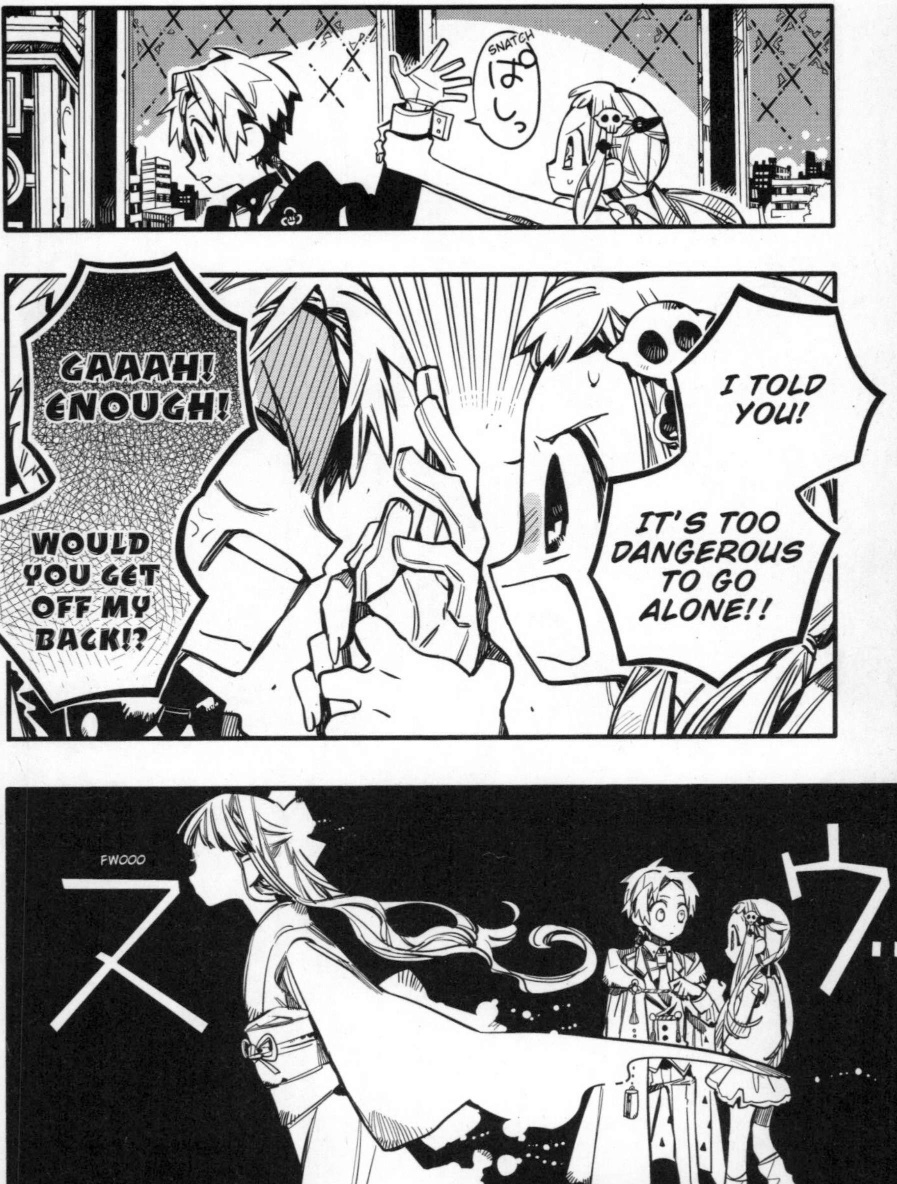
SNATCH
ぱしっ
I TOLD YOU!
IT'S TOO DANGEROUS TO GO ALONE!!
GAAAH! ENOUGH!
WOULD YOU GET OFF MY BACK!?
FWOOO
スウ..

ONE NIGHT, TWO DAWNS—

THREE GO TOGETHER...

LYING AWAKE...

...GAZING AT THE MOON...

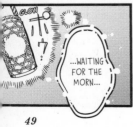

GLOW

ポゥ

...WAITING FOR THE MORN...

HUH ...?

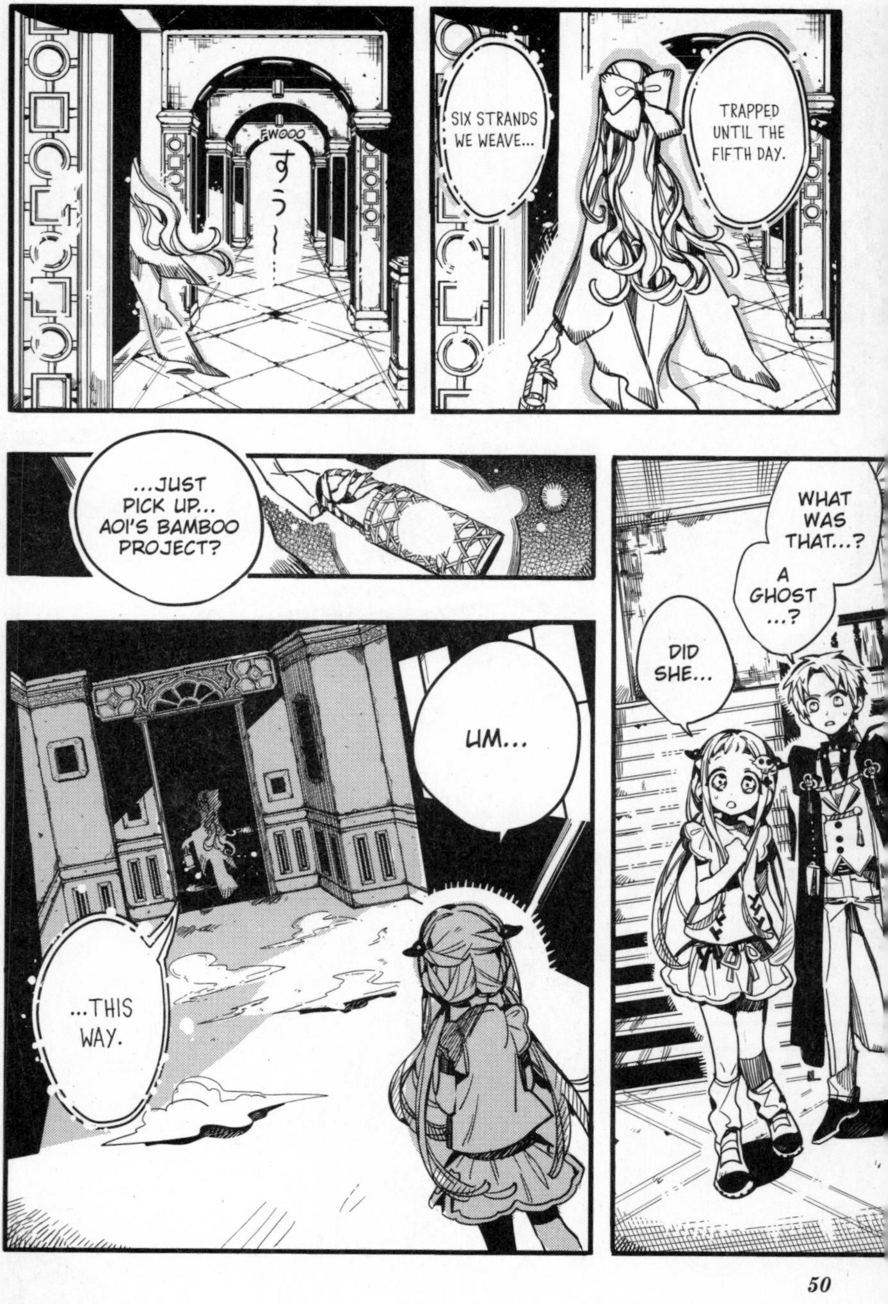
TRAPPED UNTIL THE FIFTH DAY.
SIX STRANDS WE WEAVE...
FWOOO
すう〜…
WHAT WAS THAT...?
A GHOST ...?
DID SHE...
...JUST PICK UP... AOI'S BAMBOO PROJECT?
UM...
...THIS WAY.

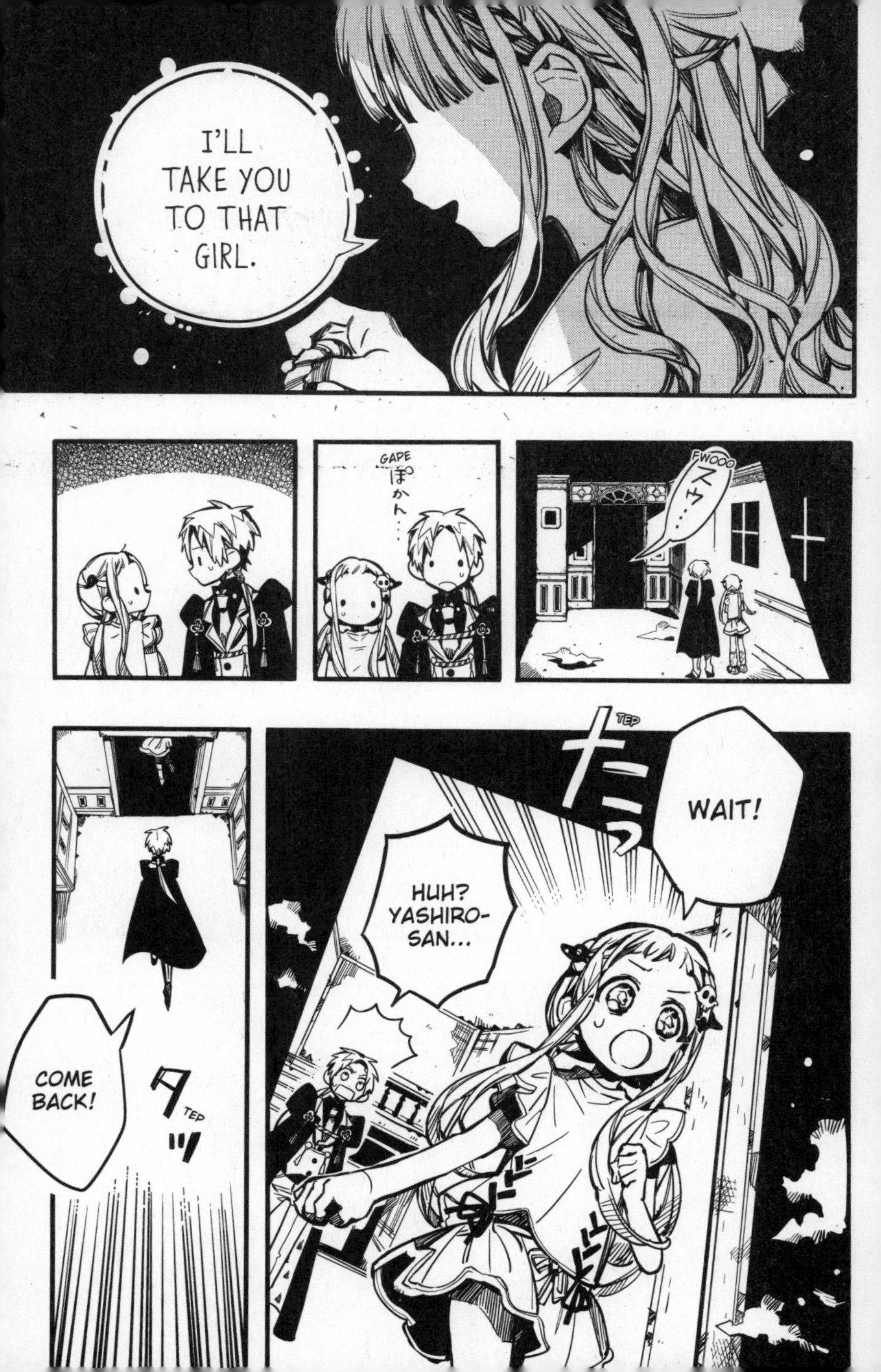
I'LL TAKE YOU TO THAT GIRL.
FWOOO
スゥ…
GAPE
ぽかん…
WAIT!
TEP
たっ
HUH? YASHIRO-SAN...
COME BACK!
タッ
TEP

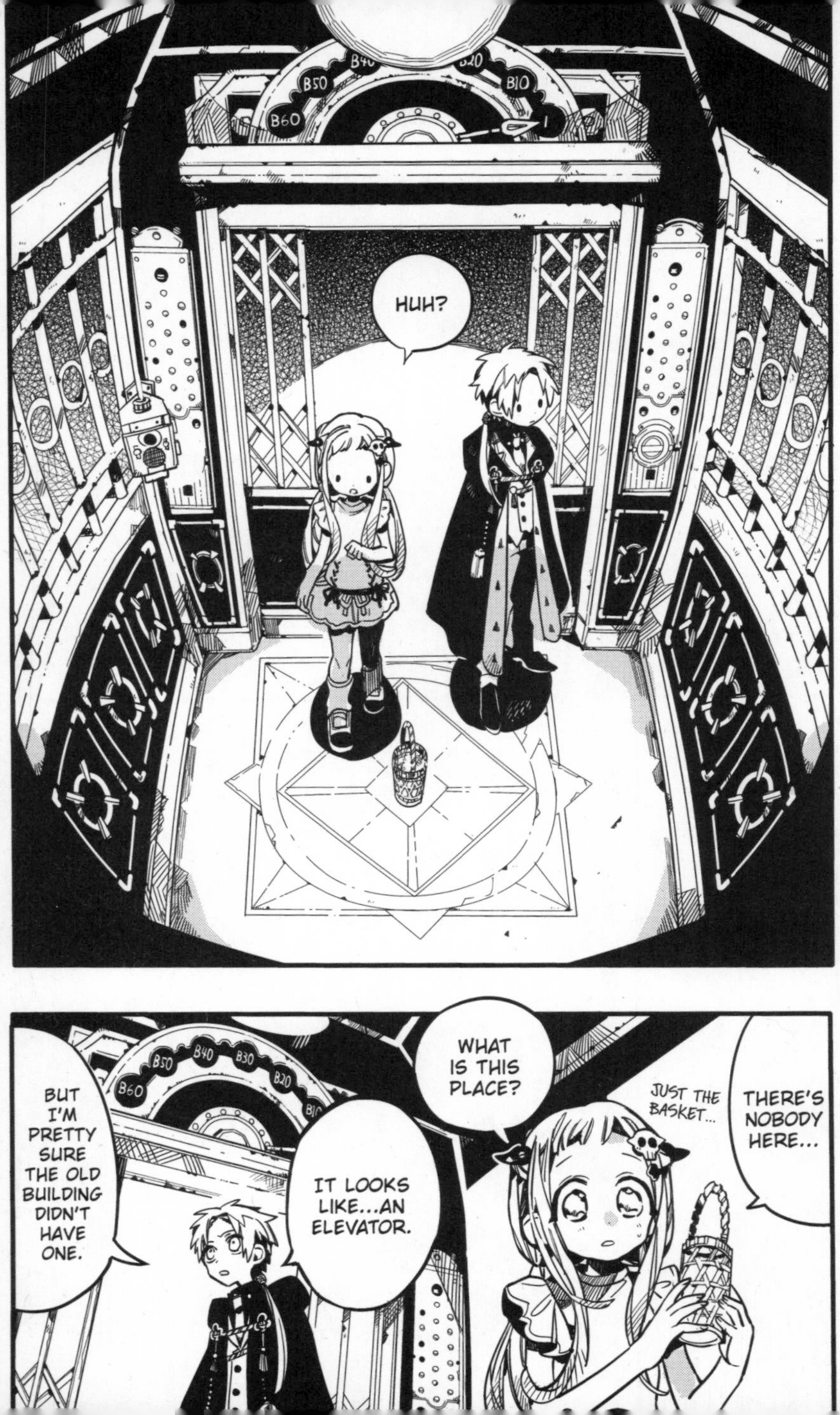
HUH?
THERE'S NOBODY HERE...
JUST THE BASKET...
WHAT IS THIS PLACE?
IT LOOKS LIKE...AN ELEVATOR.
BUT I'M PRETTY SURE THE OLD BUILDING DIDN'T HAVE ONE.

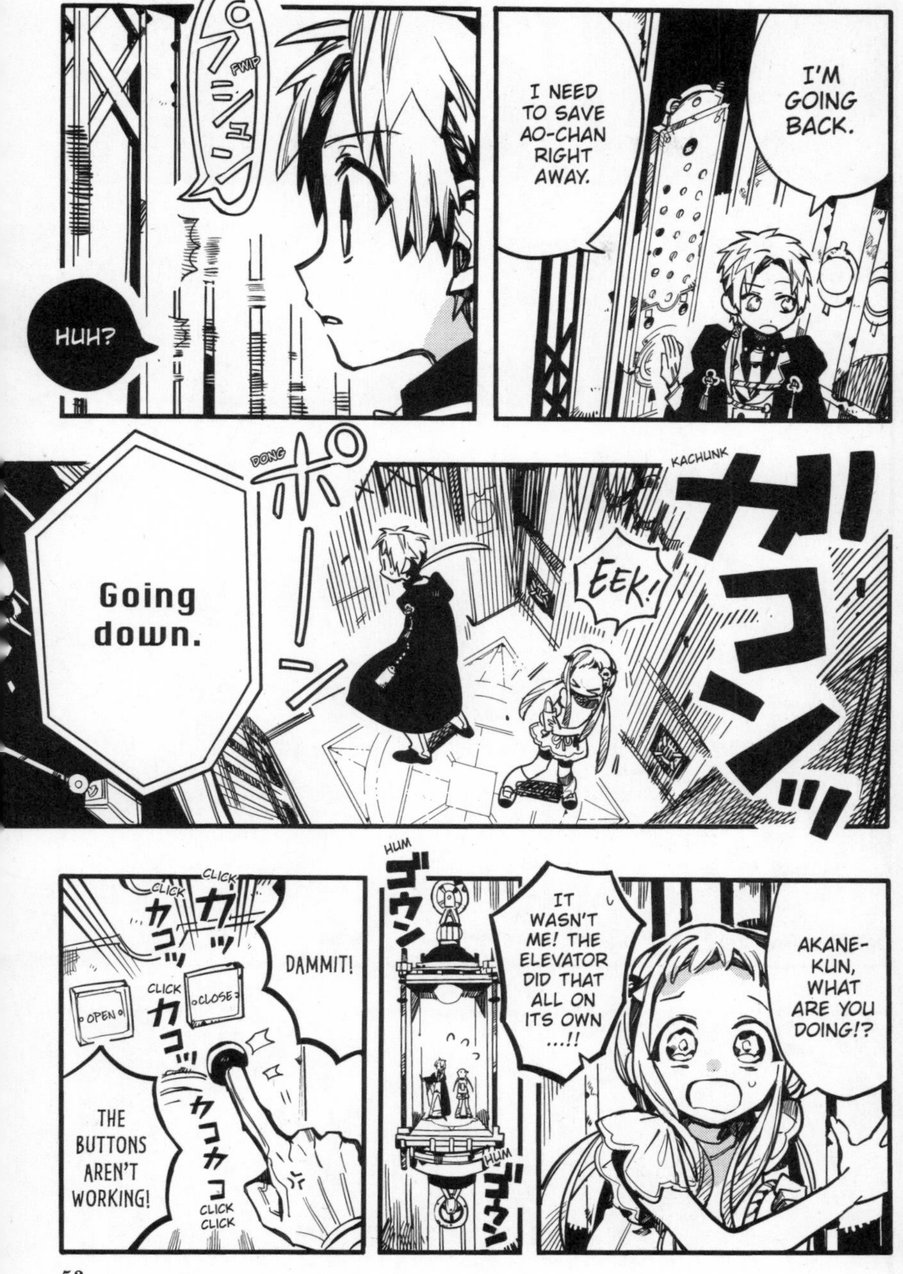
I'M GOING BACK.
I NEED TO SAVE AO-CHAN RIGHT AWAY.
FWIP
HUH?
KACHUNK
EEK!
DONG
Going down.
AKANE-KUN, WHAT ARE YOU DOING!?
IT WASN'T ME! THE ELEVATOR DID THAT ALL ON ITS OWN ...!!
HUM
HUM
DAMMIT!
CLICK
CLICK
CLOSE
OPEN
CLICK
THE BUTTONS AREN'T WORKING!
CLICK CLICK

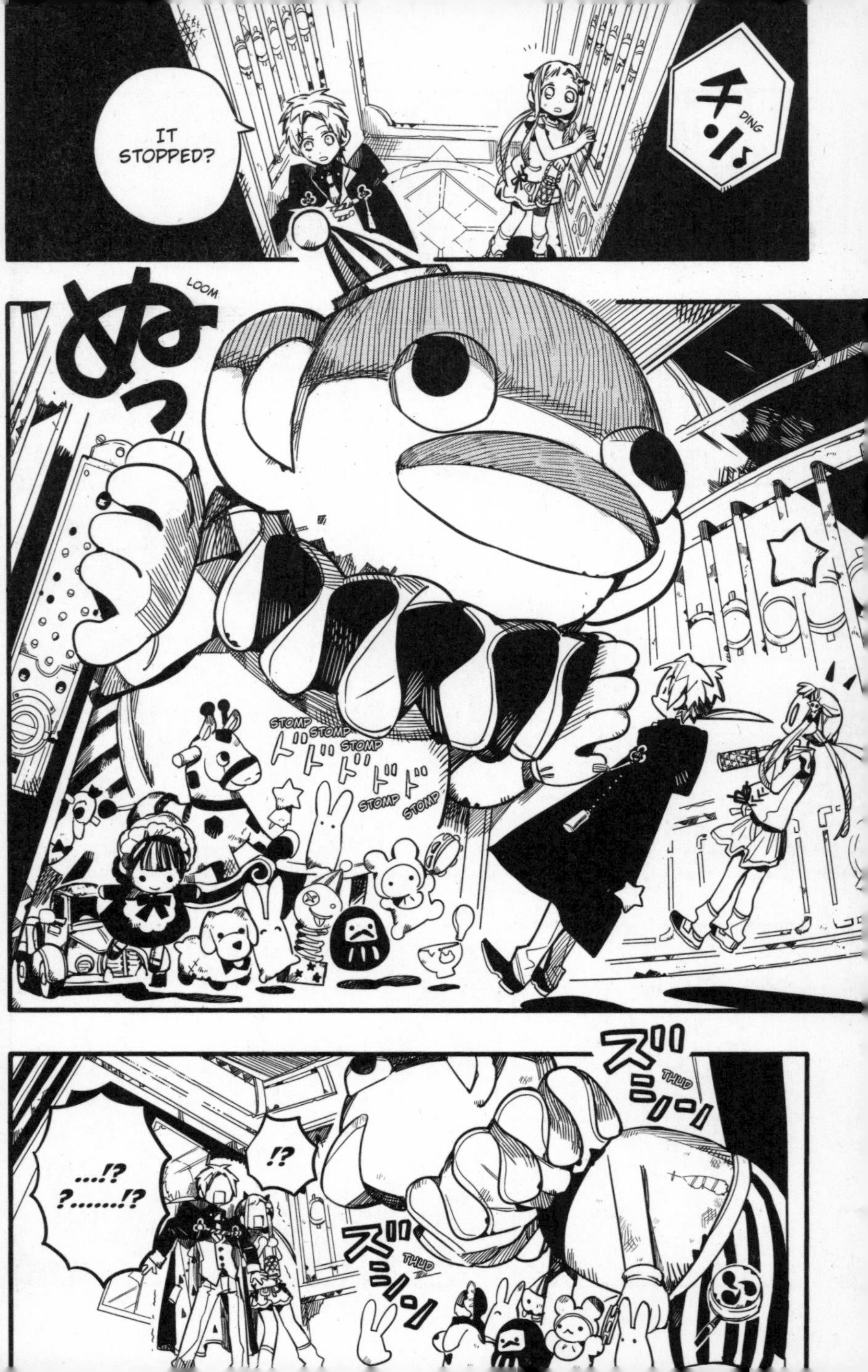
チン♪
DING
IT STOPPED?
ぬっ
LOOM
ドドドド
STOMP STOMP STOMP STOMP STOMP
THUD
!?
...!?
?.......!?
THUD

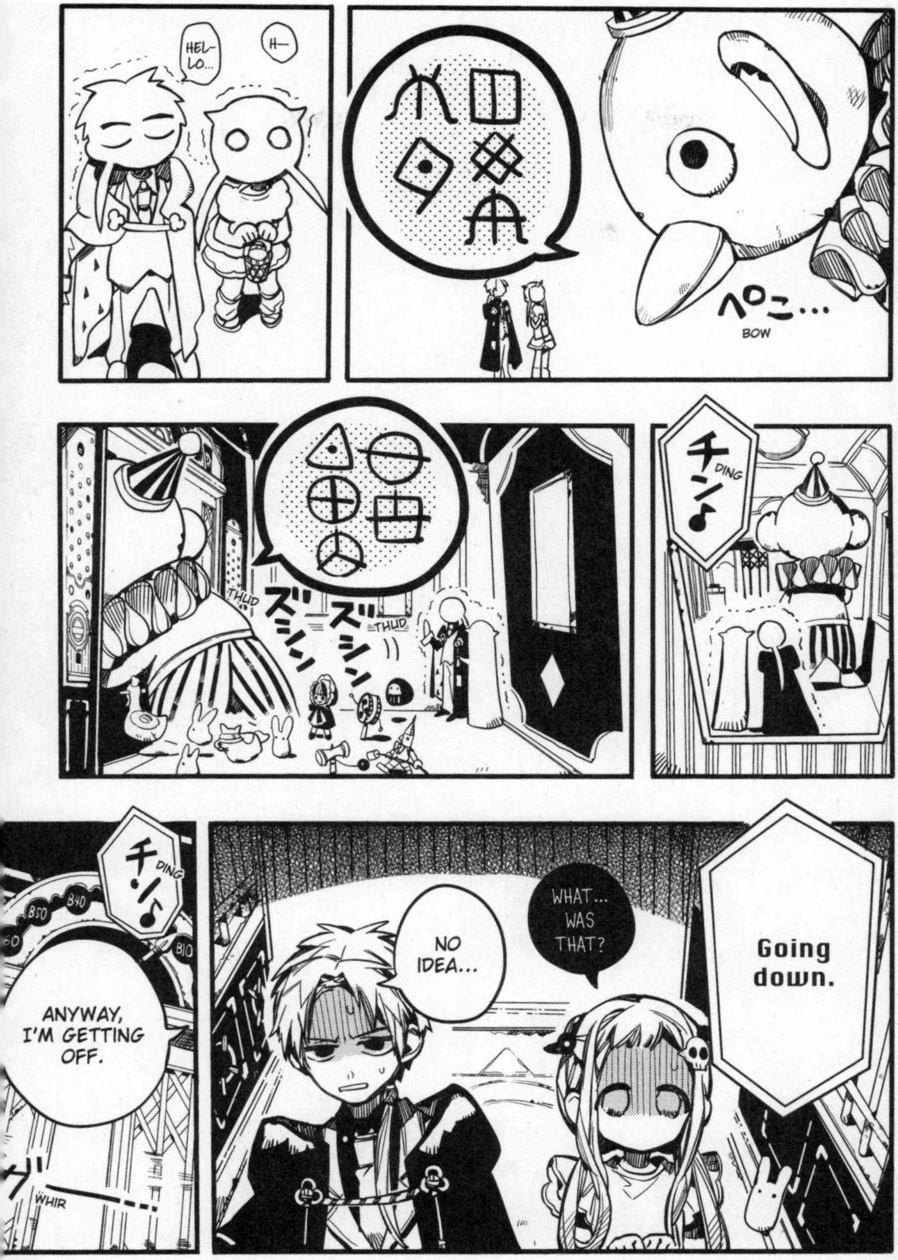
へこ…
BOW
H—
HEL-LO…
チン♪
DING
ズシン
THUD
ズシン
THUD
Going down.
WHAT… WAS THAT?
NO IDEA…
チン♪
DING
B50
B40
B10
ANYWAY, I'M GETTING OFF.
WHIR

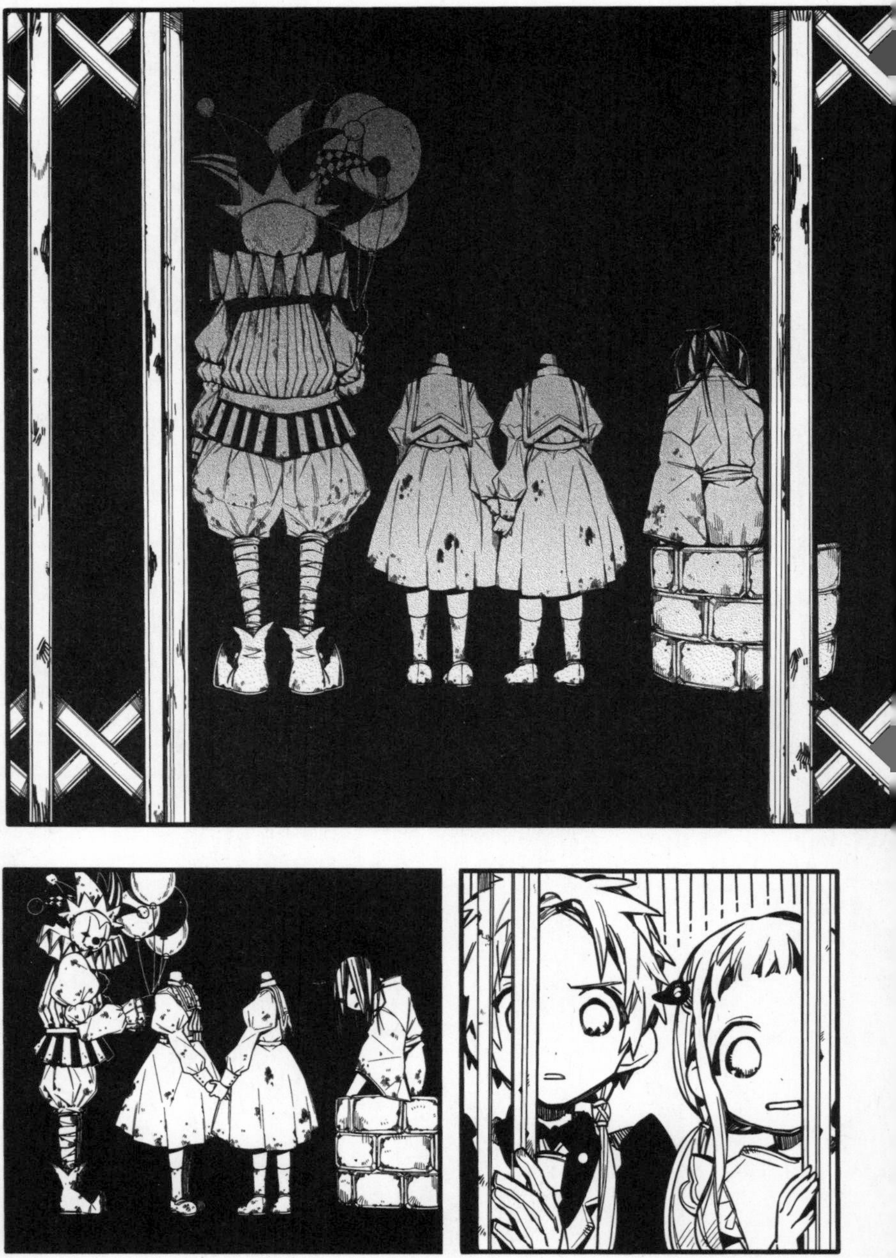

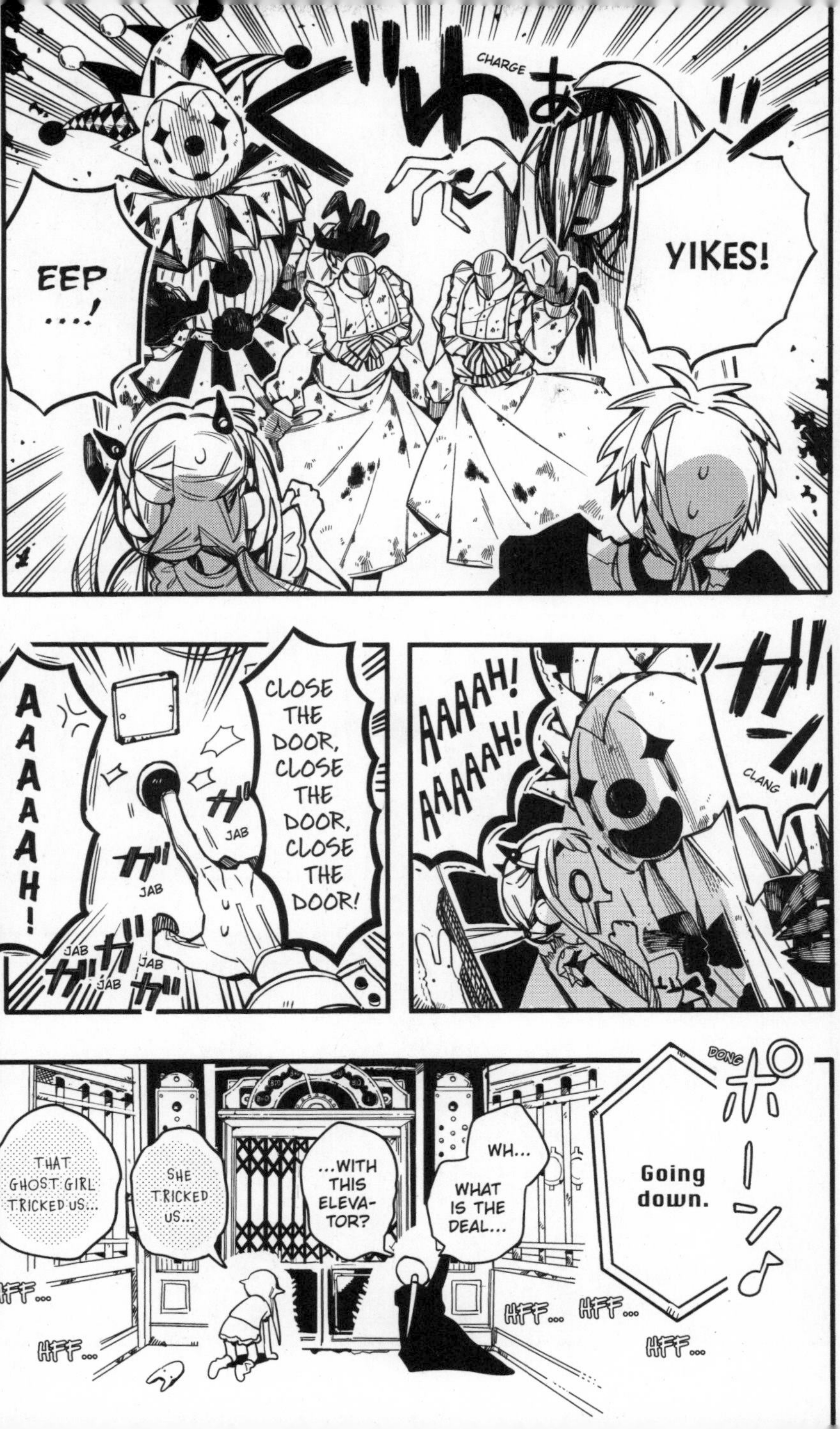
CHARGE
YIKES!
EEP ...!
CLANG
AAAAH! AAAAAH!
CLOSE THE DOOR, CLOSE THE DOOR, CLOSE THE DOOR!
JAB
JAB
JAB
JAB
JAB
AAAAAAH!
DONG
Going down.
WH... WHAT IS THE DEAL...
...WITH THIS ELEVATOR?
SHE TRICKED US...
THAT GHOST GIRL TRICKED US...
HFF...
HFF...
HFF...
HFF...
HFF...

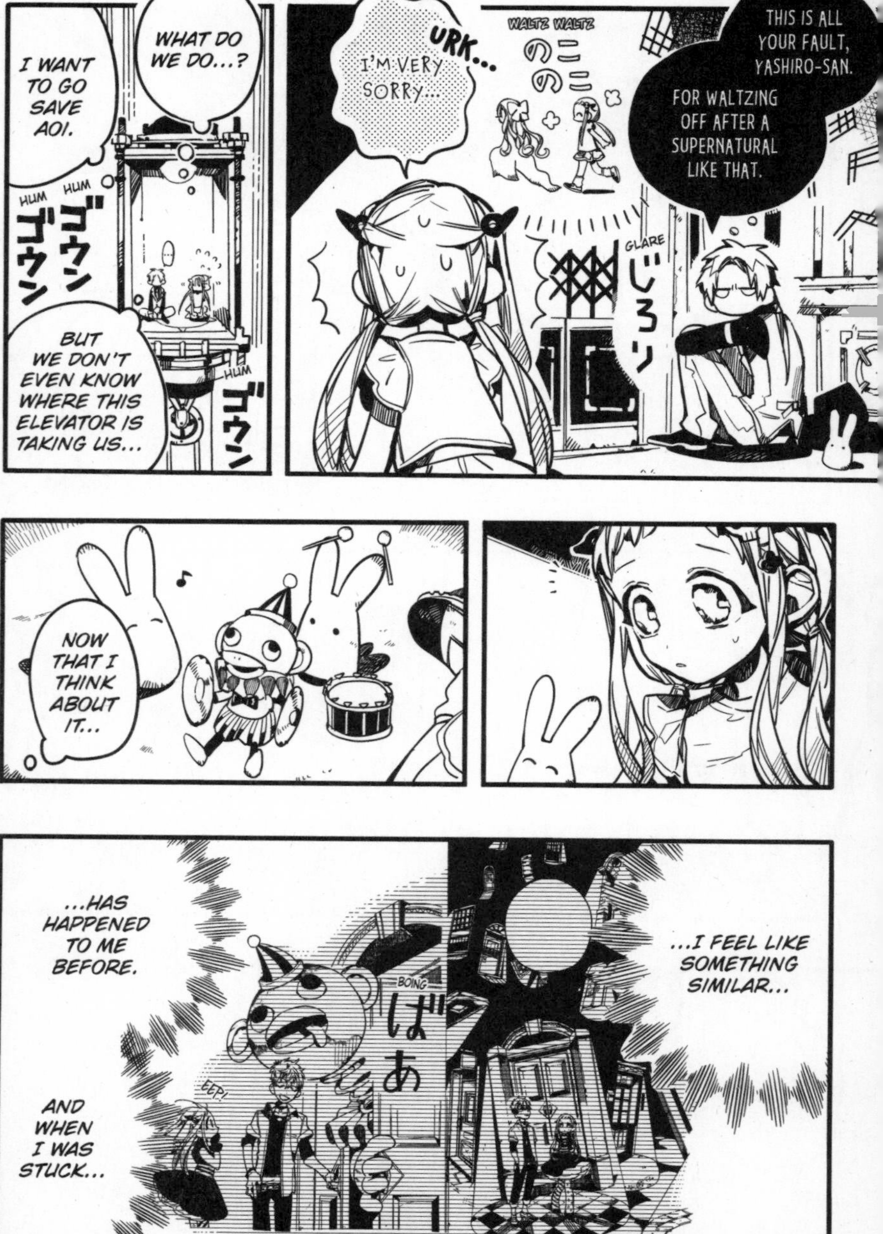
THIS IS ALL YOUR FAULT, YASHIRO-SAN.
FOR WALTZING OFF AFTER A SUPERNATURAL LIKE THAT.
WALTZ WALTZ
のこのこ
GLARE
じろり
URK...
I'M VERY SORRY...
WHAT DO WE DO...?
I WANT TO GO SAVE AOI.
HUM HUM
ゴウンゴウン
BUT WE DON'T EVEN KNOW WHERE THIS ELEVATOR IS TAKING US...
HUM
ゴウン
NOW THAT I THINK ABOUT IT...
...I FEEL LIKE SOMETHING SIMILAR...
...HAS HAPPENED TO ME BEFORE.
BOING
ばあ
EEP!
AND WHEN I WAS STUCK...

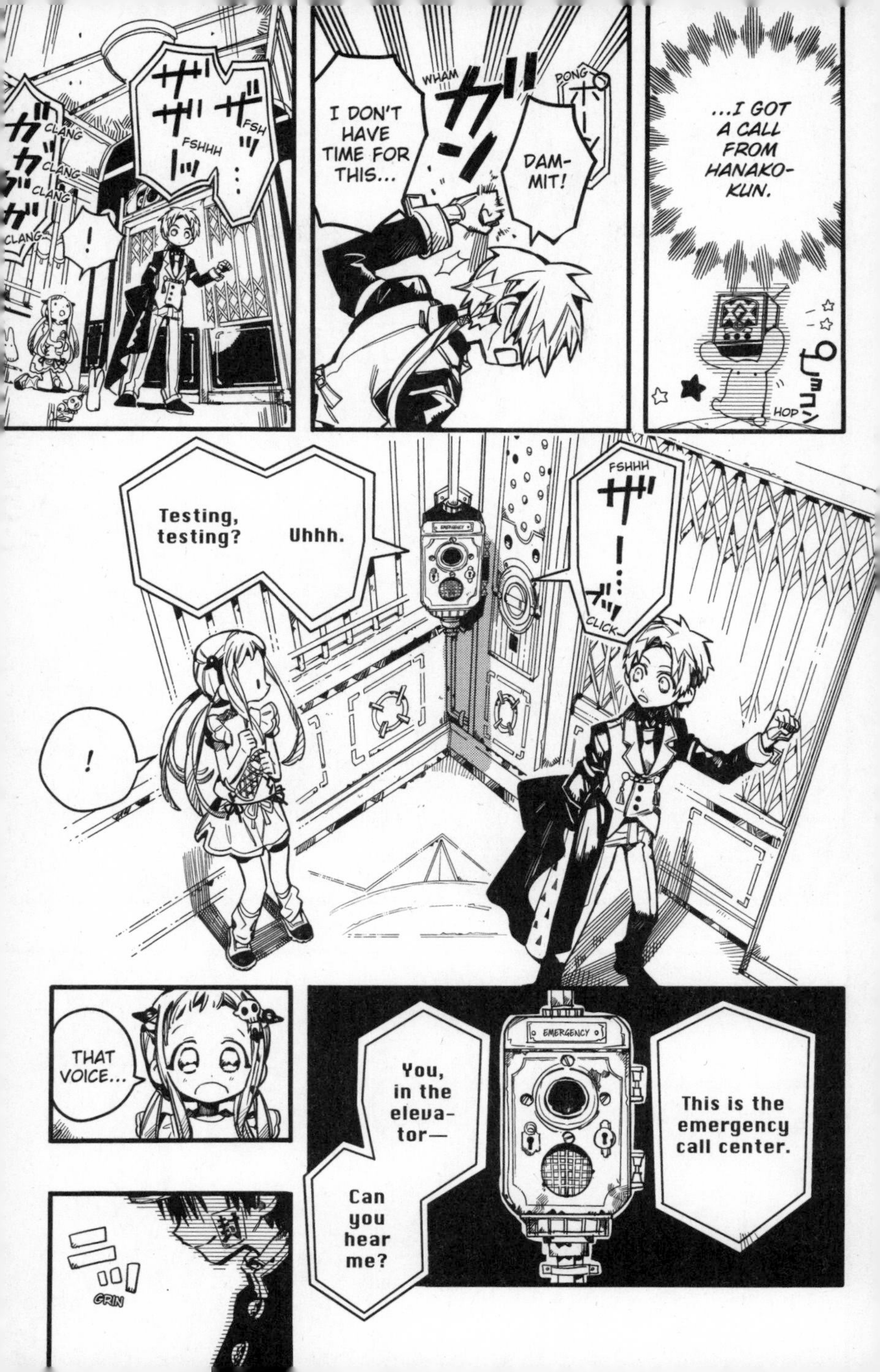
...I GOT A CALL FROM HANAKO-KUN.
HOP
PONG
DAM-MIT!
WHAM
I DON'T HAVE TIME FOR THIS...
FSH
FSHHH
CLANG
CLANG
CLANG
CLANG...
!
FSHHH
CLICK
EMERGENCY
Testing, testing? Uhhh.
!
EMERGENCY
This is the emergency call center.
You, in the elevator—
Can you hear me?
THAT VOICE...
GRIN

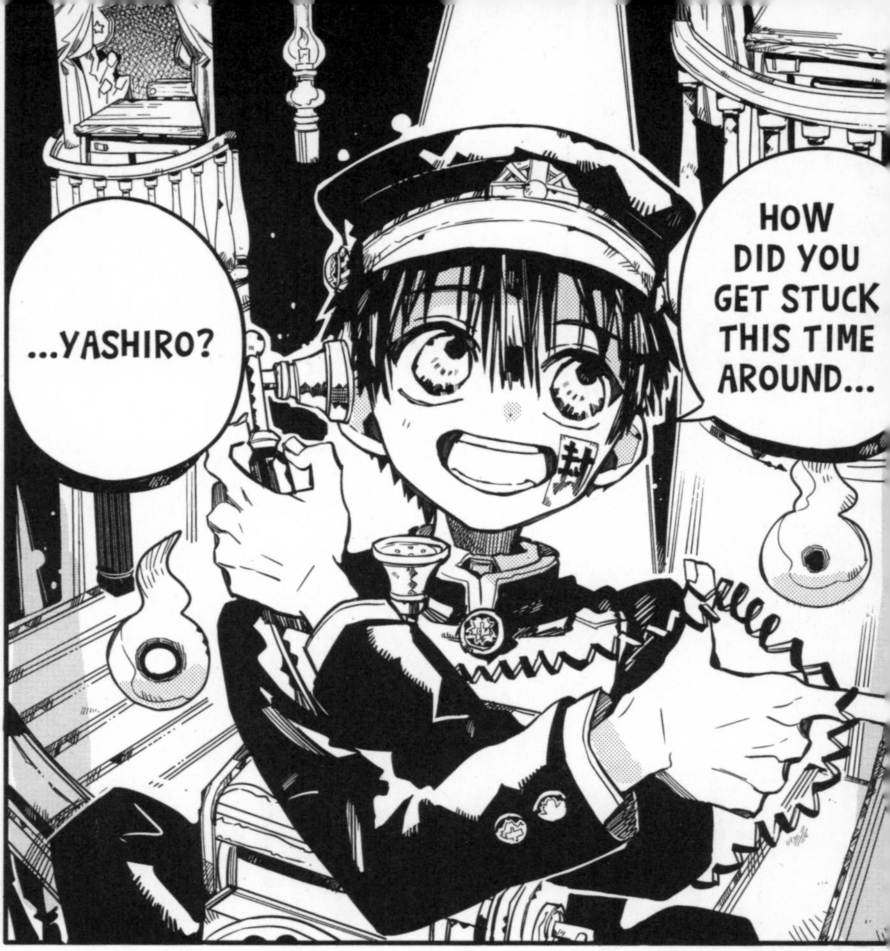
HOW DID YOU GET STUCK THIS TIME AROUND...
...YASHIRO?

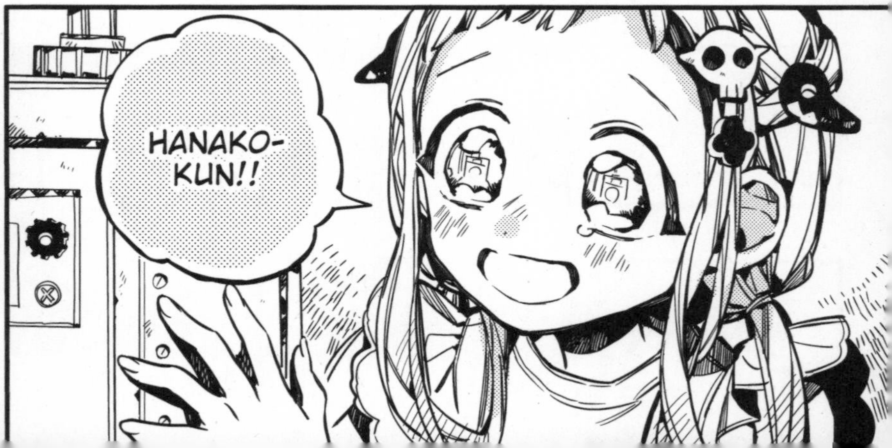
HANAKO-KUN!!

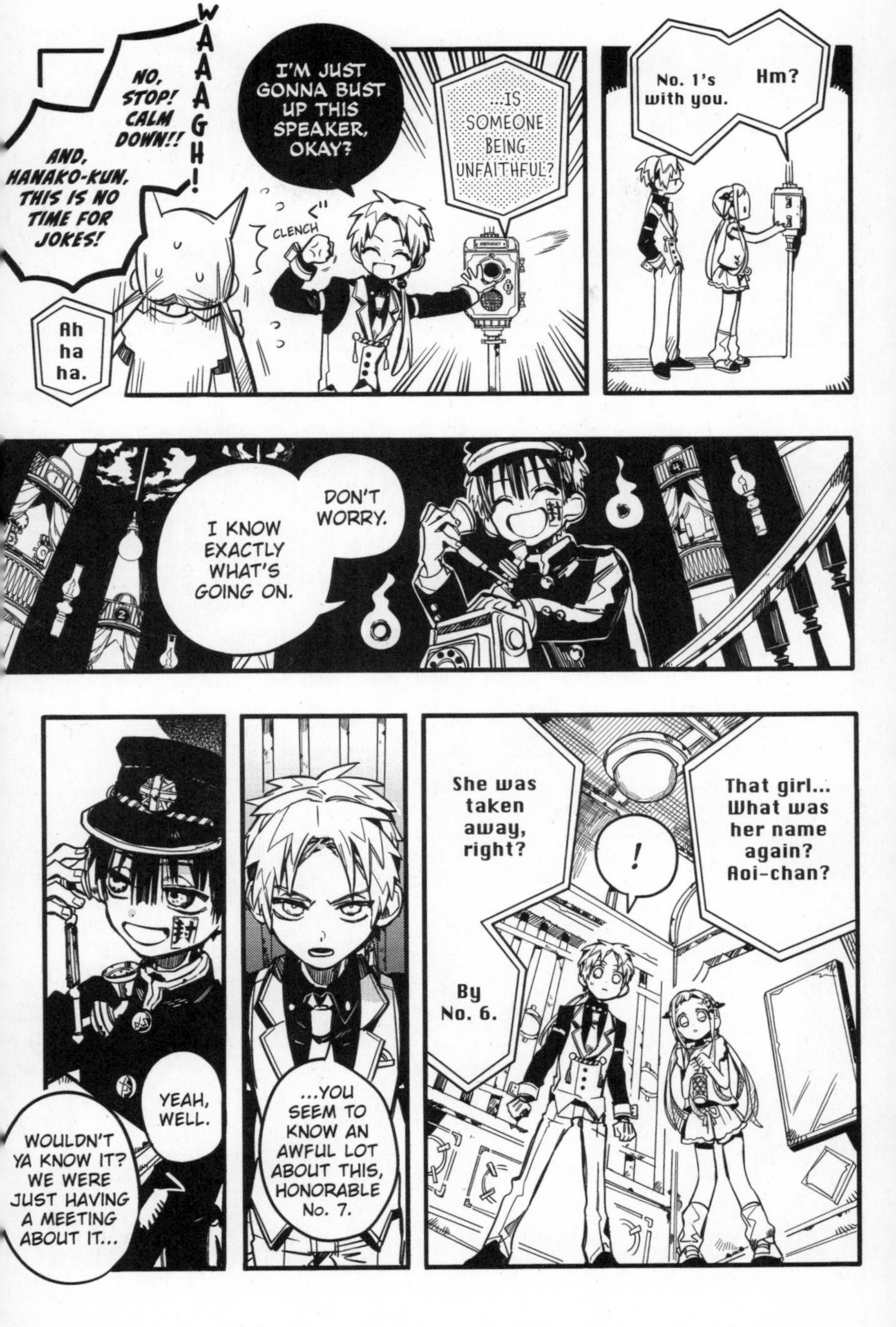
Hm?
No. 1's with you.
...IS SOMEONE BEING UNFAITHFUL?
I'M JUST GONNA BUST UP THIS SPEAKER, OKAY?
CLENCH
WAAAAGH!
NO, STOP! CALM DOWN!!
AND, HANAKO-KUN, THIS IS NO TIME FOR JOKES!
Ah ha ha.
DON'T WORRY.
I KNOW EXACTLY WHAT'S GOING ON.
That girl... What was her name again? Aoi-chan?
!
She was taken away, right?
By No. 6.
...YOU SEEM TO KNOW AN AWFUL LOT ABOUT THIS, HONORABLE No. 7.
YEAH, WELL.
WOULDN'T YA KNOW IT? WE WERE JUST HAVING A MEETING ABOUT IT...

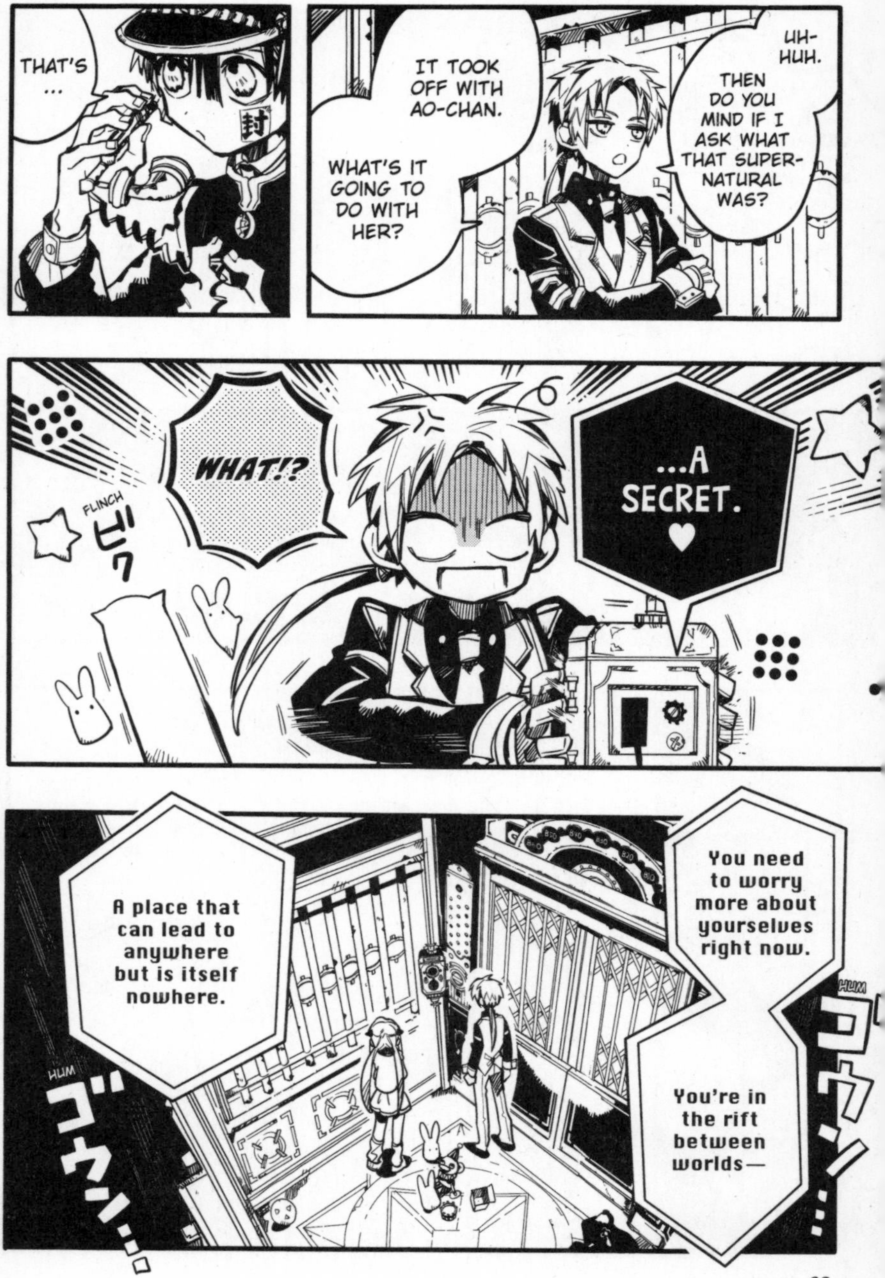
UH-HUH.
THEN DO YOU MIND IF I ASK WHAT THAT SUPER-NATURAL WAS?
IT TOOK OFF WITH AO-CHAN.
WHAT'S IT GOING TO DO WITH HER?
THAT'S ...
...A SECRET. ♥
WHAT!?
FLINCH
ビク
You need to worry more about yourselves right now.
HUM
ゴウン…
You're in the rift between worlds—
A place that can lead to anywhere but is itself nowhere.
HUM
ゴウン…

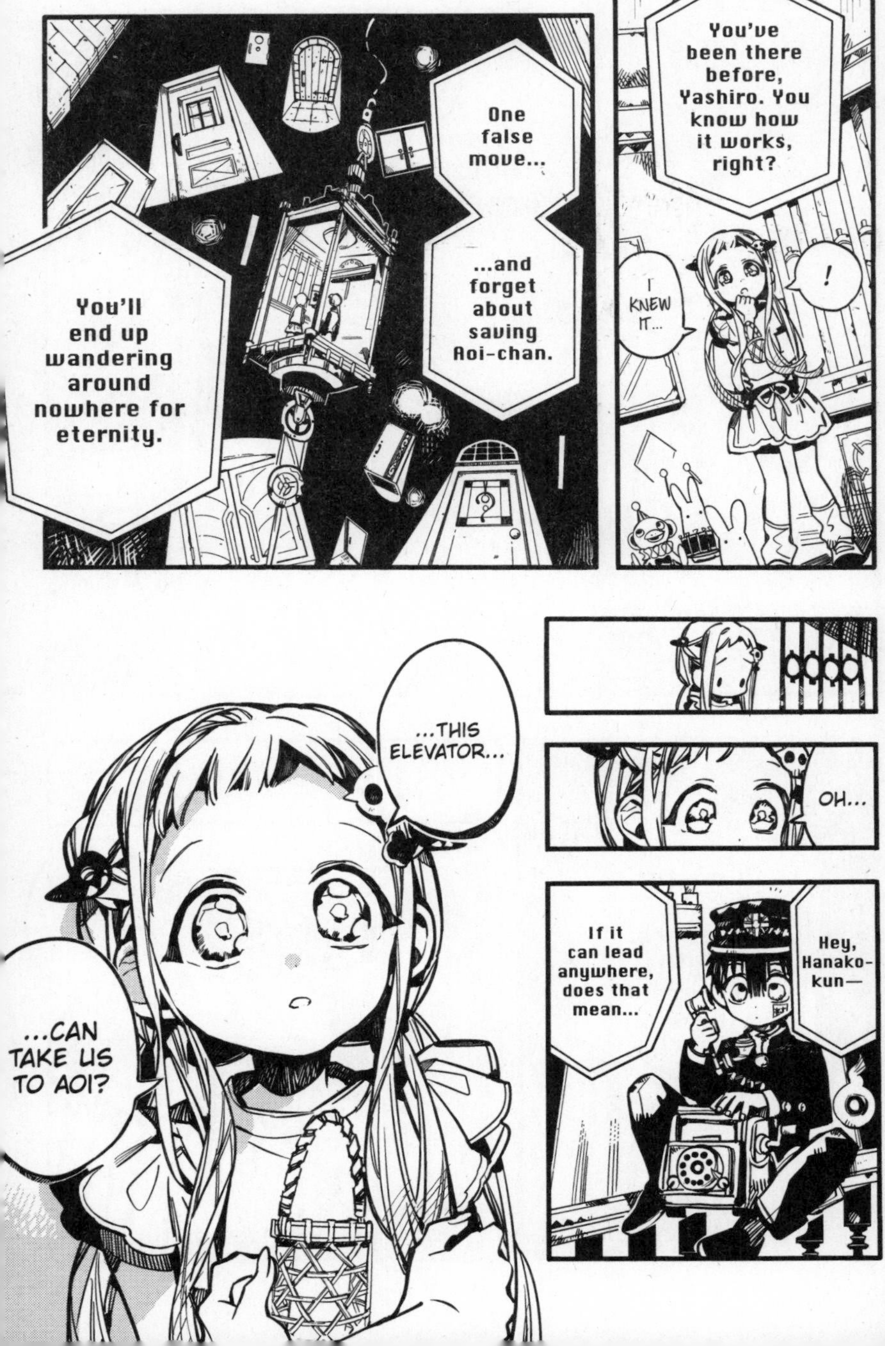
You've been there before, Yashiro. You know how it works, right?
!
I KNEW IT...
One false move...
...and forget about saving Aoi-chan.
You'll end up wandering around nowhere for eternity.
OH...
Hey, Hanako-kun—
If it can lead anywhere, does that mean...
...THIS ELEVATOR...
...CAN TAKE US TO AOI?

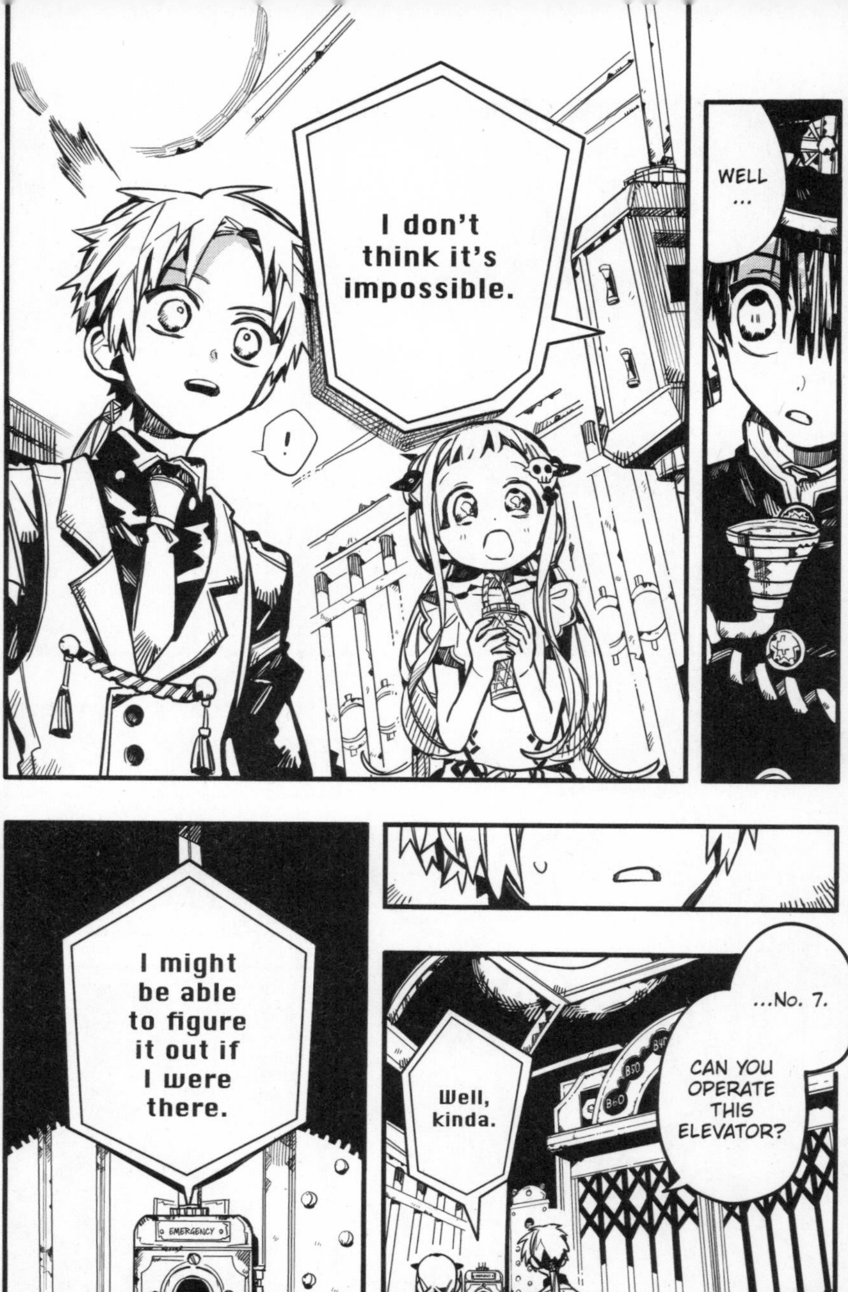
WELL ...
I don't think it's impossible.
!
...No. 7.
CAN YOU OPERATE THIS ELEVATOR?
B40
B50
B60
Well, kinda.
I might be able to figure it out if I were there.
EMERGENCY

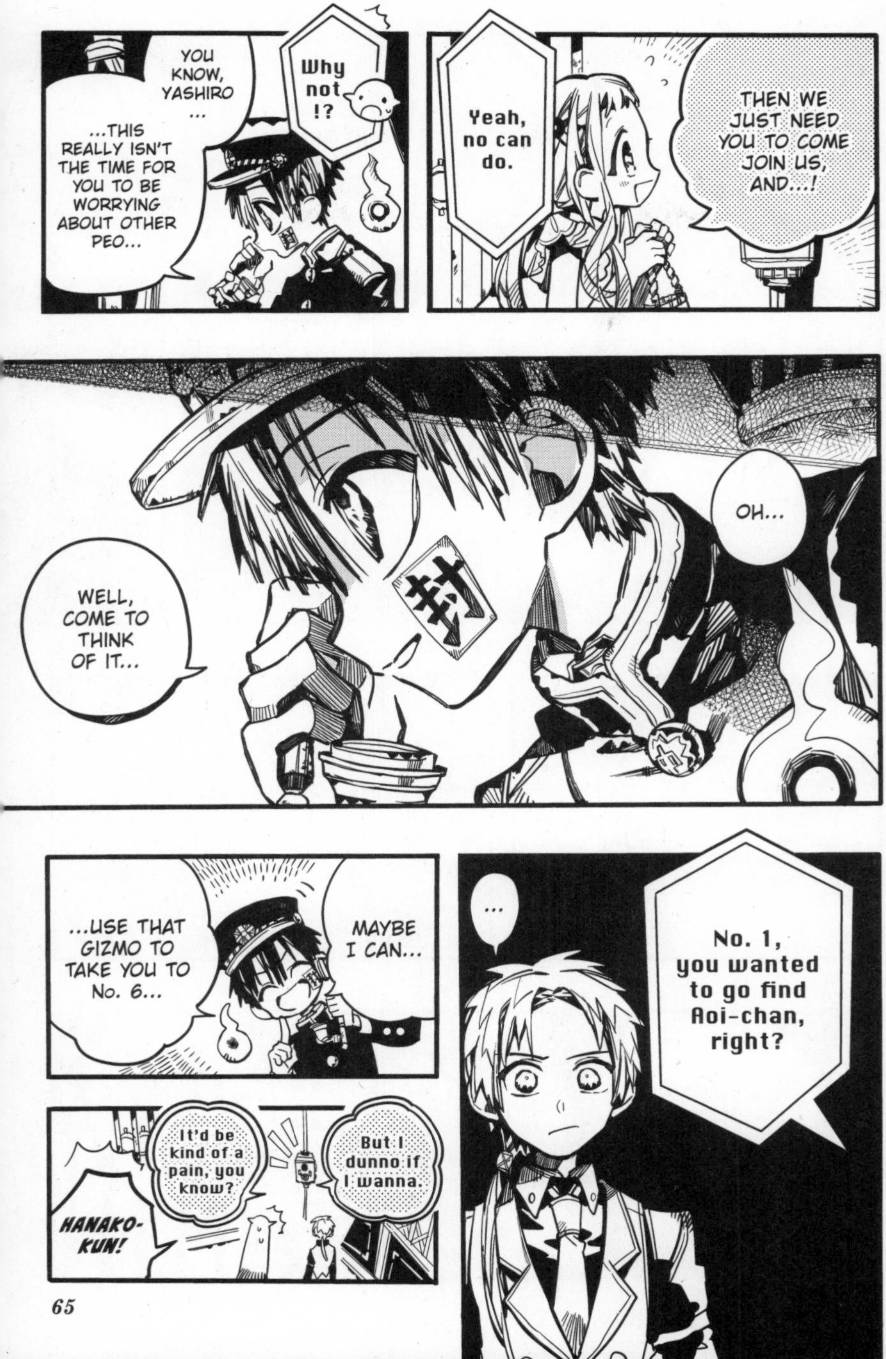
THEN WE JUST NEED YOU TO COME JOIN US, AND...!
Yeah, no can do.
Why not!?
YOU KNOW, YASHIRO...
...THIS REALLY ISN'T THE TIME FOR YOU TO BE WORRYING ABOUT OTHER PEO...
OH...
WELL, COME TO THINK OF IT...
No. 1, you wanted to go find Aoi-chan, right?
...
MAYBE I CAN...
...USE THAT GIZMO TO TAKE YOU TO No. 6...
But I dunno if I wanna.
It'd be kind of a pain, you know?
HANAKO-KUN!

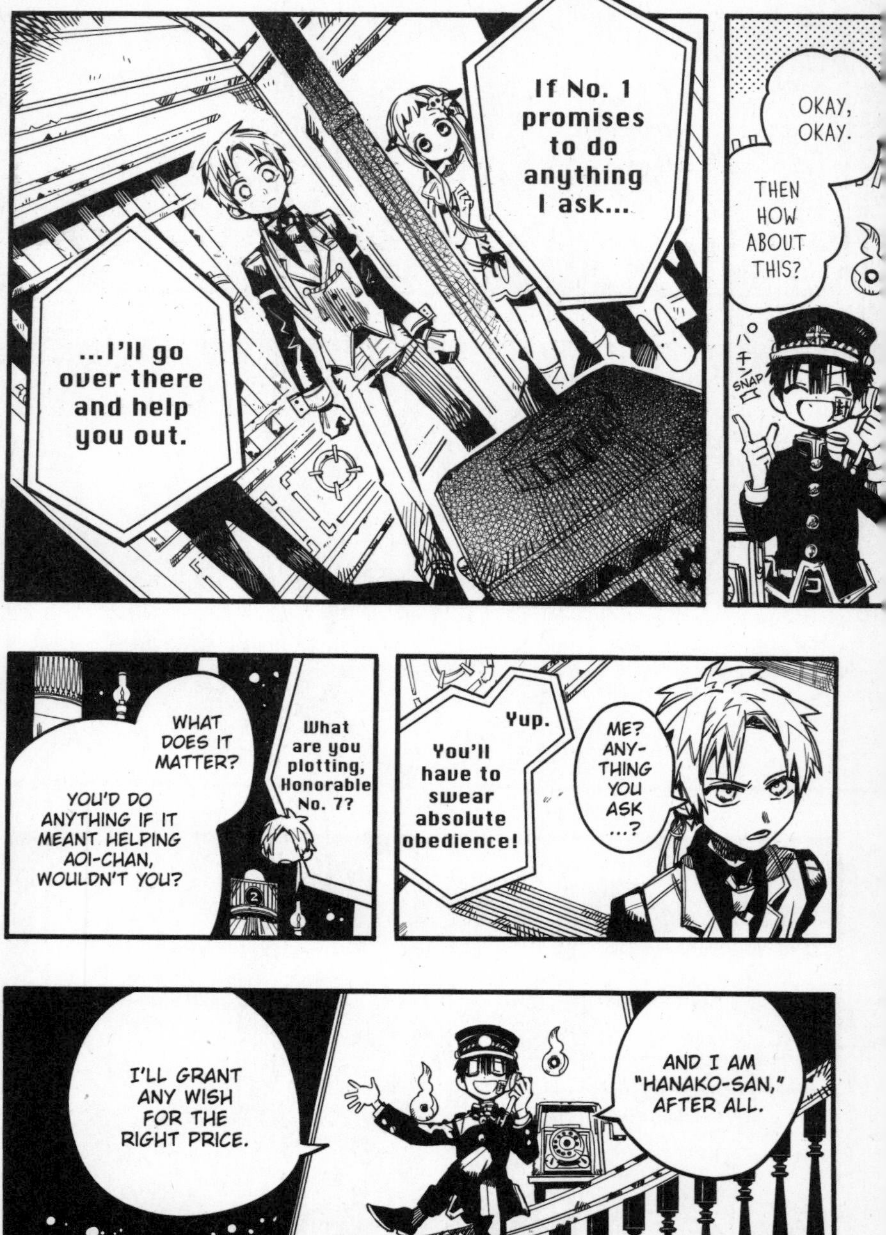
OKAY, OKAY.
THEN HOW ABOUT THIS?
パチン
SNAP
If No. 1 promises to do anything I ask...
...I'll go over there and help you out.
ME? ANYTHING YOU ASK ...?
Yup.
You'll have to swear absolute obedience!
What are you plotting, Honorable No. 7?
WHAT DOES IT MATTER?
YOU'D DO ANYTHING IF IT MEANT HELPING AOI-CHAN, WOULDN'T YOU?
AND I AM "HANAKO-SAN," AFTER ALL.
I'LL GRANT ANY WISH FOR THE RIGHT PRICE.

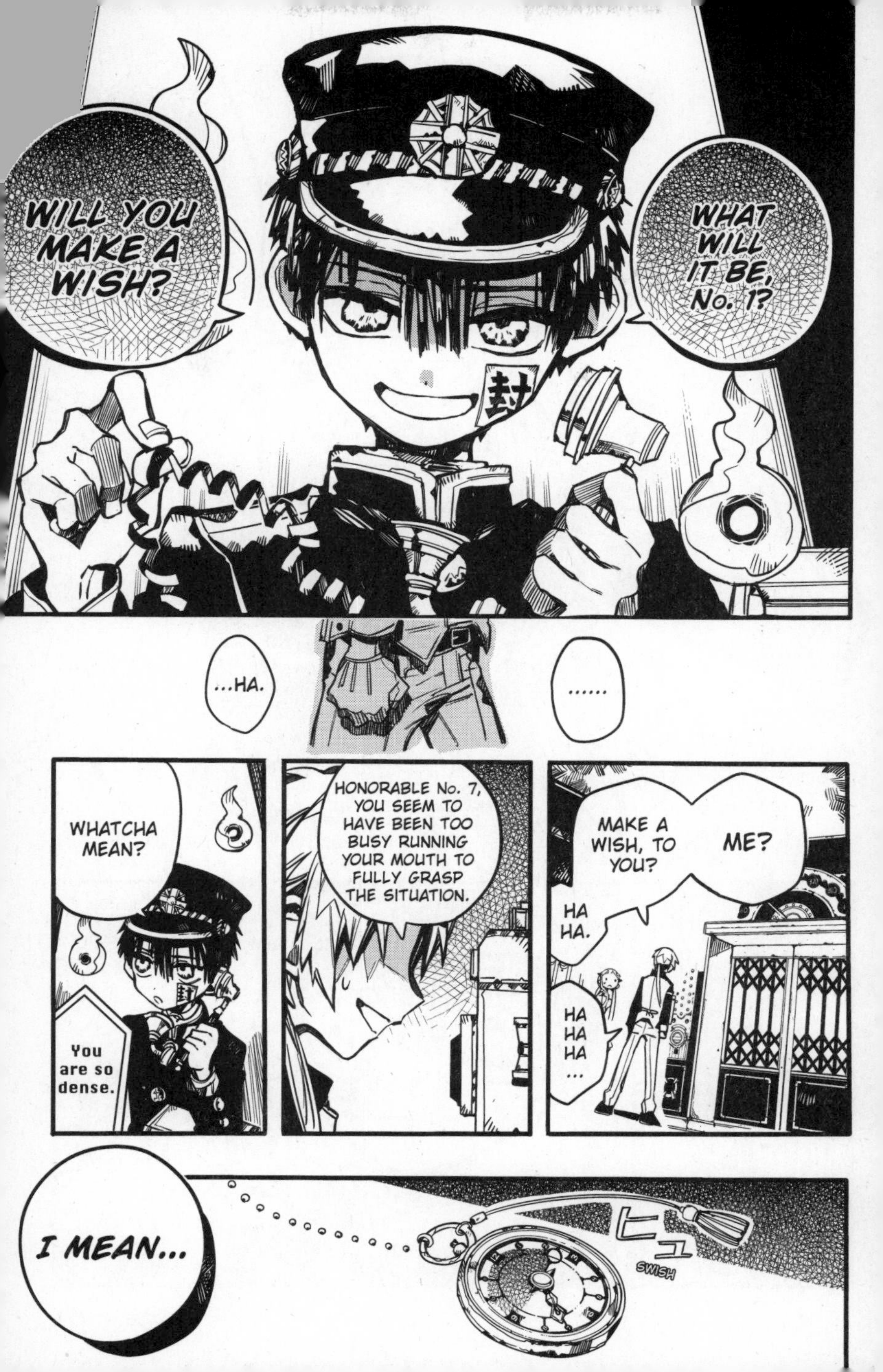
WHAT WILL IT BE, No. 1?
WILL YOU MAKE A WISH?
......
...HA.
MAKE A WISH, TO YOU?
ME?
HA HA.
HA HA HA...
HONORABLE No. 7, YOU SEEM TO HAVE BEEN TOO BUSY RUNNING YOUR MOUTH TO FULLY GRASP THE SITUATION.
WHATCHA MEAN?
You are so dense.
I MEAN...
ヒュ
SWISH

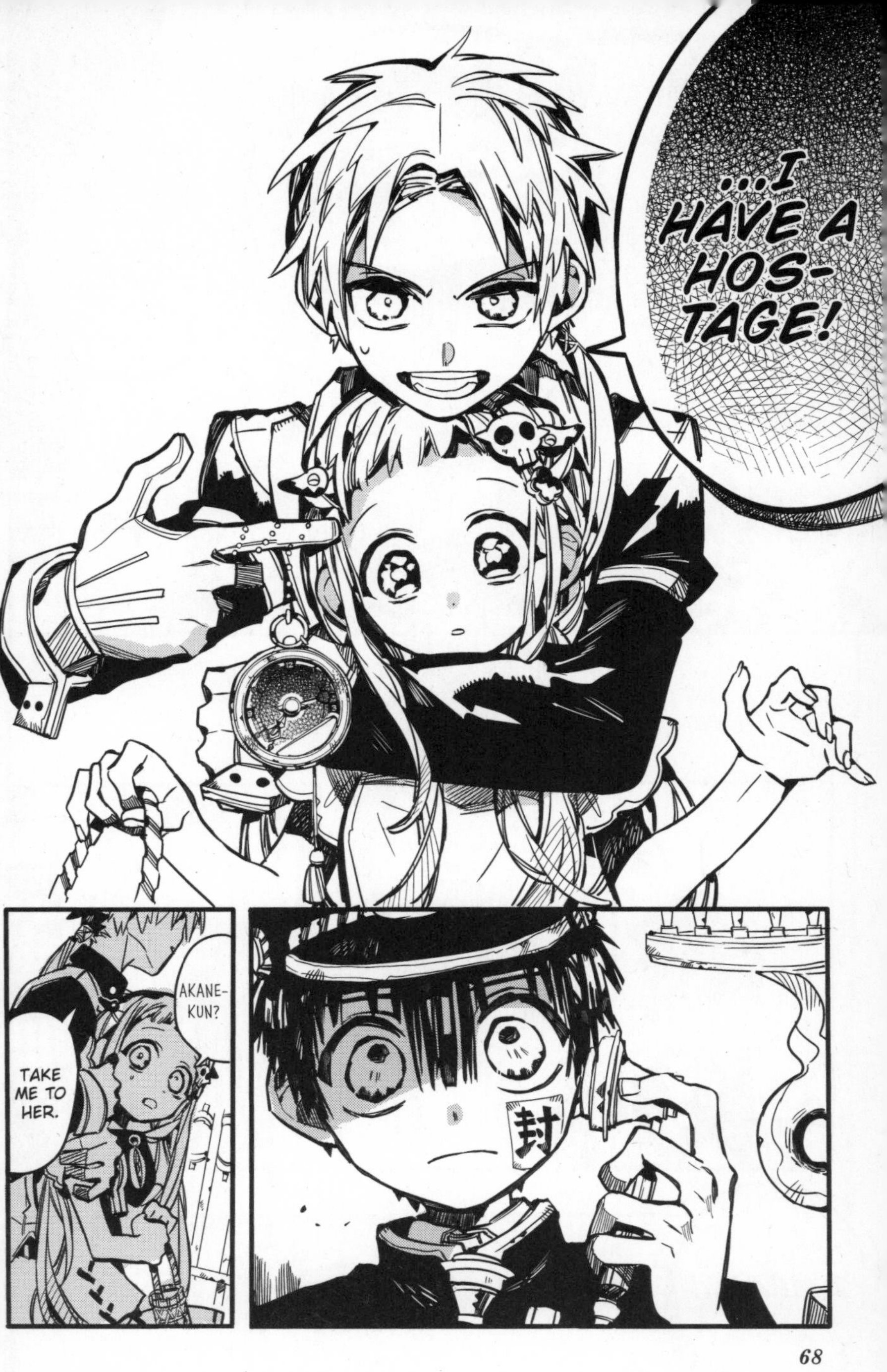
...I HAVE A HOS-TAGE!
封
AKANE-KUN?
TAKE ME TO HER.

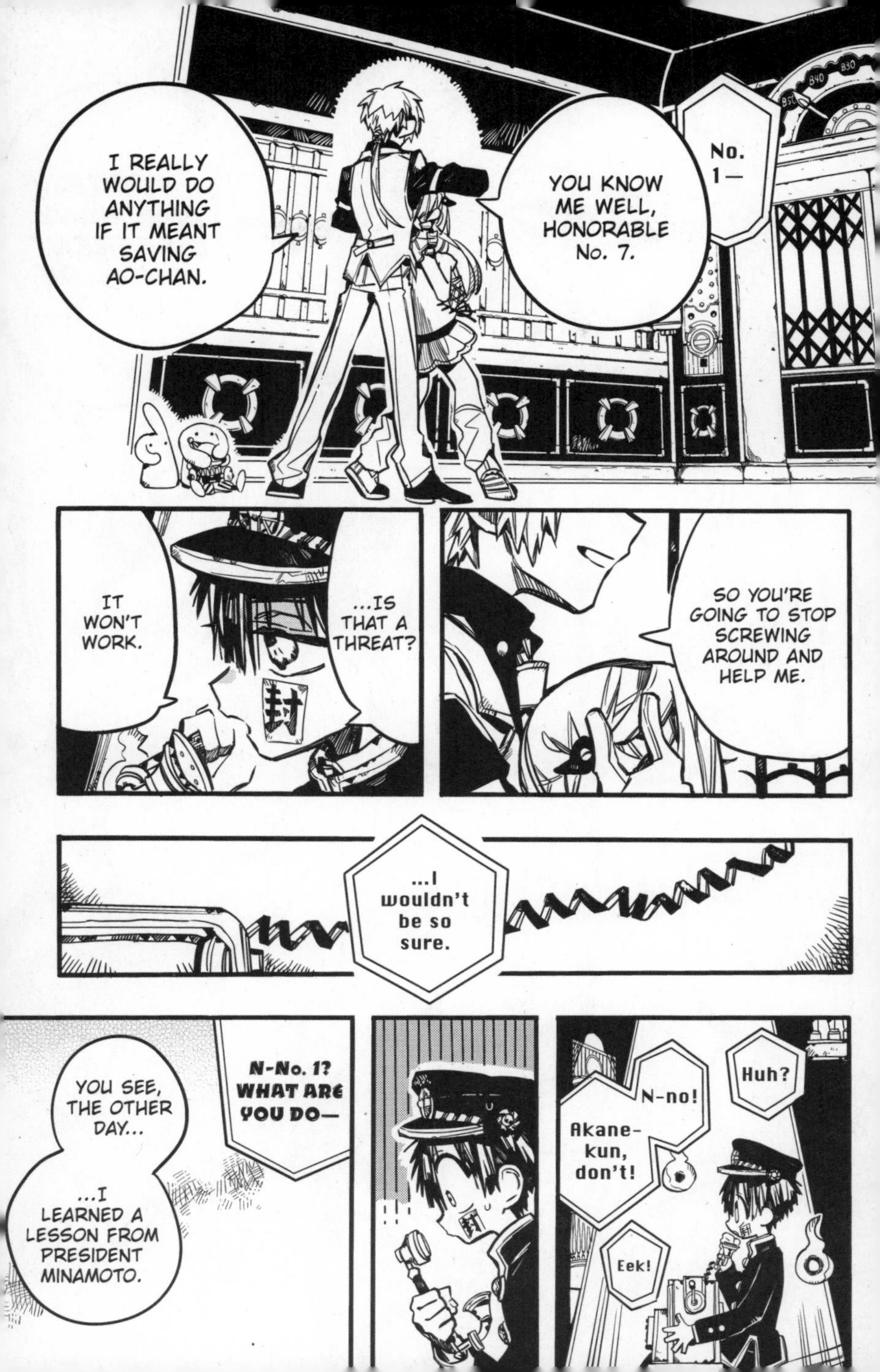
No. 1—
YOU KNOW ME WELL, HONORABLE No. 7.
I REALLY WOULD DO ANYTHING IF IT MEANT SAVING AO-CHAN.
SO YOU'RE GOING TO STOP SCREWING AROUND AND HELP ME.
...IS THAT A THREAT?
IT WON'T WORK.
...I wouldn't be so sure.
Huh?
N-no!
Akane-kun, don't!
Eek!
!!
N-No. 1? WHAT ARE YOU DO—
YOU SEE, THE OTHER DAY...
...I LEARNED A LESSON FROM PRESIDENT MINAMOTO.

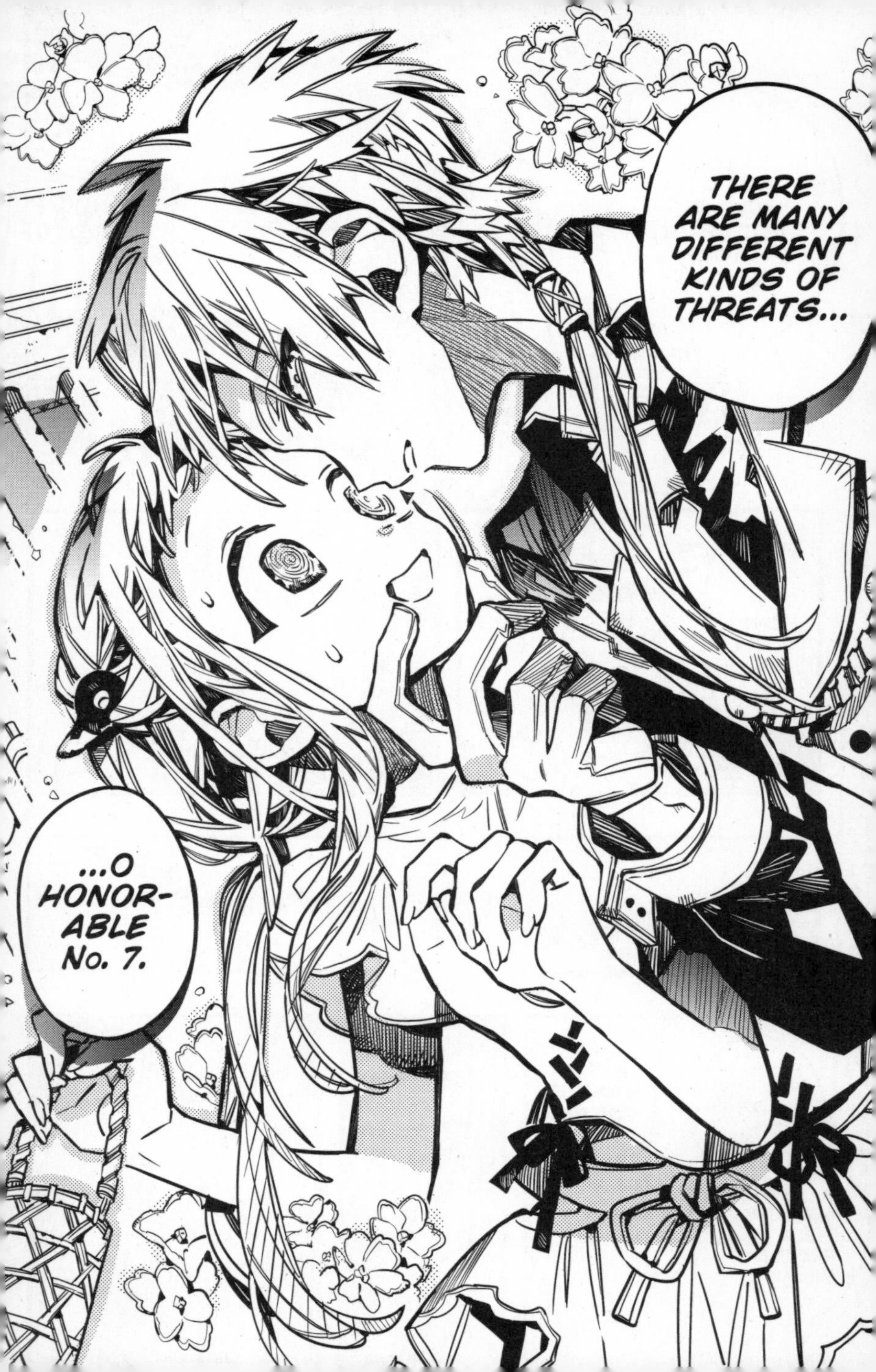
THERE ARE MANY DIFFERENT KINDS OF THREATS...
...O HONORABLE No. 7.

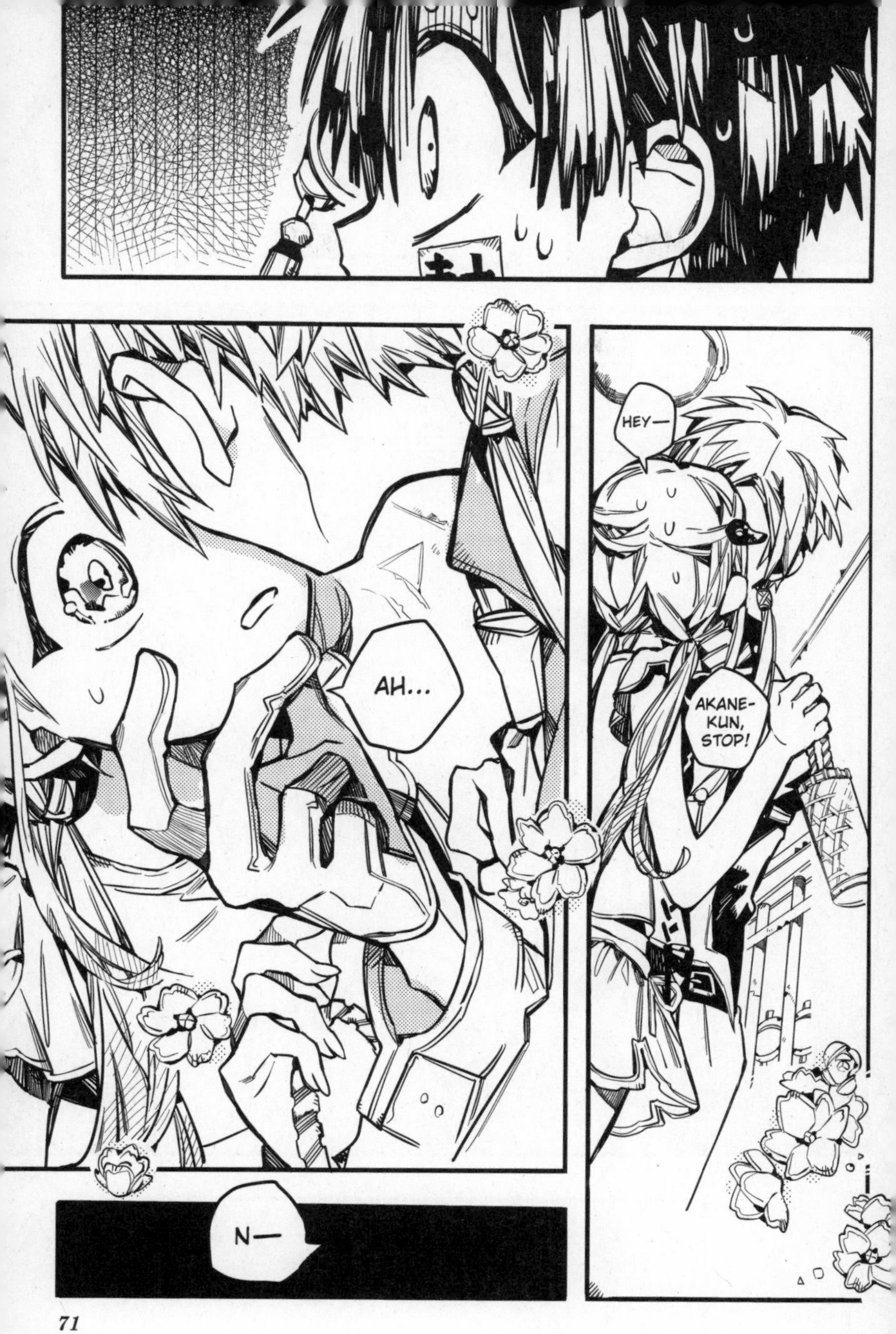
HEY—
AKANE-KUN, STOP!
AH...
N—

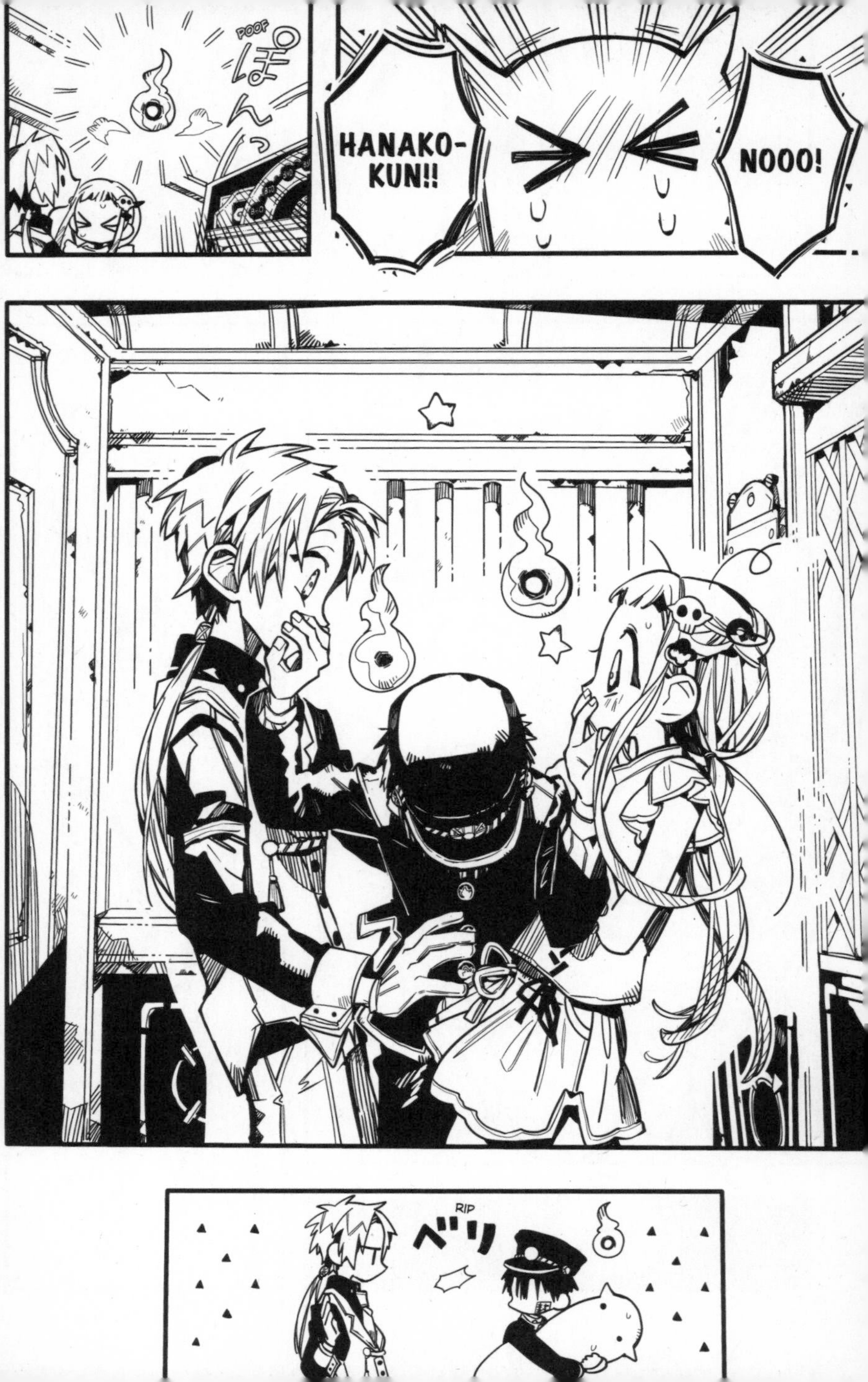
NOOO!
HANAKO-KUN!!
POOF
ぽんっ
RIP
ベリ

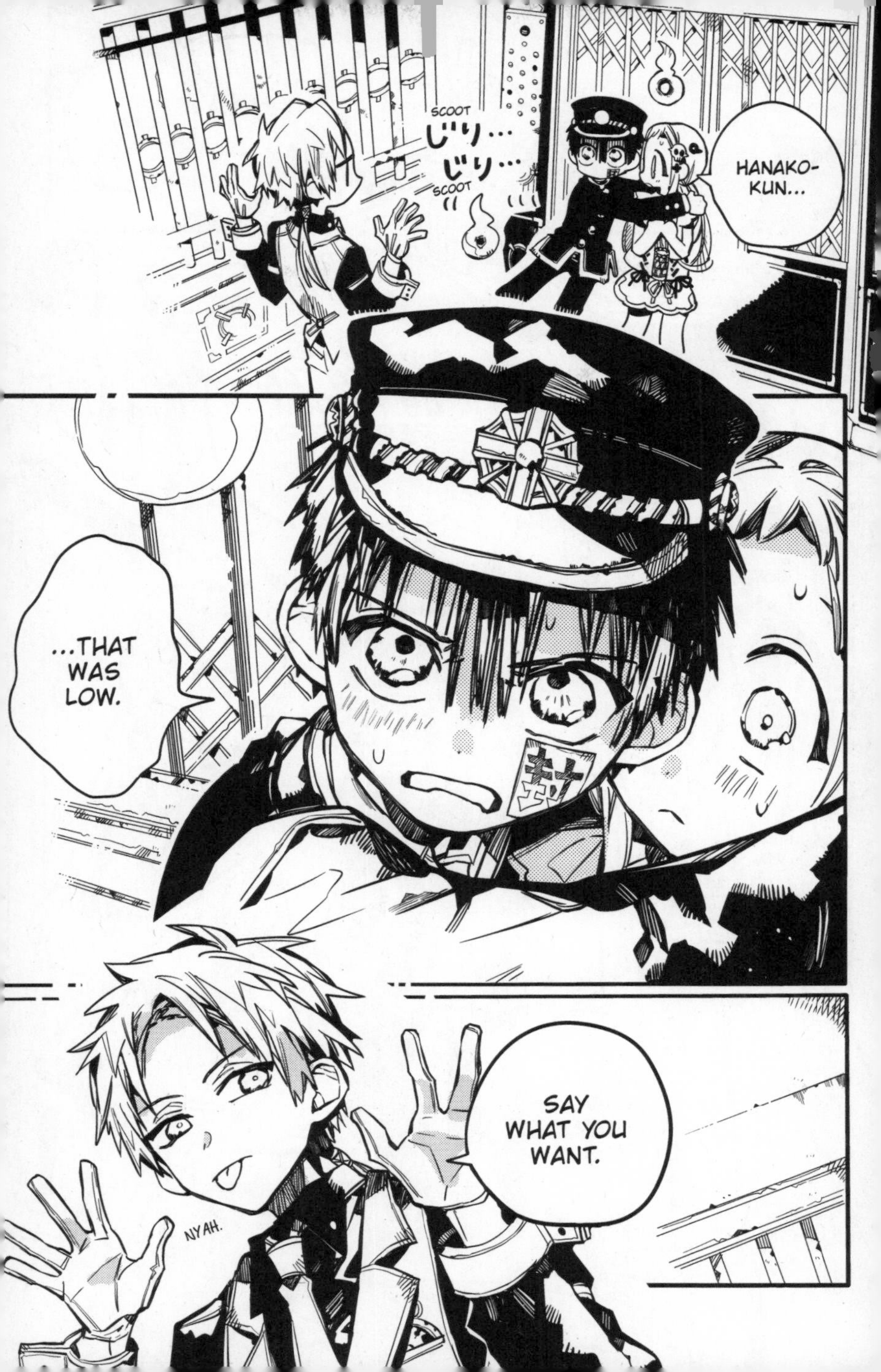
HANAKO-KUN...
SCOOT
じり…
じり…
SCOOT
...THAT WAS LOW.
SAY WHAT YOU WANT.
NYAH.

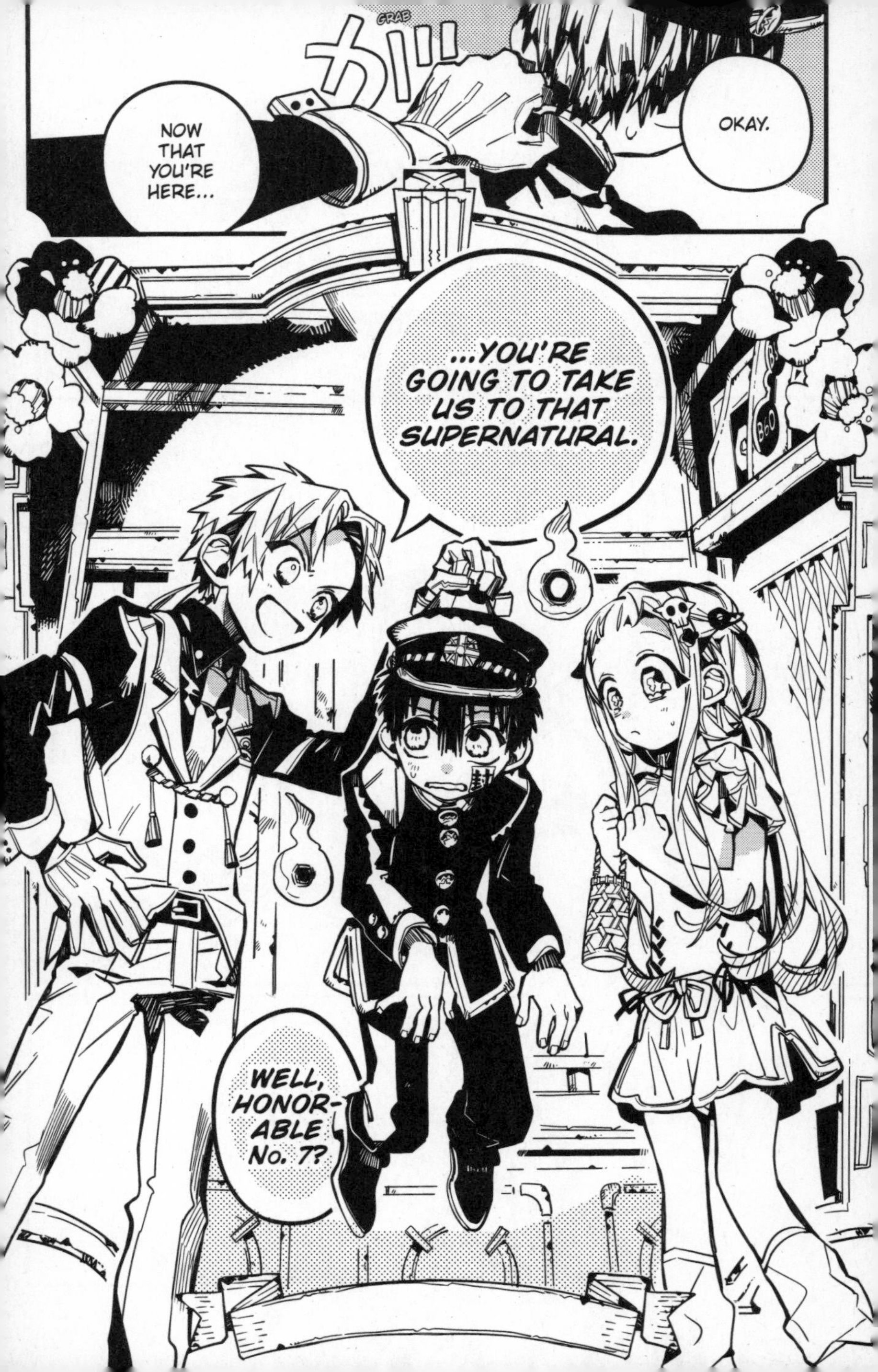
GRAB
OKAY.
NOW THAT YOU'RE HERE...
...YOU'RE GOING TO TAKE US TO THAT SUPERNATURAL.
WELL, HONOR-ABLE No. 7?

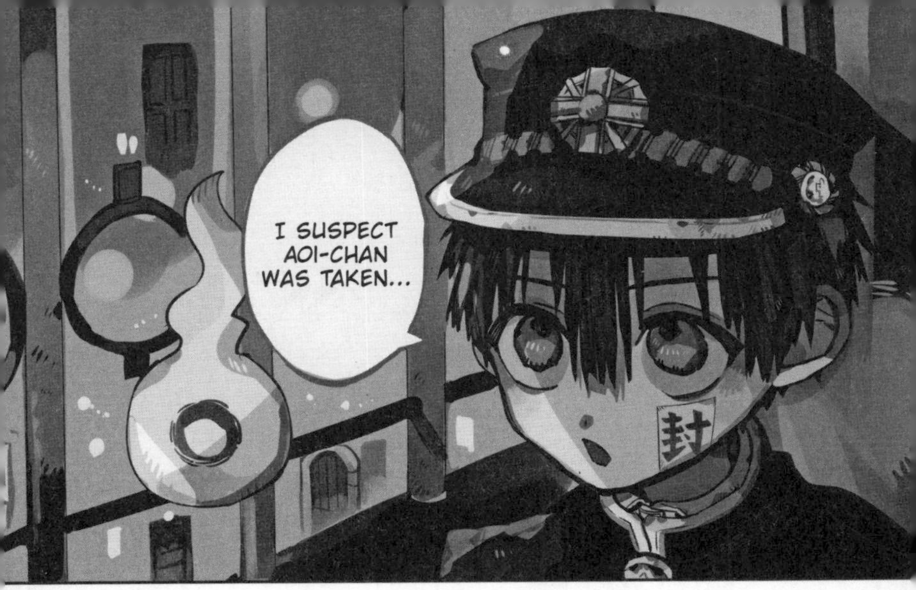
I SUSPECT AOI-CHAN WAS TAKEN...
封
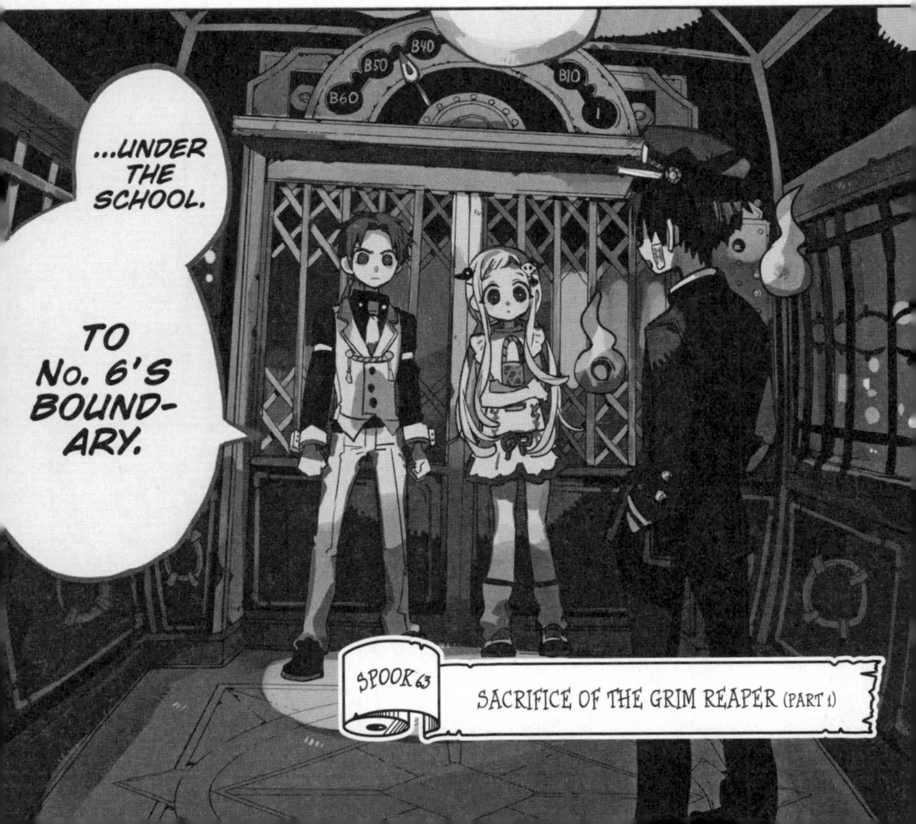
B40
B50
B60
B10
1
...UNDER THE SCHOOL.
TO No. 6'S BOUNDARY.
SPOOK 63
SACRIFICE OF THE GRIM REAPER (PART 1)

CLICK
ポチ

15

7

BEEP

BEEP

HANAKO-KUN? WHAT ARE YOU DOING...?

TO WORK THE ELEVATOR...

...YOU HAVE TO PUSH THE BUTTONS IN A SPECIFIC ORDER.

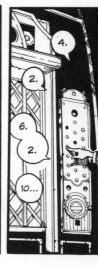

4.

2.

6.

2.

10...

NOW, THEN—

IT'S MOVING...

HUM
ゴウン...

!

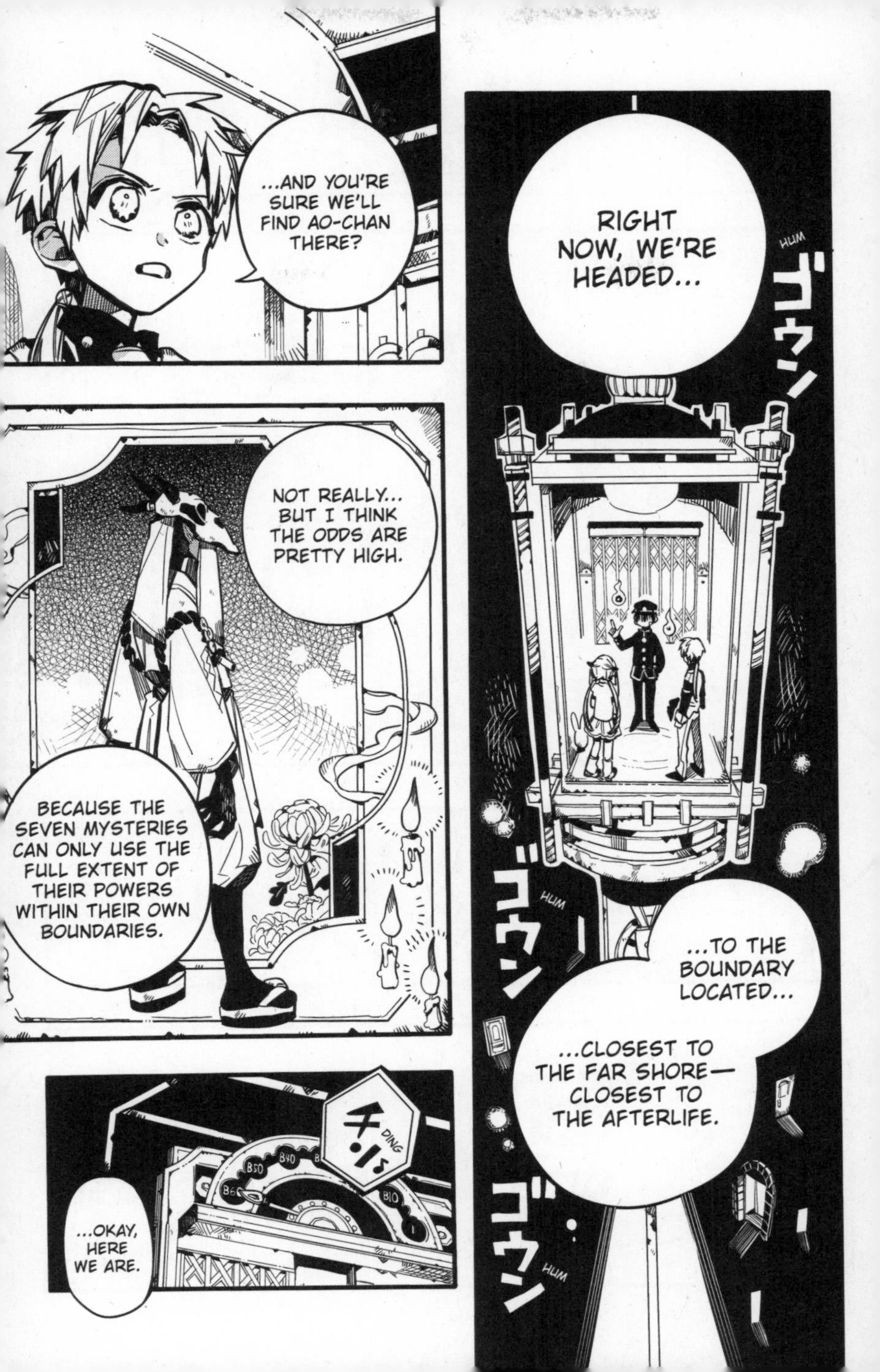
RIGHT NOW, WE'RE HEADED...
HUM
ゴウン
HUM
ゴウン
...TO THE BOUNDARY LOCATED...
...CLOSEST TO THE FAR SHORE—CLOSEST TO THE AFTERLIFE.
HUM
ゴウン
...AND YOU'RE SURE WE'LL FIND AO-CHAN THERE?
NOT REALLY... BUT I THINK THE ODDS ARE PRETTY HIGH.
BECAUSE THE SEVEN MYSTERIES CAN ONLY USE THE FULL EXTENT OF THEIR POWERS WITHIN THEIR OWN BOUNDARIES.
チーン
DING
...OKAY, HERE WE ARE.

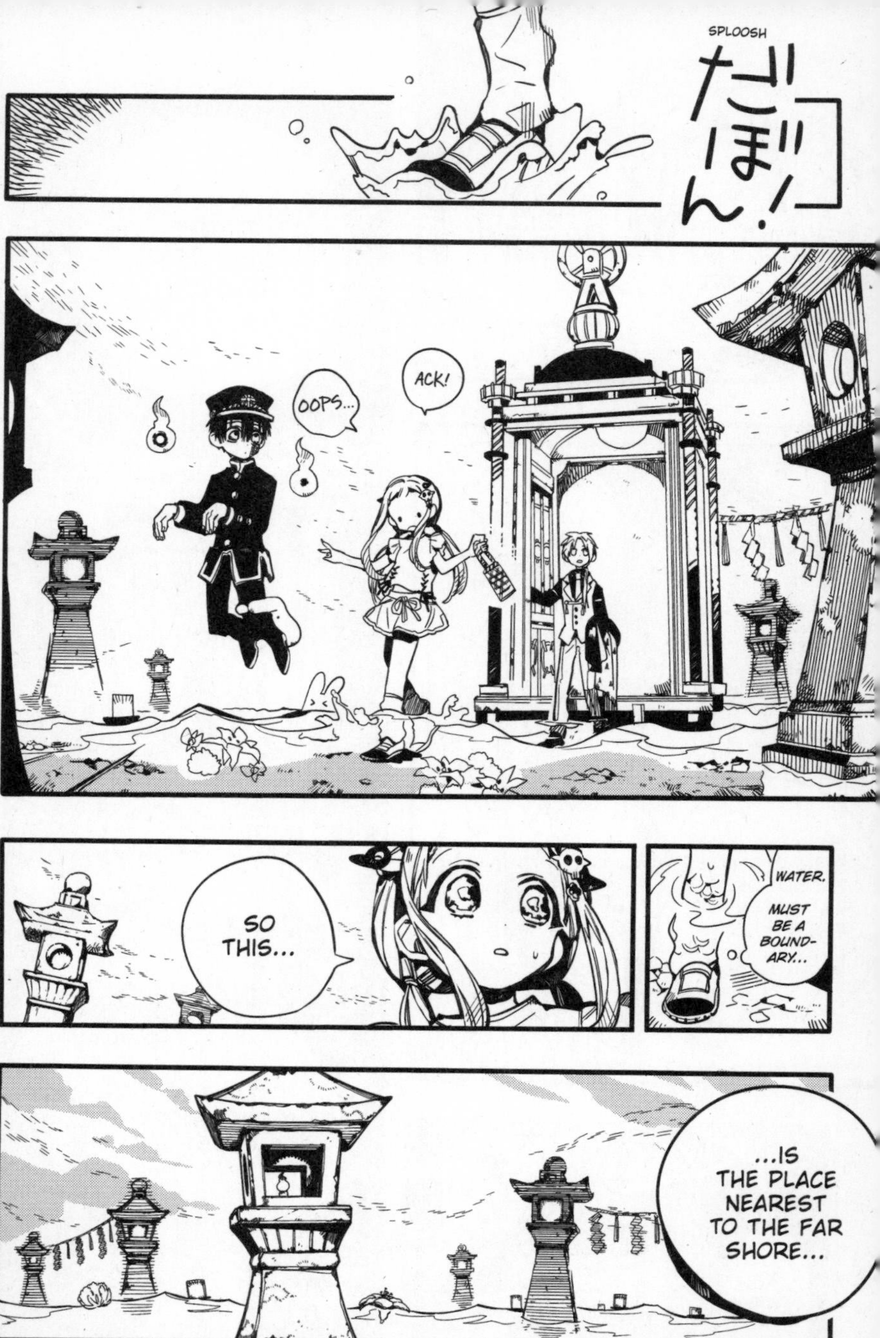
SPLOOSH
ざぼん!
ACK!
OOPS...
WATER.
MUST BE A BOUNDARY...
SO THIS...
...IS THE PLACE NEAREST TO THE FAR SHORE...

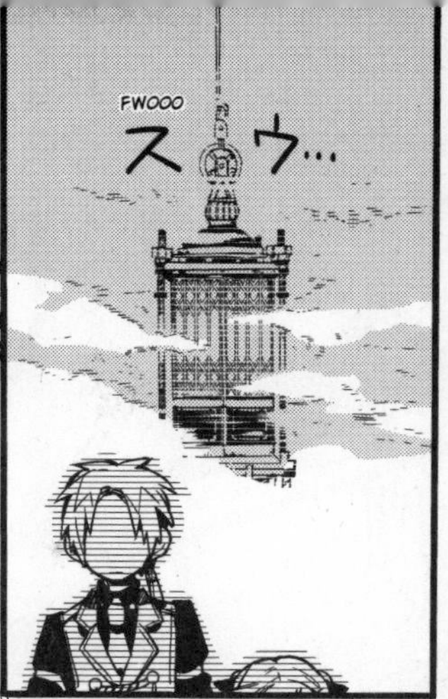
FWOOO
スゥ…
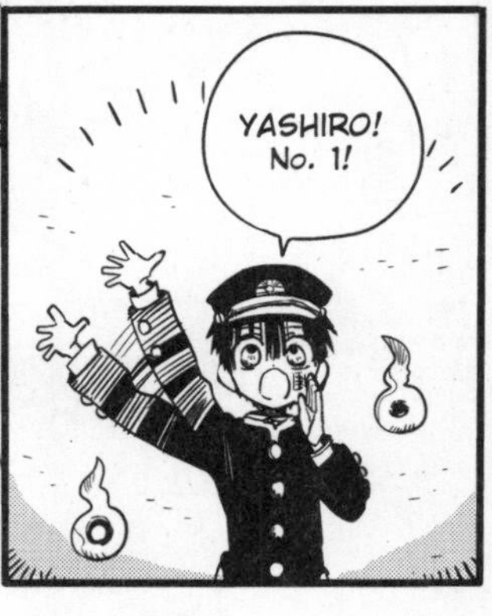
YASHIRO! No. 1!
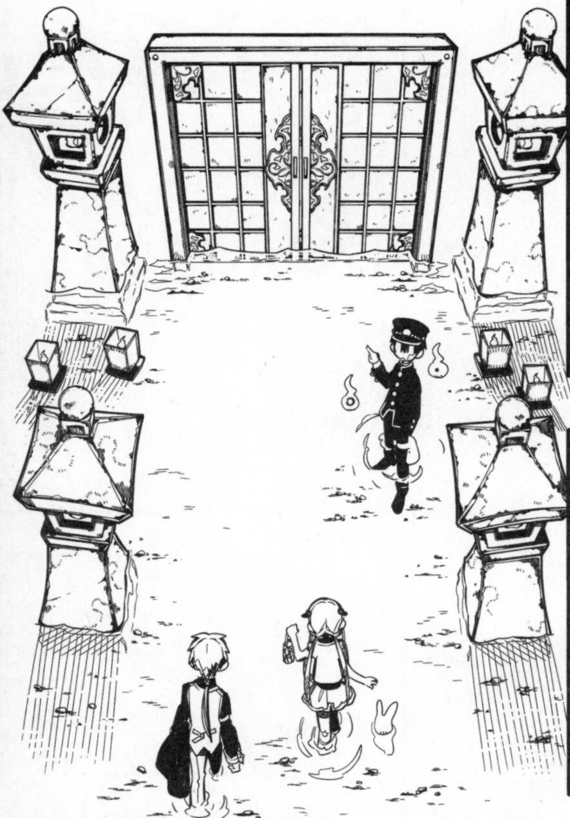
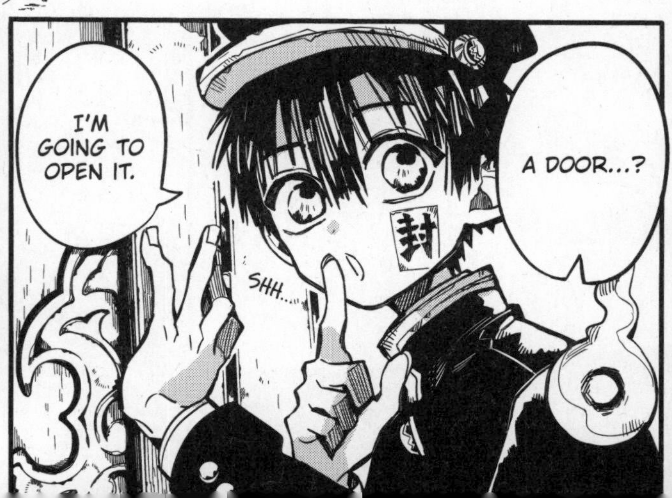
A DOOR...?
I'M GOING TO OPEN IT.
SHH...
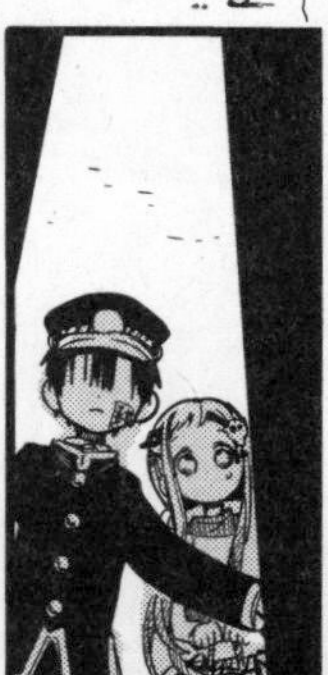

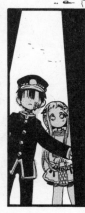

WHOOSH

ビュュォ

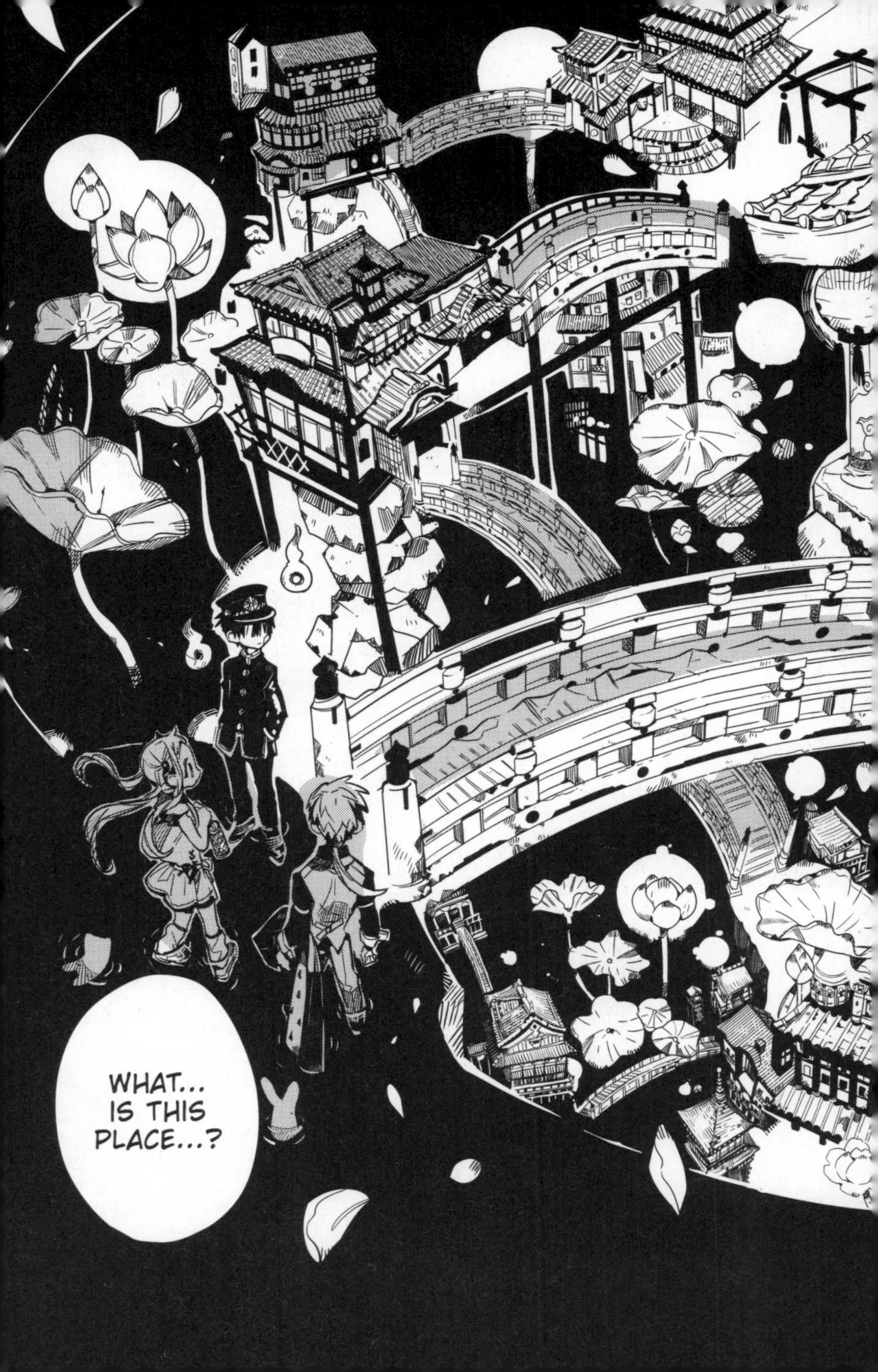
WHAT... IS THIS PLACE...?

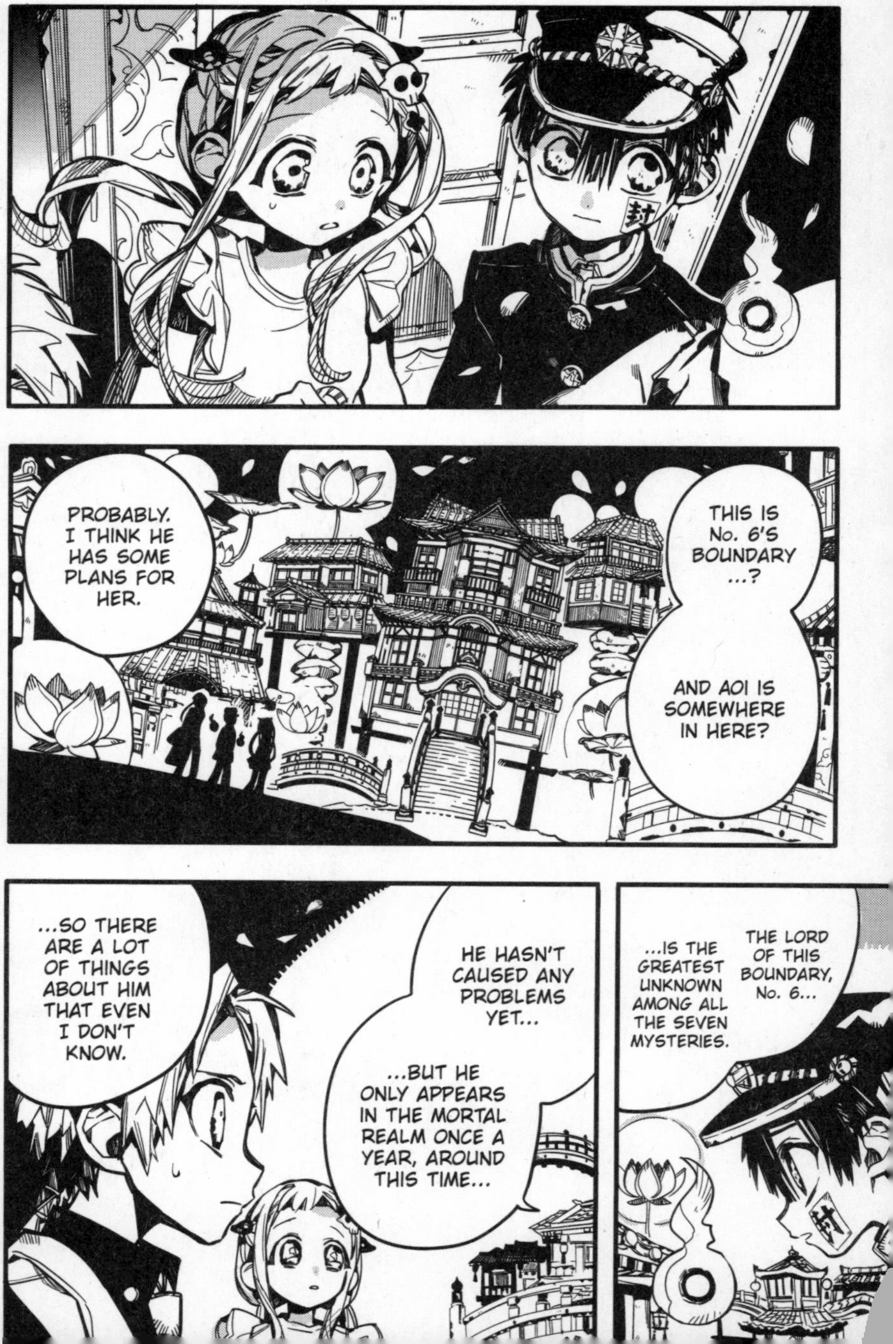
THIS IS No. 6'S BOUNDARY ...?
AND AOI IS SOMEWHERE IN HERE?
PROBABLY. I THINK HE HAS SOME PLANS FOR HER.
THE LORD OF THIS BOUNDARY, No. 6...
...IS THE GREATEST UNKNOWN AMONG ALL THE SEVEN MYSTERIES.
HE HASN'T CAUSED ANY PROBLEMS YET...
...BUT HE ONLY APPEARS IN THE MORTAL REALM ONCE A YEAR, AROUND THIS TIME...
...SO THERE ARE A LOT OF THINGS ABOUT HIM THAT EVEN I DON'T KNOW.

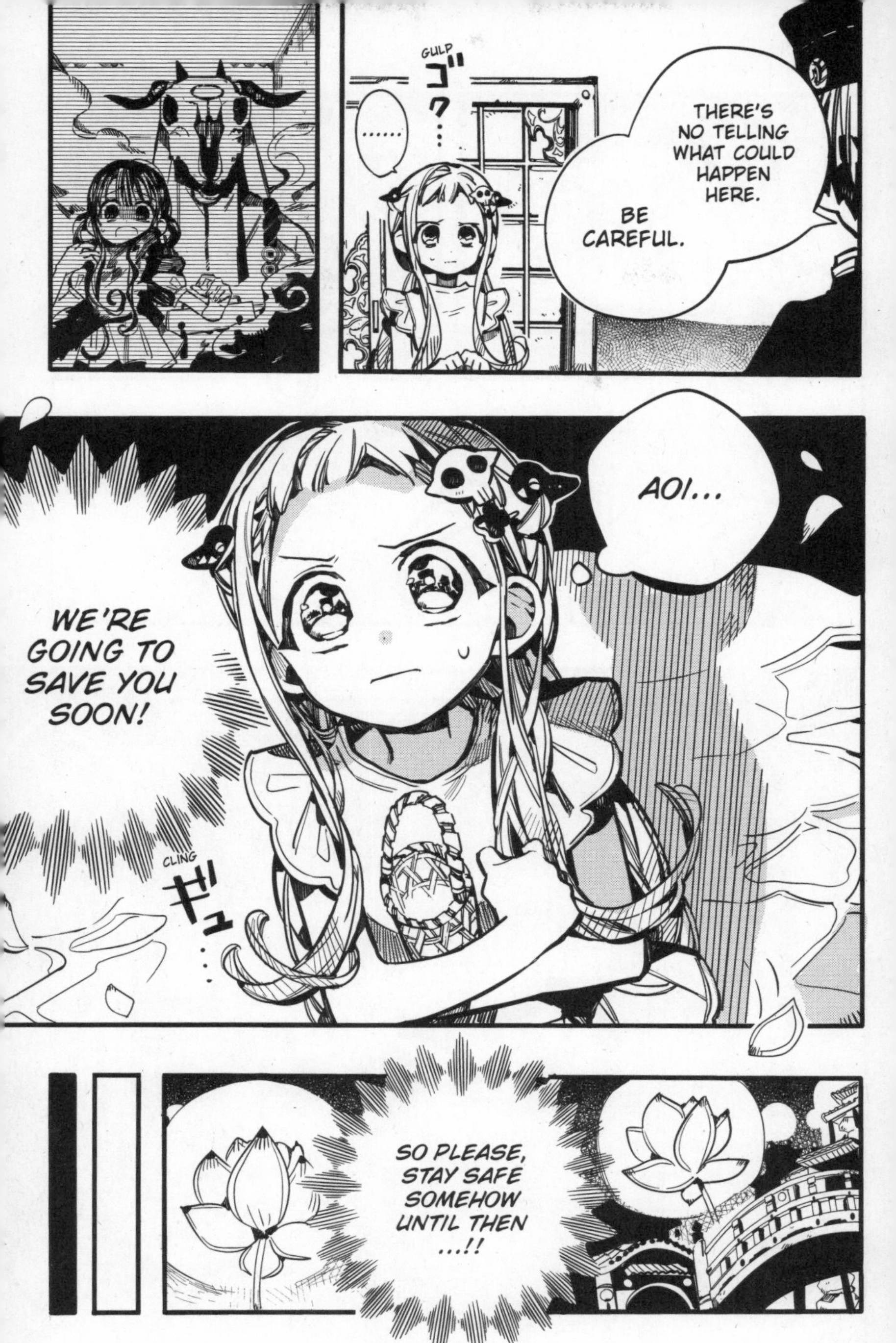
THERE'S NO TELLING WHAT COULD HAPPEN HERE.
BE CAREFUL.
GULP
ゴク…
……
AOI...
WE'RE GOING TO SAVE YOU SOON!
CLING
ギュ…
SO PLEASE, STAY SAFE SOMEHOW UNTIL THEN ...!!

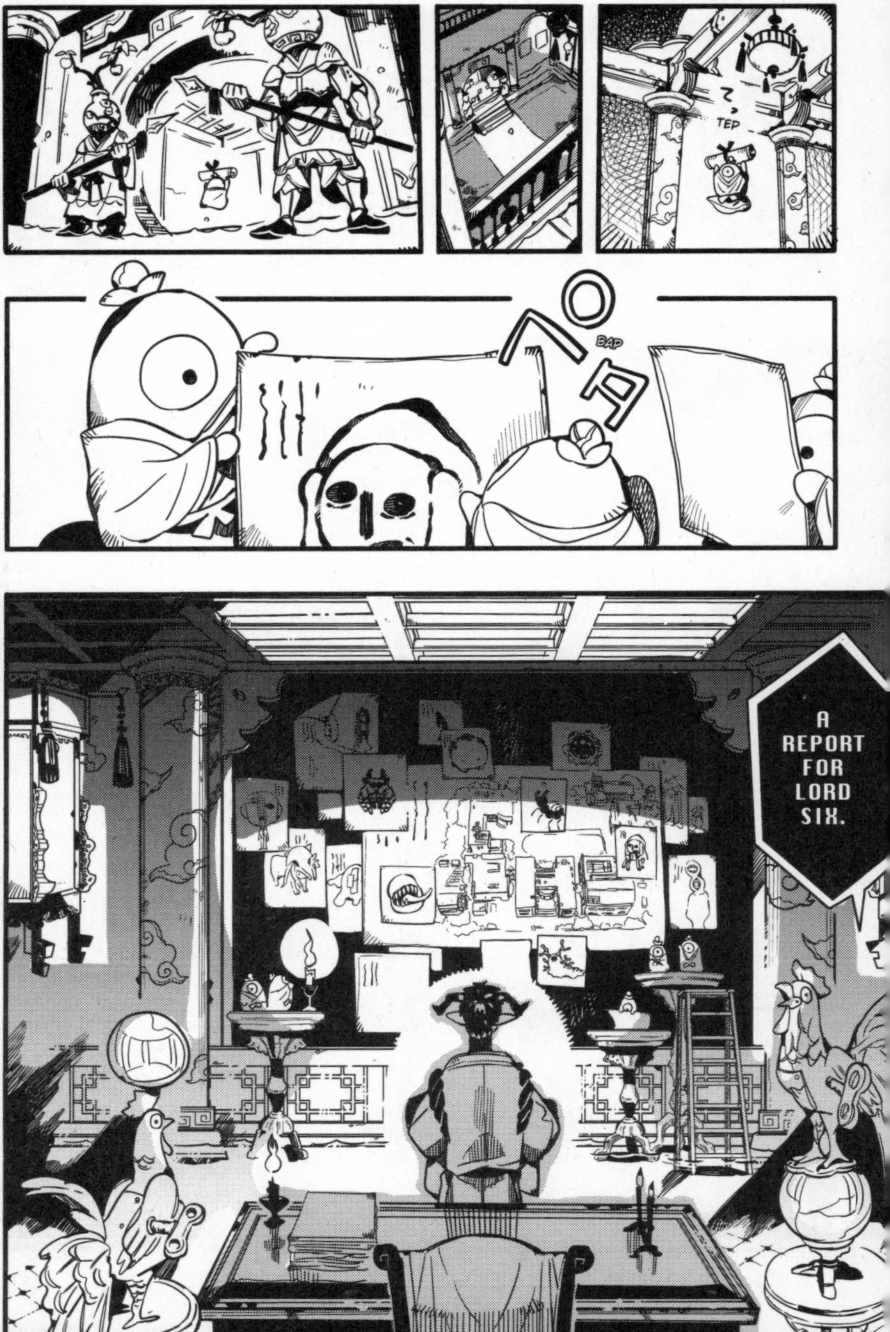
TEP
ペタ
BAP
A REPORT FOR LORD SIX.

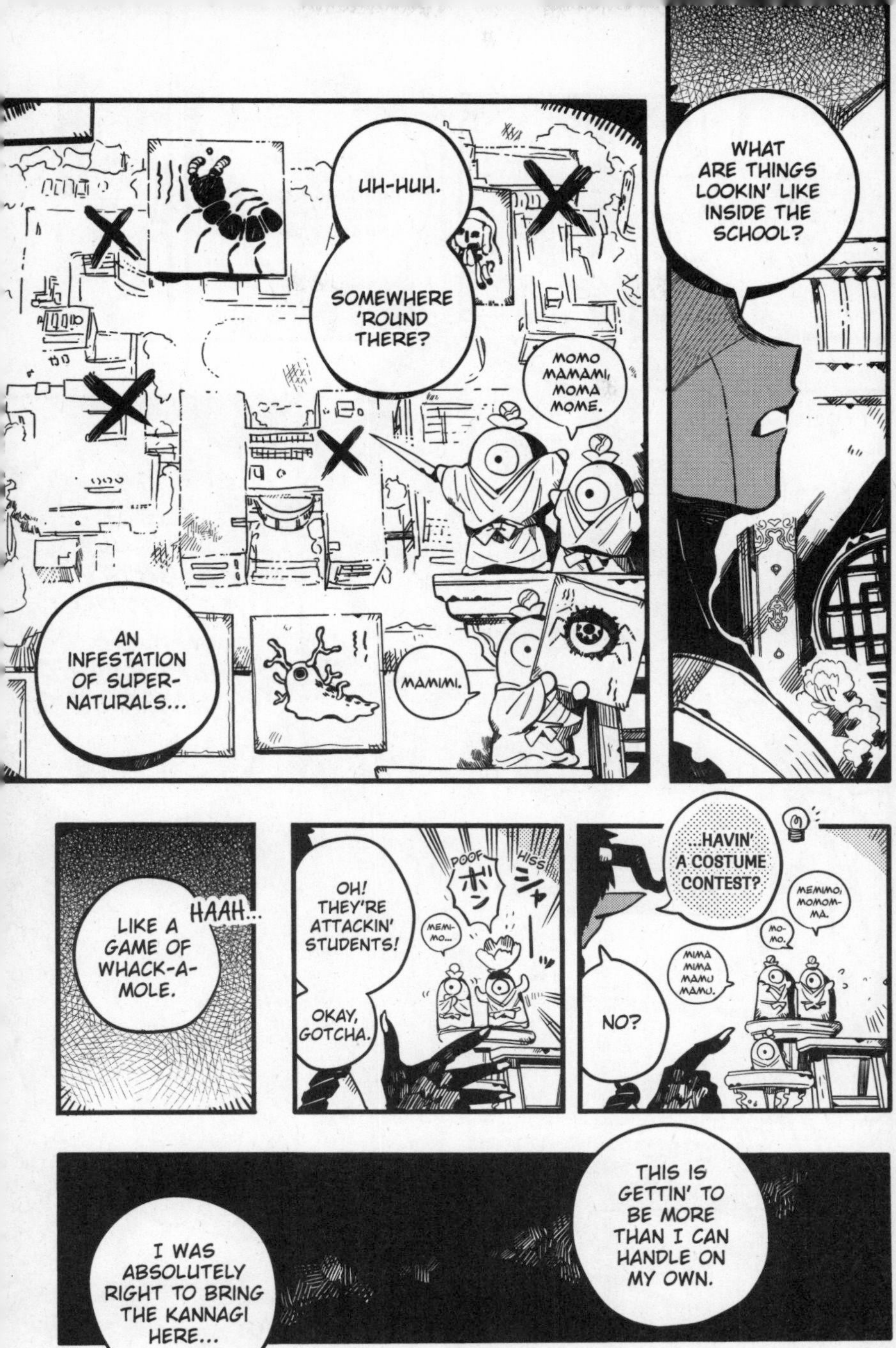
WHAT ARE THINGS LOOKIN' LIKE INSIDE THE SCHOOL?
UH-HUH.
SOMEWHERE 'ROUND THERE?
MOMO MAMAMI, MOMA MOME.
MAMIMI.
AN INFESTATION OF SUPER-NATURALS...
...HAVIN' A COSTUME CONTEST?
MEMIMO, MOMOM-MA.
MO-MO.
MIMA MIMA MAMU MAMU.
NO?
HISS
シャー
POOF
ボン
OH! THEY'RE ATTACKIN' STUDENTS!
MEMI-MO...
OKAY, GOTCHA.
HAAH...
LIKE A GAME OF WHACK-A-MOLE.
THIS IS GETTIN' TO BE MORE THAN I CAN HANDLE ON MY OWN.
I WAS ABSOLUTELY RIGHT TO BRING THE KANNAGI HERE...

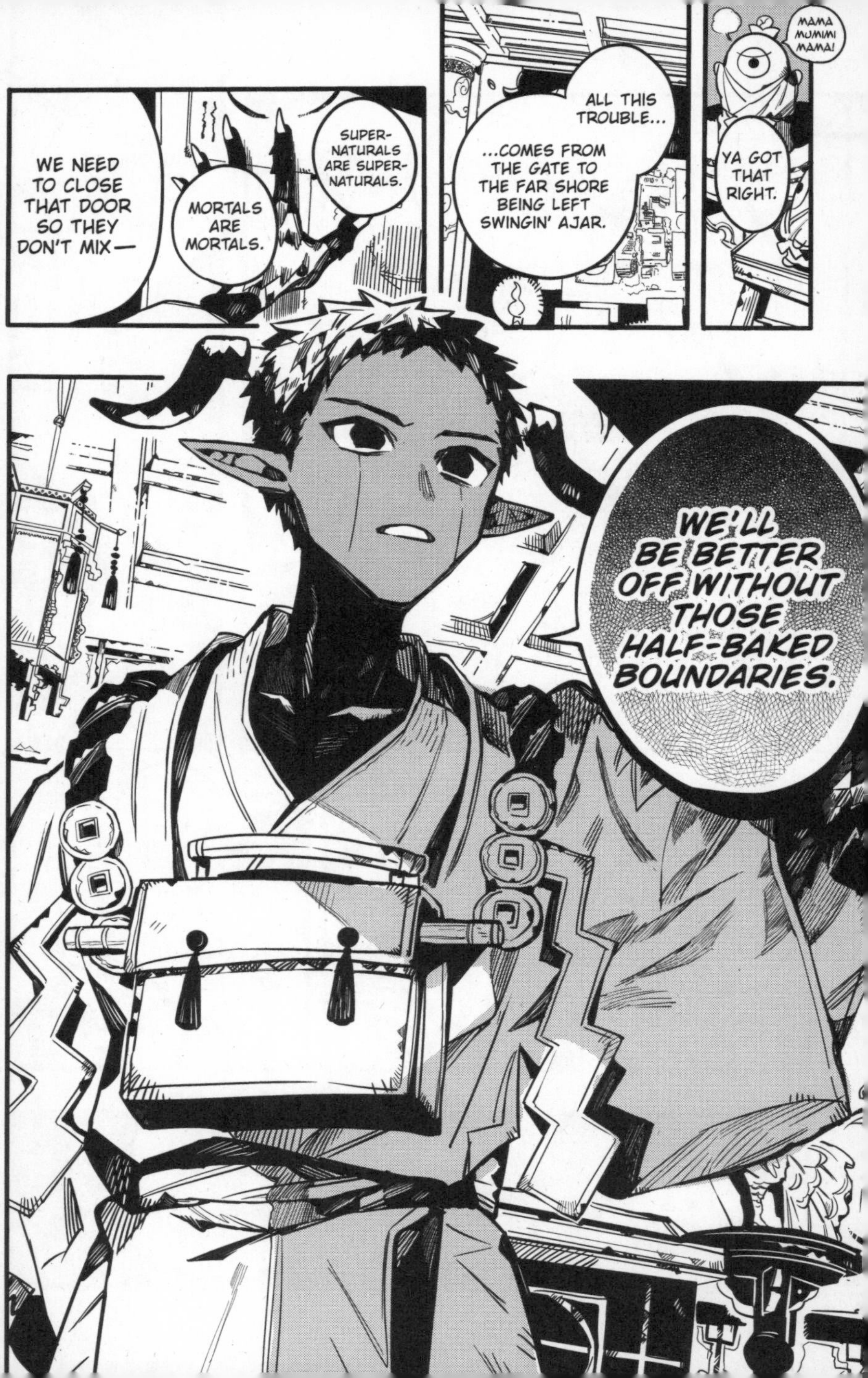
MAMA MUMIMI MAMA!
YA GOT THAT RIGHT.
ALL THIS TROUBLE...
...COMES FROM THE GATE TO THE FAR SHORE BEING LEFT SWINGIN' AJAR.
SUPER-NATURALS ARE SUPER-NATURALS.
MORTALS ARE MORTALS.
WE NEED TO CLOSE THAT DOOR SO THEY DON'T MIX—
WE'LL BE BETTER OFF WITHOUT THOSE HALF-BAKED BOUNDARIES.

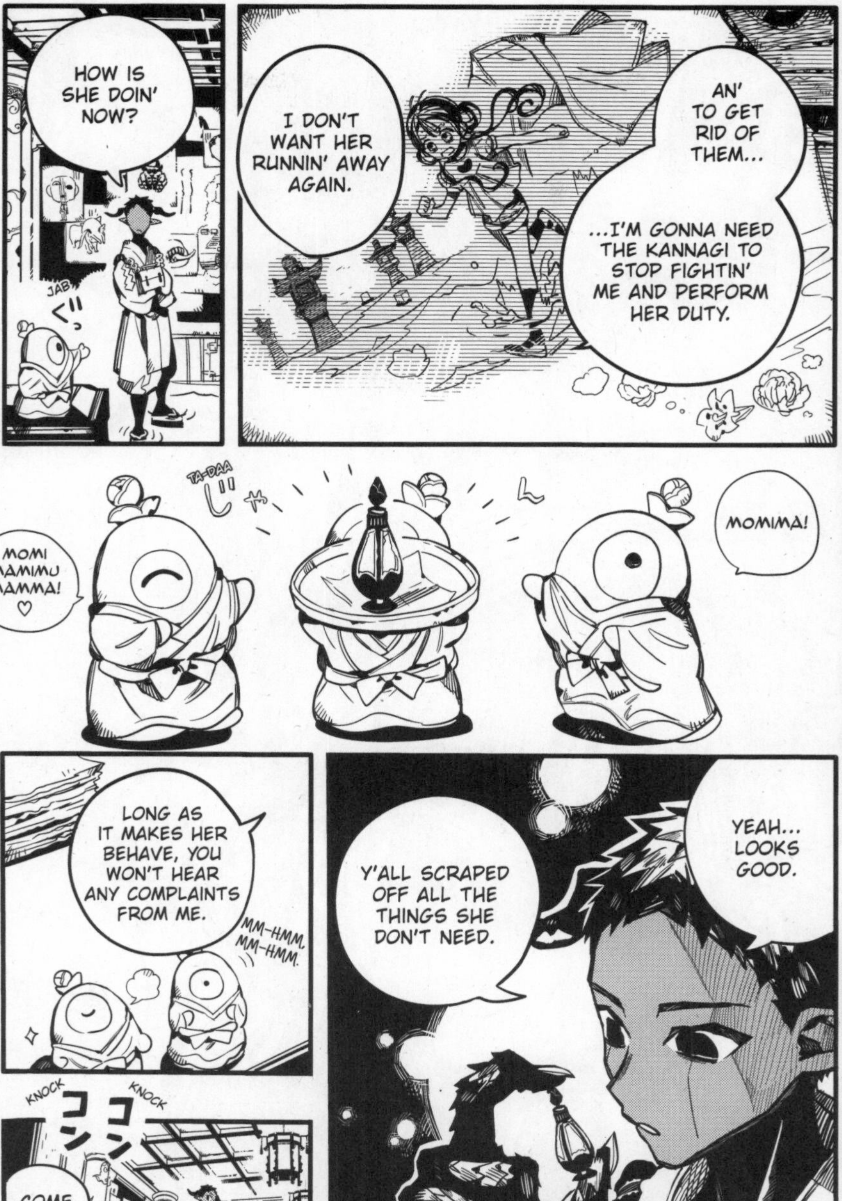
AN' TO GET RID OF THEM...
...I'M GONNA NEED THE KANNAGI TO STOP FIGHTIN' ME AND PERFORM HER DUTY.
I DON'T WANT HER RUNNIN' AWAY AGAIN.
HOW IS SHE DOIN' NOW?
JAB
MOMIMA!
TA-DAA
MOMI MAMIMU MAMMA! ♡
YEAH... LOOKS GOOD.
Y'ALL SCRAPED OFF ALL THE THINGS SHE DON'T NEED.
LONG AS IT MAKES HER BEHAVE, YOU WON'T HEAR ANY COMPLAINTS FROM ME.
MM-HMM, MM-HMM.
KNOCK KNOCK
COME IN.

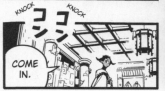

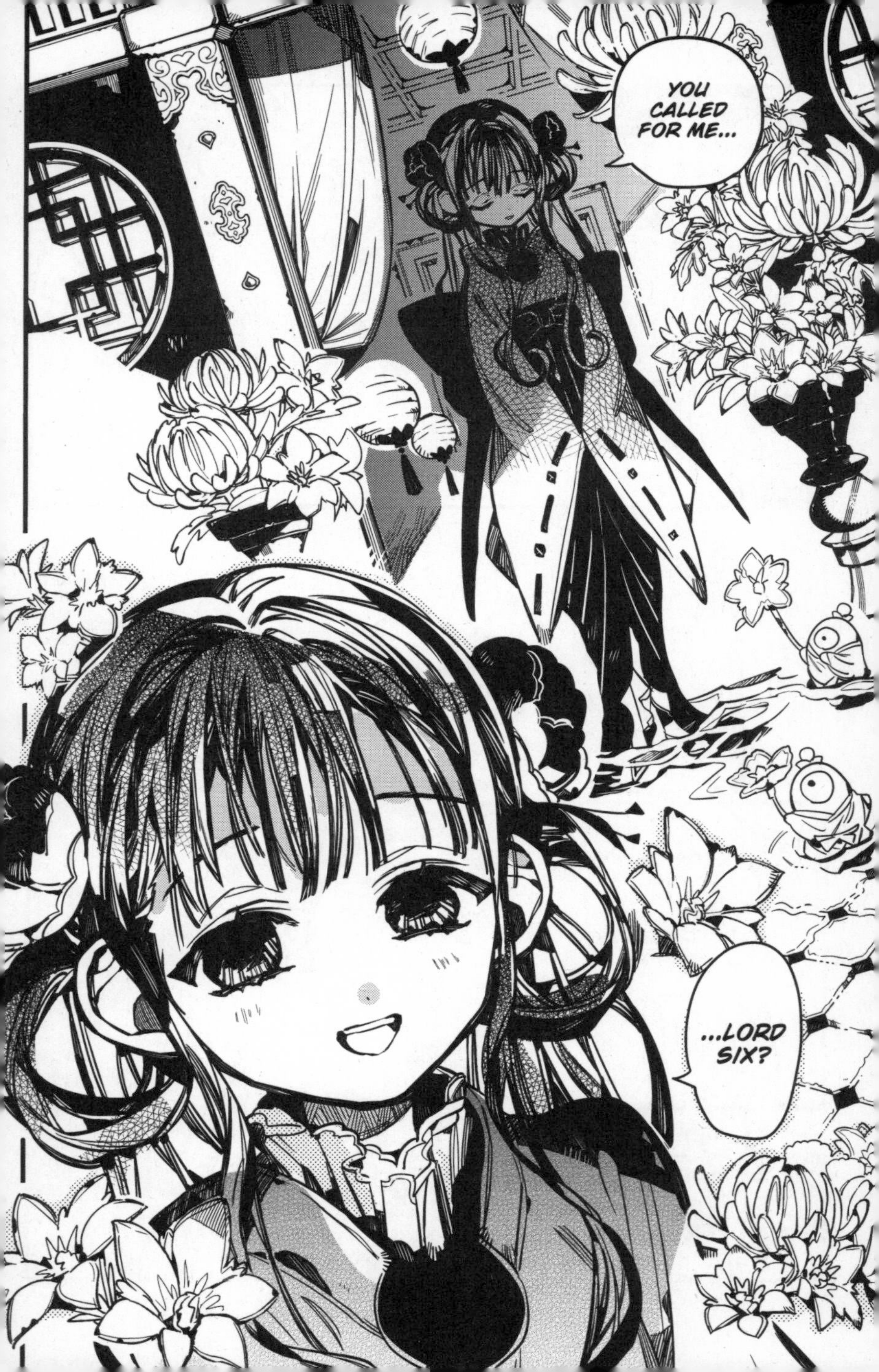
YOU CALLED FOR ME...
...LORD SIX?

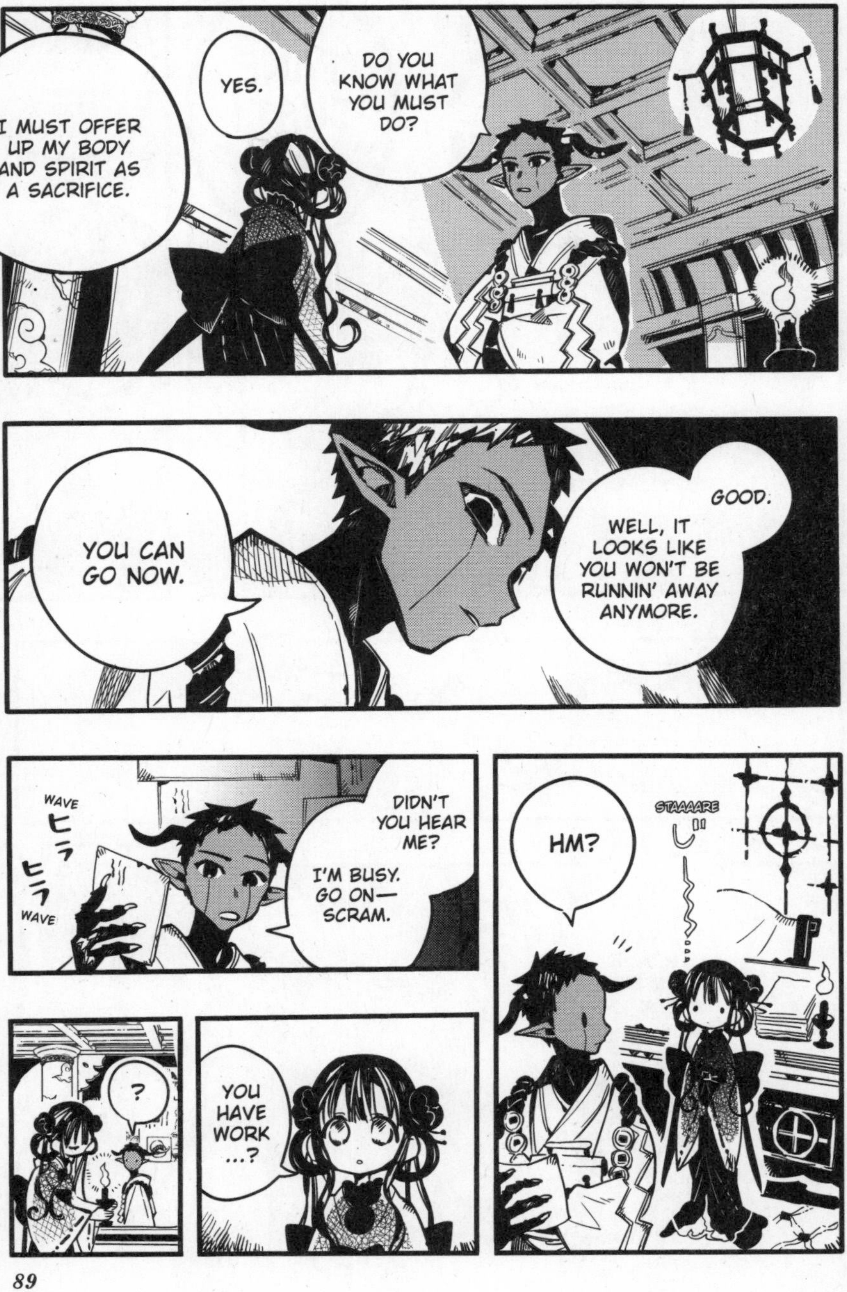
DO YOU KNOW WHAT YOU MUST DO?
YES.
I MUST OFFER UP MY BODY AND SPIRIT AS A SACRIFICE.
GOOD.
WELL, IT LOOKS LIKE YOU WON'T BE RUNNIN' AWAY ANYMORE.
YOU CAN GO NOW.
STAAAARE
じー
HM?
DIDN'T YOU HEAR ME?
I'M BUSY. GO ON— SCRAM.
WAVE
ヒラ
ヒラ
WAVE
YOU HAVE WORK ...?
?

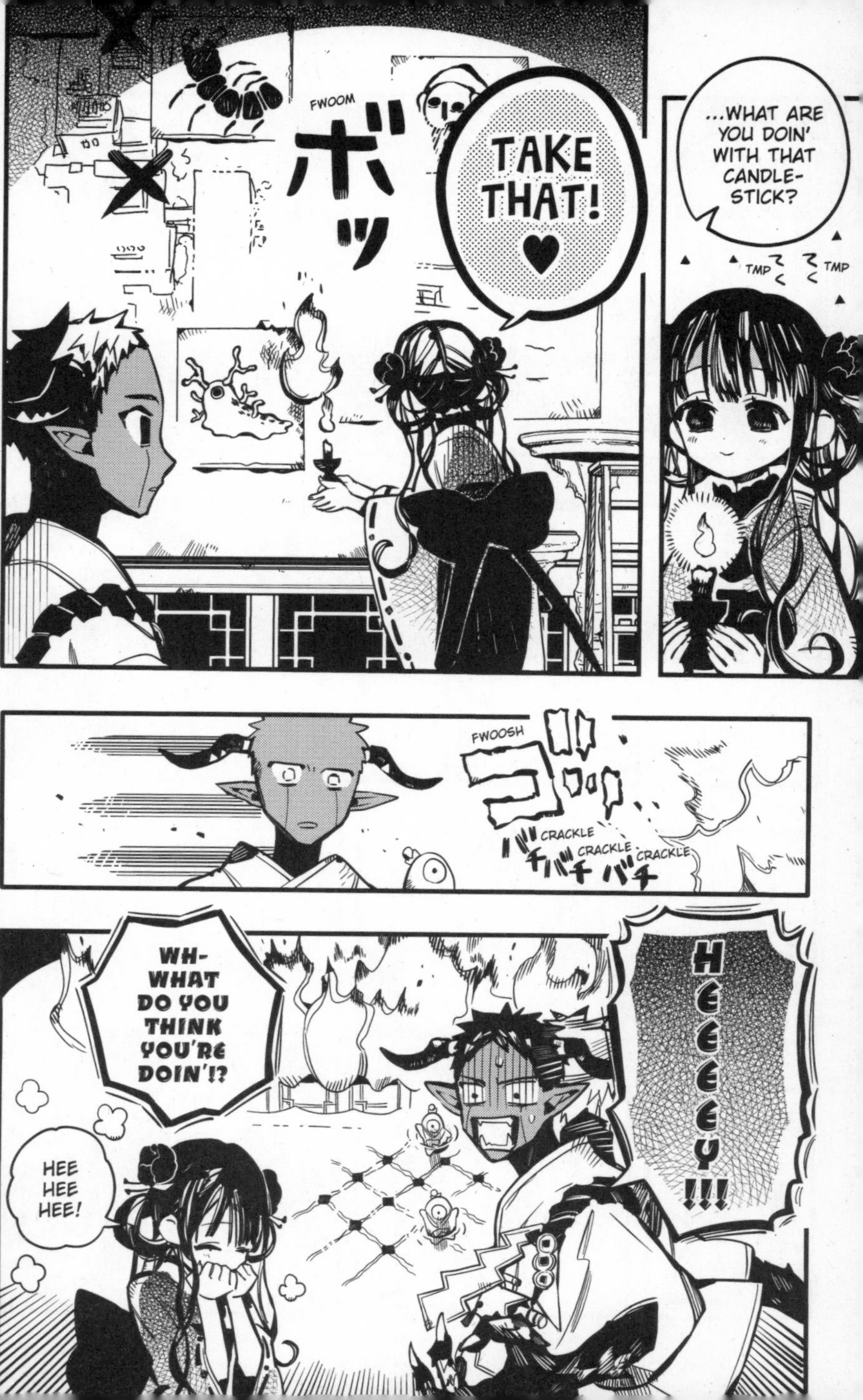
...WHAT ARE YOU DOIN' WITH THAT CANDLE-STICK?
TMP TMP
FWOOM
ボッ
TAKE THAT! ♥
FWOOSH
ゴォッ
CRACKLE CRACKLE CRACKLE
バチバチバチ
HEEEEEY!!!
WH-WHAT DO YOU THINK YOU'RE DOIN'!?
HEE HEE HEE!

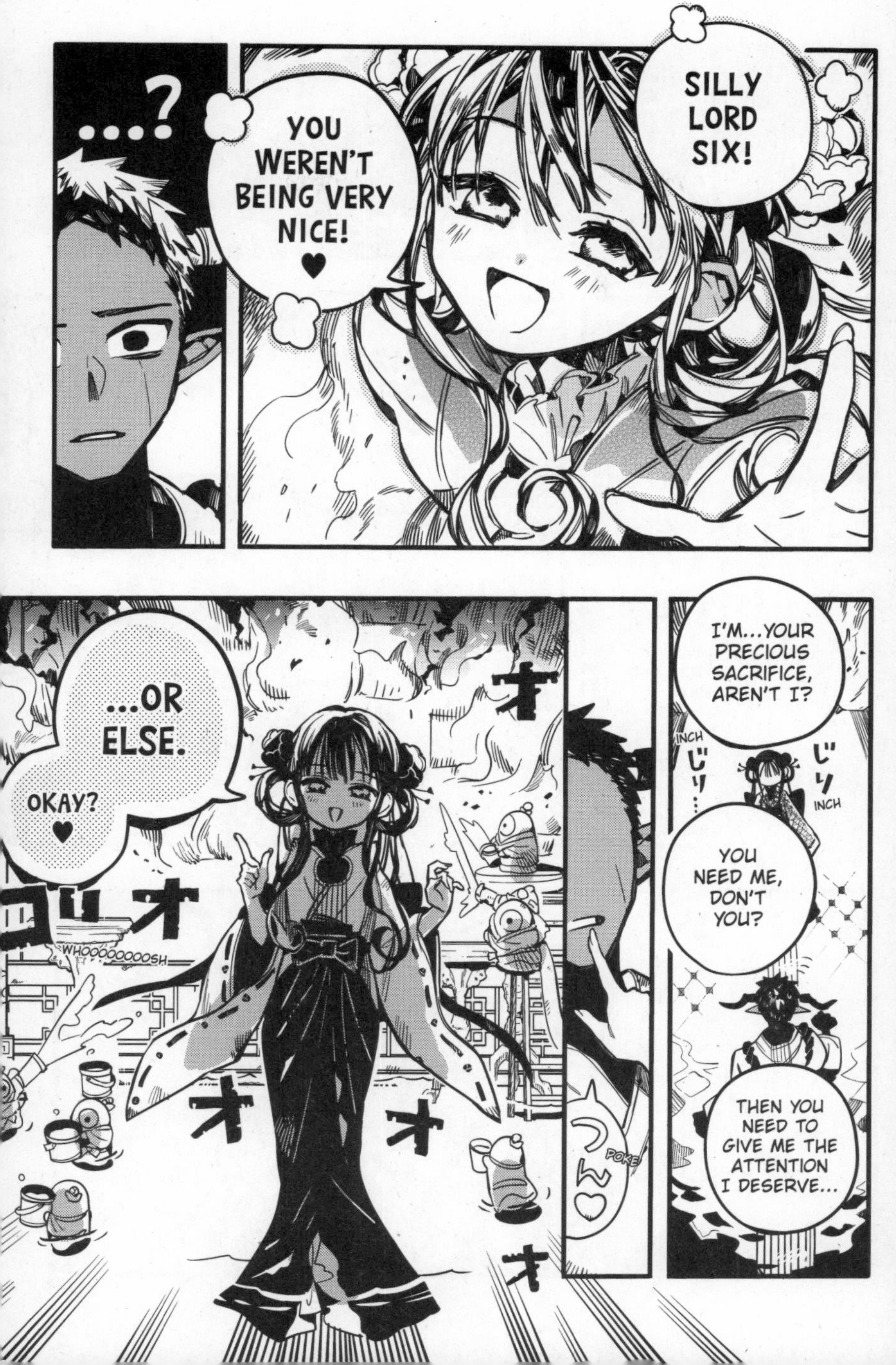
SILLY LORD SIX!
YOU WEREN'T BEING VERY NICE! ♥
...?
I'M...YOUR PRECIOUS SACRIFICE, AREN'T I?
じりじり...
INCH INCH
YOU NEED ME, DON'T YOU?
THEN YOU NEED TO GIVE ME THE ATTENTION I DESERVE...
つん♡
POKE
...OR ELSE.
OKAY? ♥
ゴオオ
WHOOOOOOOOOSH

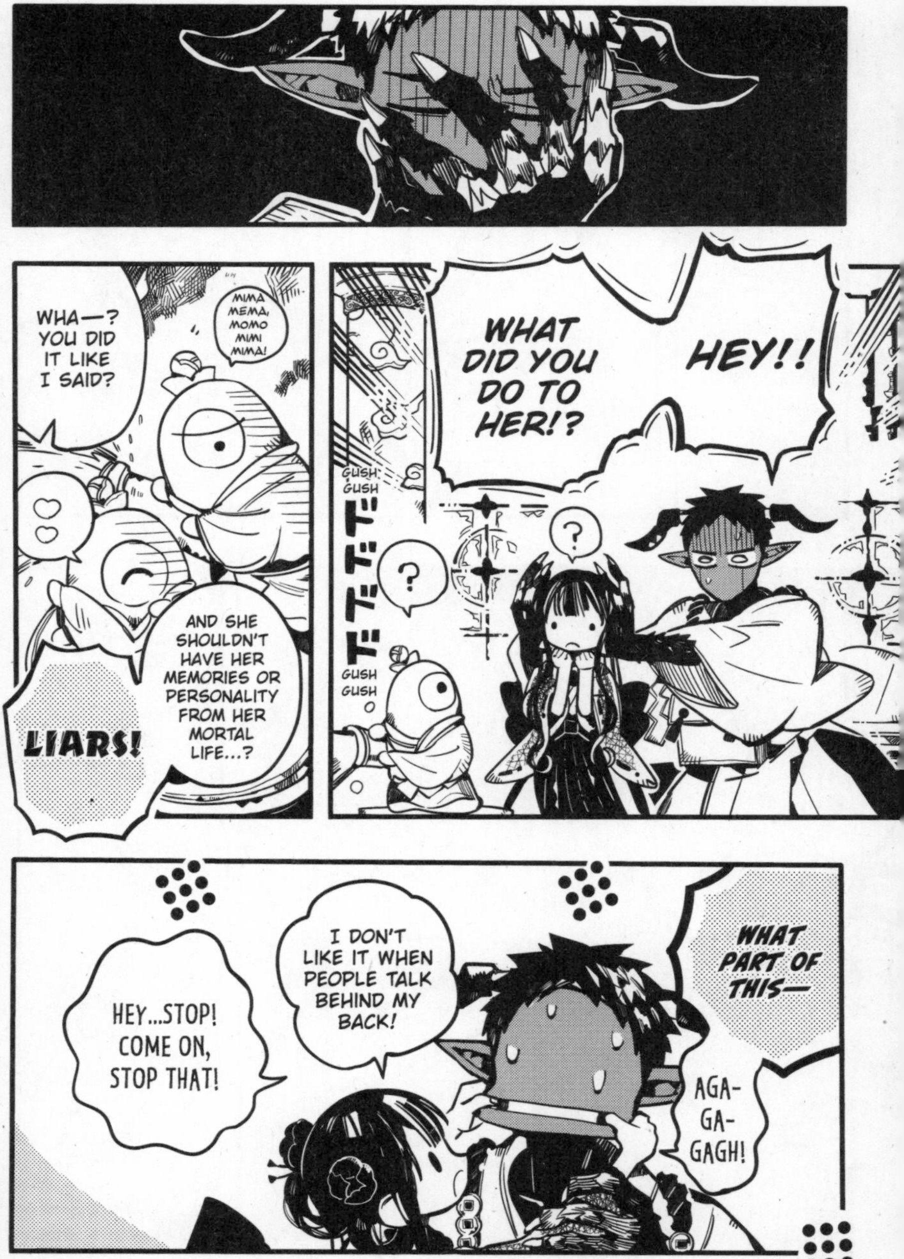
HEY!!
WHAT DID YOU DO TO HER!?
GUSH GUSH
ドドドドド
?
?
GUSH GUSH
MIMA MEMA, MOMO MIMI MIMA!
WHA—? YOU DID IT LIKE I SAID?
AND SHE SHOULDN'T HAVE HER MEMORIES OR PERSONALITY FROM HER MORTAL LIFE...?
LIARS!
WHAT PART OF THIS—
AGA-GA-GAGH!
I DON'T LIKE IT WHEN PEOPLE TALK BEHIND MY BACK!
HEY...STOP! COME ON, STOP THAT!

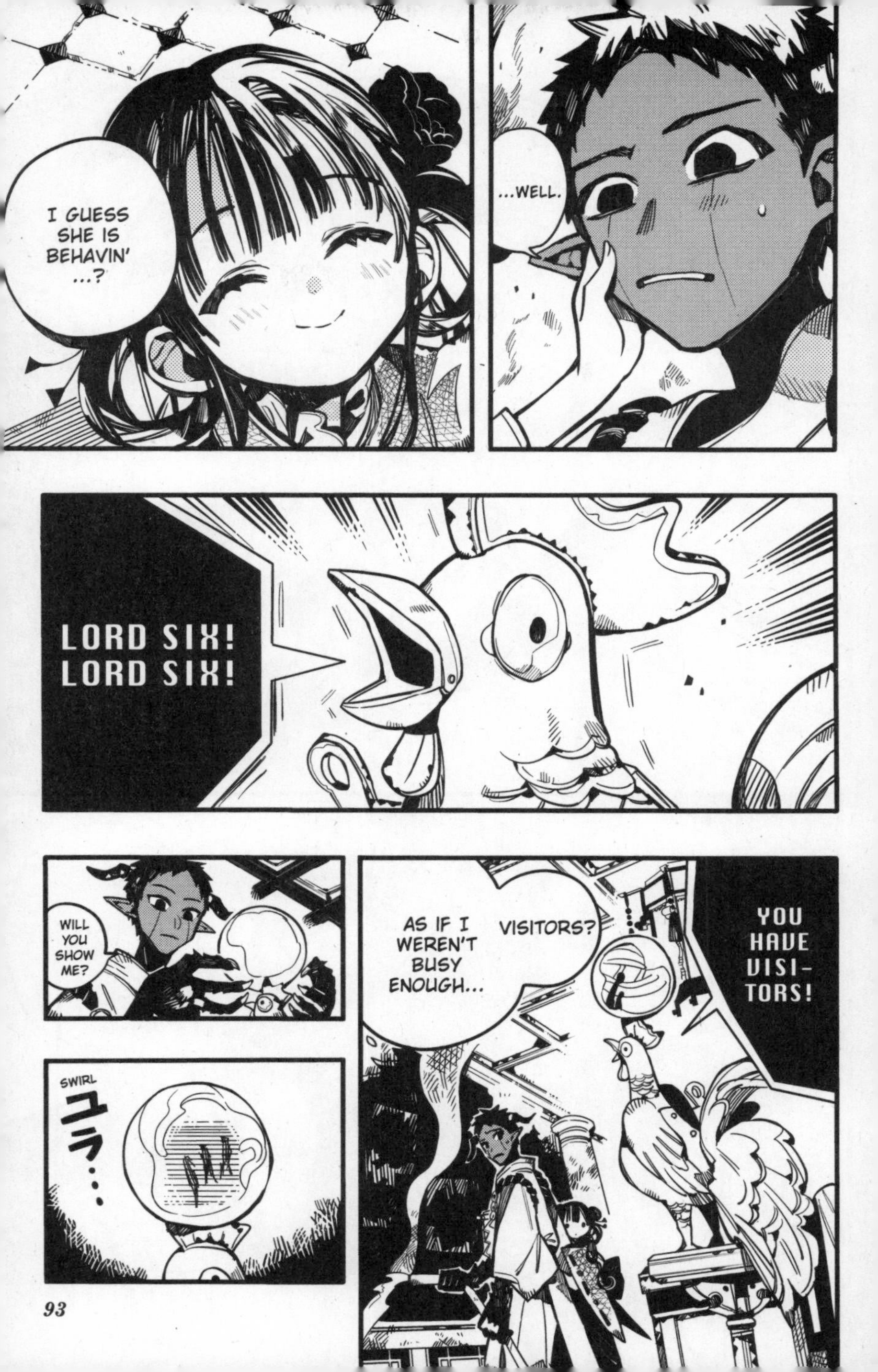
...WELL.
I GUESS SHE IS BEHAVIN' ...?
LORD SIX! LORD SIX!
YOU HAVE VISI- TORS!
VISITORS?
AS IF I WEREN'T BUSY ENOUGH...
WILL YOU SHOW ME?
SWIRL
ユラ…

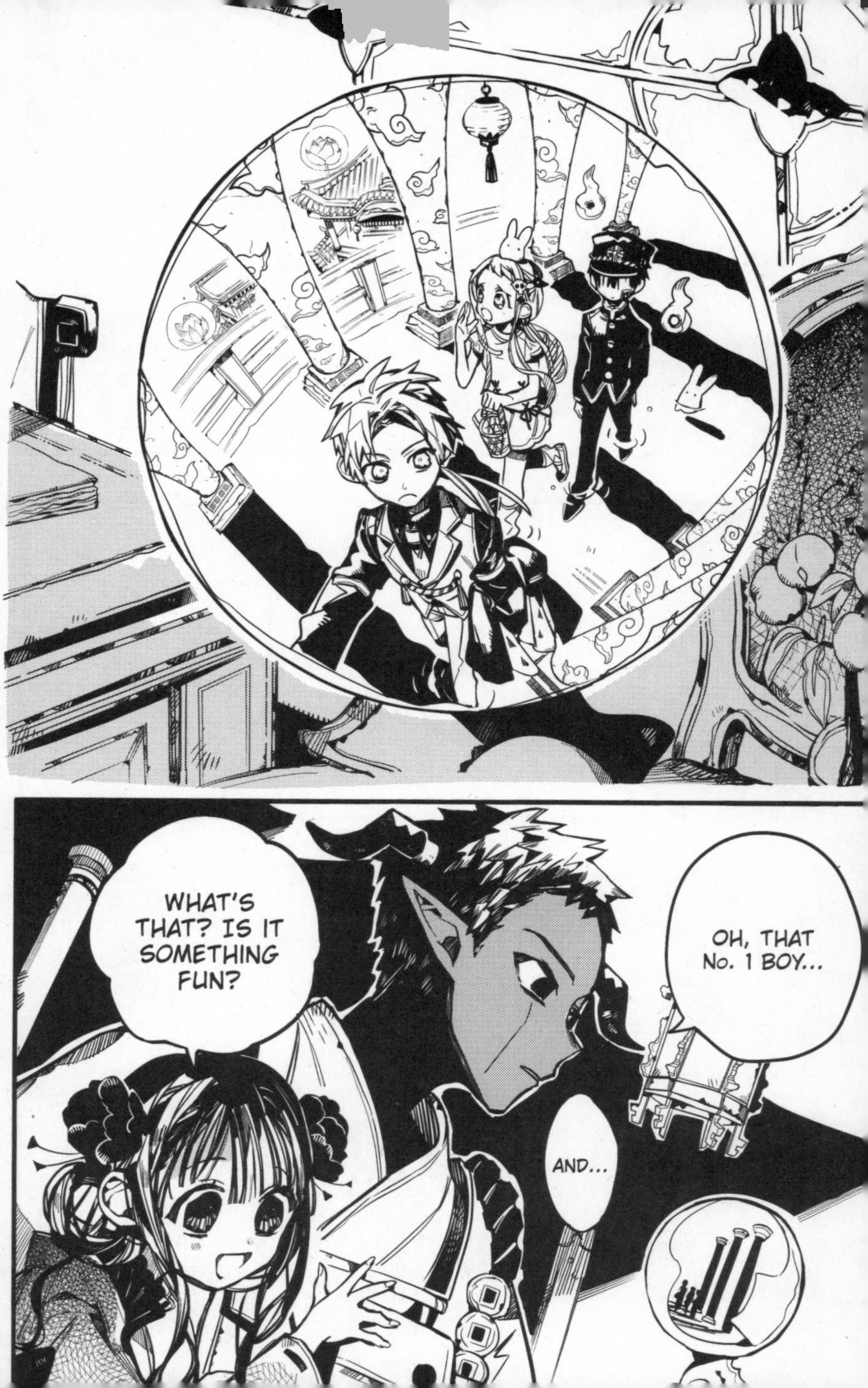
OH, THAT No. 1 BOY...
AND...
WHAT'S THAT? IS IT SOMETHING FUN?

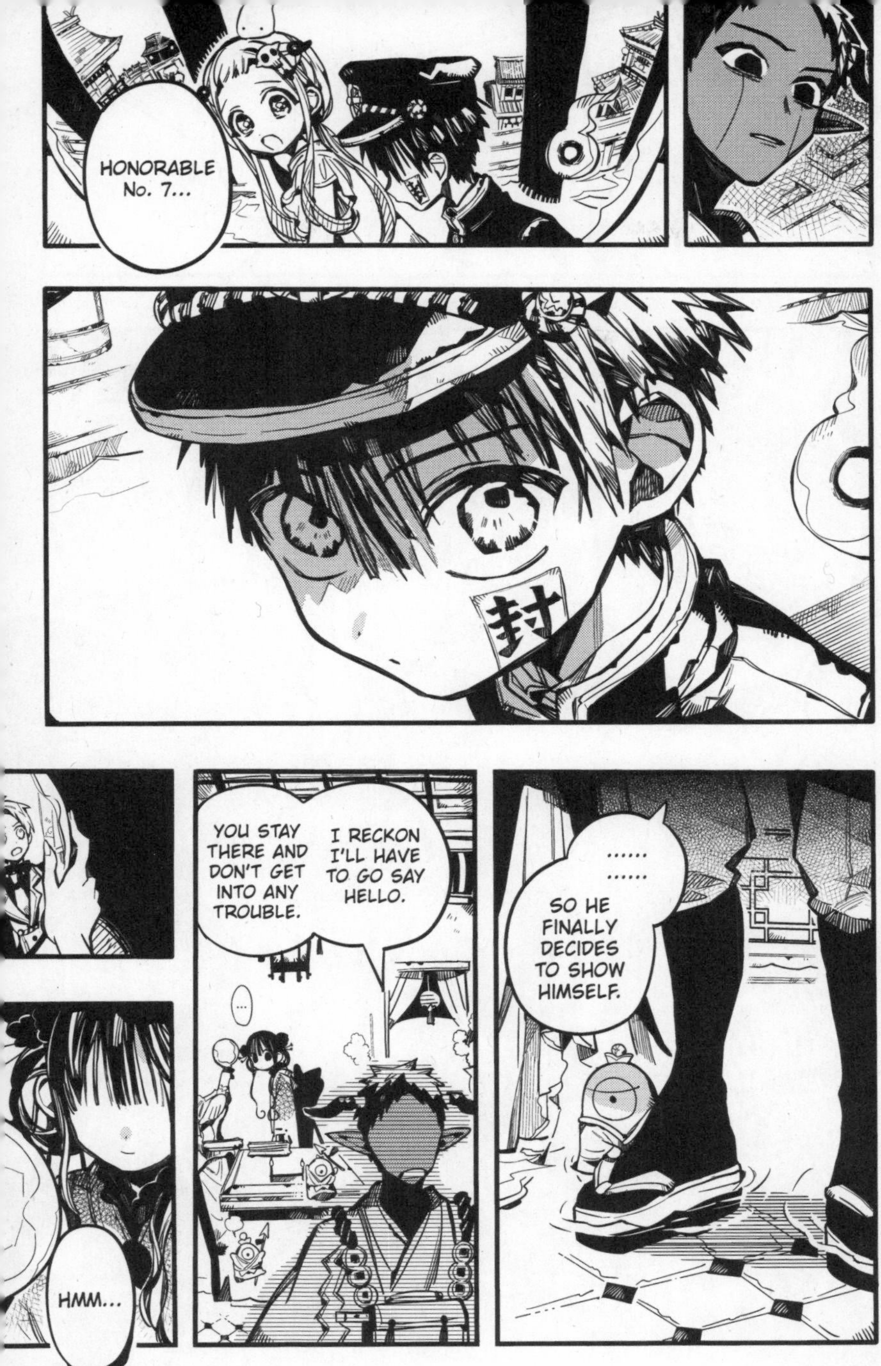
HONORABLE No. 7...
......
......
SO HE FINALLY DECIDES TO SHOW HIMSELF.
I RECKON I'LL HAVE TO GO SAY HELLO.
YOU STAY THERE AND DON'T GET INTO ANY TROUBLE.
...
HMM...

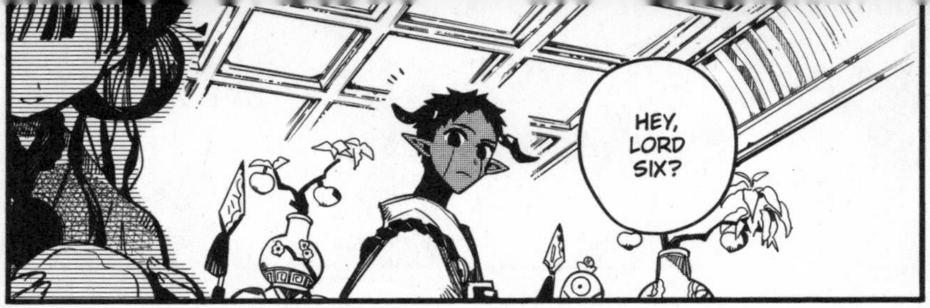
HEY, LORD SIX?

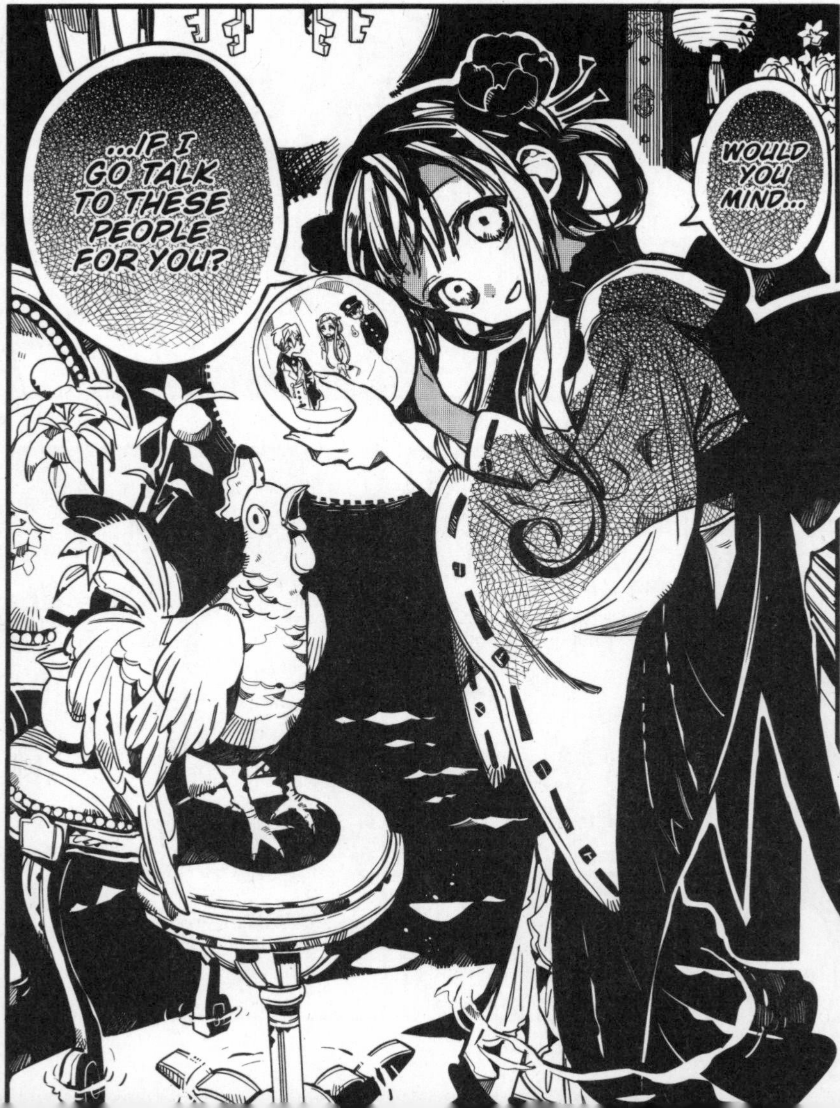
WOULD YOU MIND...
...IF I GO TALK TO THESE PEOPLE FOR YOU?

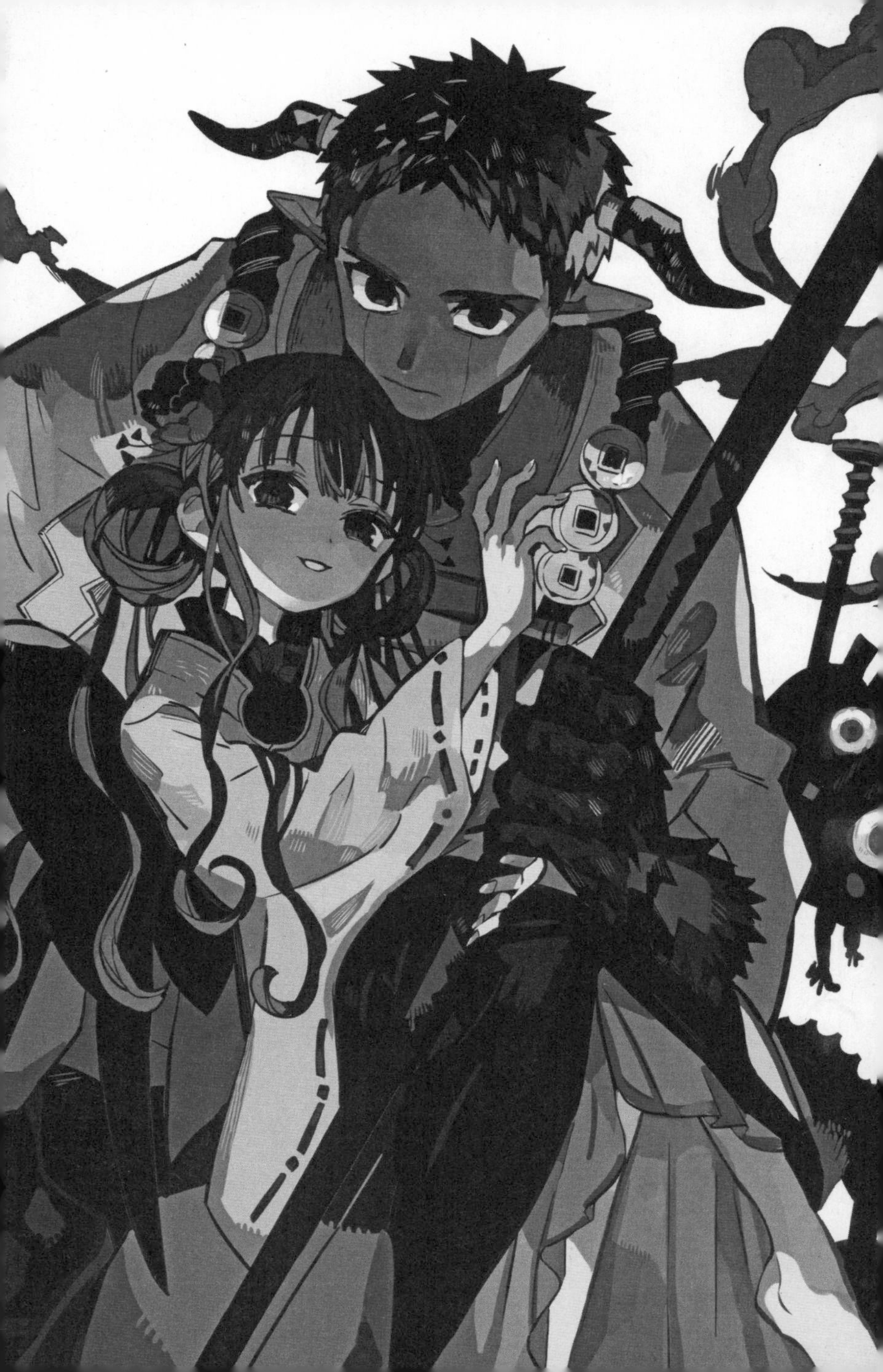

SPOOK 64
SACRIFICE OF THE GRIM REAPER (PART 2)

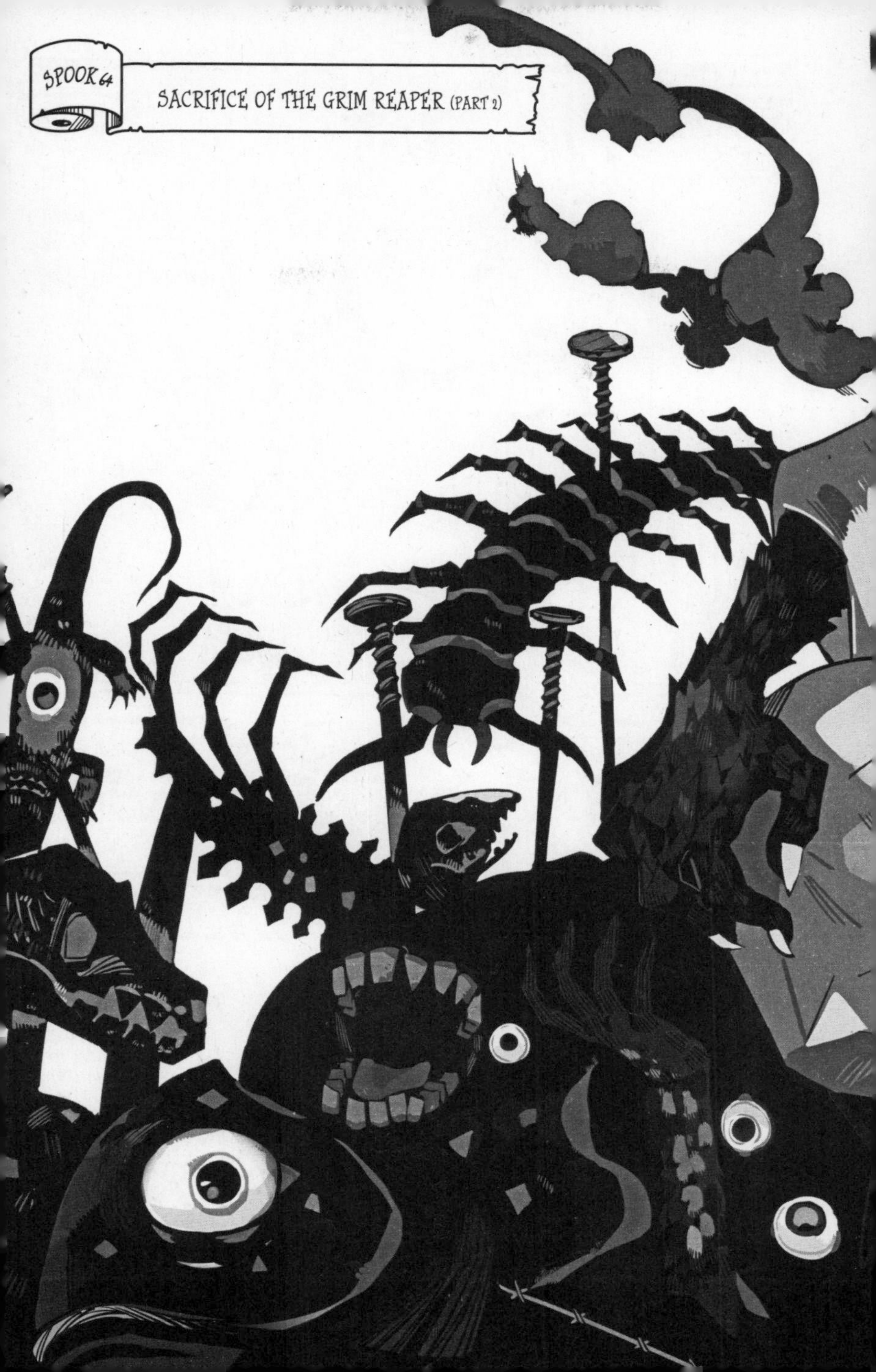

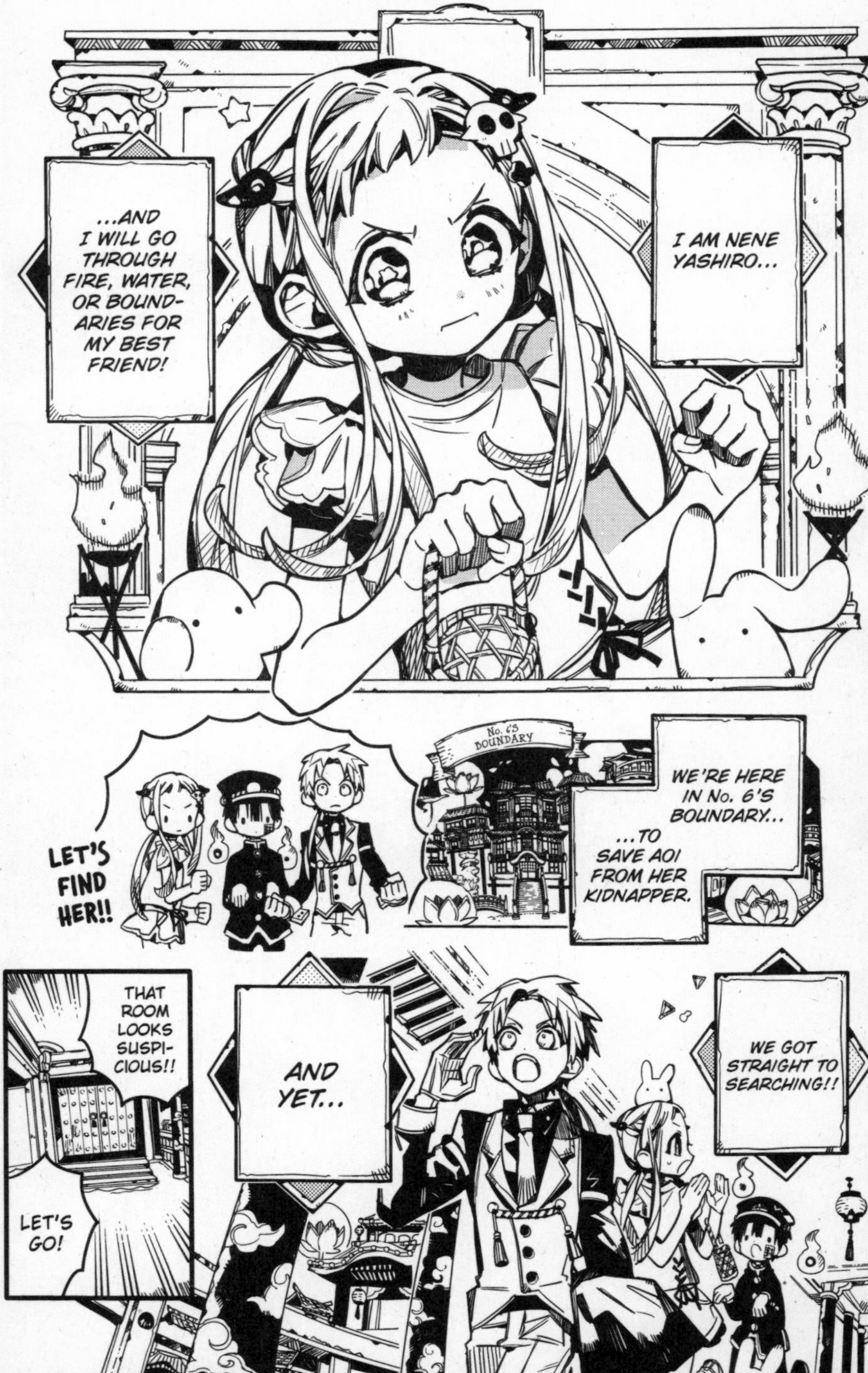
I AM NENE YASHIRO...
...AND I WILL GO THROUGH FIRE, WATER, OR BOUNDARIES FOR MY BEST FRIEND!
No. 6'S BOUNDARY
WE'RE HERE IN No. 6'S BOUNDARY...
...TO SAVE AOI FROM HER KIDNAPPER.
LET'S FIND HER!!
WE GOT STRAIGHT TO SEARCHING!!
AND YET...
THAT ROOM LOOKS SUSPICIOUS!!
LET'S GO!

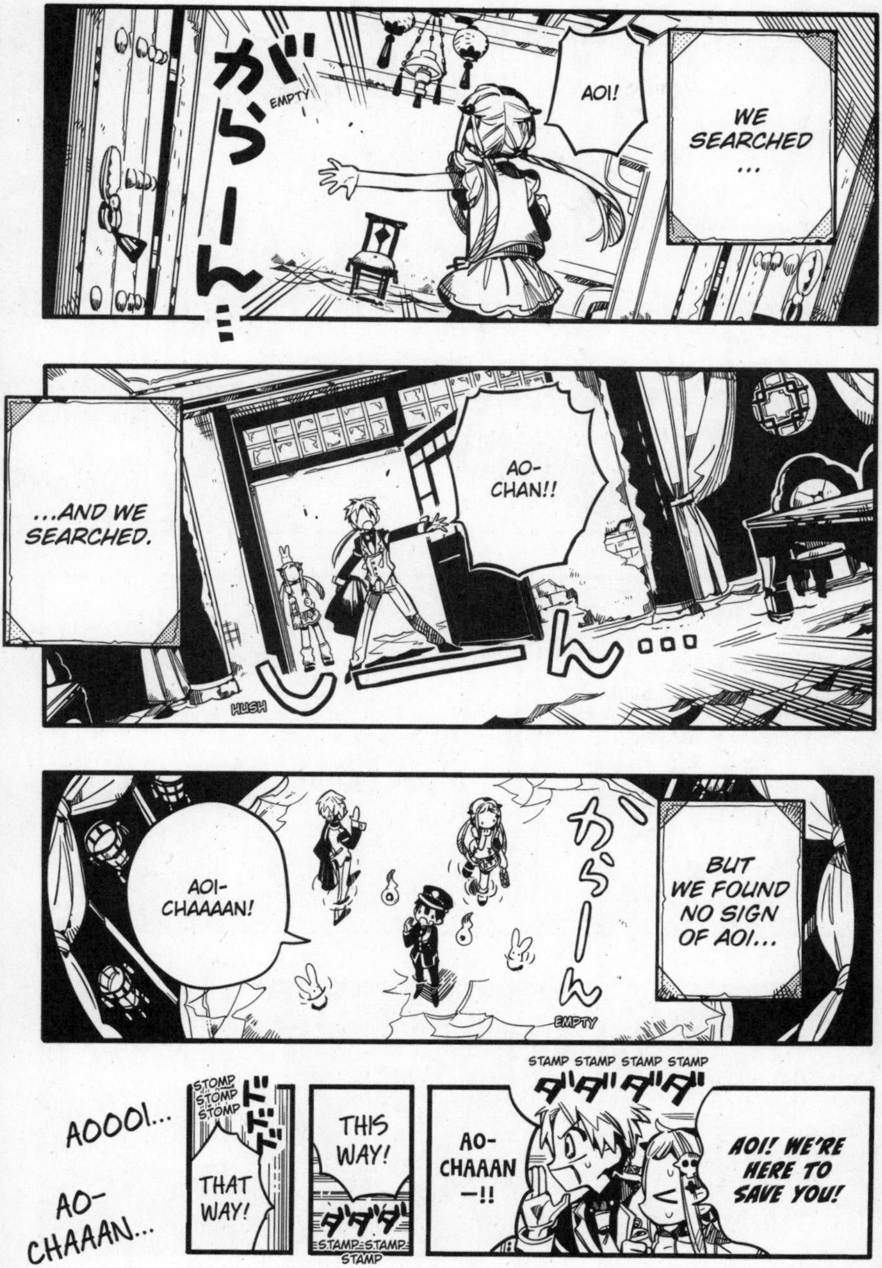

WE SEARCHED ...
AOI!
がらーん
EMPTY
AO-CHAN!!
...AND WE SEARCHED.
しん...
HUSH
BUT WE FOUND NO SIGN OF AOI...
からーん
EMPTY
AOI-CHAAAAN!
ダダダダ
STAMP STAMP STAMP STAMP
AOI! WE'RE HERE TO SAVE YOU!
AO-CHAAAN—!!
THIS WAY!
ダダダ
STAMP STAMP STAMP
ドドド
STOMP STOMP STOMP
THAT WAY!
AOOOI...
AO-CHAAAN...

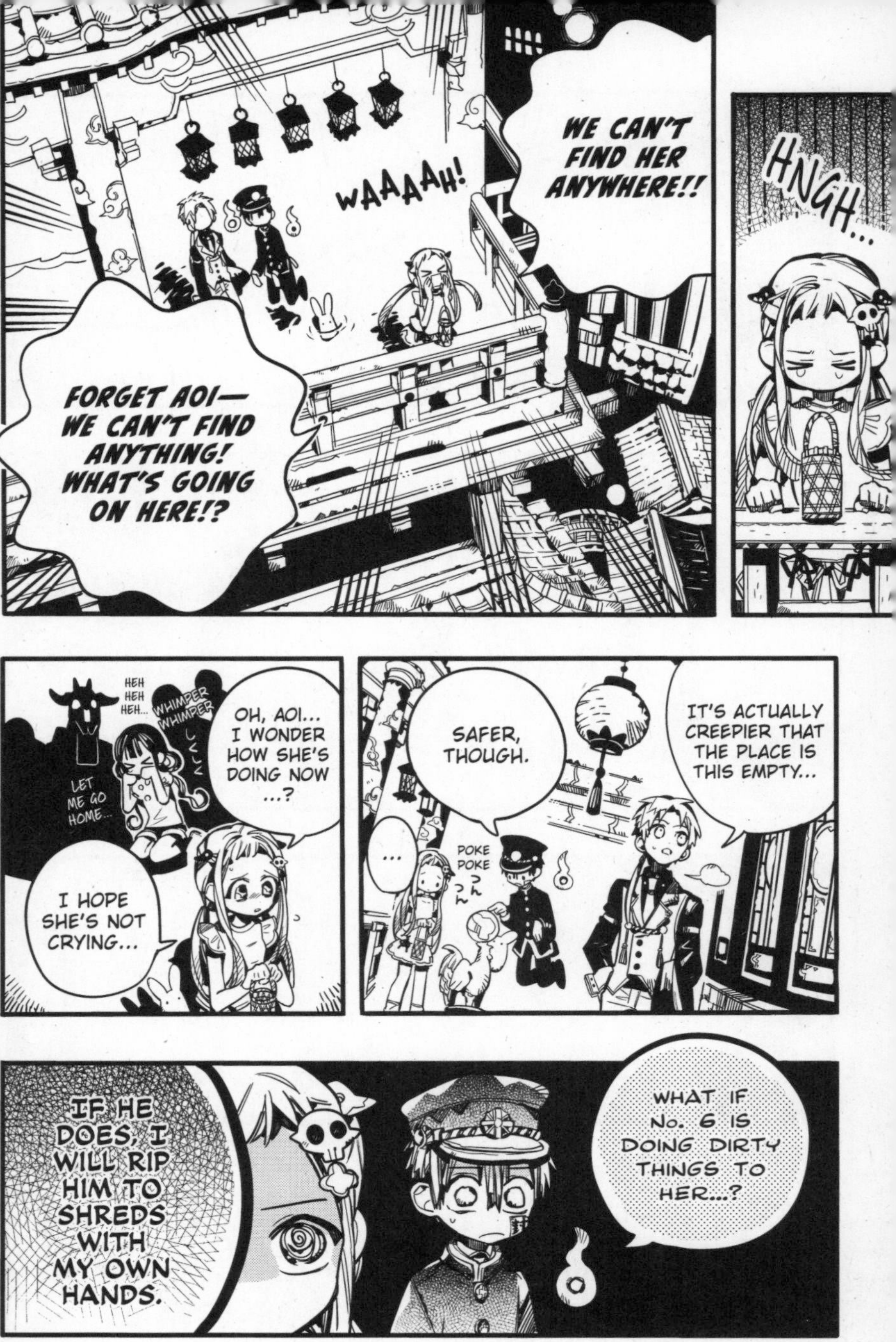
HNGH...
WE CAN'T FIND HER ANYWHERE!!
WAAAAH!
FORGET AOI— WE CAN'T FIND ANYTHING! WHAT'S GOING ON HERE!?
IT'S ACTUALLY CREEPIER THAT THE PLACE IS THIS EMPTY...
SAFER, THOUGH.
POKE POKE
...
OH, AOI... I WONDER HOW SHE'S DOING NOW ...?
HEH HEH HEH...
WHIMPER WHIMPER
LET ME GO HOME...
I HOPE SHE'S NOT CRYING...
WHAT IF No. 6 IS DOING DIRTY THINGS TO HER...?
IF HE DOES, I WILL RIP HIM TO SHREDS WITH MY OWN HANDS.

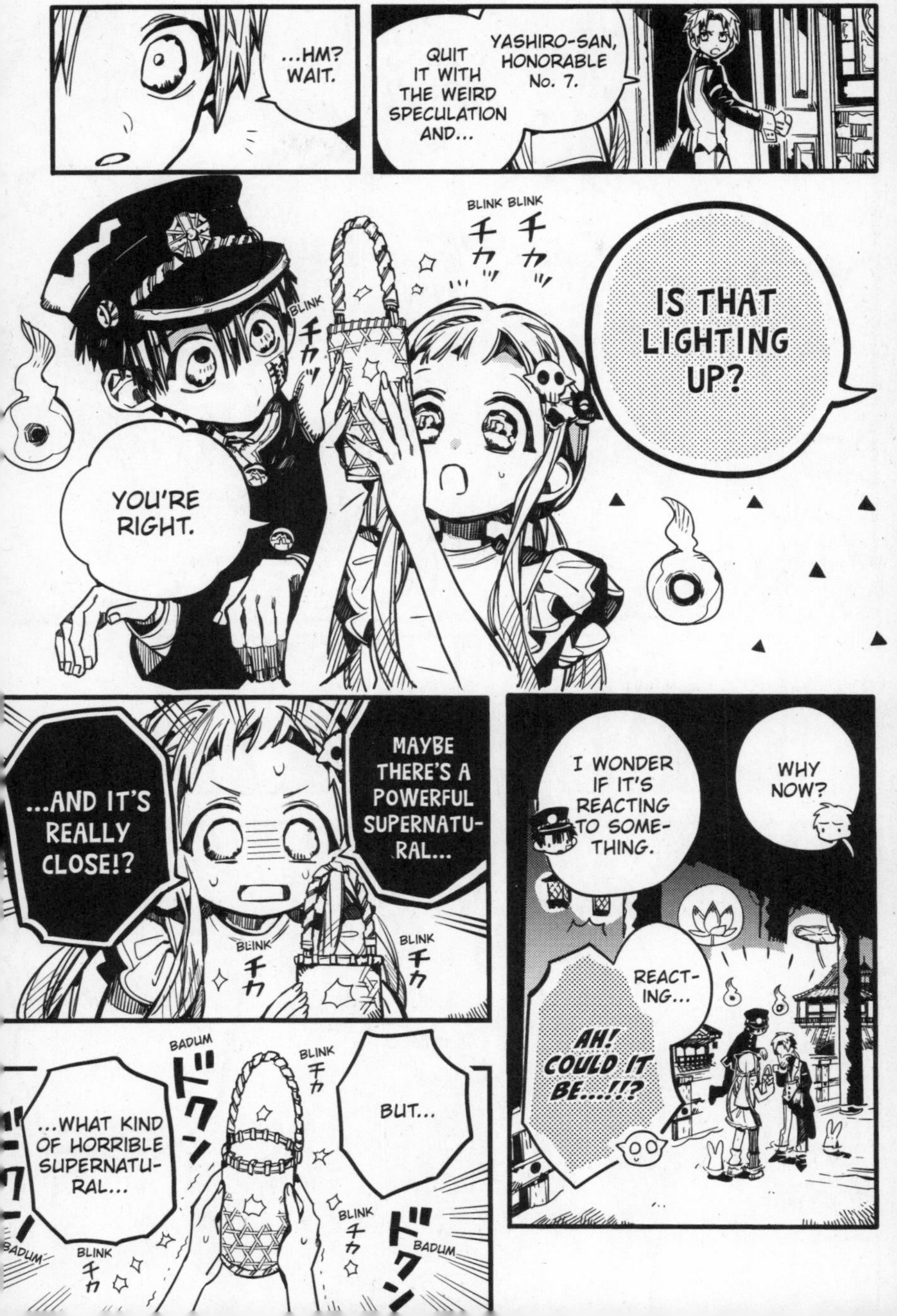
YASHIRO-SAN, HONORABLE No. 7.
QUIT IT WITH THE WEIRD SPECULATION AND...
...HM? WAIT.
BLINK BLINK
IS THAT LIGHTING UP?
BLINK
YOU'RE RIGHT.
WHY NOW?
I WONDER IF IT'S REACTING TO SOME-THING.
REACT-ING...
AH! COULD IT BE...!!?
MAYBE THERE'S A POWERFUL SUPERNATU-RAL...
...AND IT'S REALLY CLOSE!?
BLINK
BLINK
BLINK
BADUM
BUT...
...WHAT KIND OF HORRIBLE SUPERNATU-RAL...
BLINK
BADUM
BLINK
BADUM

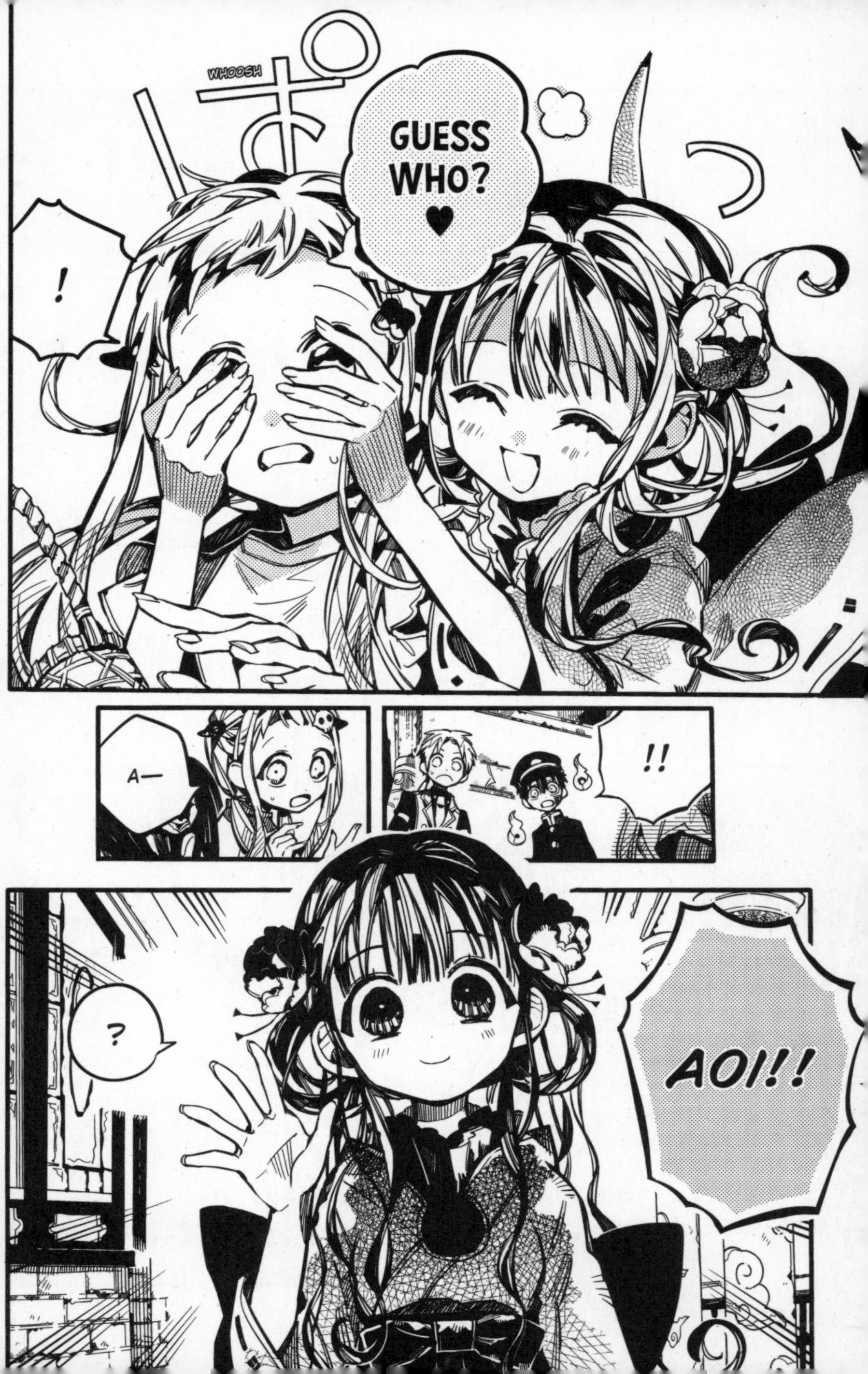
GUESS WHO? ♥
WHOOSH
!
!!
A—
AOI!!
?

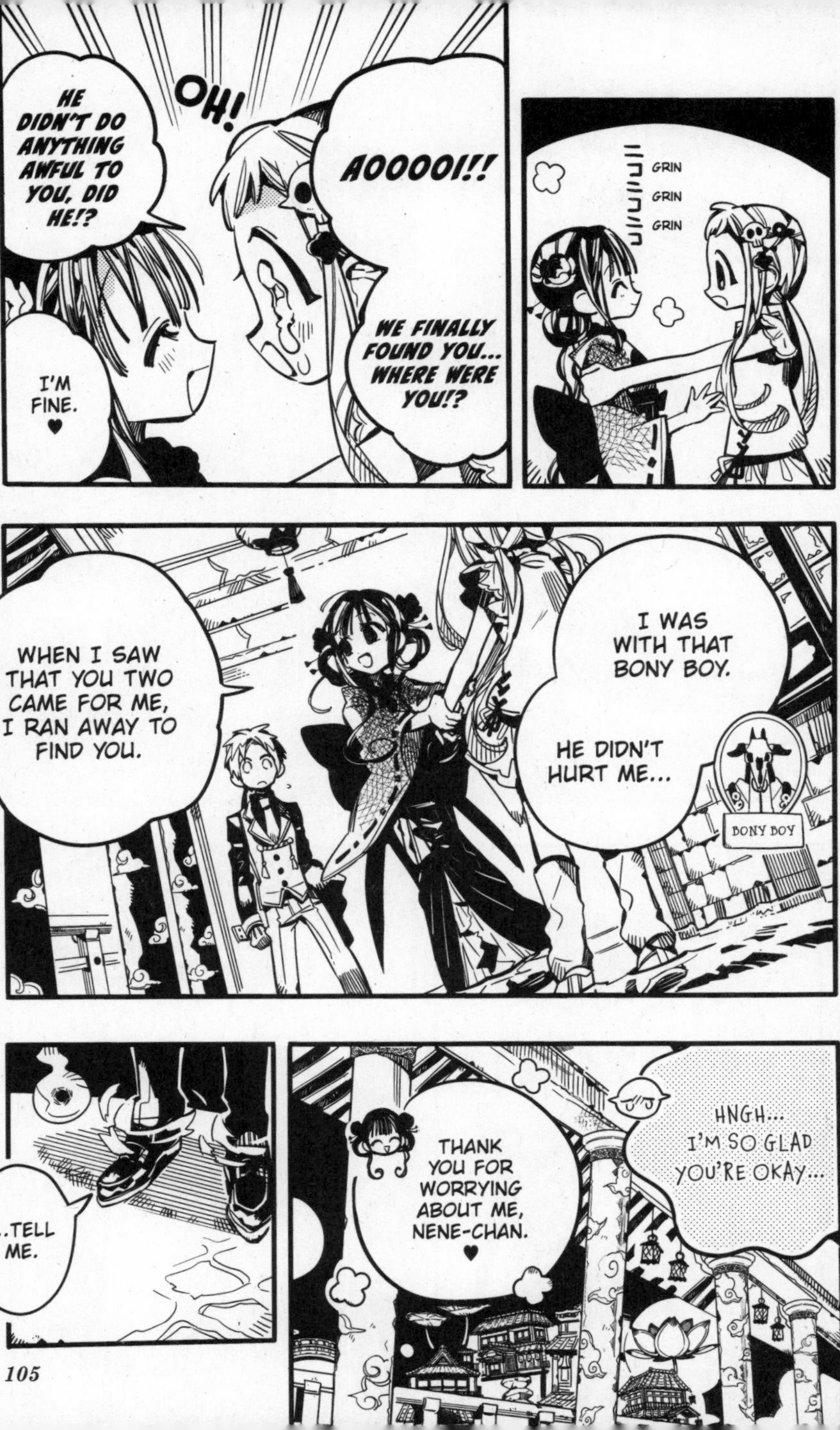
GRIN GRIN GRIN
AOOOOI!!
OH!
HE DIDN'T DO ANYTHING AWFUL TO YOU, DID HE!?
WE FINALLY FOUND YOU... WHERE WERE YOU!?
I'M FINE. ♥
I WAS WITH THAT BONY BOY.
HE DIDN'T HURT ME...
BONY BOY
WHEN I SAW THAT YOU TWO CAME FOR ME, I RAN AWAY TO FIND YOU.
HNGH... I'M SO GLAD YOU'RE OKAY...
THANK YOU FOR WORRYING ABOUT ME, NENE-CHAN. ♥
...TELL ME.

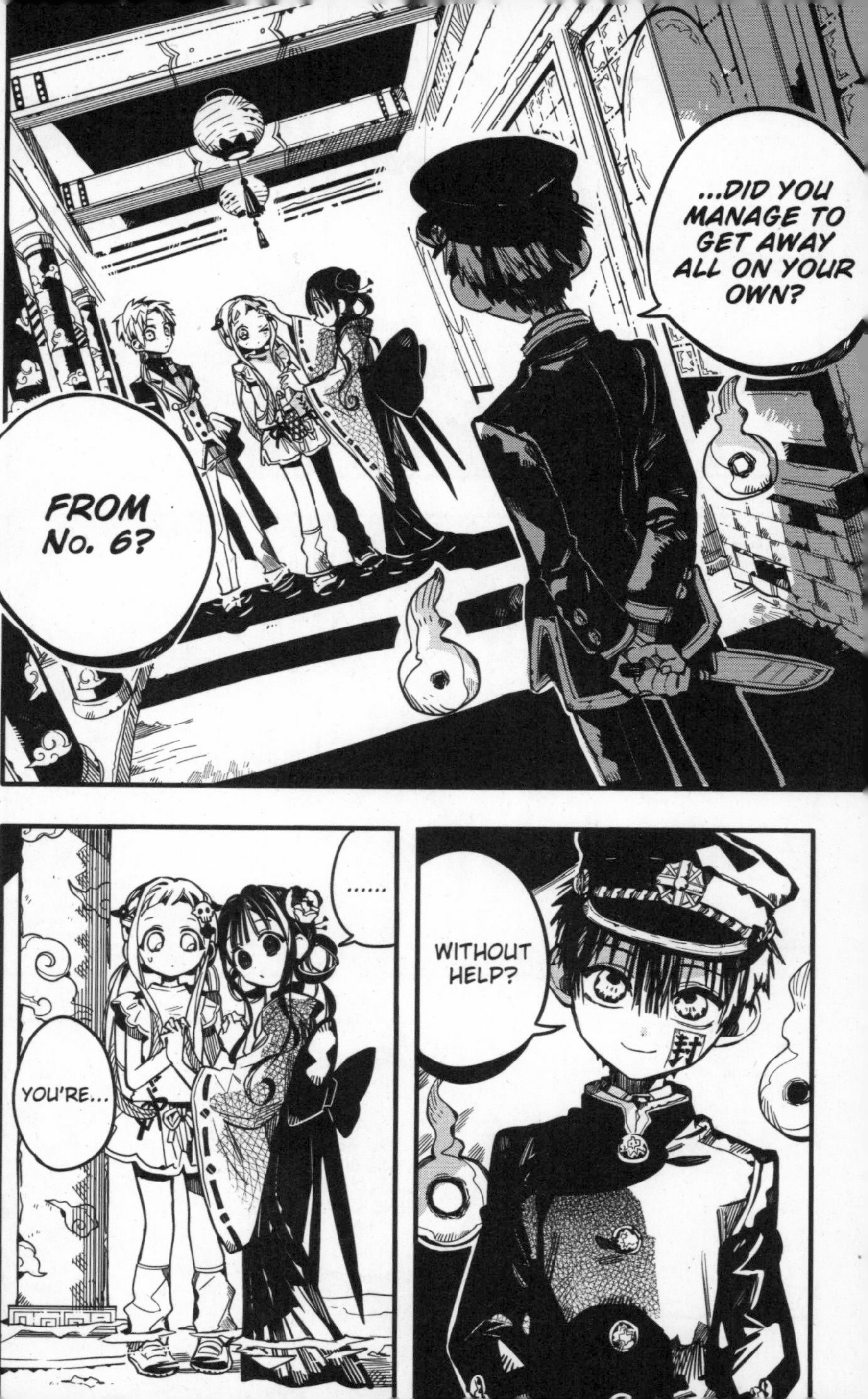
...DID YOU MANAGE TO GET AWAY ALL ON YOUR OWN?
FROM No. 6?
WITHOUT HELP?
......
YOU'RE...

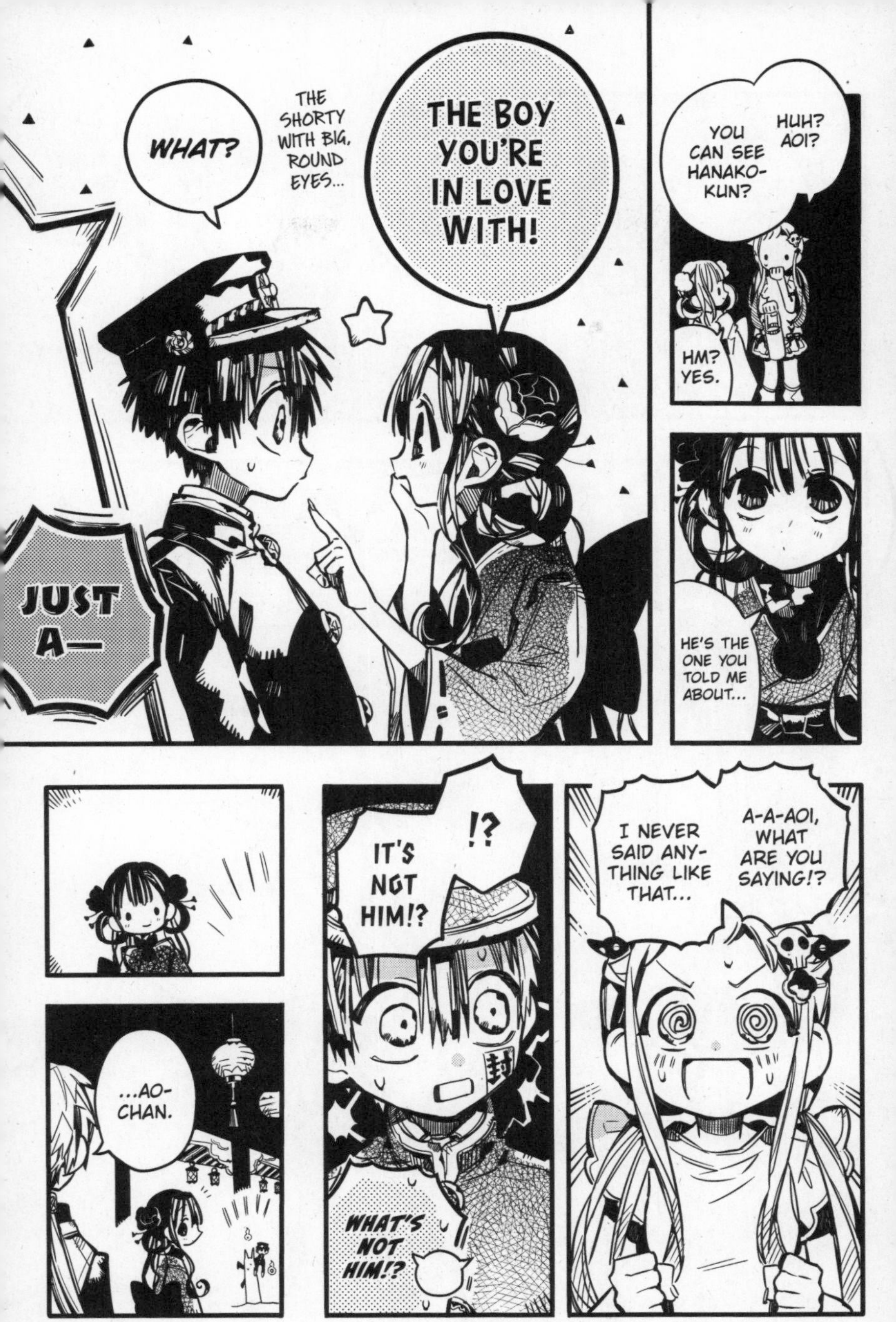
HUH? AOI?
YOU CAN SEE HANAKO-KUN?
HM? YES.
HE'S THE ONE YOU TOLD ME ABOUT...
THE BOY YOU'RE IN LOVE WITH!
THE SHORTY WITH BIG, ROUND EYES...
WHAT?
JUST A—
A-A-AOI, WHAT ARE YOU SAYING!?
I NEVER SAID ANYTHING LIKE THAT...
!?
IT'S NOT HIM!?
WHAT'S NOT HIM!?
...AO-CHAN.

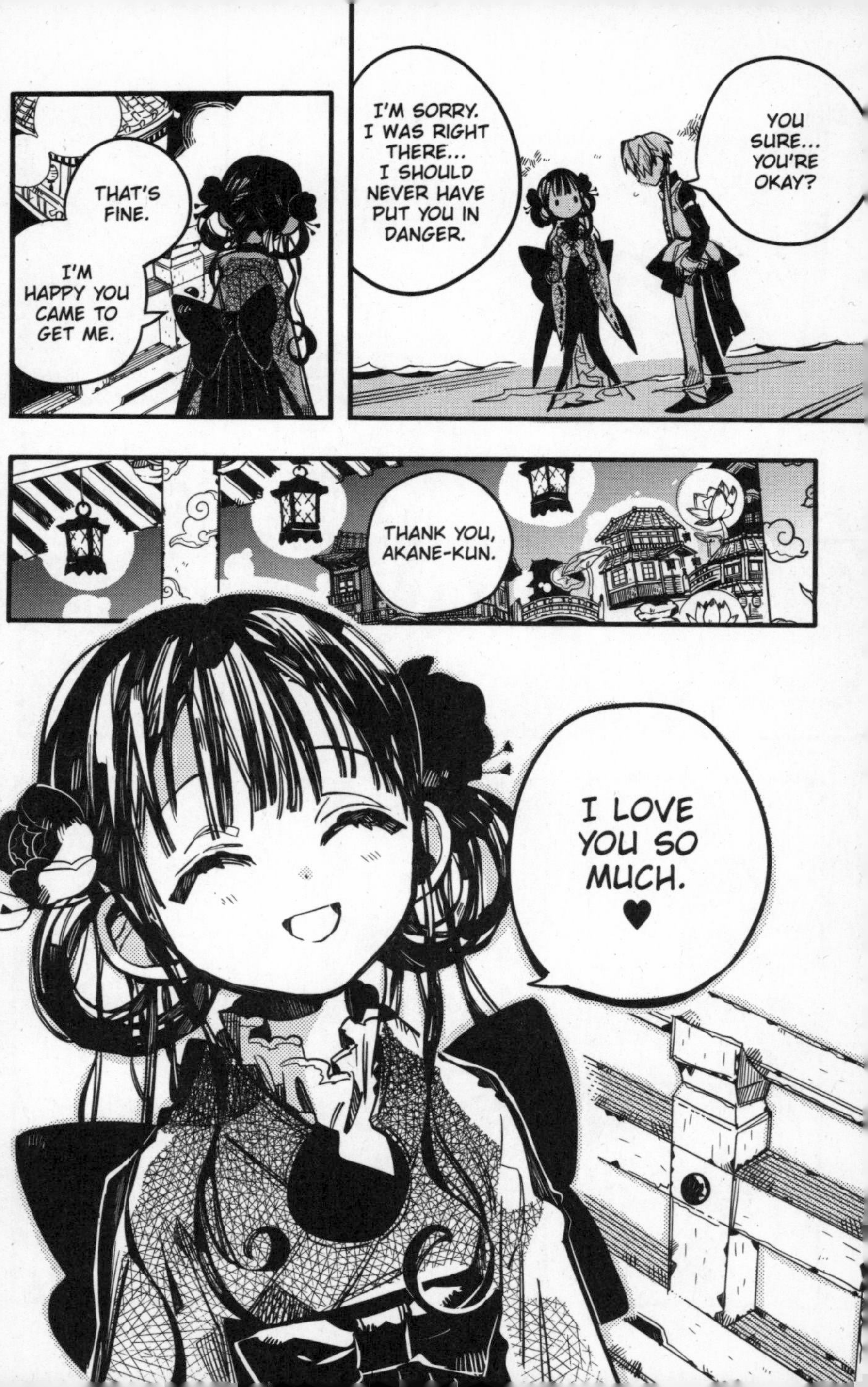
YOU SURE... YOU'RE OKAY?
I'M SORRY. I WAS RIGHT THERE... I SHOULD NEVER HAVE PUT YOU IN DANGER.
THAT'S FINE.
I'M HAPPY YOU CAME TO GET ME.
THANK YOU, AKANE-KUN.
I LOVE YOU SO MUCH. ♥

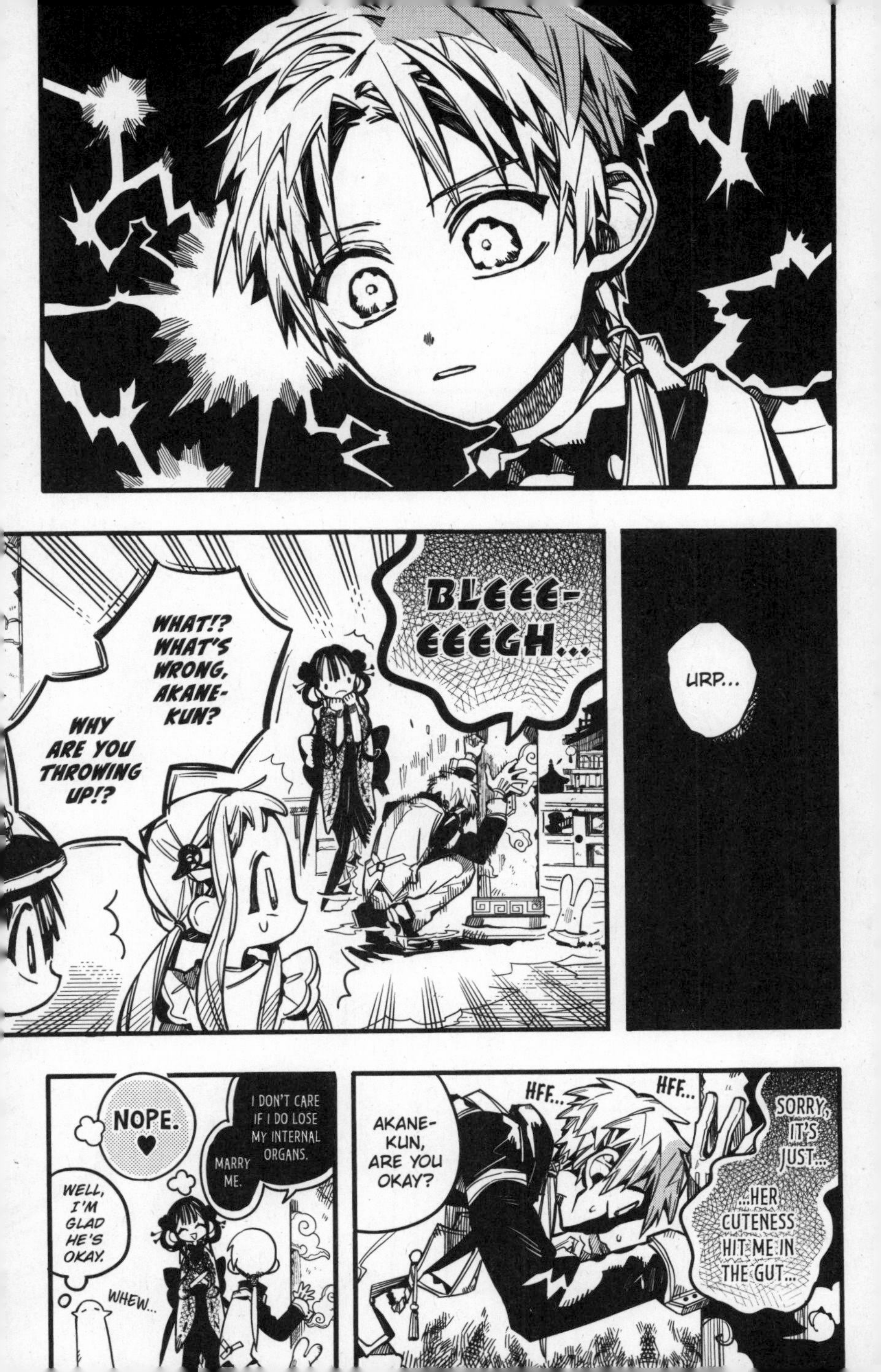
URP...
BLEEE-EEEGH...
WHAT!? WHAT'S WRONG, AKANE-KUN?
WHY ARE YOU THROWING UP!?
HFF... HFF...
AKANE-KUN, ARE YOU OKAY?
SORRY, IT'S JUST...
...HER CUTENESS HIT ME IN THE GUT...
I DON'T CARE IF I DO LOSE MY INTERNAL ORGANS.
MARRY ME.
NOPE. ♥
WELL, I'M GLAD HE'S OKAY.
WHEW...

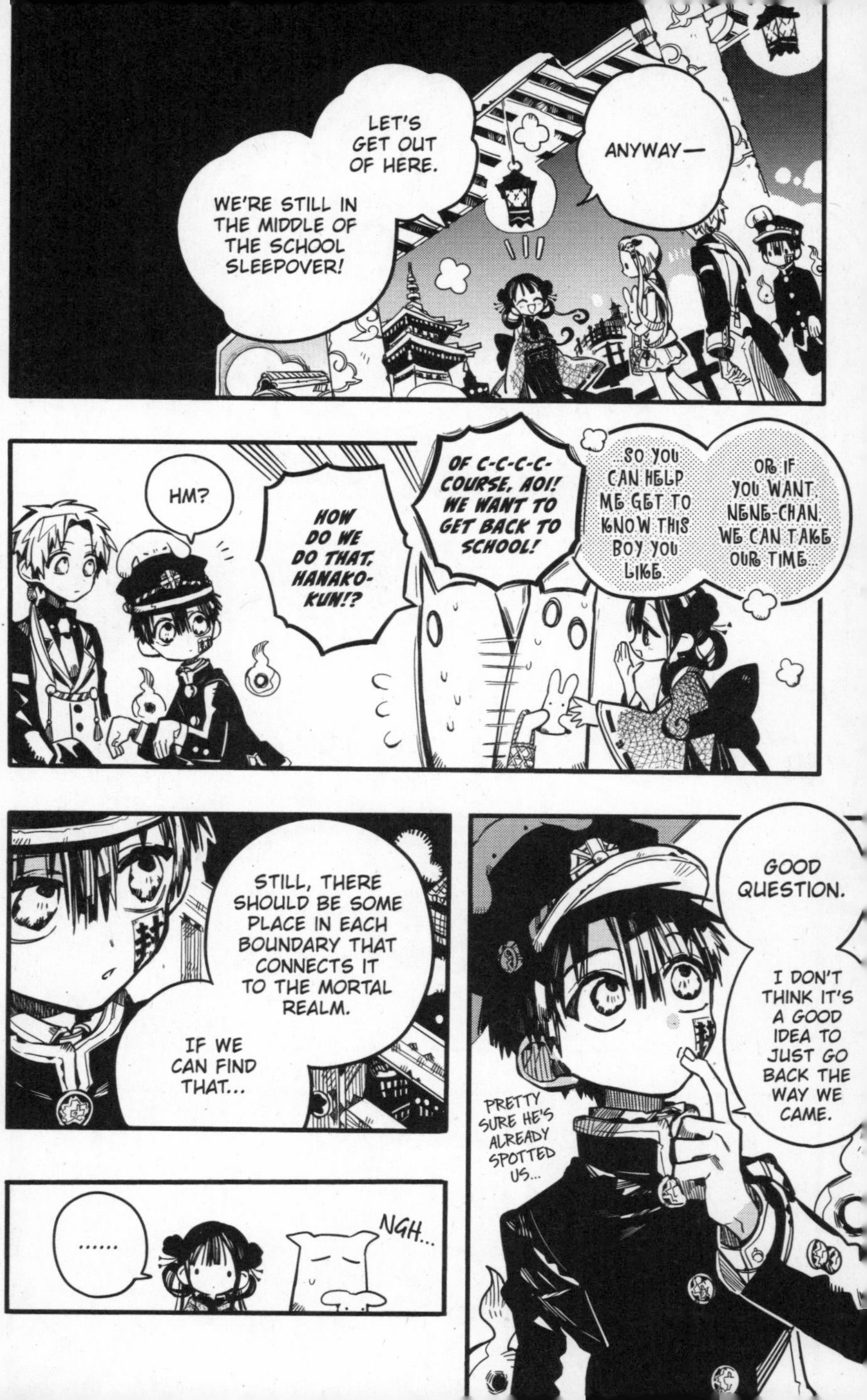
ANYWAY—
LET'S GET OUT OF HERE.
WE'RE STILL IN THE MIDDLE OF THE SCHOOL SLEEPOVER!
OR IF YOU WANT, NENE-CHAN, WE CAN TAKE OUR TIME...
...SO YOU CAN HELP ME GET TO KNOW THIS BOY YOU LIKE.
OF C-C-C-C-COURSE, AOI! WE WANT TO GET BACK TO SCHOOL!
HOW DO WE DO THAT, HANAKO-KUN!?
HM?
GOOD QUESTION.
I DON'T THINK IT'S A GOOD IDEA TO JUST GO BACK THE WAY WE CAME.
PRETTY SURE HE'S ALREADY SPOTTED US...
STILL, THERE SHOULD BE SOME PLACE IN EACH BOUNDARY THAT CONNECTS IT TO THE MORTAL REALM.
IF WE CAN FIND THAT...
NGH...
......

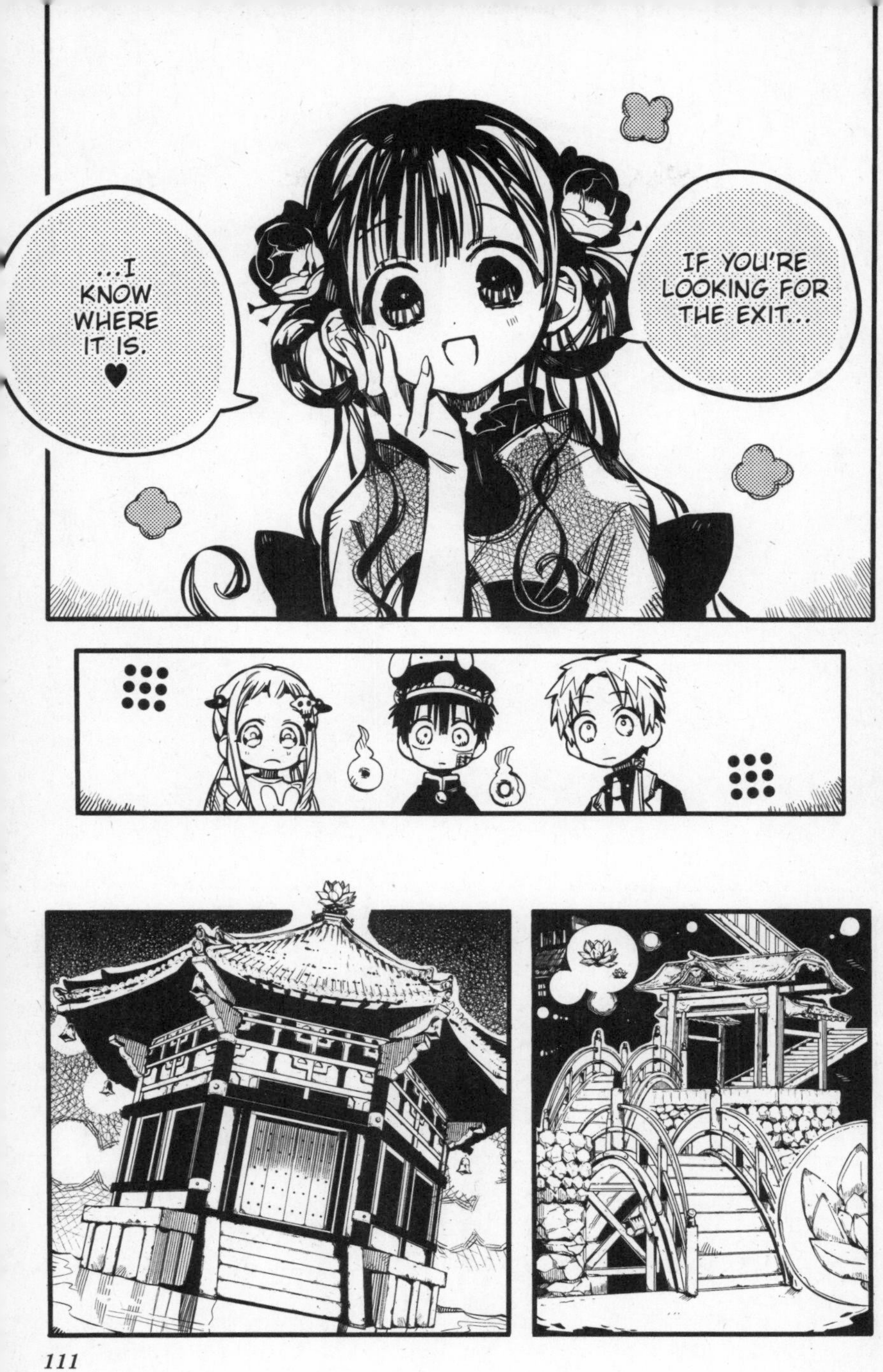
IF YOU'RE LOOKING FOR THE EXIT...
...I KNOW WHERE IT IS. ♥

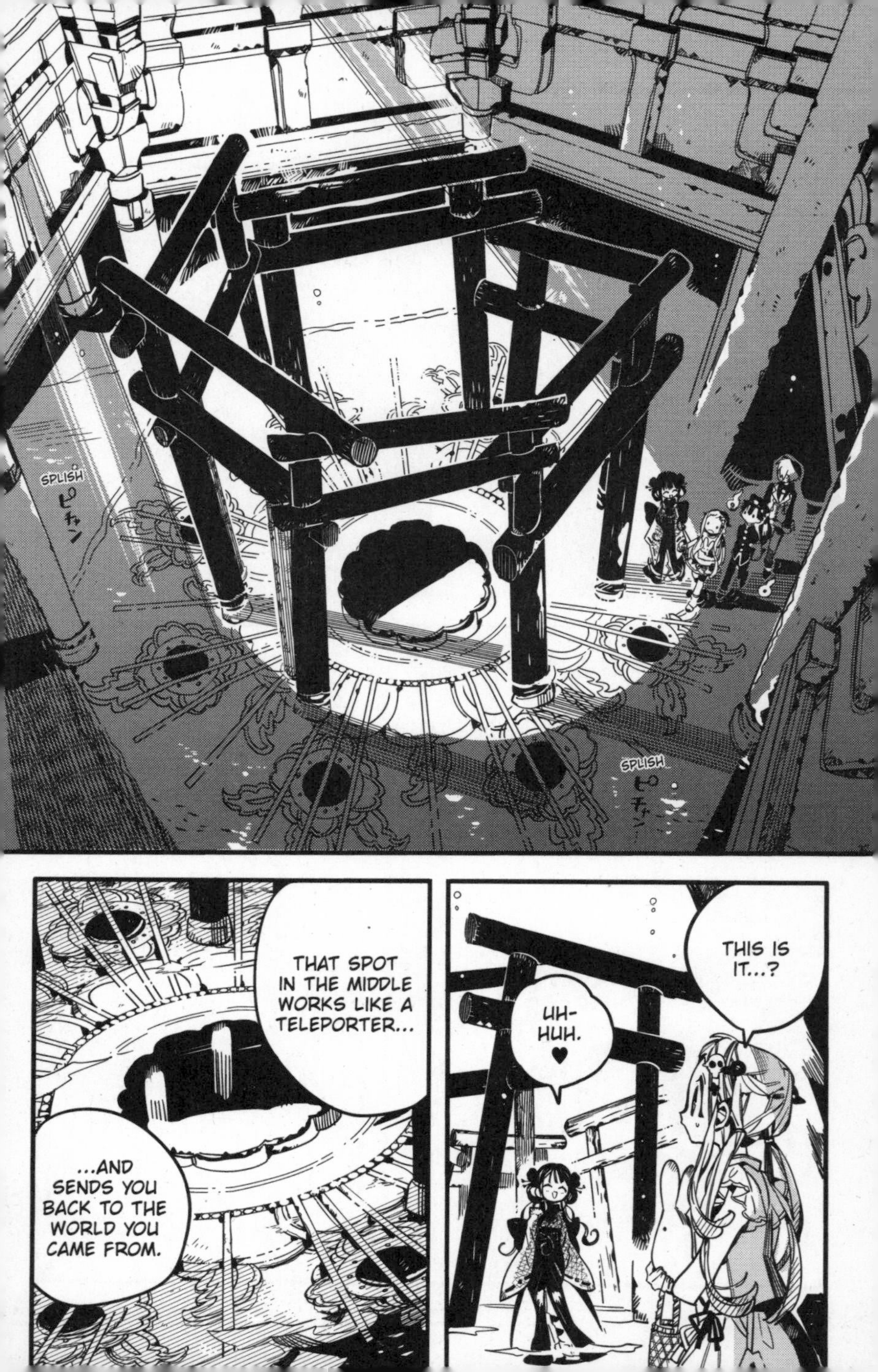
SPLISH
ピチャン
SPLISH
ピチャン
THIS IS IT...?
UH-HUH. ♥
THAT SPOT IN THE MIDDLE WORKS LIKE A TELEPORTER...
...AND SENDS YOU BACK TO THE WORLD YOU CAME FROM.

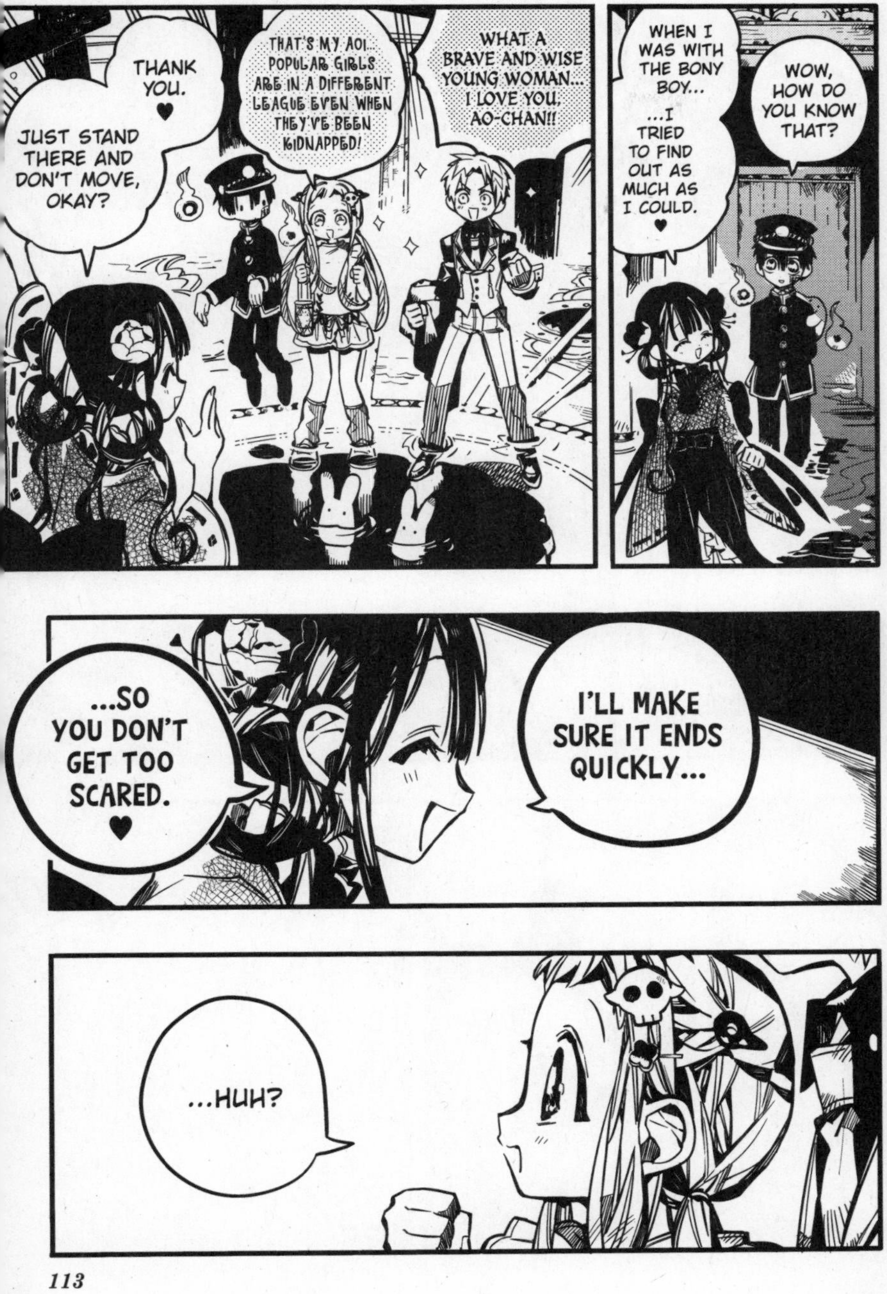
WOW, HOW DO YOU KNOW THAT?
WHEN I WAS WITH THE BONY BOY... ...I TRIED TO FIND OUT AS MUCH AS I COULD. ♥
WHAT A BRAVE AND WISE YOUNG WOMAN... I LOVE YOU, AO-CHAN!!
THAT'S MY AOI... POPULAR GIRLS ARE IN A DIFFERENT LEAGUE EVEN WHEN THEY'VE BEEN KIDNAPPED!
THANK YOU. ♥
JUST STAND THERE AND DON'T MOVE, OKAY?
I'LL MAKE SURE IT ENDS QUICKLY...
...SO YOU DON'T GET TOO SCARED. ♥
...HUH?

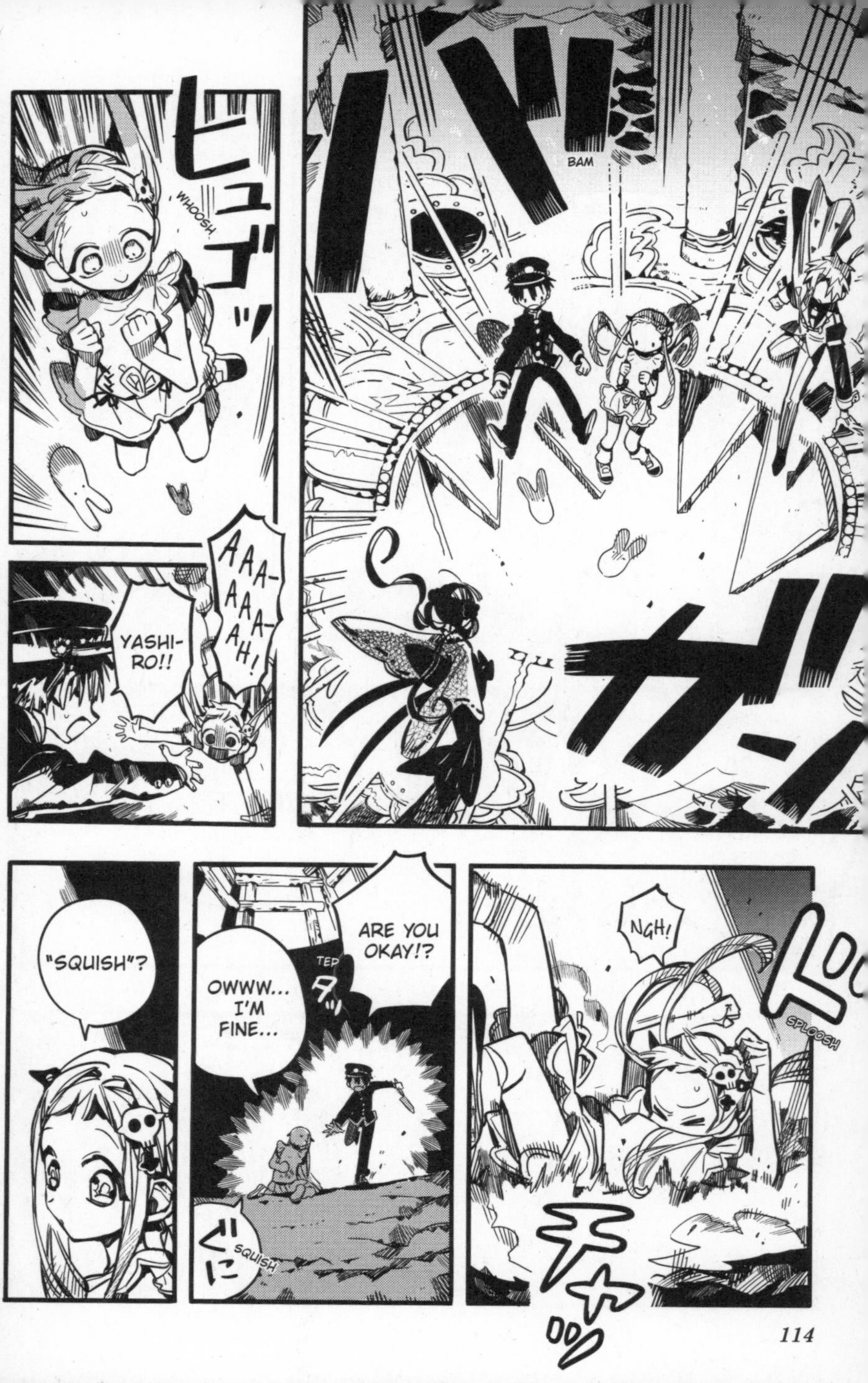
BAM
ビュゴッ
WHOOSH
AAAAAAAH!
YASHIRO!!
NGH!
SPLOOSH
ARE YOU OKAY!?
TEP
OWWW... I'M FINE...
ぐに
SQUISH
"SQUISH"?

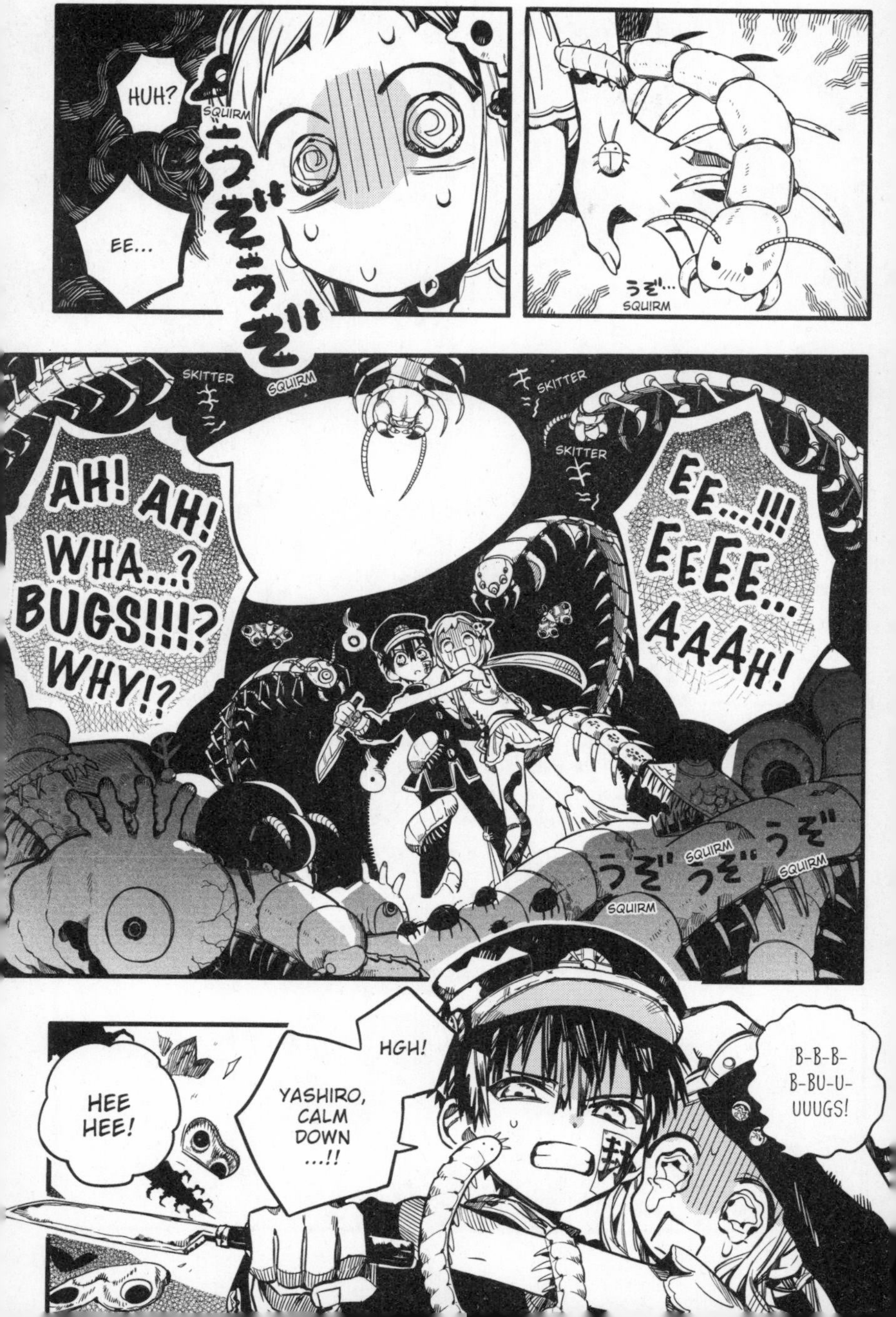
うぞ…
SQUIRM
うぞうぞ
SQUIRM
HUH?
EE...
SKITTER
SKITTER
EE...!!! EEEE... AAAH!
SQUIRM
SKITTER
AH! AH! WHA...? BUGS!!!!? WHY!?
うぞ
SQUIRM
うぞ
SQUIRM
うぞ
SQUIRM
B-B-B-B-BU-U-UUUGS!
HGH!
YASHIRO, CALM DOWN ...!!
HEE HEE!

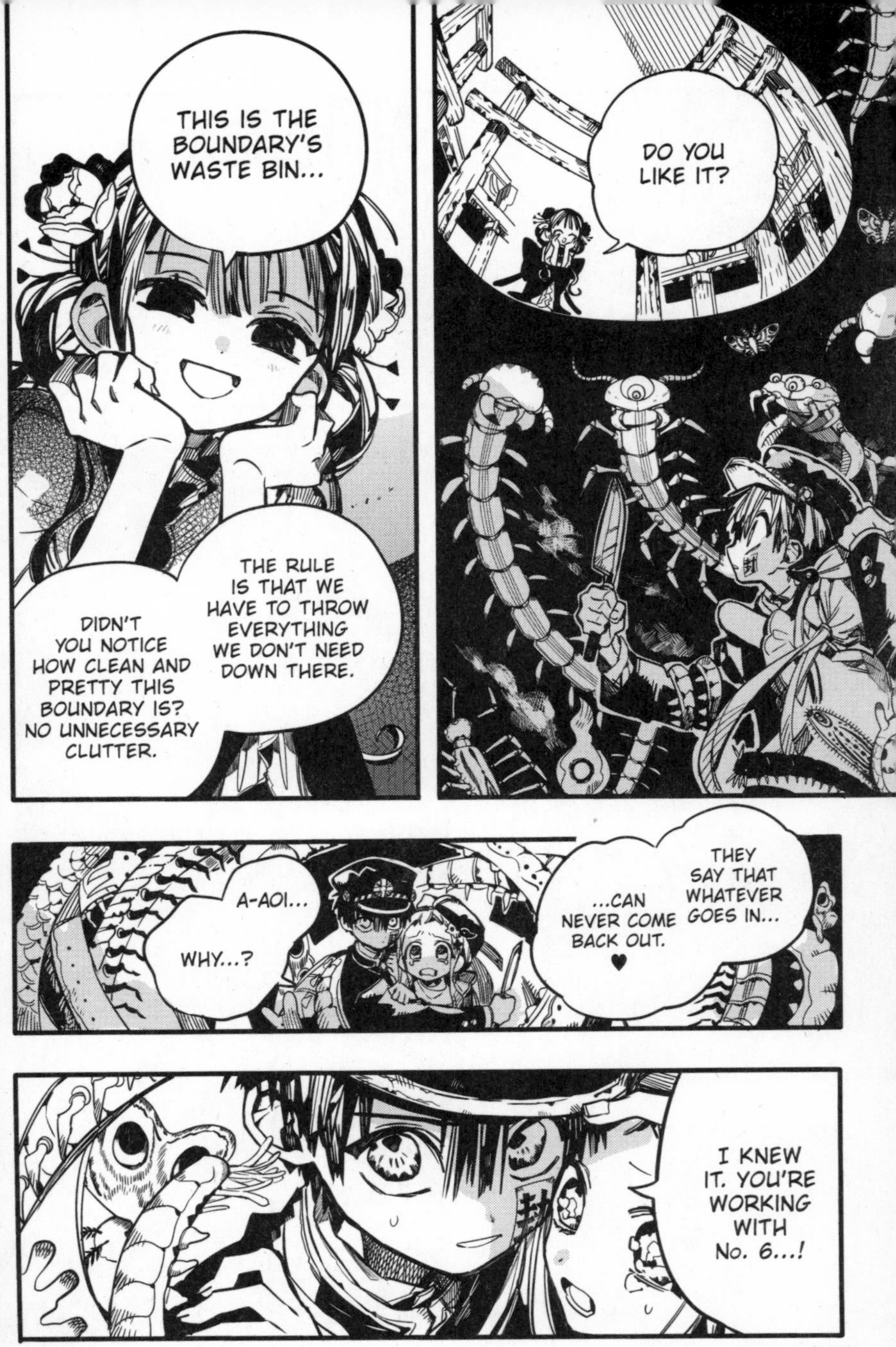
DO YOU LIKE IT?
THIS IS THE BOUNDARY'S WASTE BIN...
THE RULE IS THAT WE HAVE TO THROW EVERYTHING WE DON'T NEED DOWN THERE.
DIDN'T YOU NOTICE HOW CLEAN AND PRETTY THIS BOUNDARY IS? NO UNNECESSARY CLUTTER.
THEY SAY THAT WHATEVER GOES IN...
...CAN NEVER COME BACK OUT. ♥
A-AOI...
WHY...?
I KNEW IT. YOU'RE WORKING WITH No. 6...!

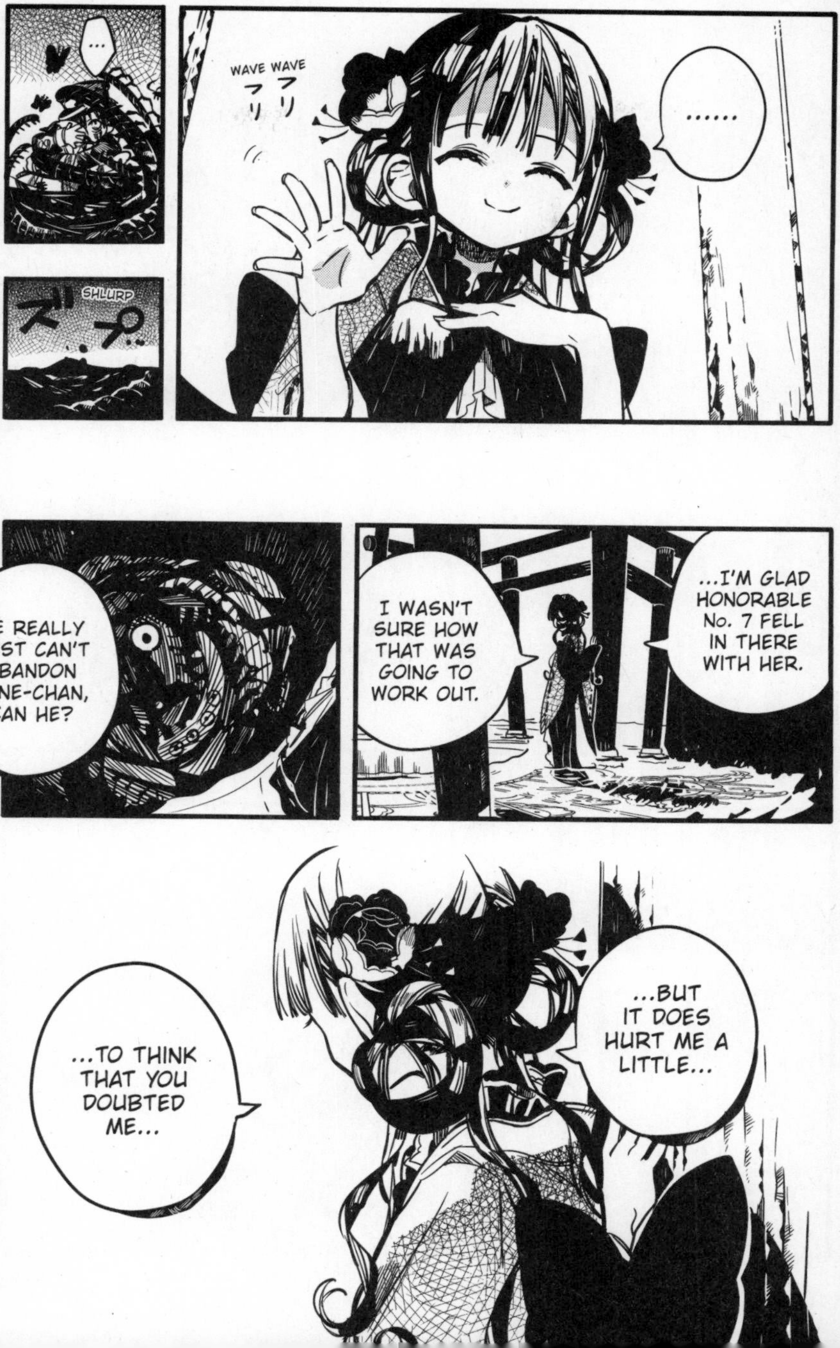
WAVE WAVE
フリフリ
......
...
SHLURP
...I'M GLAD HONORABLE No. 7 FELL IN THERE WITH HER.
I WASN'T SURE HOW THAT WAS GOING TO WORK OUT.
HE REALLY JUST CAN'T ABANDON NENE-CHAN, CAN HE?
...BUT IT DOES HURT ME A LITTLE...
...TO THINK THAT YOU DOUBTED ME...

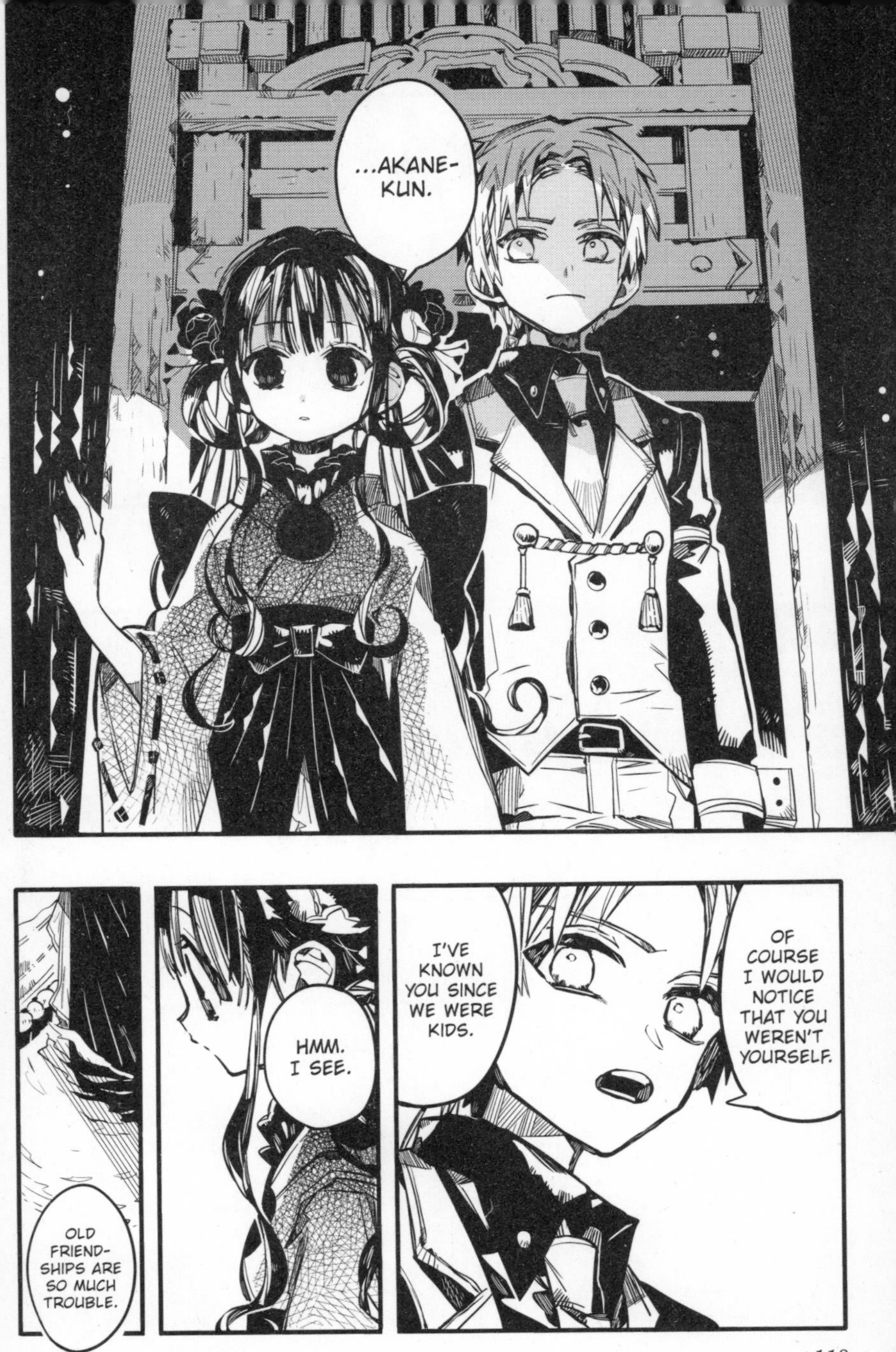
...AKANE-KUN.
OF COURSE I WOULD NOTICE THAT YOU WEREN'T YOURSELF.
I'VE KNOWN YOU SINCE WE WERE KIDS.
HMM. I SEE.
OLD FRIENDSHIPS ARE SO MUCH TROUBLE.

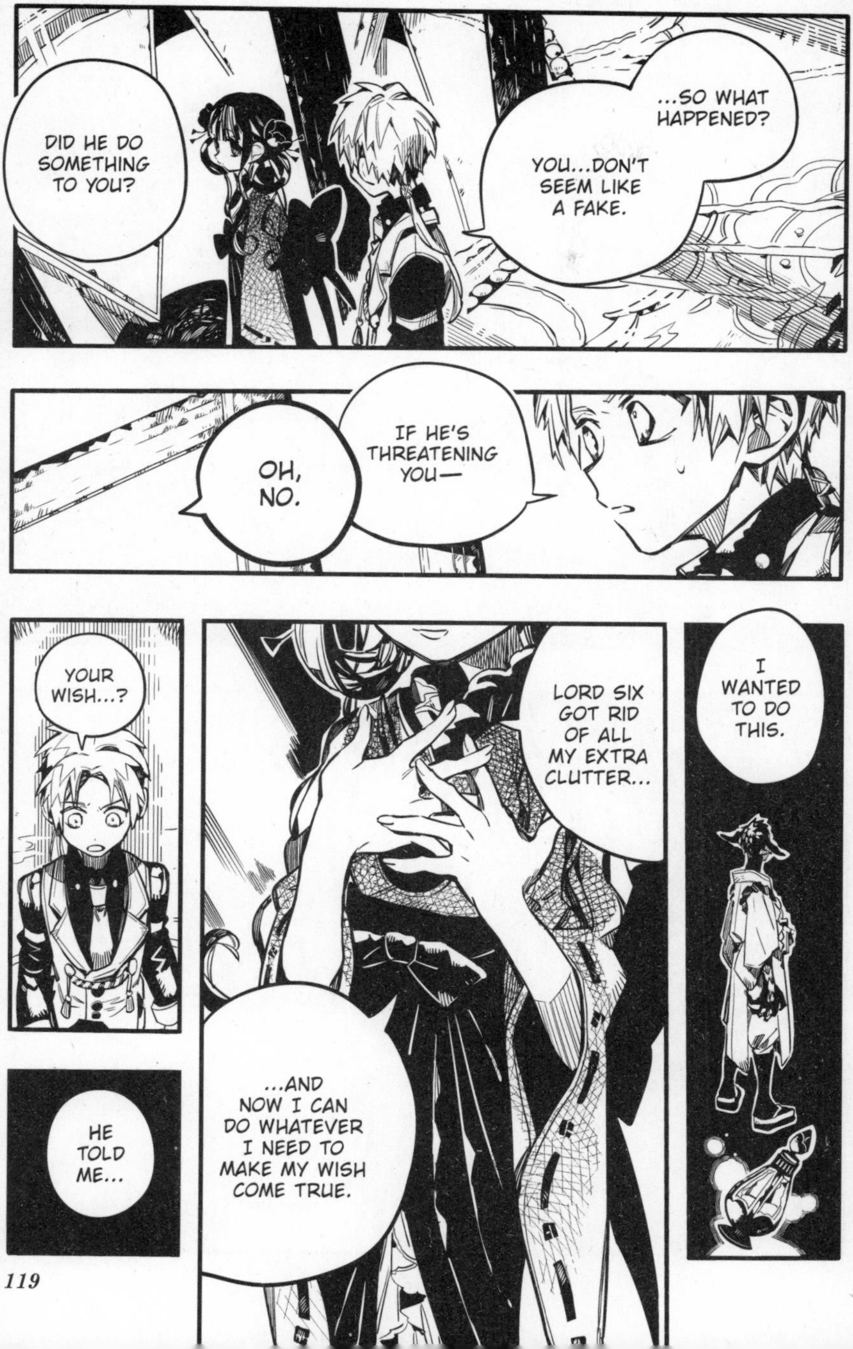
...SO WHAT HAPPENED?
YOU...DON'T SEEM LIKE A FAKE.
DID HE DO SOMETHING TO YOU?
IF HE'S THREATENING YOU—
OH, NO.
I WANTED TO DO THIS.
LORD SIX GOT RID OF ALL MY EXTRA CLUTTER...
...AND NOW I CAN DO WHATEVER I NEED TO MAKE MY WISH COME TRUE.
YOUR WISH...?
HE TOLD ME...

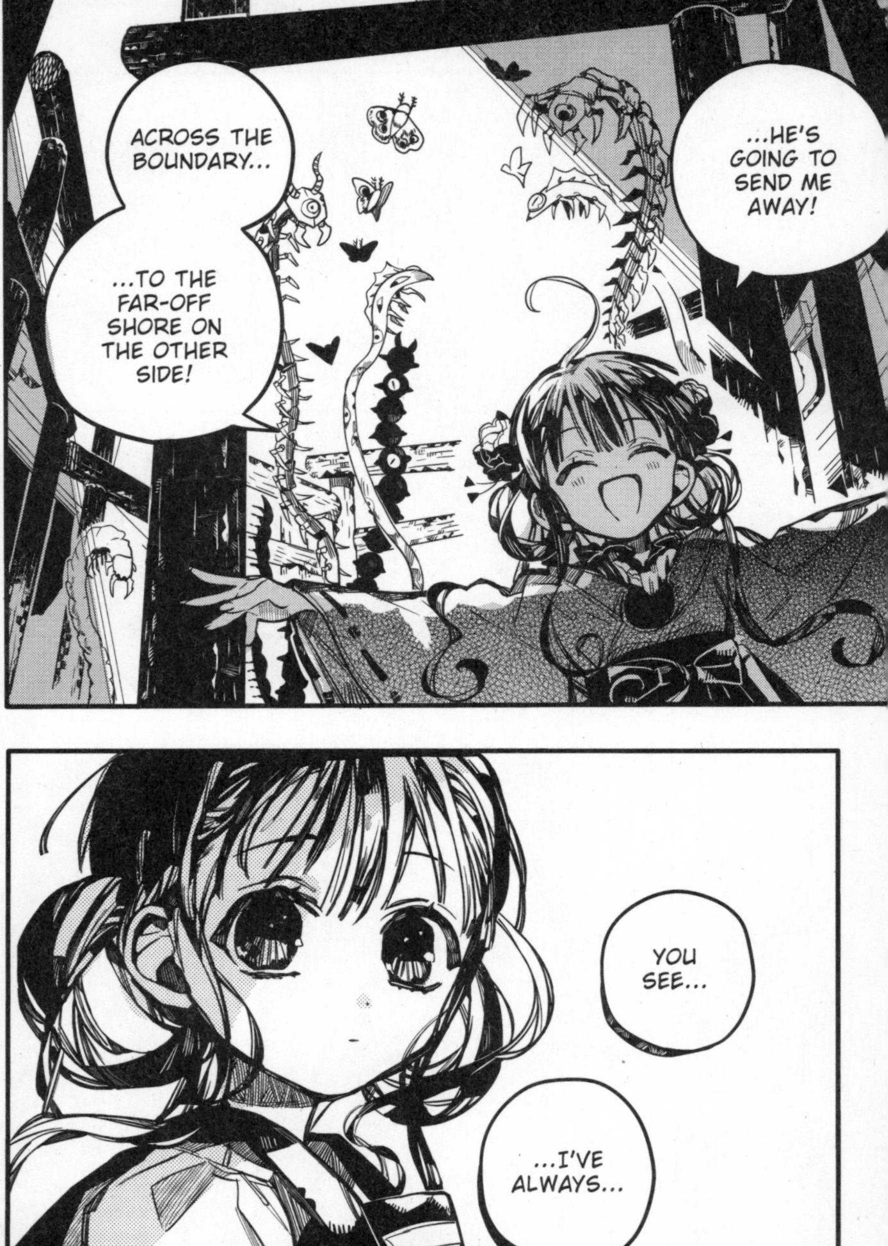
...HE'S GOING TO SEND ME AWAY!
ACROSS THE BOUNDARY...
...TO THE FAR-OFF SHORE ON THE OTHER SIDE!
YOU SEE...
...I'VE ALWAYS...

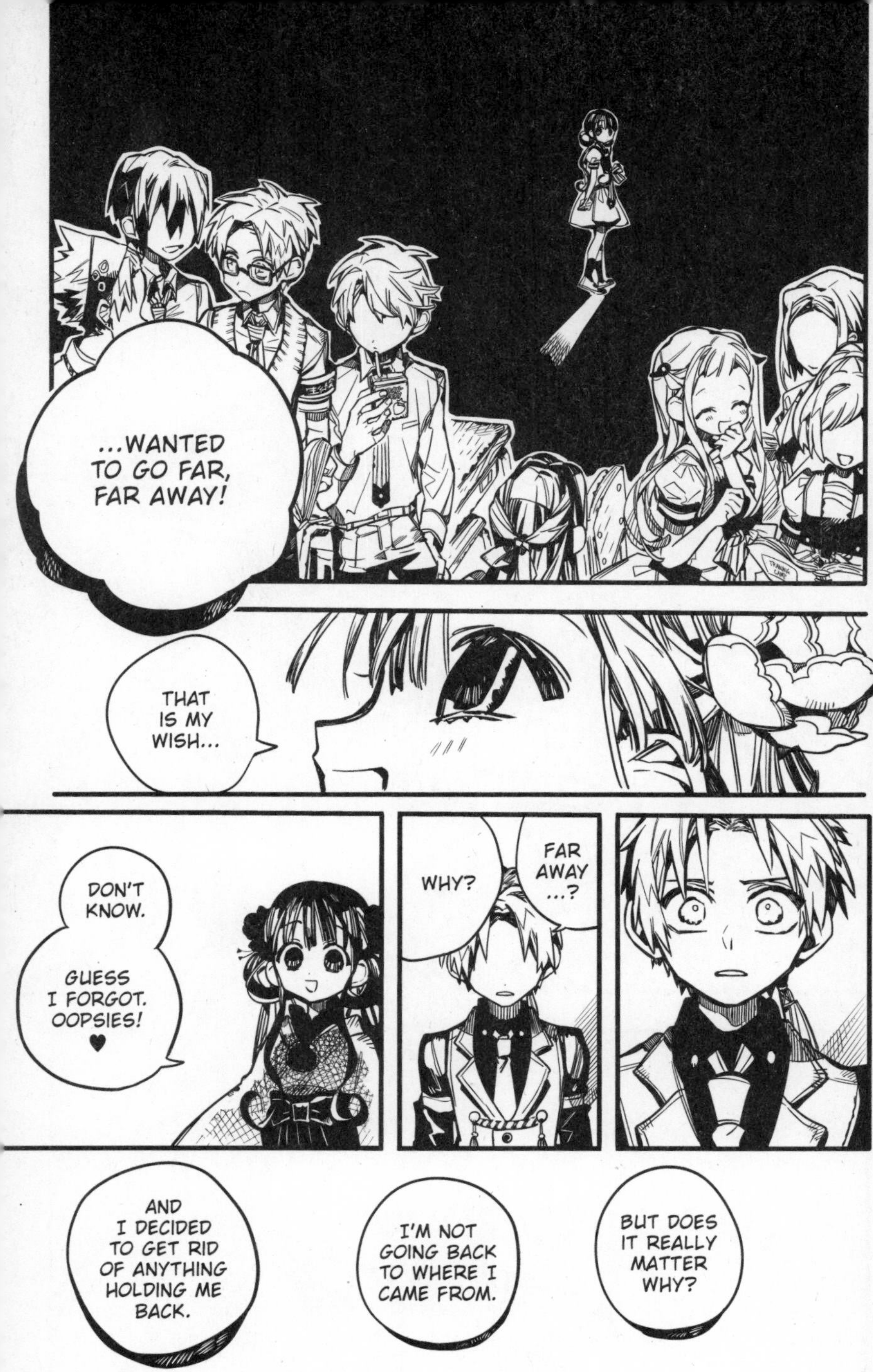
...WANTED TO GO FAR, FAR AWAY!
THAT IS MY WISH...
FAR AWAY ...?
WHY?
DON'T KNOW.
GUESS I FORGOT. OOPSIES! ♥
BUT DOES IT REALLY MATTER WHY?
I'M NOT GOING BACK TO WHERE I CAME FROM.
AND I DECIDED TO GET RID OF ANYTHING HOLDING ME BACK.

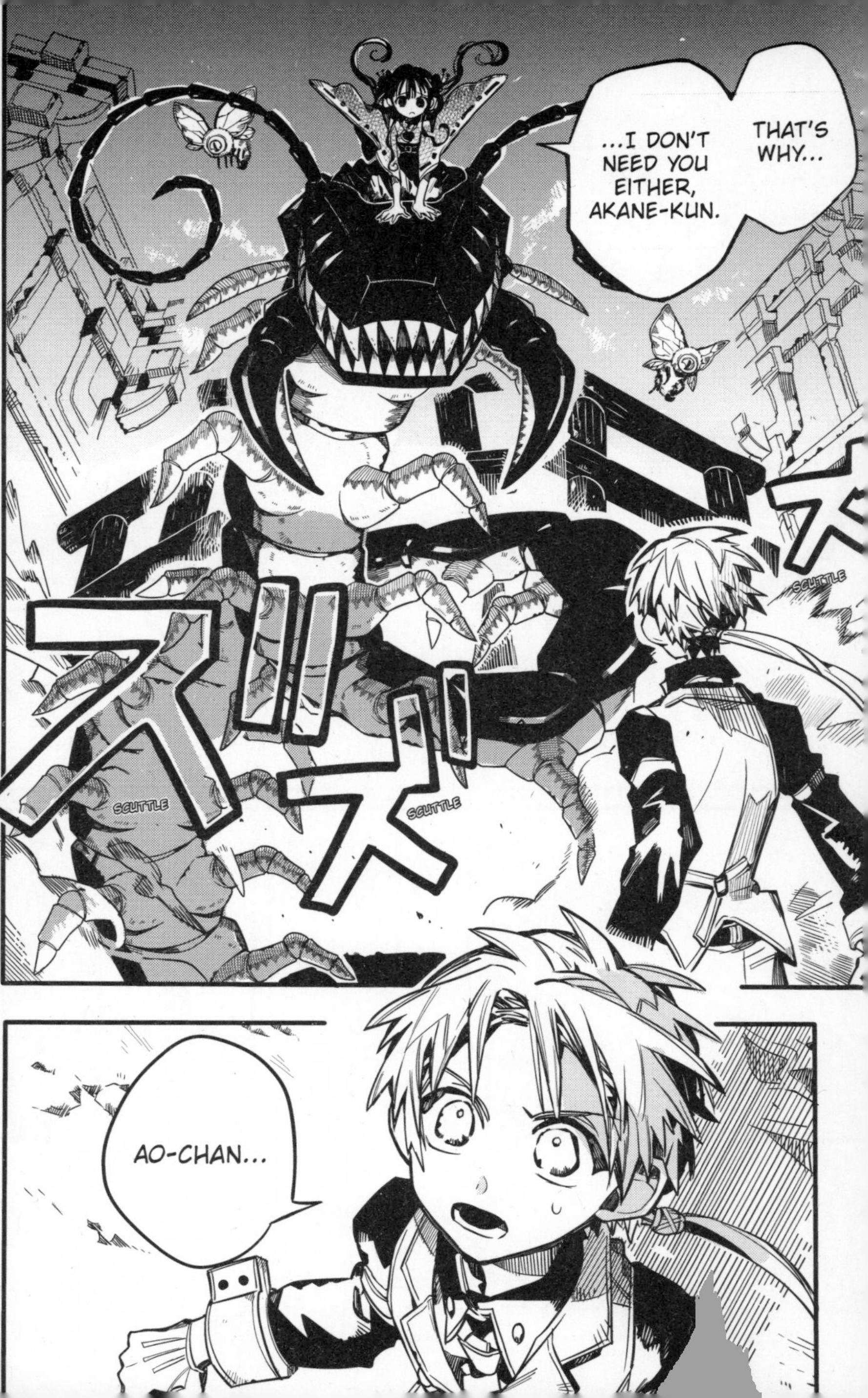
THAT'S WHY...
...I DON'T NEED YOU EITHER, AKANE-KUN.
SCUTTLE
SCUTTLE
SCUTTLE
AO-CHAN...

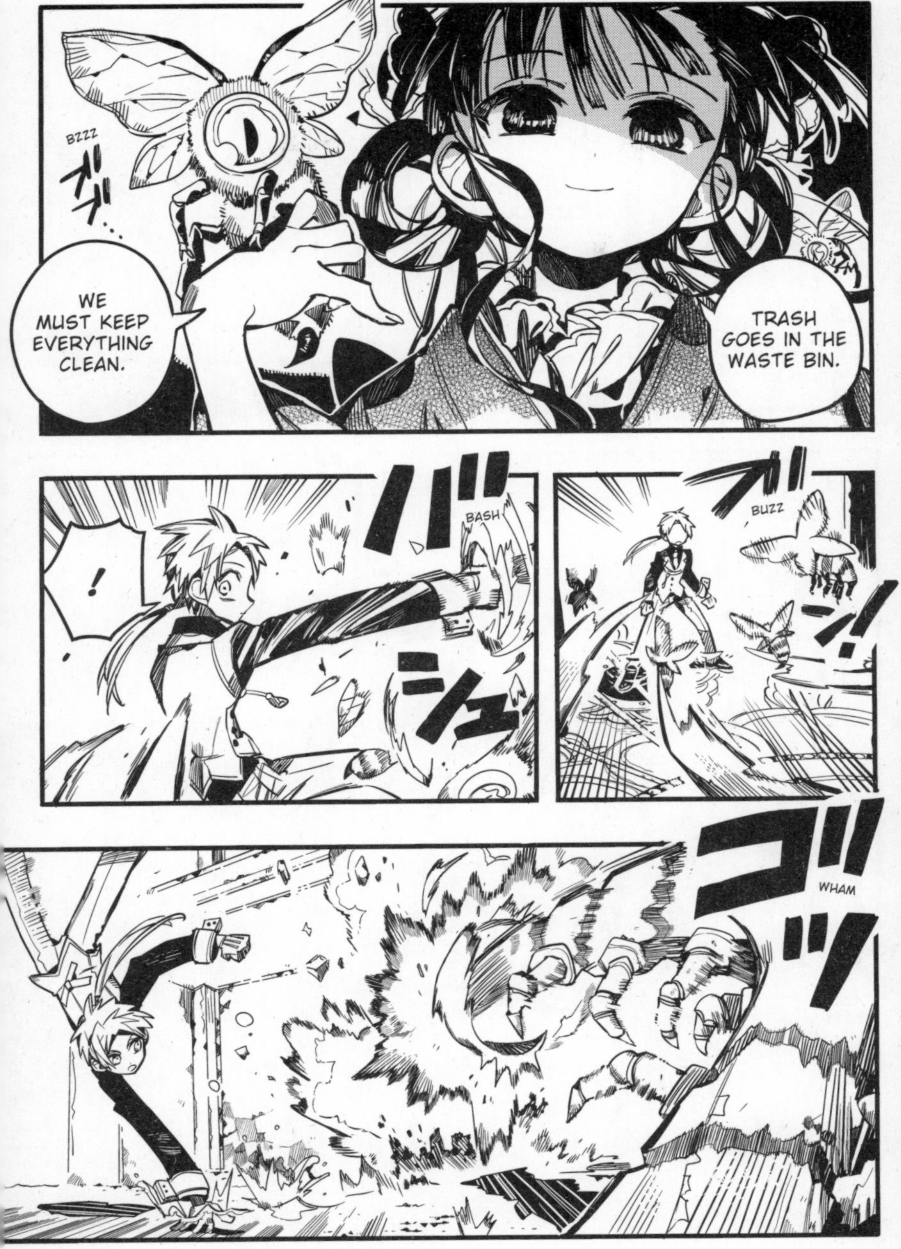
TRASH GOES IN THE WASTE BIN.
WE MUST KEEP EVERYTHING CLEAN.
BZZZ
ブブ…
ブン!
BUZZ
バ
BASH
!
シュ
ゴッ
WHAM

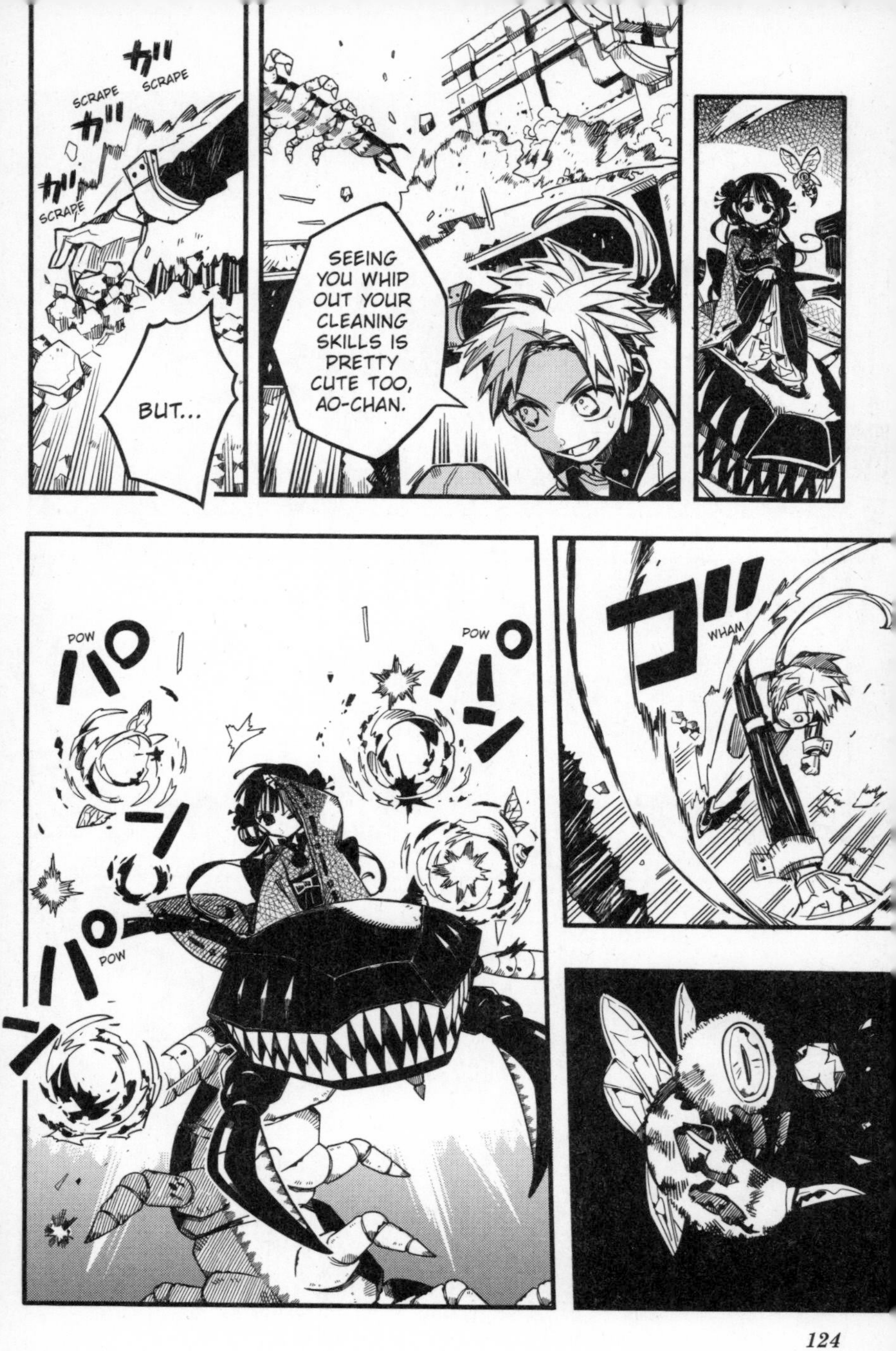
SEEING YOU WHIP OUT YOUR CLEANING SKILLS IS PRETTY CUTE TOO, AO-CHAN.
ガ SCRAPE
ガ SCRAPE
ガ SCRAPE
BUT...
ゴッ WHAM
パン POW
パーン POW
パン POW

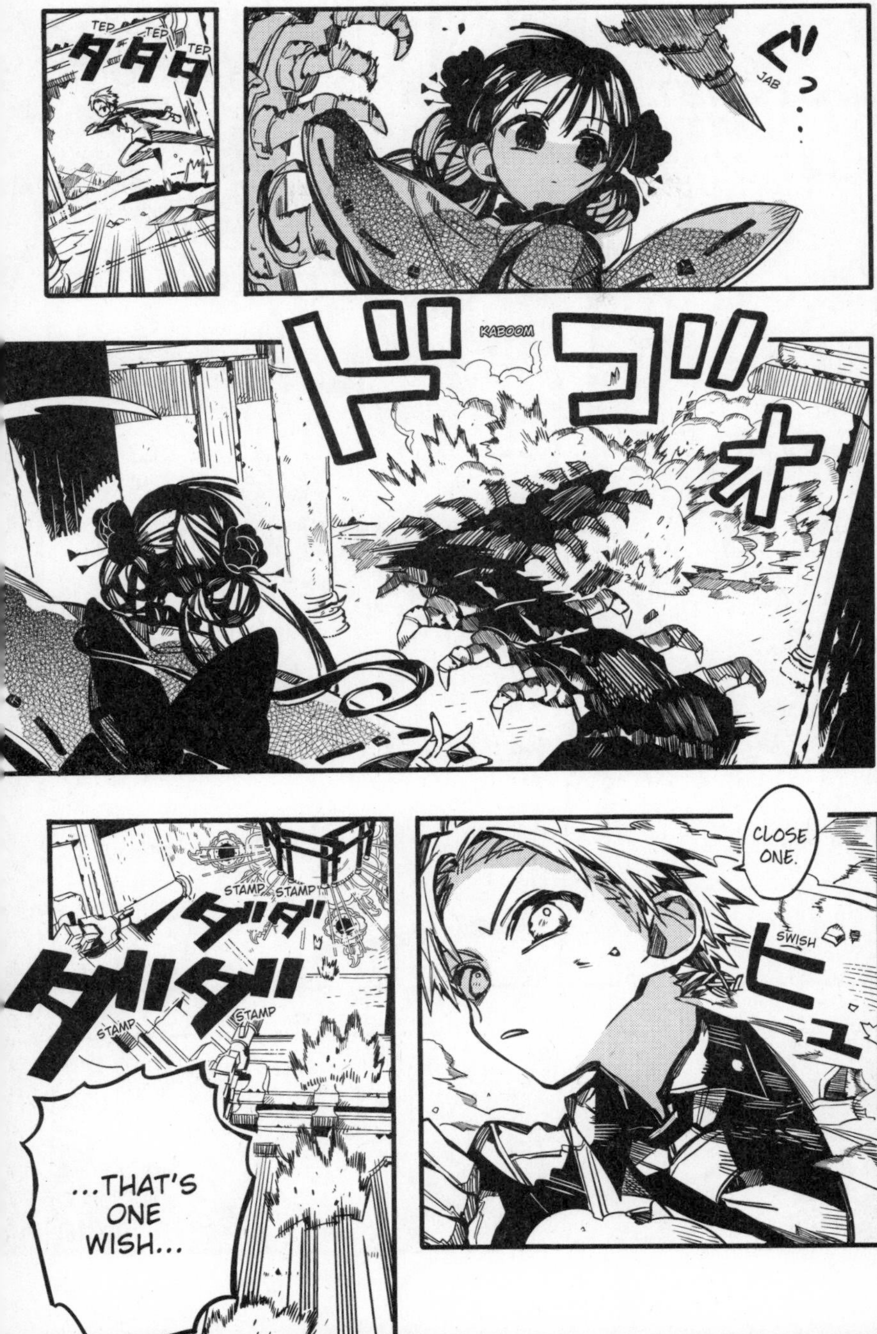
ぐっ…
JAB
タタタ
TEP TEP TEP
ドゴォ
KABOOM
CLOSE ONE.
ヒュ
SWISH
ダッダッ
STAMP STAMP
ダッダッ
STAMP STAMP
...THAT'S ONE WISH...

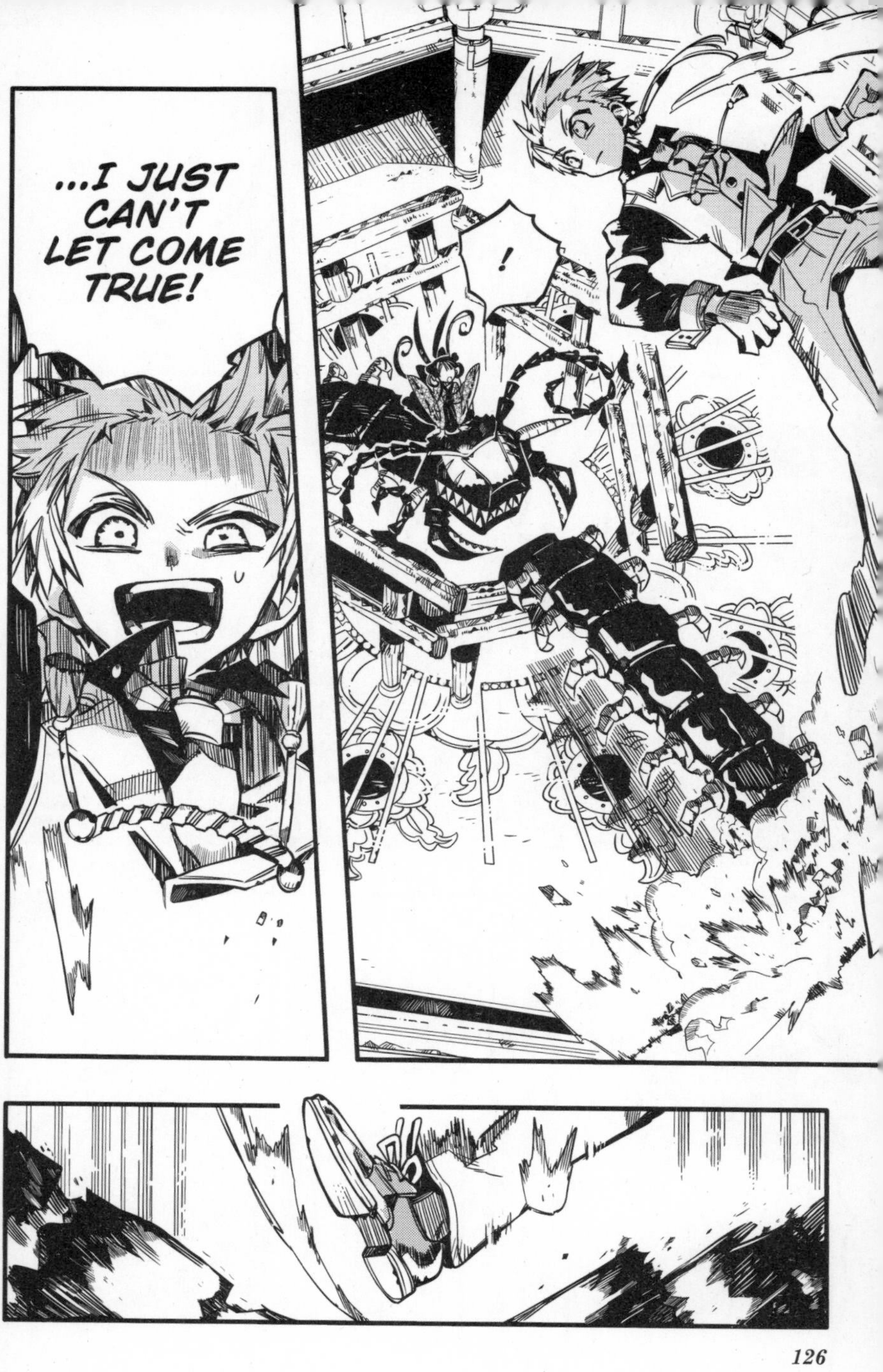
!
...I JUST CAN'T LET COME TRUE!

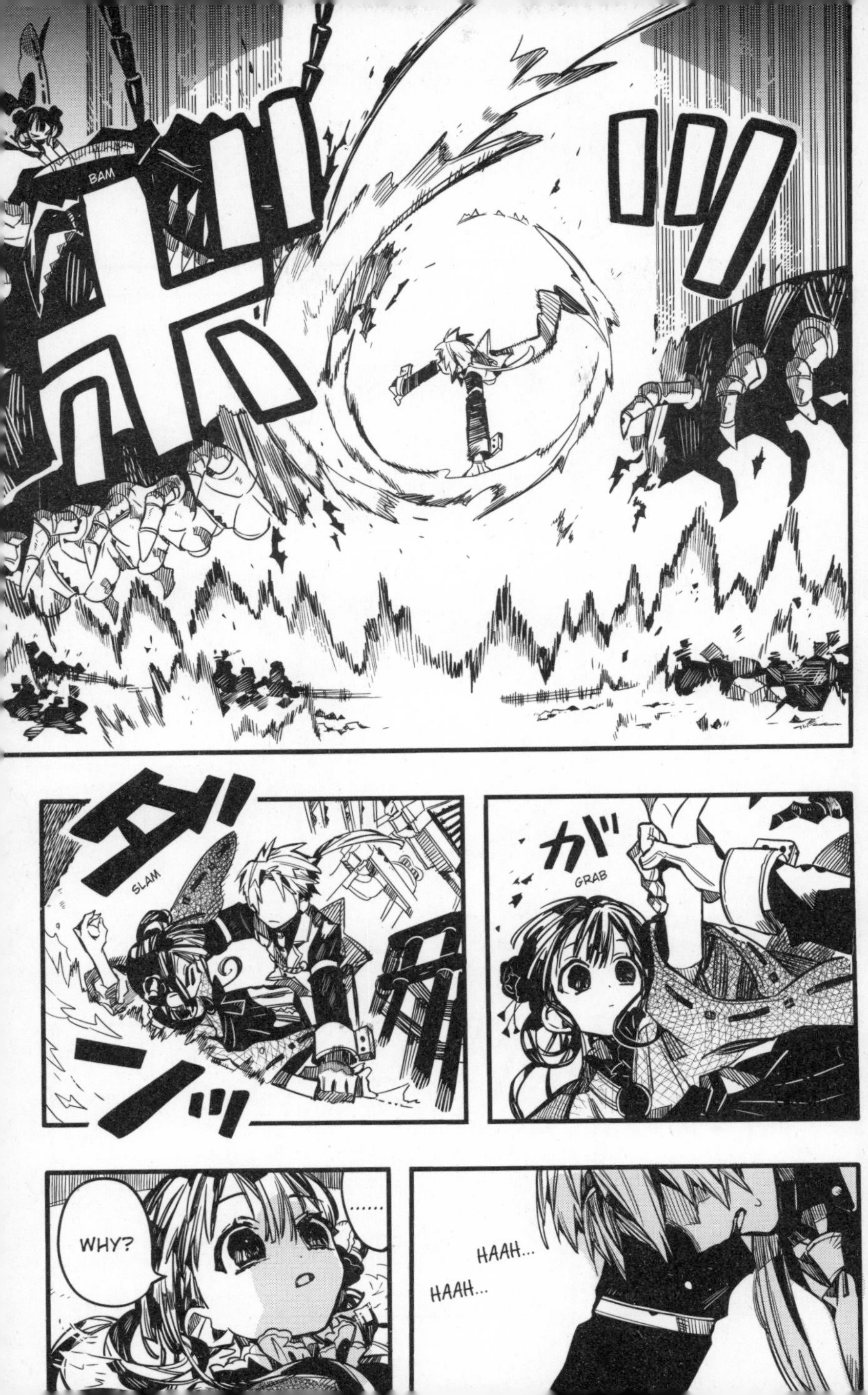
BAM
GRAB
SLAM
HAAH...
HAAH...
......
WHY?

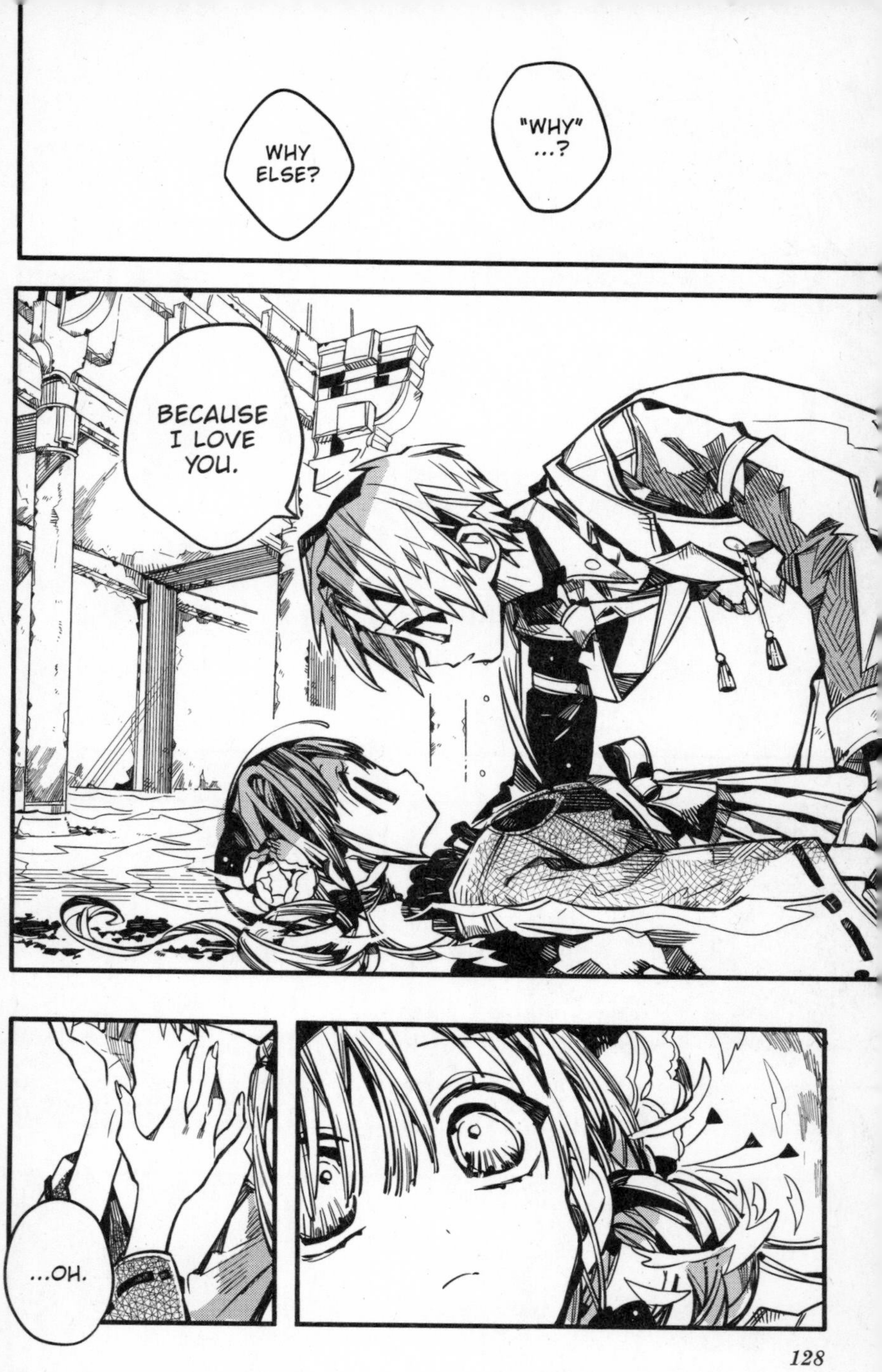
"WHY"
...?
WHY
ELSE?
BECAUSE
I LOVE
YOU.
...OH.

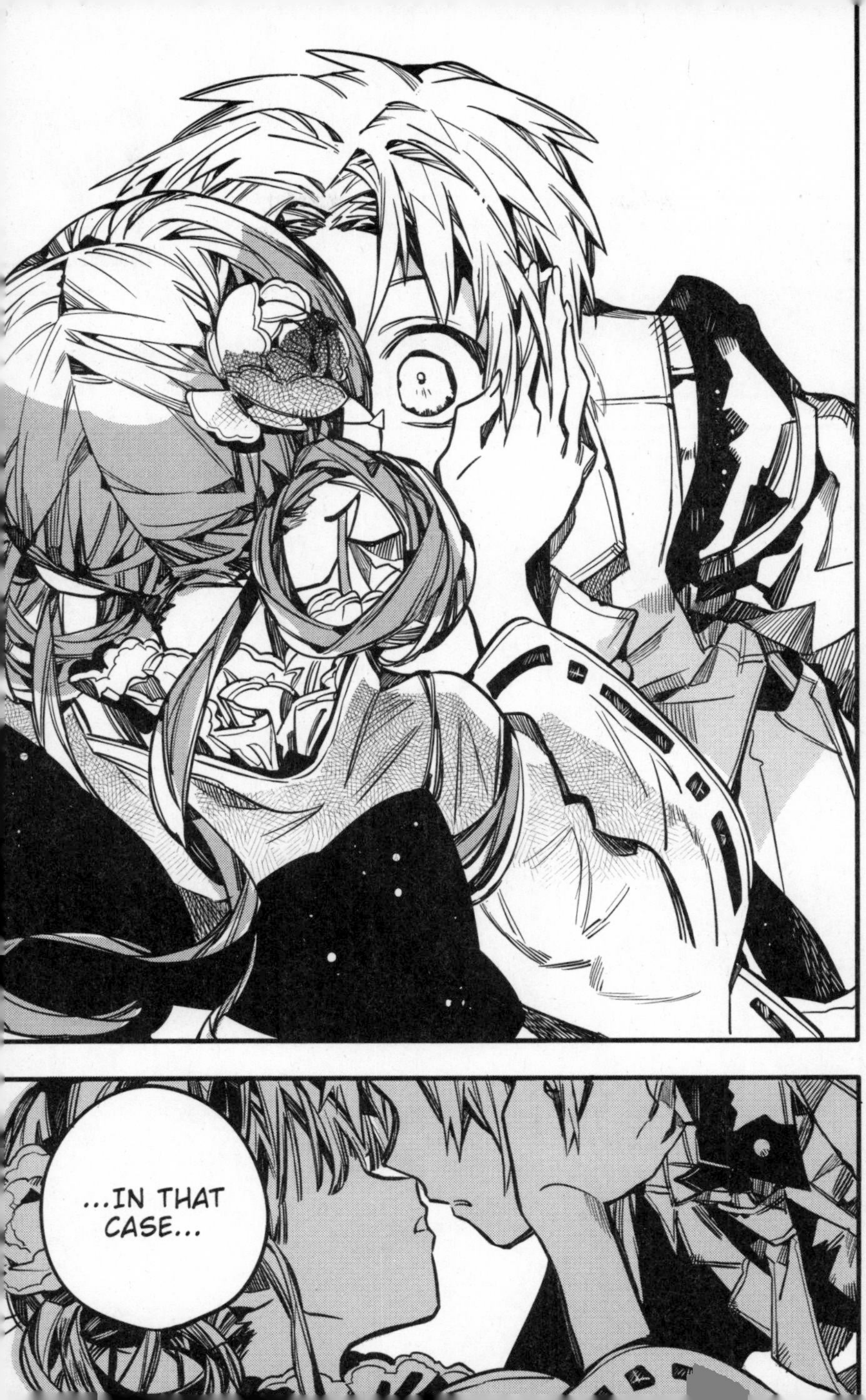
...IN THAT CASE...

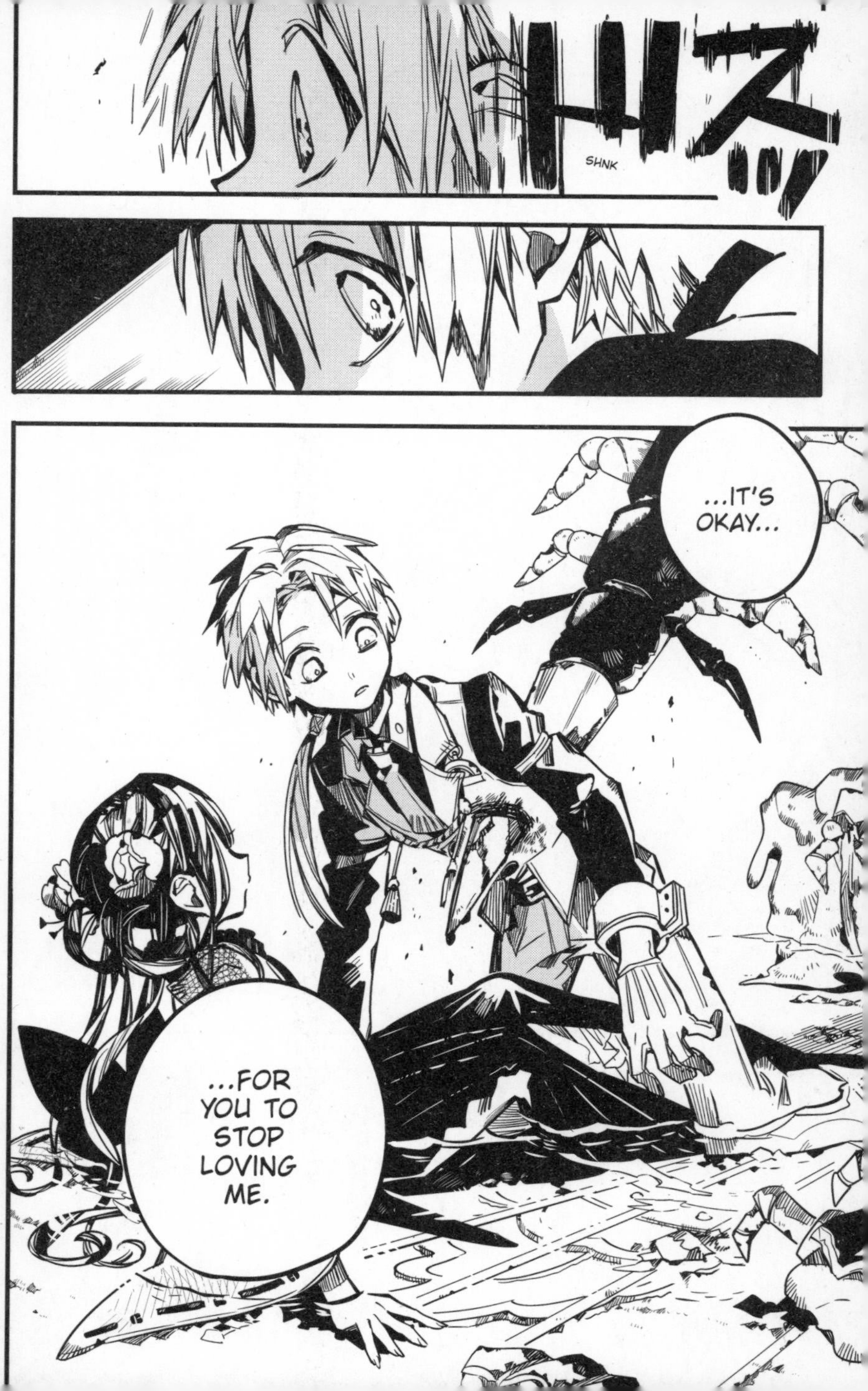
SHNK
...IT'S OKAY...
...FOR YOU TO STOP LOVING ME.

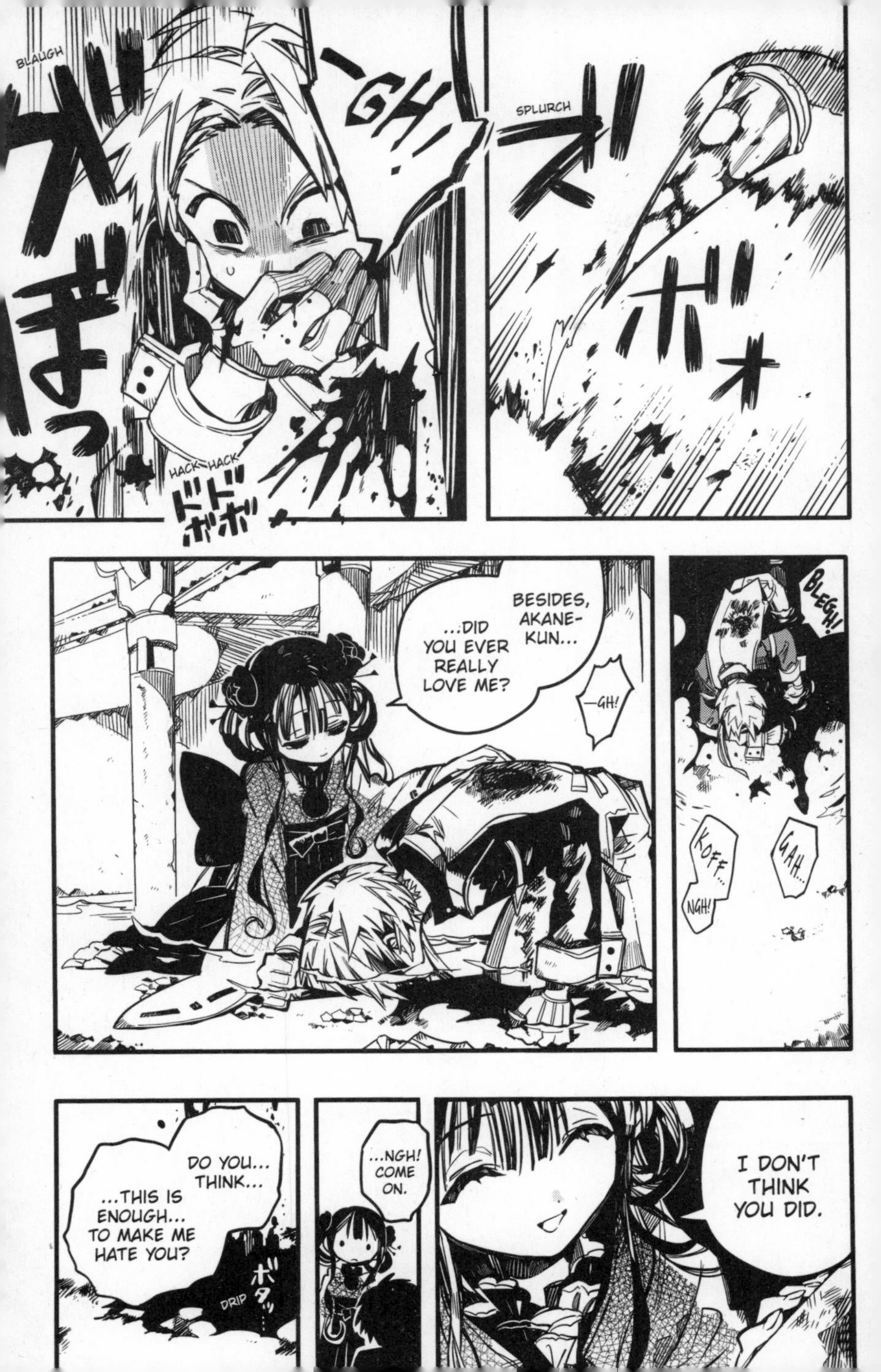
SPLURCH
BLAUGH
—GH!
HACK HACK
BLEGH!
KOFF...
GAH...
NGH!
BESIDES, AKANE-KUN...
...DID YOU EVER REALLY LOVE ME?
—GH!
I DON'T THINK YOU DID.
...NGH! COME ON.
DO YOU... THINK...
...THIS IS ENOUGH... TO MAKE ME HATE YOU?
DRIP

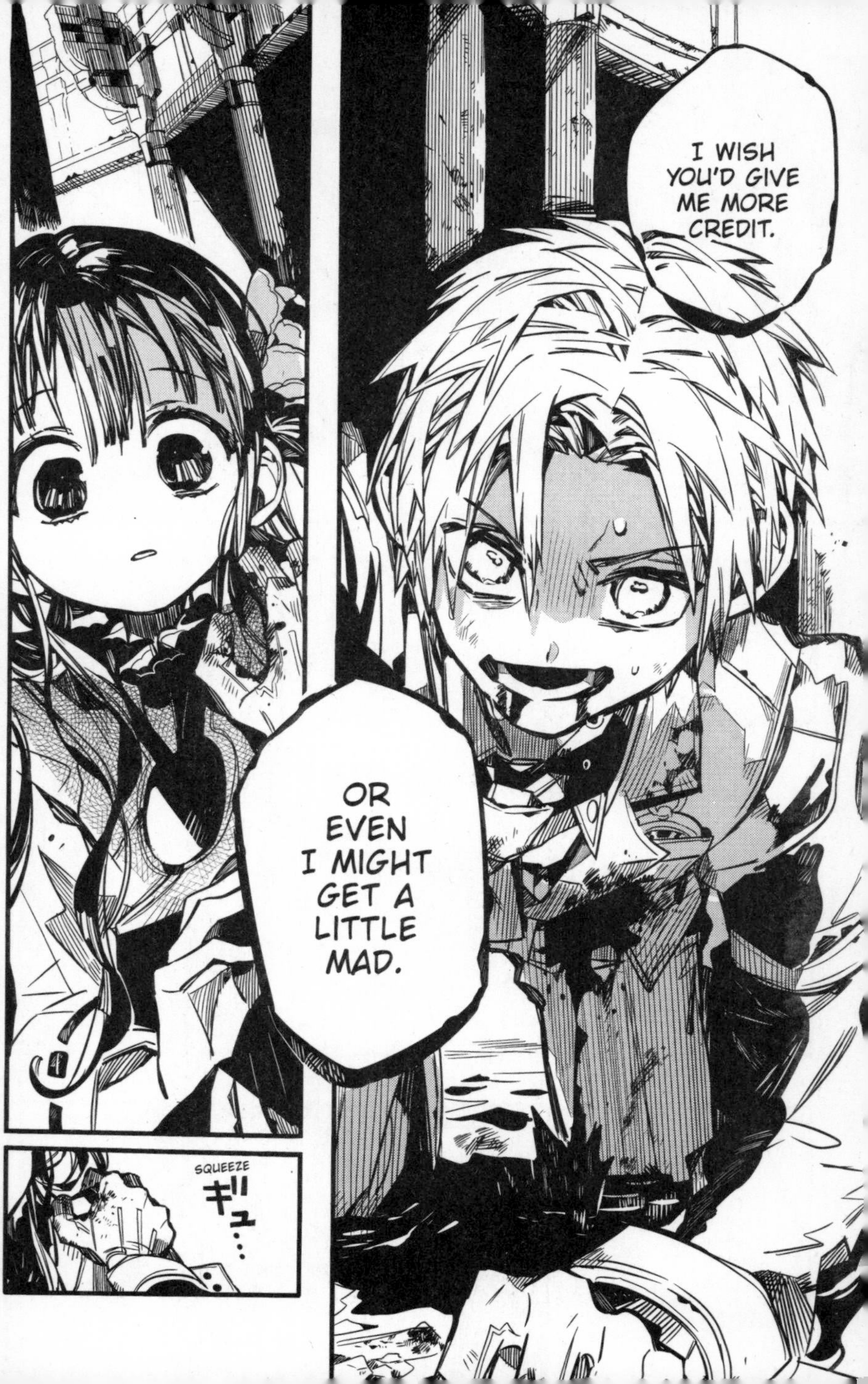
I WISH YOU'D GIVE ME MORE CREDIT.
OR EVEN I MIGHT GET A LITTLE MAD.
SQUEEZE
ギュ…

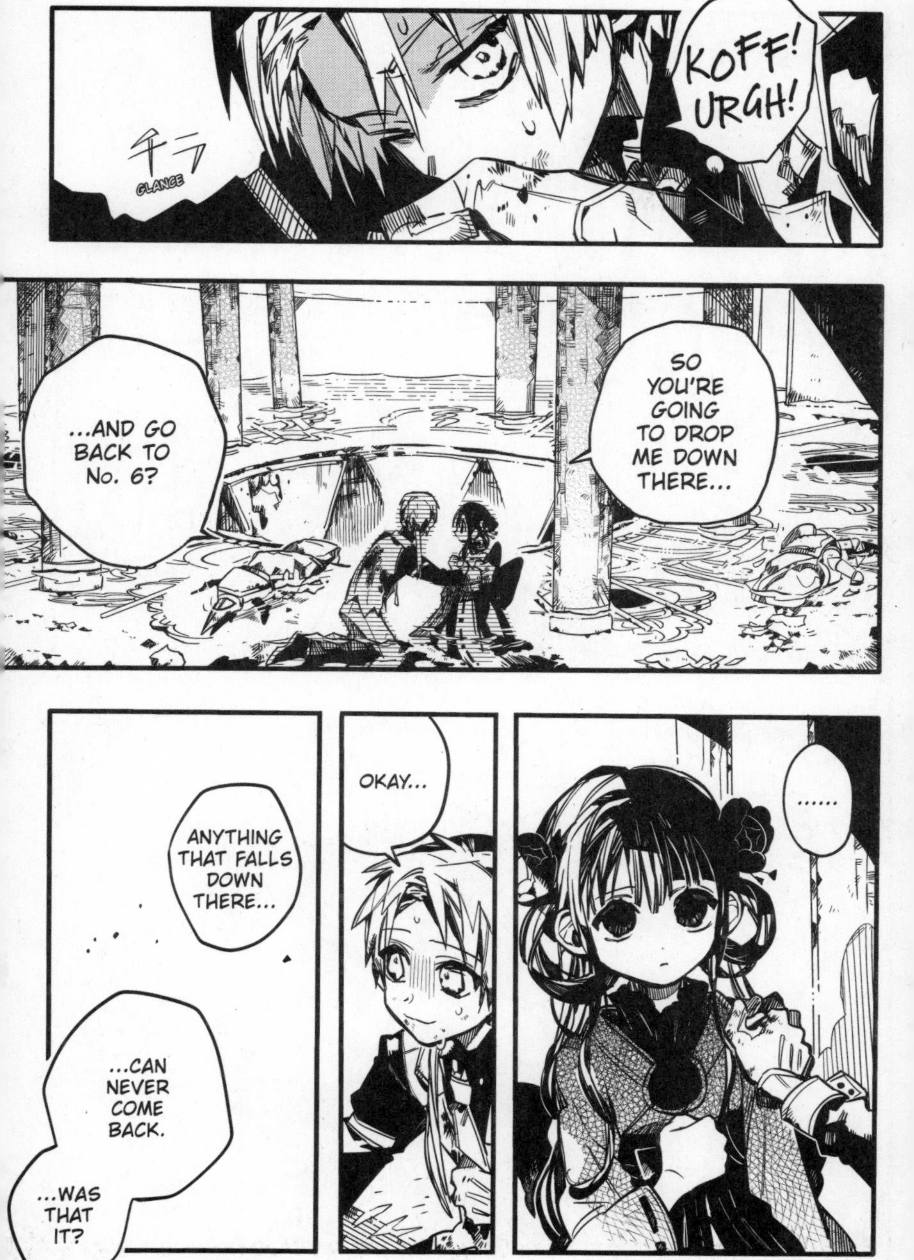
KOFF! URGH!
チラ
GLANCE
SO YOU'RE GOING TO DROP ME DOWN THERE...
...AND GO BACK TO No. 6?
......
OKAY...
ANYTHING THAT FALLS DOWN THERE...
...CAN NEVER COME BACK.
...WAS THAT IT?

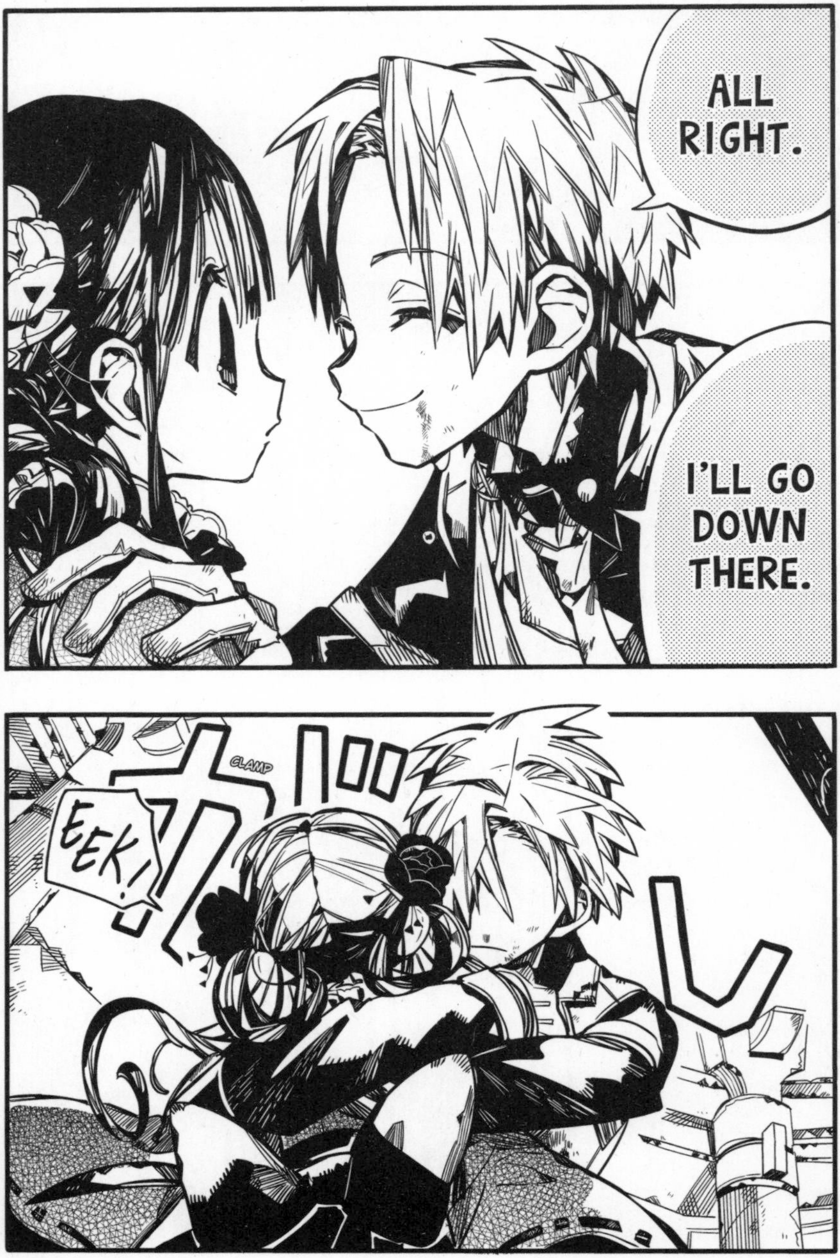
ALL RIGHT.
I'LL GO DOWN THERE.
CLAMP
EEK!

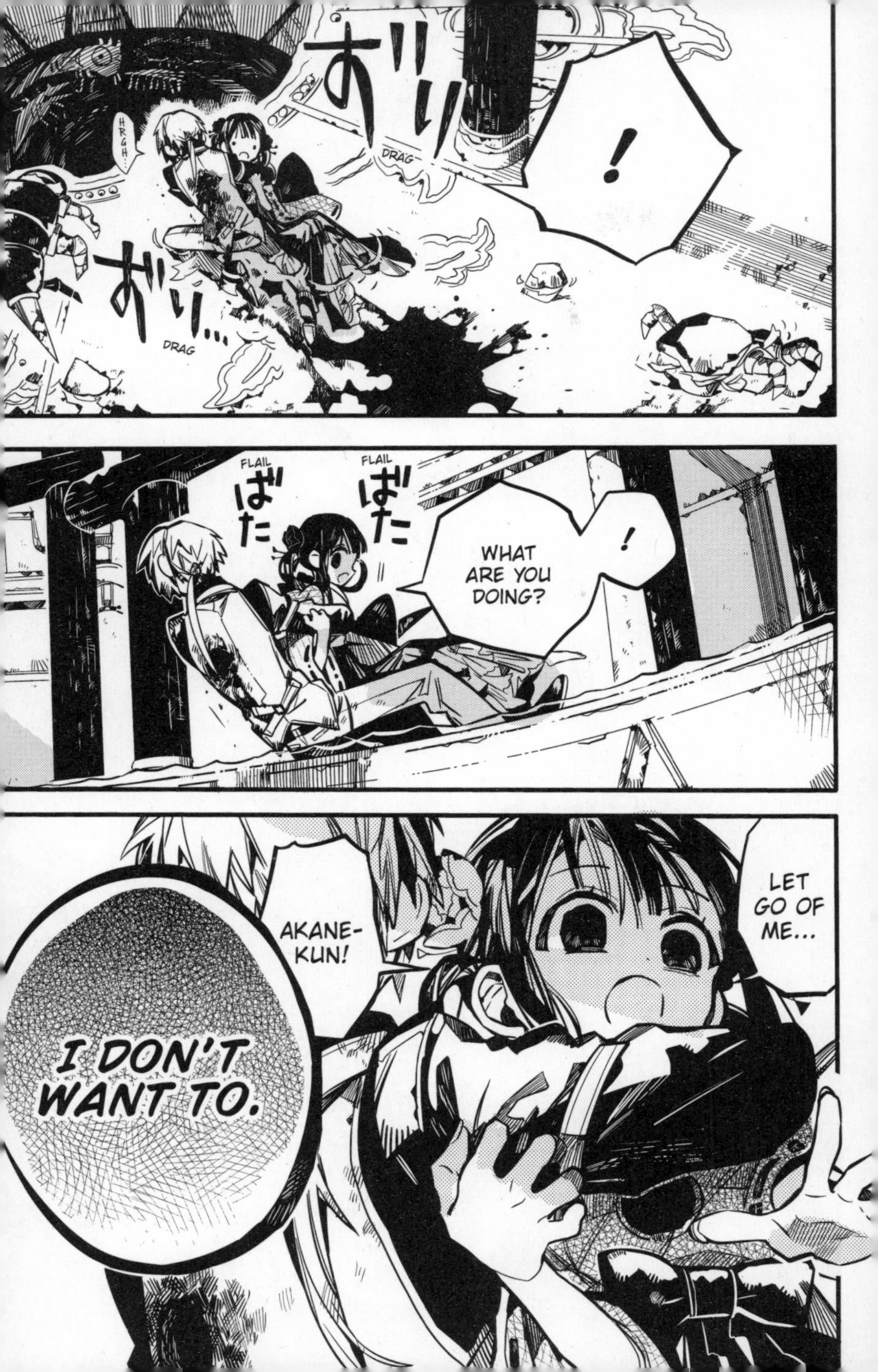
!
DRAG
HRGH...
DRAG
!
WHAT ARE YOU DOING?
FLAIL
ばた
FLAIL
ばた
LET GO OF ME...
AKANE-KUN!
I DON'T WANT TO.

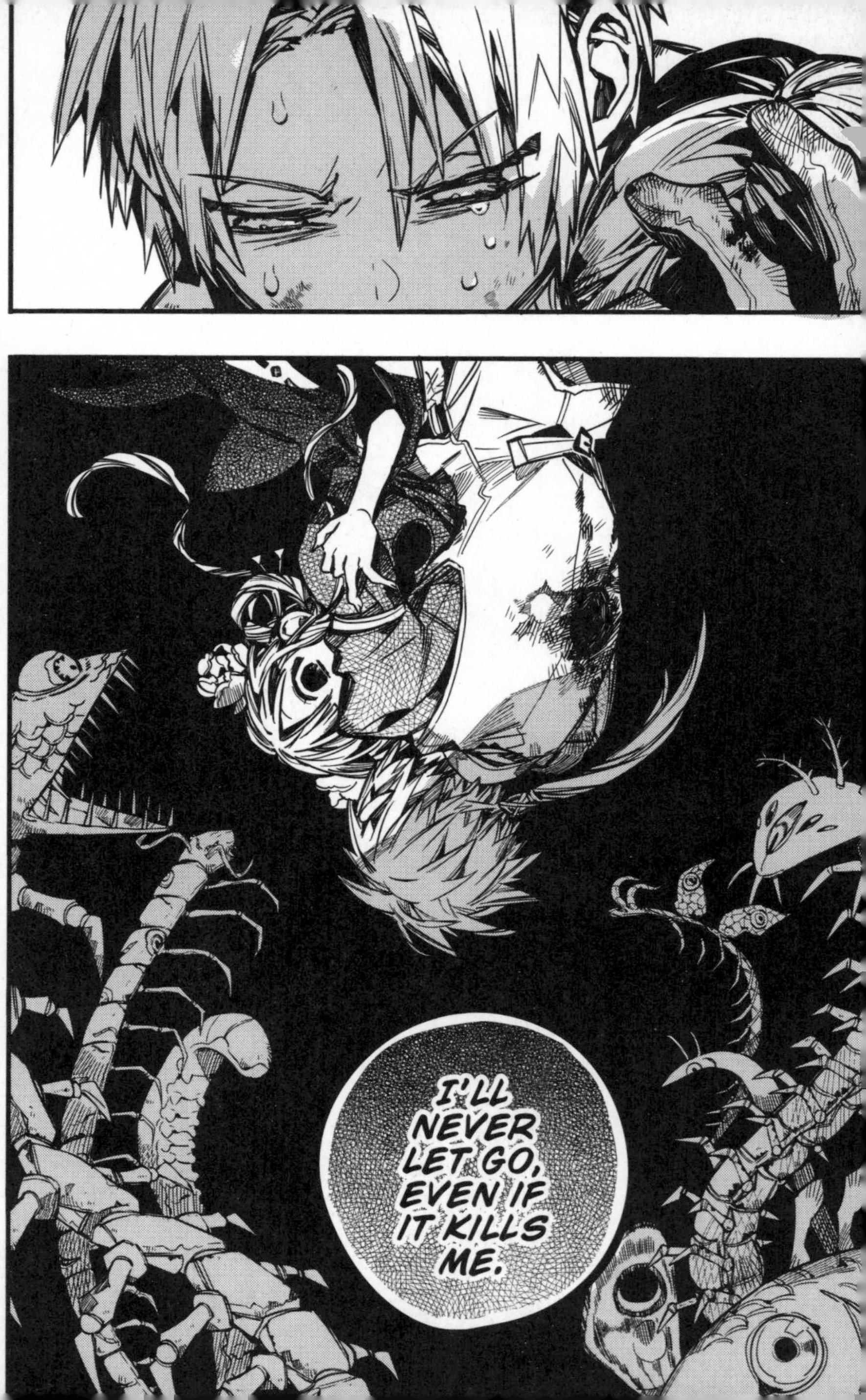
I'LL NEVER LET GO, EVEN IF IT KILLS ME.

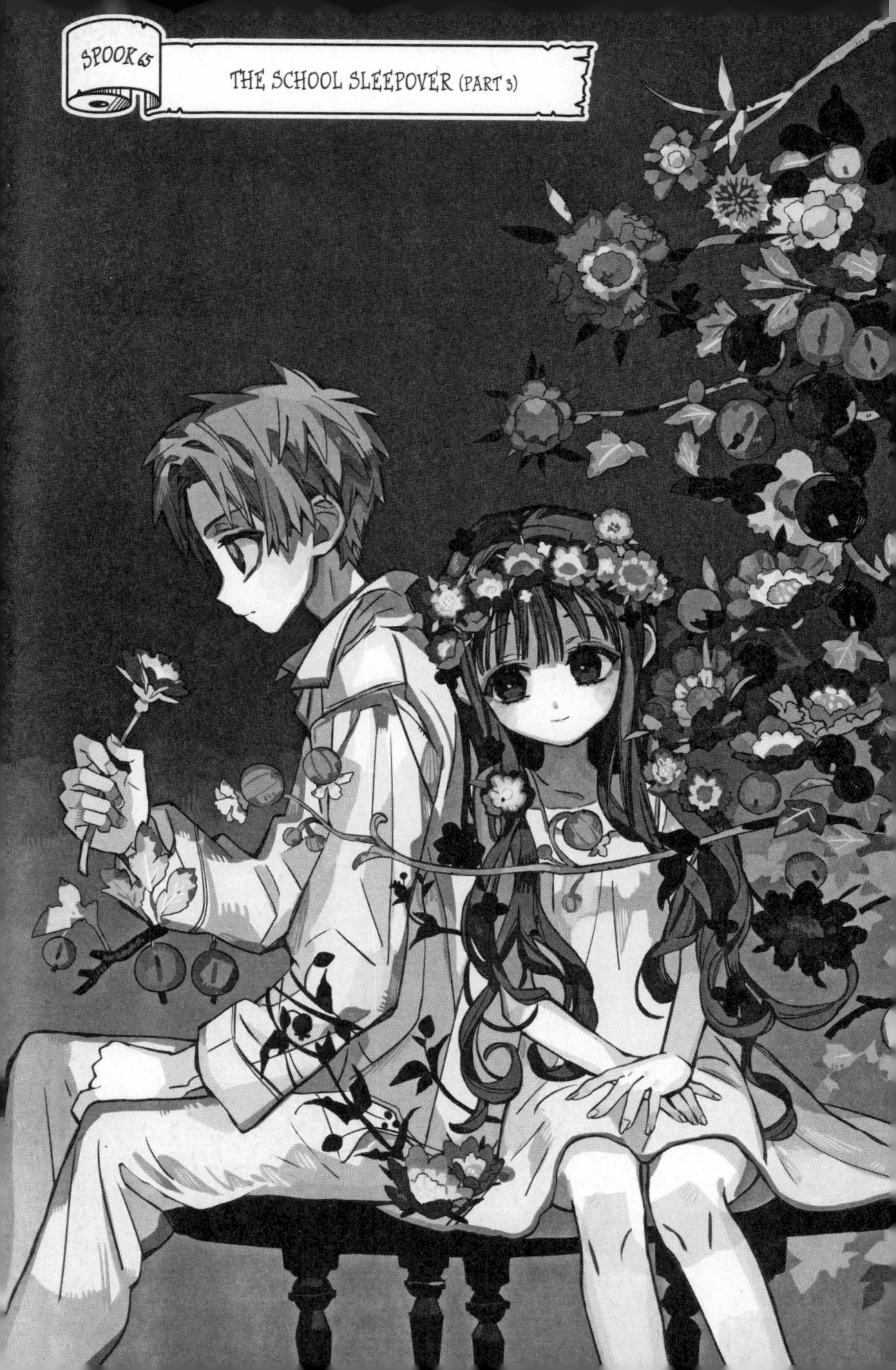
SPOOK 65
THE SCHOOL SLEEPOVER (PART 3)

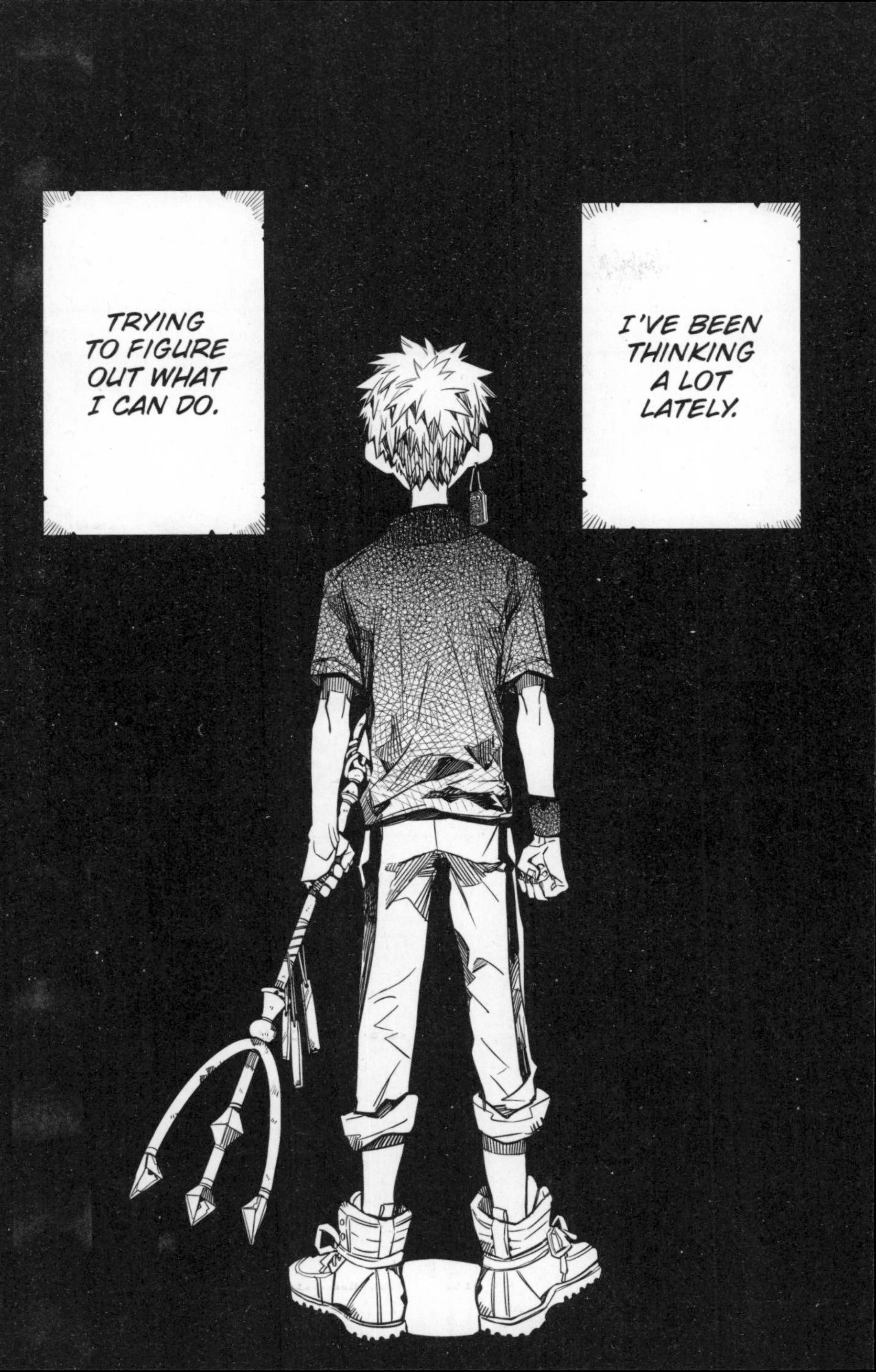
I'VE BEEN THINKING A LOT LATELY.
TRYING TO FIGURE OUT WHAT I CAN DO.

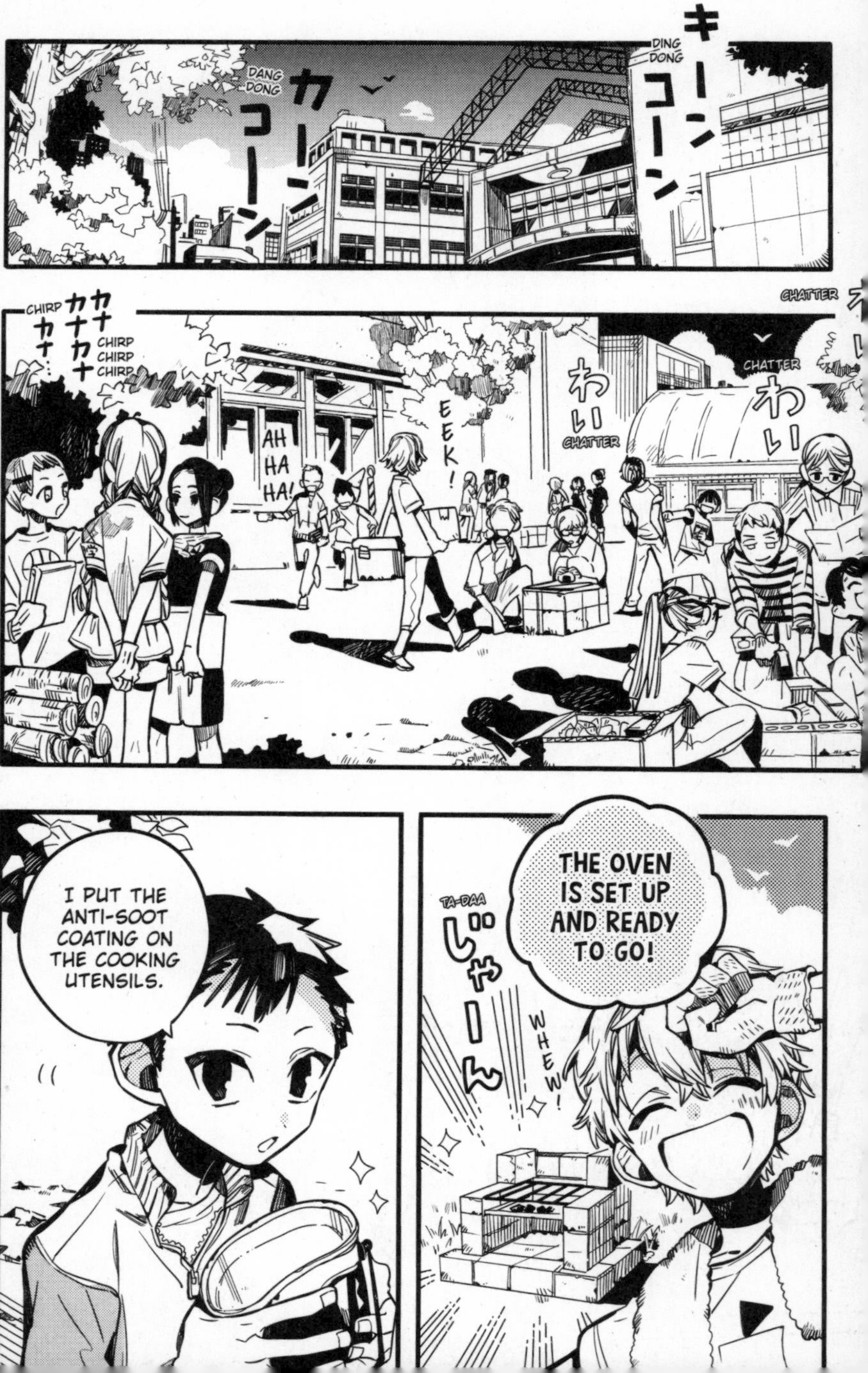
キーンコーン
DING DONG
カーンコーン
DANG DONG
CHATTER
わい
CHATTER
わい
CHATTER
EEK!
AH HA HA!
カナカナカナカナ…
CHIRP CHIRP CHIRP CHIRP
THE OVEN IS SET UP AND READY TO GO!
TA-DAA
じゃーん
WHEW!
I PUT THE ANTI-SOOT COATING ON THE COOKING UTENSILS.

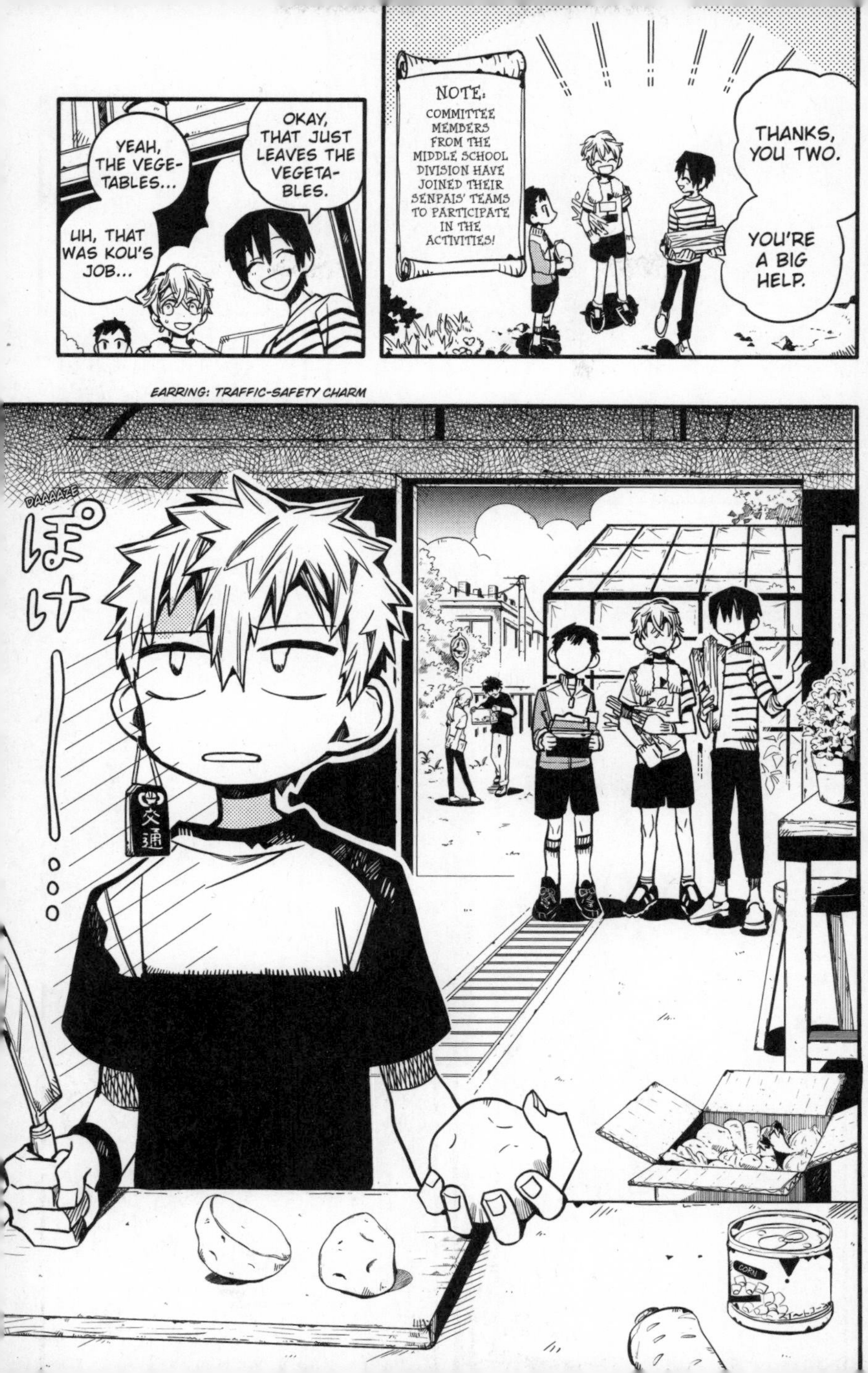
THANKS, YOU TWO.
YOU'RE A BIG HELP.
NOTE: COMMITTEE MEMBERS FROM THE MIDDLE SCHOOL DIVISION HAVE JOINED THEIR SENPAIS' TEAMS TO PARTICIPATE IN THE ACTIVITIES!
OKAY, THAT JUST LEAVES THE VEGETA-BLES.
YEAH, THE VEGE-TABLES...
UH, THAT WAS KOU'S JOB...
EARRING: TRAFFIC-SAFETY CHARM
DAAAAZE
ぽけー…
交通
CORN

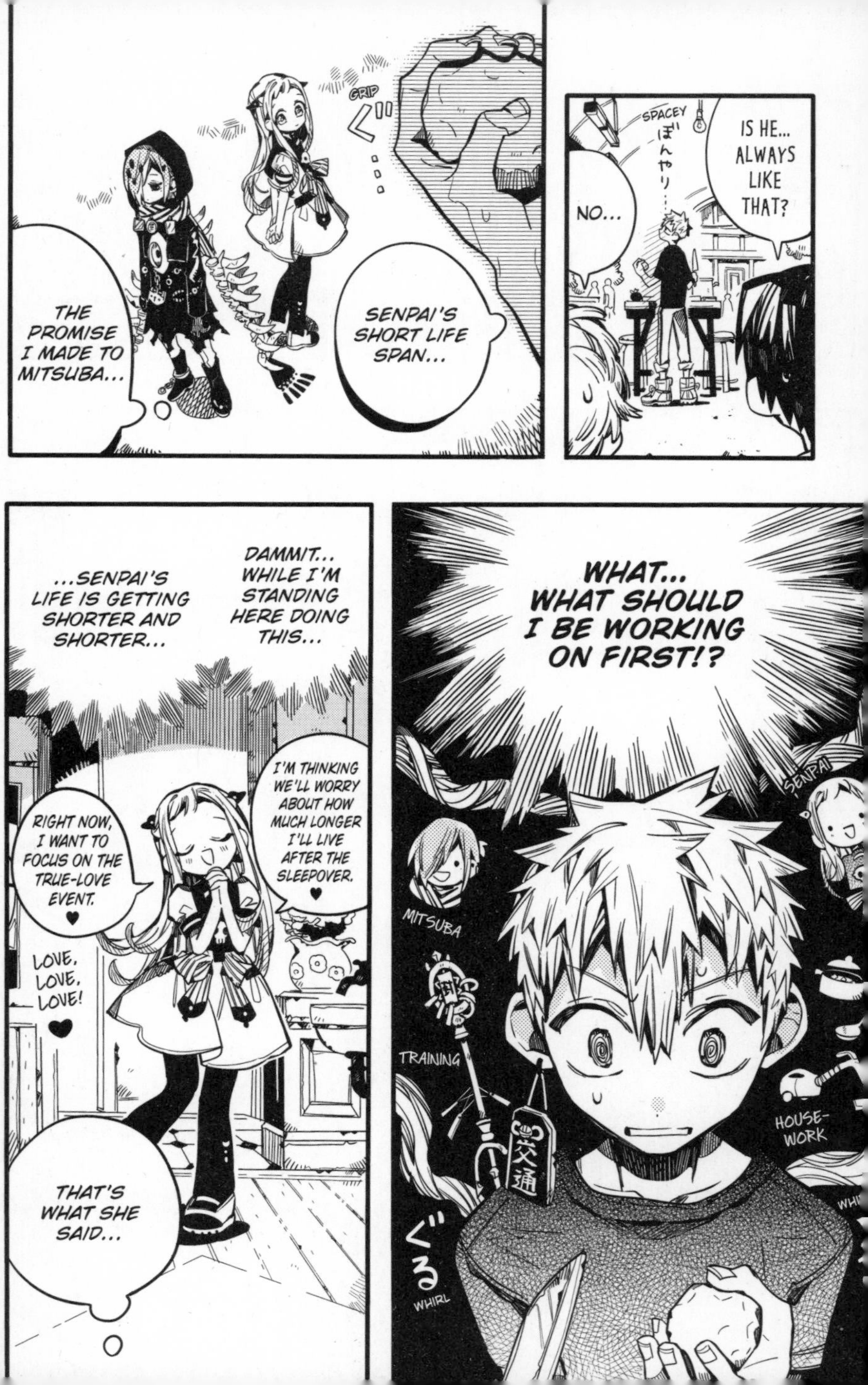
SPACEY
ぼんやり…
IS HE... ALWAYS LIKE THAT?
NO...
GRIP
ぐ"
SENPAI'S SHORT LIFE SPAN...
THE PROMISE I MADE TO MITSUBA...
WHAT... WHAT SHOULD I BE WORKING ON FIRST!?
SENPAI
MITSUBA
TRAINING
HOUSE-WORK
ぐる
WHIRL
DAMMIT... WHILE I'M STANDING HERE DOING THIS...
...SENPAI'S LIFE IS GETTING SHORTER AND SHORTER...
I'M THINKING WE'LL WORRY ABOUT HOW MUCH LONGER I'LL LIVE AFTER THE SLEEPOVER. ♥
RIGHT NOW, I WANT TO FOCUS ON THE TRUE-LOVE EVENT. ♥
LOVE, LOVE, LOVE! ♥
THAT'S WHAT SHE SAID...

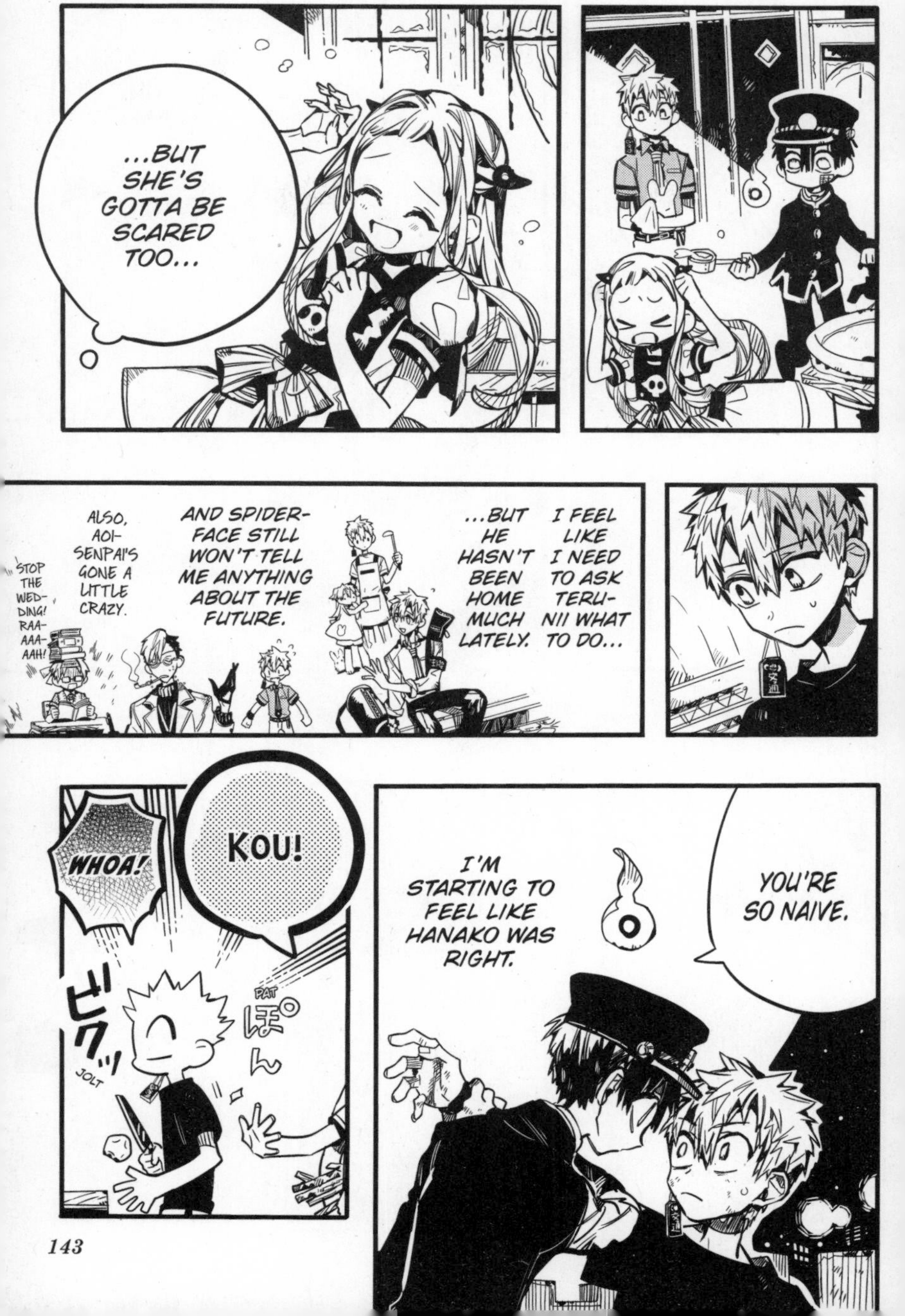
...BUT SHE'S GOTTA BE SCARED TOO...
I FEEL LIKE I NEED TO ASK TERU-NII WHAT TO DO...
...BUT HE HASN'T BEEN HOME MUCH LATELY.
AND SPIDER-FACE STILL WON'T TELL ME ANYTHING ABOUT THE FUTURE.
ALSO, AOI-SENPAI'S GONE A LITTLE CRAZY.
STOP THE WEDDING! RAAAAAAH!
YOU'RE SO NAIVE.
I'M STARTING TO FEEL LIKE HANAKO WAS RIGHT.
KOU!
PAT
ぽん
WHOA!
ビクッ
JOLT

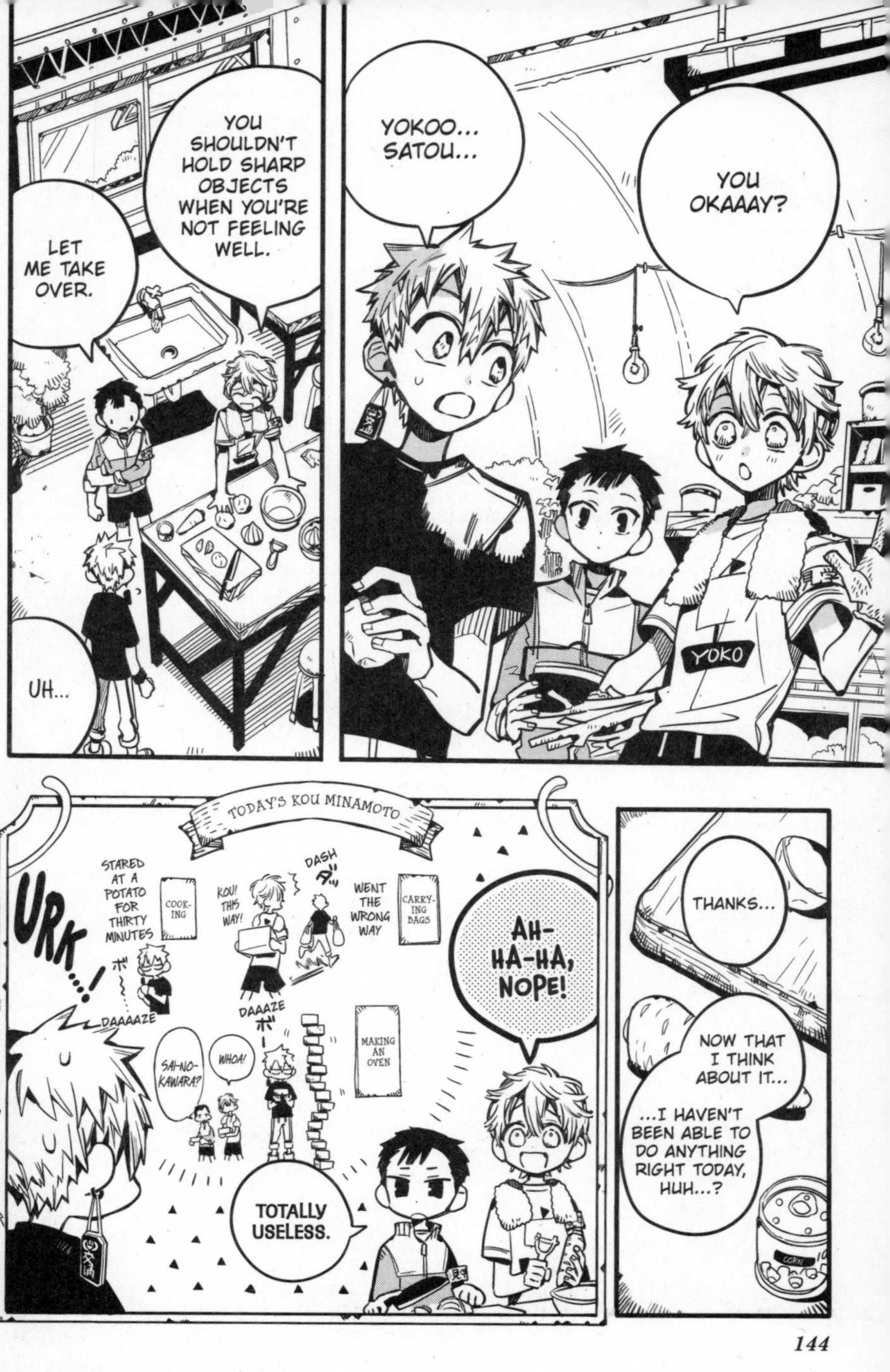
YOU OKAAAY?
YOKOO... SATOU...
YOU SHOULDN'T HOLD SHARP OBJECTS WHEN YOU'RE NOT FEELING WELL.
LET ME TAKE OVER.
UH...
YOKO
THANKS...
NOW THAT I THINK ABOUT IT...
...I HAVEN'T BEEN ABLE TO DO ANYTHING RIGHT TODAY, HUH...?
CORN
TODAY'S KOU MINAMOTO
AH-HA-HA, NOPE!
WENT THE WRONG WAY
CARRY-ING BAGS
DASH
KOU! THIS WAY!
STARED AT A POTATO FOR THIRTY MINUTES
COOK-ING
MAKING AN OVEN
DAAAZE
WHOA!
SAI-NO-KAWARA?
DAAAAAZE
URK...!
TOTALLY USELESS.

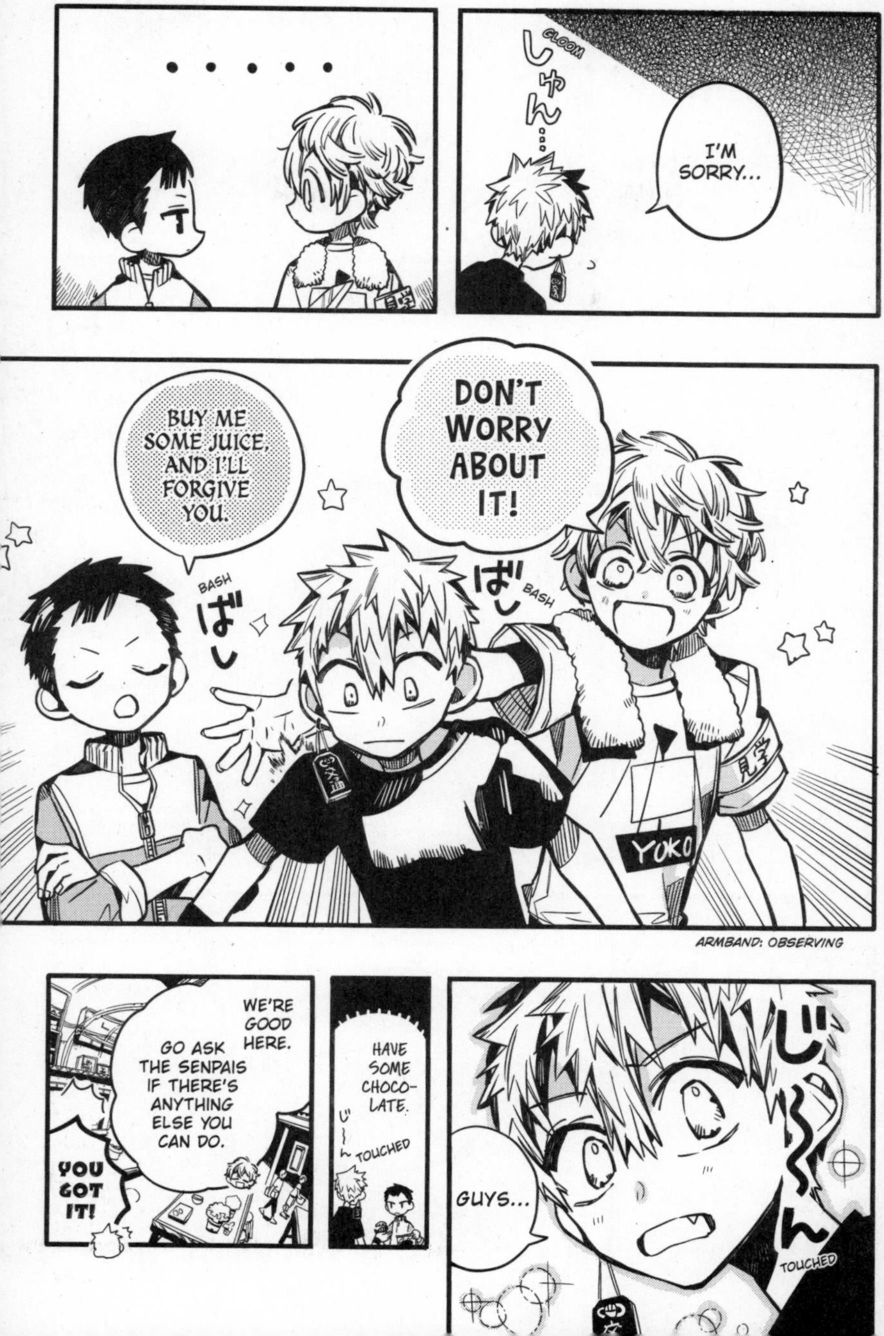
GLOOM
しゅん…
I'M SORRY…
• • • • •
DON'T WORRY ABOUT IT!
ばし
BASH
BUY ME SOME JUICE, AND I'LL FORGIVE YOU.
ばし
BASH
YOKO
ARMBAND: OBSERVING
じ〜ん
TOUCHED
GUYS…
HAVE SOME CHOCOLATE.
じ〜ん
TOUCHED
WE'RE GOOD HERE.
GO ASK THE SENPAIS IF THERE'S ANYTHING ELSE YOU CAN DO.
YOU GOT IT!

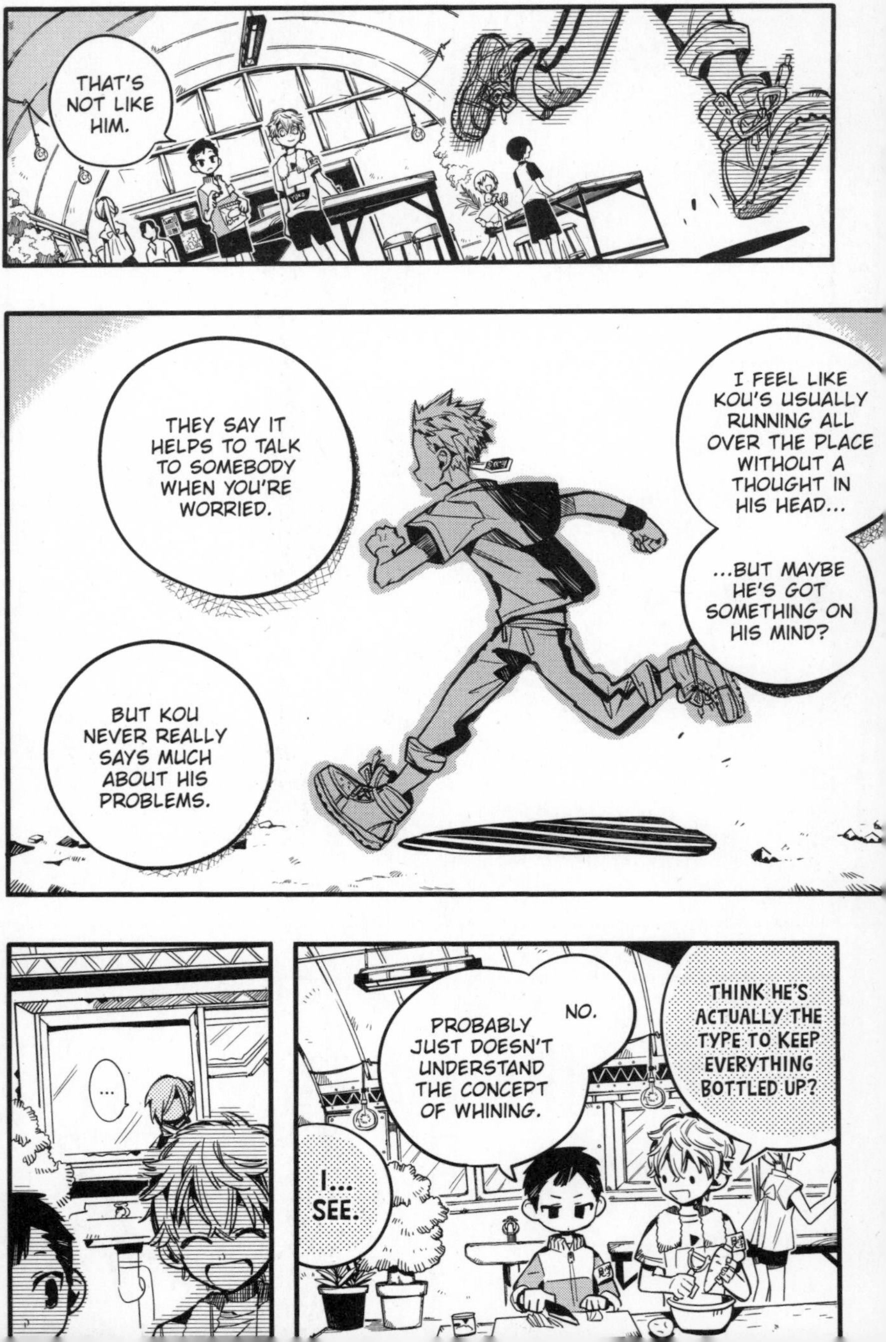
THAT'S NOT LIKE HIM.
I FEEL LIKE KOU'S USUALLY RUNNING ALL OVER THE PLACE WITHOUT A THOUGHT IN HIS HEAD...
...BUT MAYBE HE'S GOT SOMETHING ON HIS MIND?
THEY SAY IT HELPS TO TALK TO SOMEBODY WHEN YOU'RE WORRIED.
BUT KOU NEVER REALLY SAYS MUCH ABOUT HIS PROBLEMS.
THINK HE'S ACTUALLY THE TYPE TO KEEP EVERYTHING BOTTLED UP?
NO.
PROBABLY JUST DOESN'T UNDERSTAND THE CONCEPT OF WHINING.
I... SEE.
...

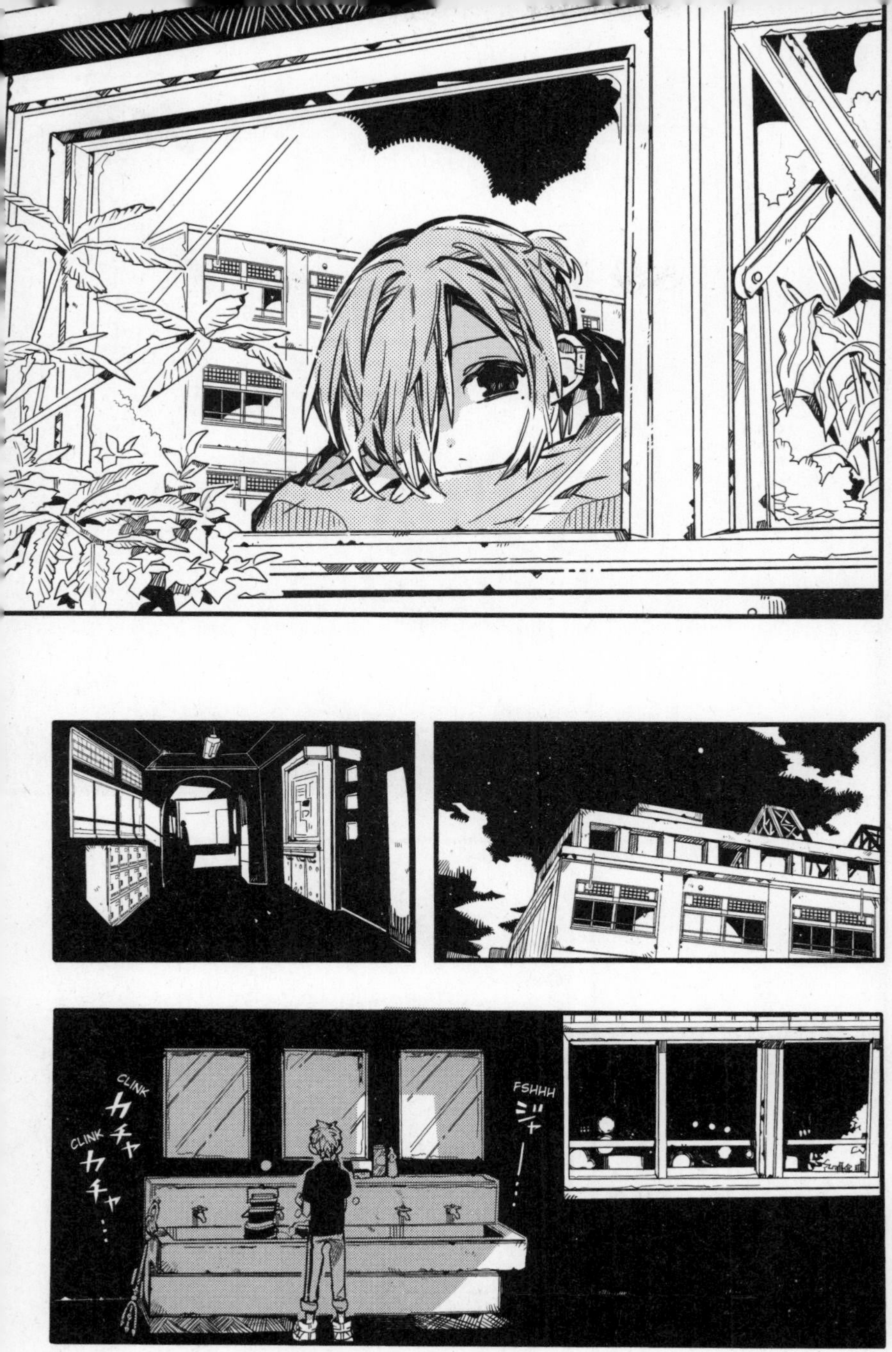
FSHHH
ジャー…
CLINK
カチャ
CLINK
カチャ…

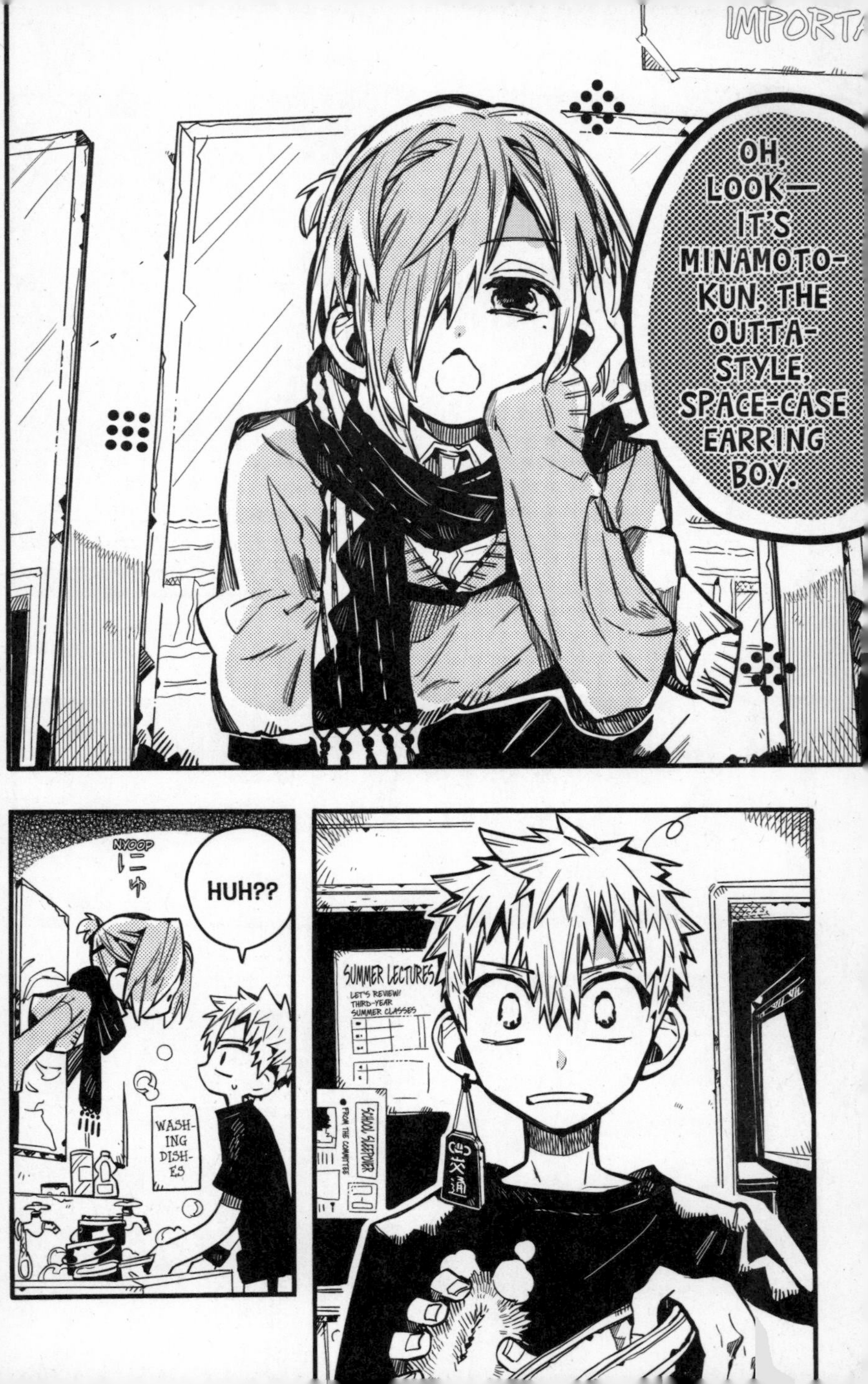
IMPORTA
OH, LOOK—IT'S MINAMOTO-KUN, THE OUTTA-STYLE, SPACE-CASE EARRING BOY.
SUMMER LECTURES
LET'S REVIEW! THIRD-YEAR SUMMER CLASSES
SCHOOL SLEEPOVER
FROM THE COMMITTEE
NYOOP
HUH??
WASH-ING DISH-ES

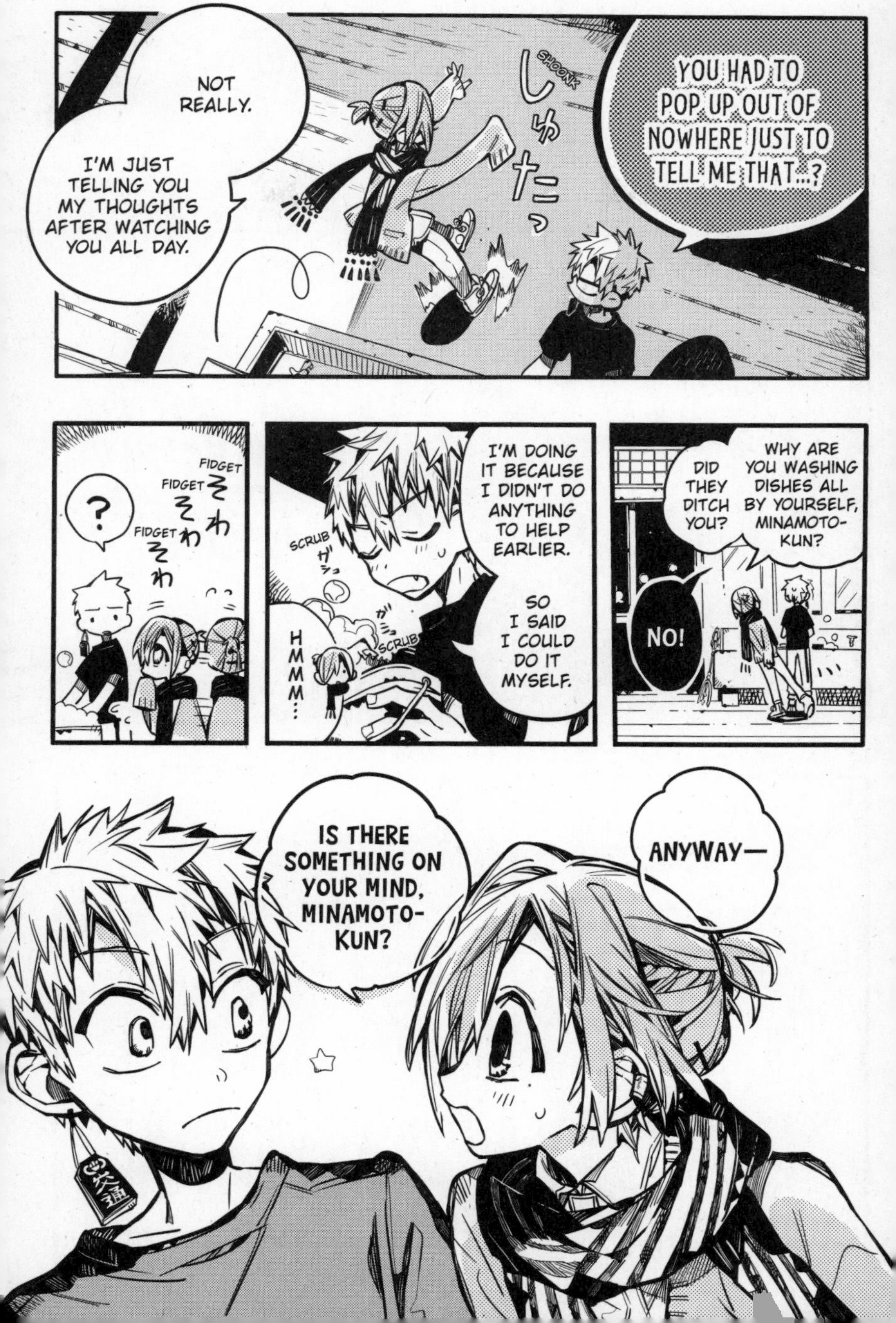
YOU HAD TO POP UP OUT OF NOWHERE JUST TO TELL ME THAT...?
SHOONK
しゅたっ
NOT REALLY.
I'M JUST TELLING YOU MY THOUGHTS AFTER WATCHING YOU ALL DAY.
WHY ARE YOU WASHING DISHES ALL BY YOURSELF, MINAMOTO-KUN?
DID THEY DITCH YOU?
NO!
I'M DOING IT BECAUSE I DIDN'T DO ANYTHING TO HELP EARLIER.
SO I SAID I COULD DO IT MYSELF.
SCRUB
ガシュ
SCRUB
ガシュ
HMMM...
FIDGET
そわ
FIDGET
そわ
FIDGET
そわ
?
ANYWAY—
IS THERE SOMETHING ON YOUR MIND, MINAMOTO-KUN?

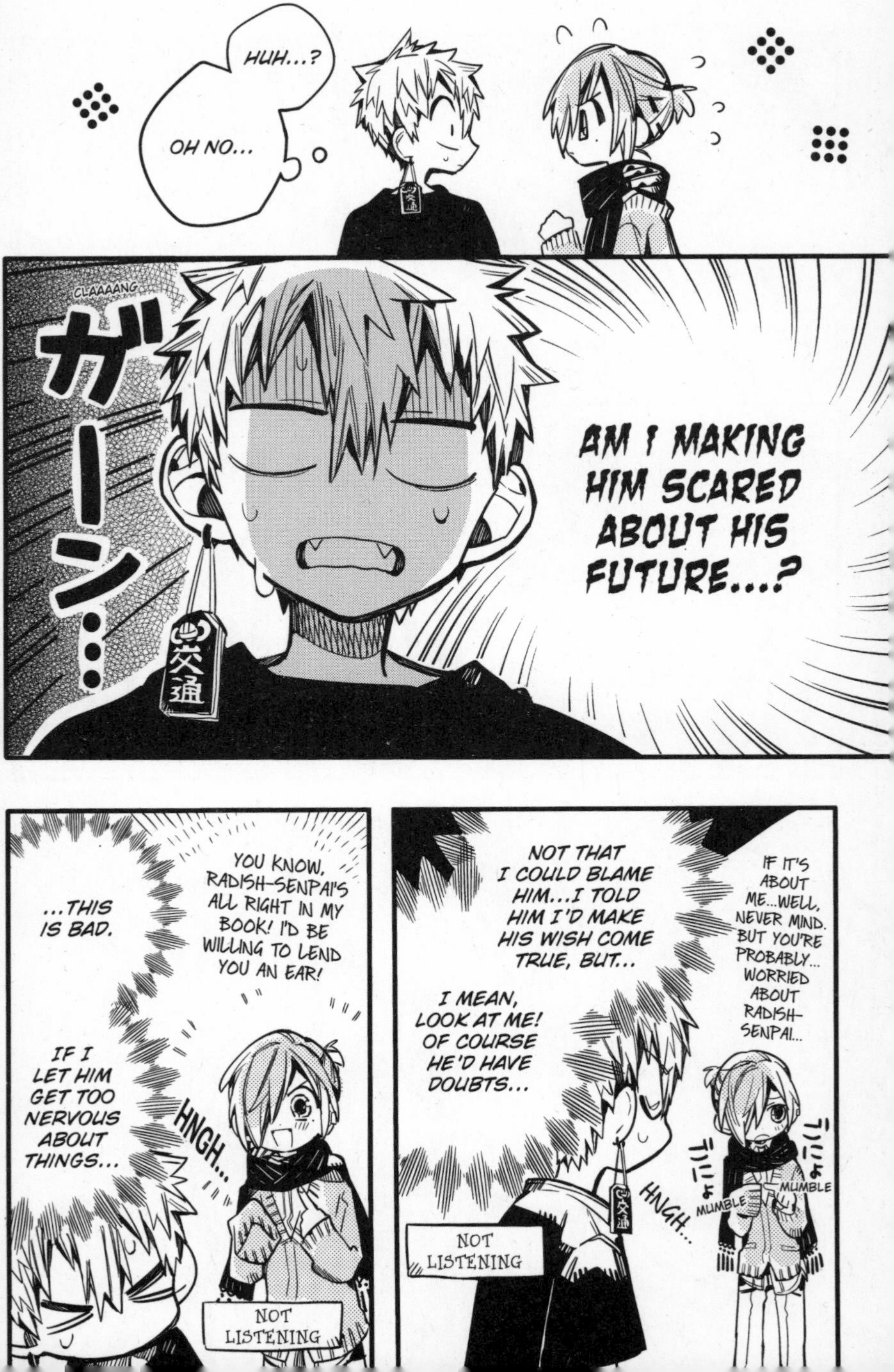
HUH...?
OH NO...
CLAAAANG
ガーン...
AM I MAKING HIM SCARED ABOUT HIS FUTURE...?
IF IT'S ABOUT ME...WELL, NEVER MIND. BUT YOU'RE PROBABLY... WORRIED ABOUT RADISH-SENPAI...
NOT THAT I COULD BLAME HIM...I TOLD HIM I'D MAKE HIS WISH COME TRUE, BUT...
I MEAN, LOOK AT ME! OF COURSE HE'D HAVE DOUBTS...
ごにょ MUMBLE
ごにょ MUMBLE
HNGH...
NOT LISTENING
YOU KNOW, RADISH-SENPAI'S ALL RIGHT IN MY BOOK! I'D BE WILLING TO LEND YOU AN EAR!
...THIS IS BAD.
IF I LET HIM GET TOO NERVOUS ABOUT THINGS...
HNGH...
NOT LISTENING

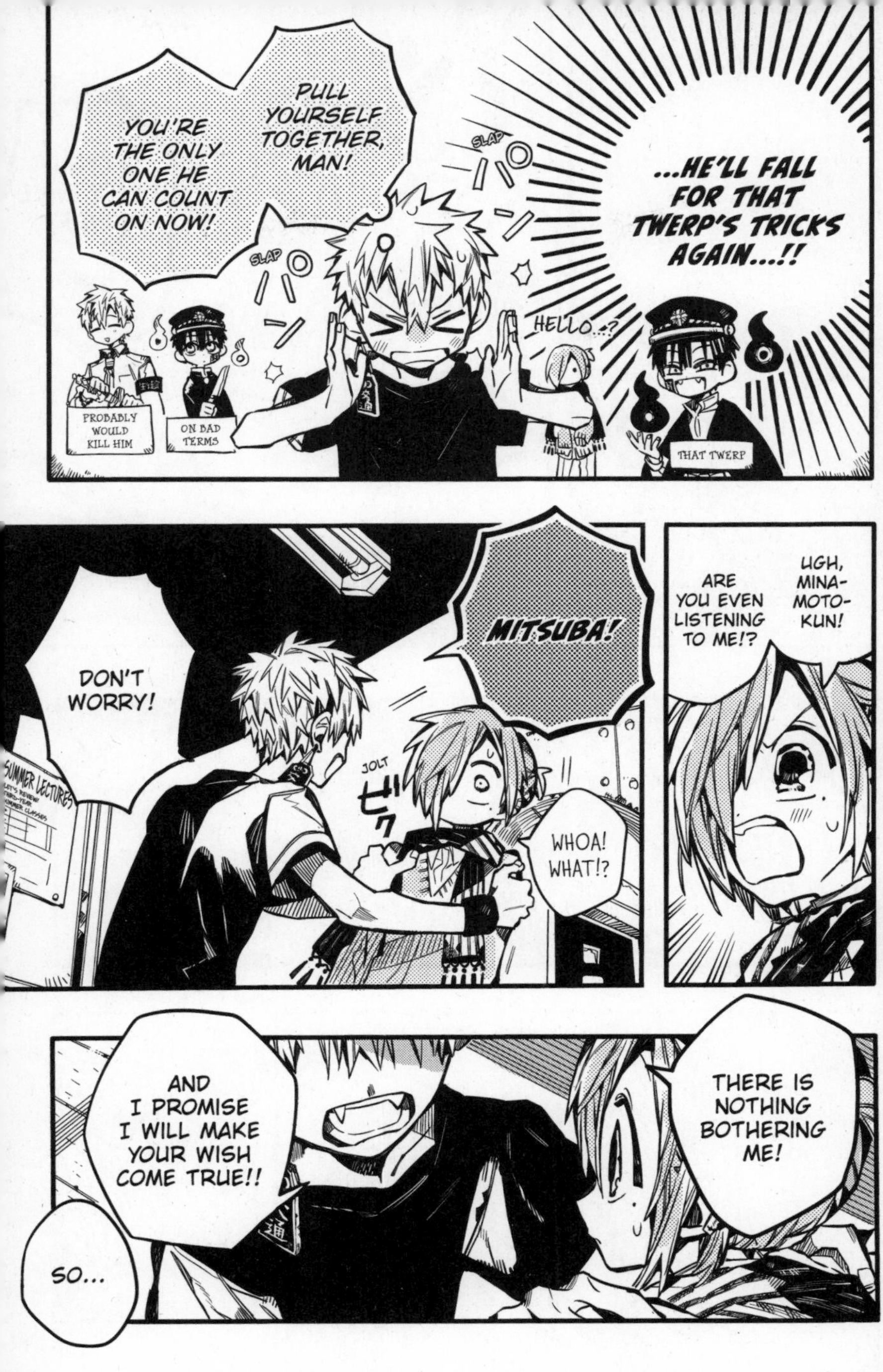
...HE'LL FALL FOR THAT TWERP'S TRICKS AGAIN...!!
SLAP
PULL YOURSELF TOGETHER, MAN!
YOU'RE THE ONLY ONE HE CAN COUNT ON NOW!
SLAP
HELLO...?
THAT TWERP
ON BAD TERMS
PROBABLY WOULD KILL HIM
UGH, MINA-MOTO-KUN!
ARE YOU EVEN LISTENING TO ME!?
MITSUBA!
JOLT
WHOA! WHAT!?
DON'T WORRY!
SUMMER LECTURES
THERE IS NOTHING BOTHERING ME!
AND I PROMISE I WILL MAKE YOUR WISH COME TRUE!!
SO...

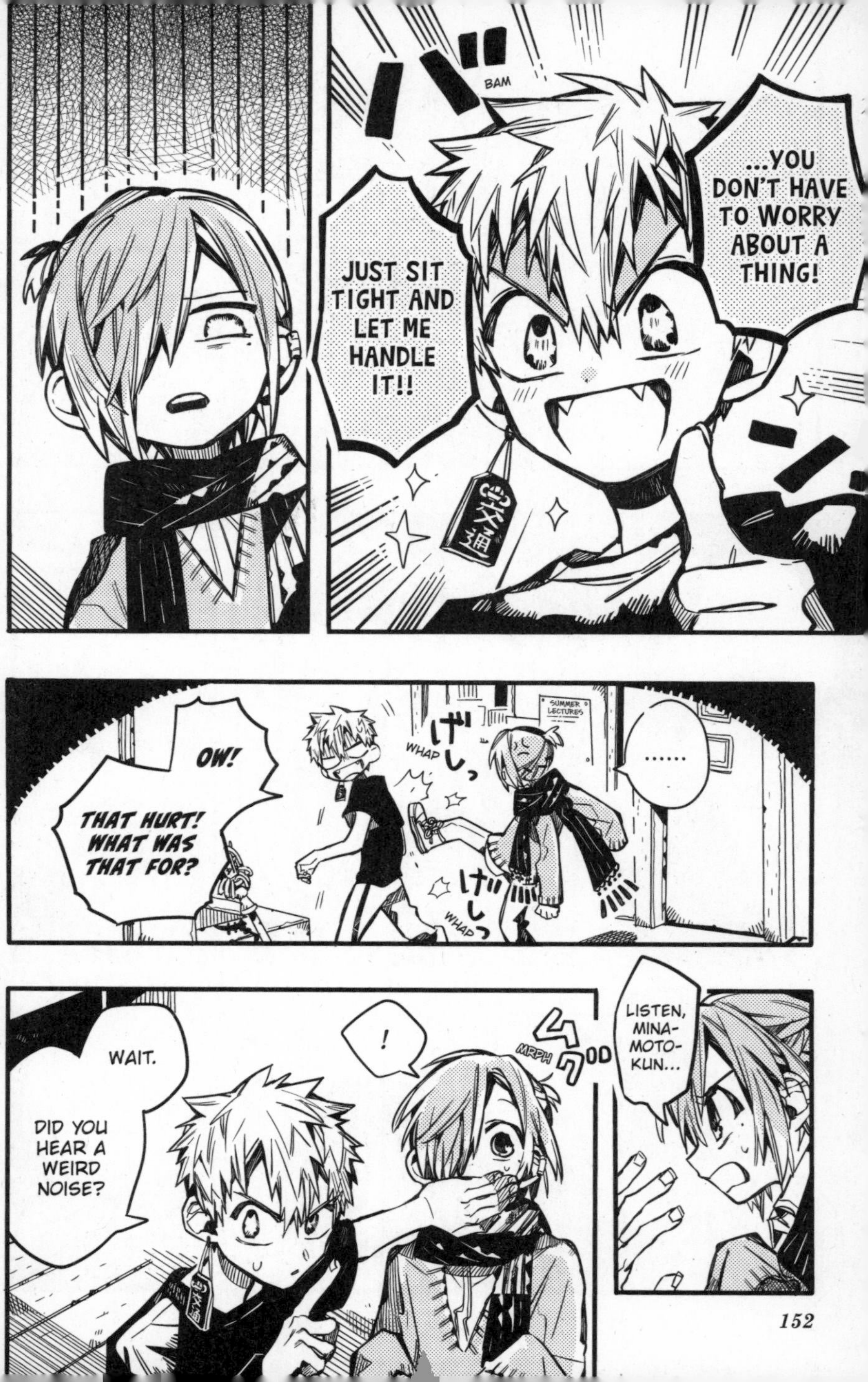
BAM
...YOU DON'T HAVE TO WORRY ABOUT A THING!
JUST SIT TIGHT AND LET ME HANDLE IT!!
SUMMER LECTURES
......
WHAP
WHAP
OW!
THAT HURT! WHAT WAS THAT FOR?
LISTEN, MINA-MOTO-KUN...
MRPH
!
WAIT.
DID YOU HEAR A WEIRD NOISE?

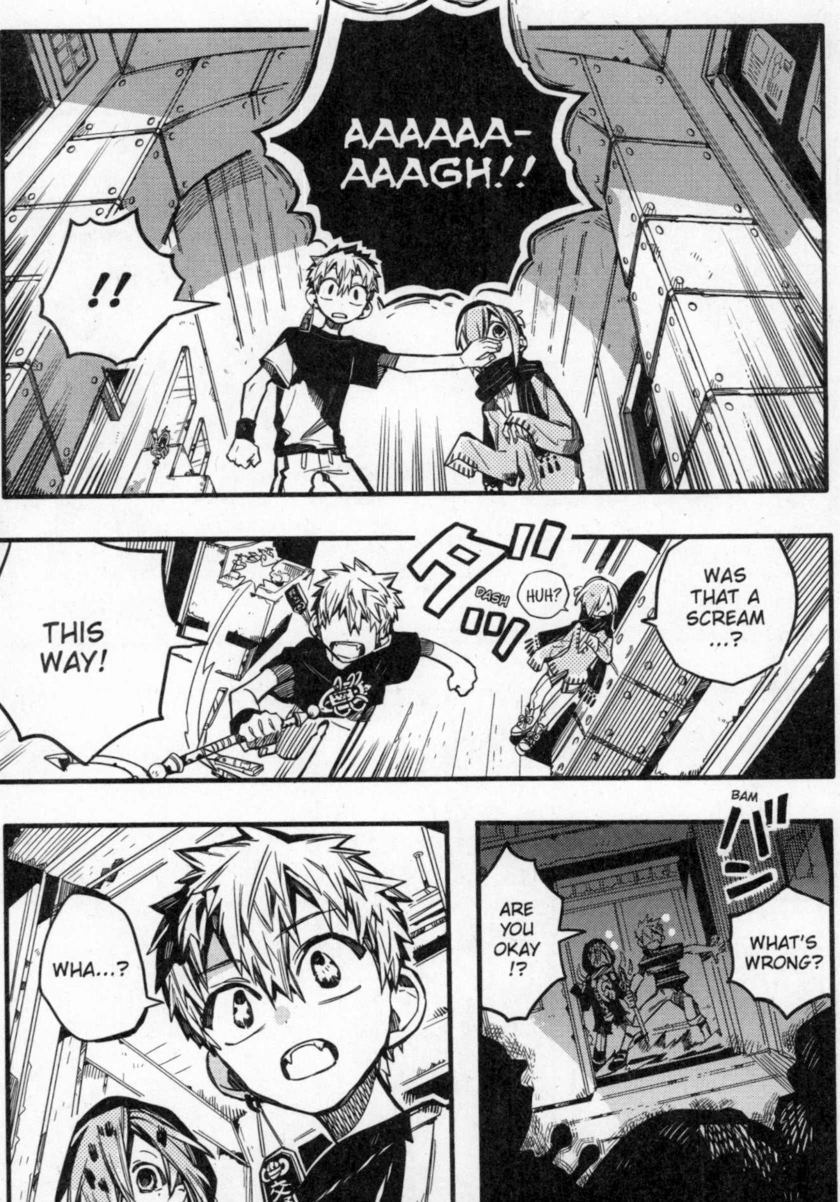
AAAAAA-AAAGH!!
!!
WAS THAT A SCREAM ...?
HUH?
DASH
THIS WAY!
BAM
WHAT'S WRONG?
ARE YOU OKAY !?
WHA...?

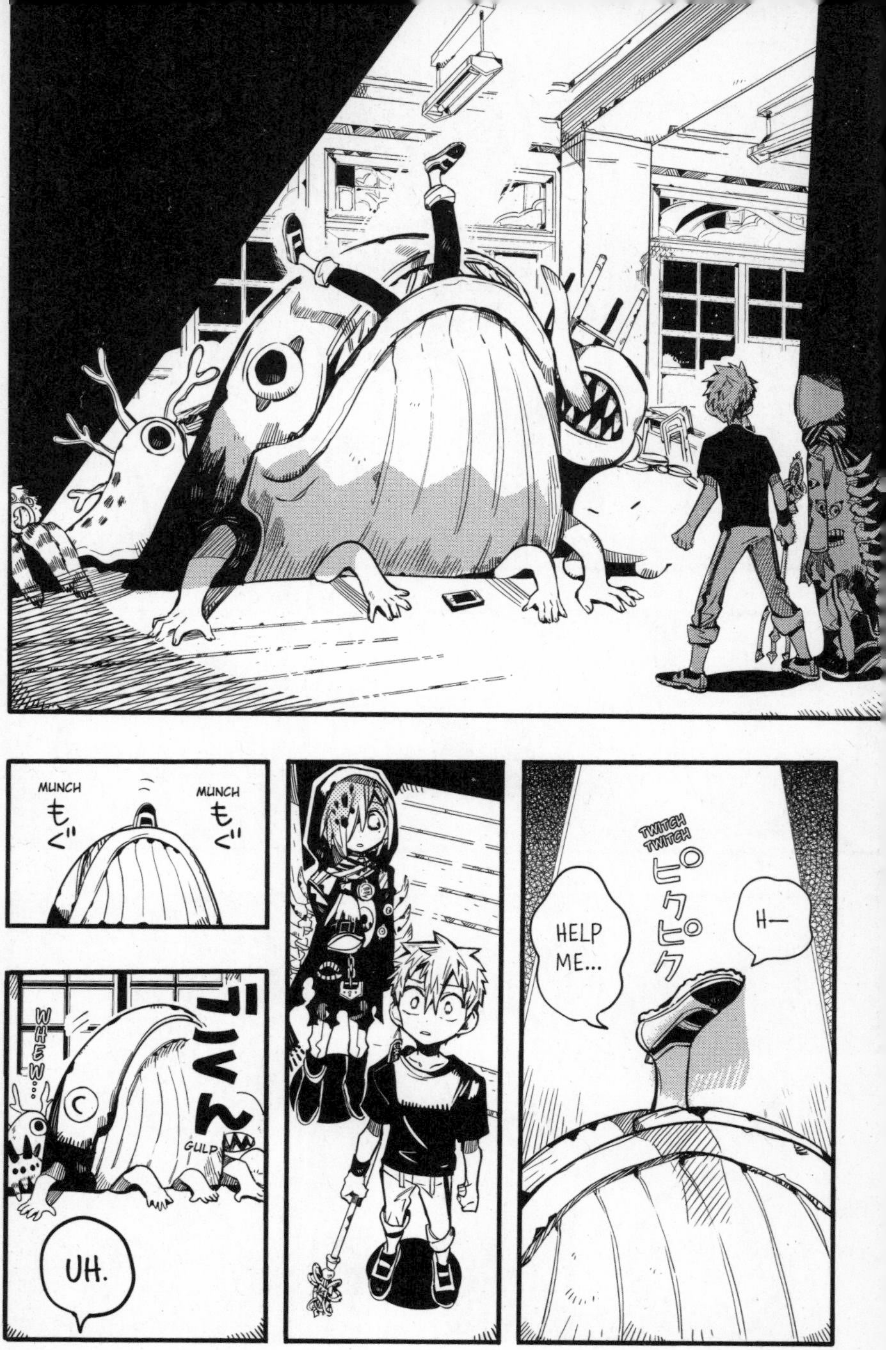

TWITCH TWITCH
ピクピク
H—
HELP ME...
MUNCH
もぐ
MUNCH
もぐ
GULP
WHEW...
UH.

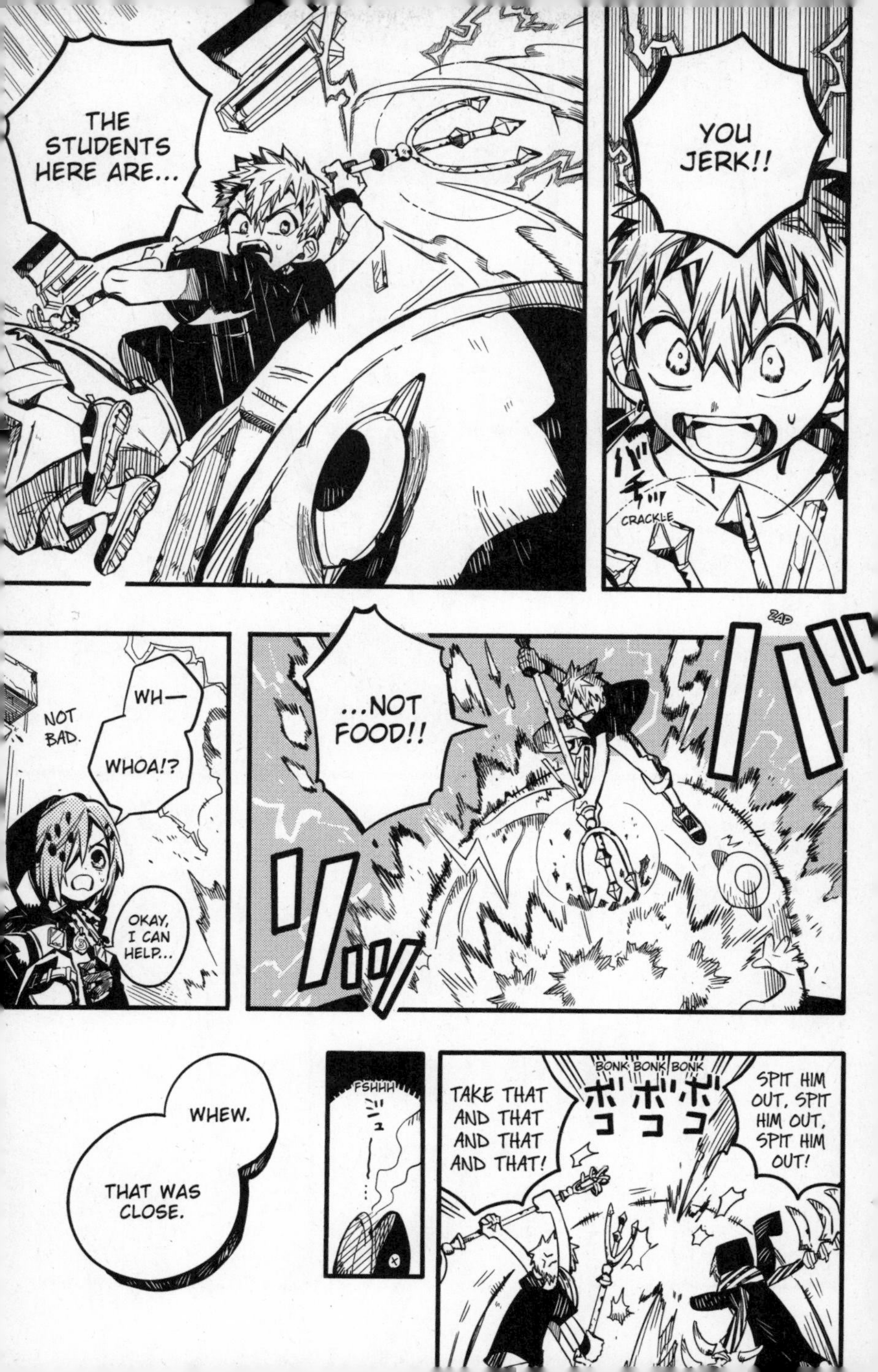
YOU JERK!!
CRACKLE
THE STUDENTS HERE ARE...
ZAP
...NOT FOOD!!
WH—
WHOA!?
NOT BAD.
OKAY, I CAN HELP...
SPIT HIM OUT, SPIT HIM OUT, SPIT HIM OUT!
BONK BONK BONK
TAKE THAT AND THAT AND THAT AND THAT!
FSHHH
WHEW.
THAT WAS CLOSE.

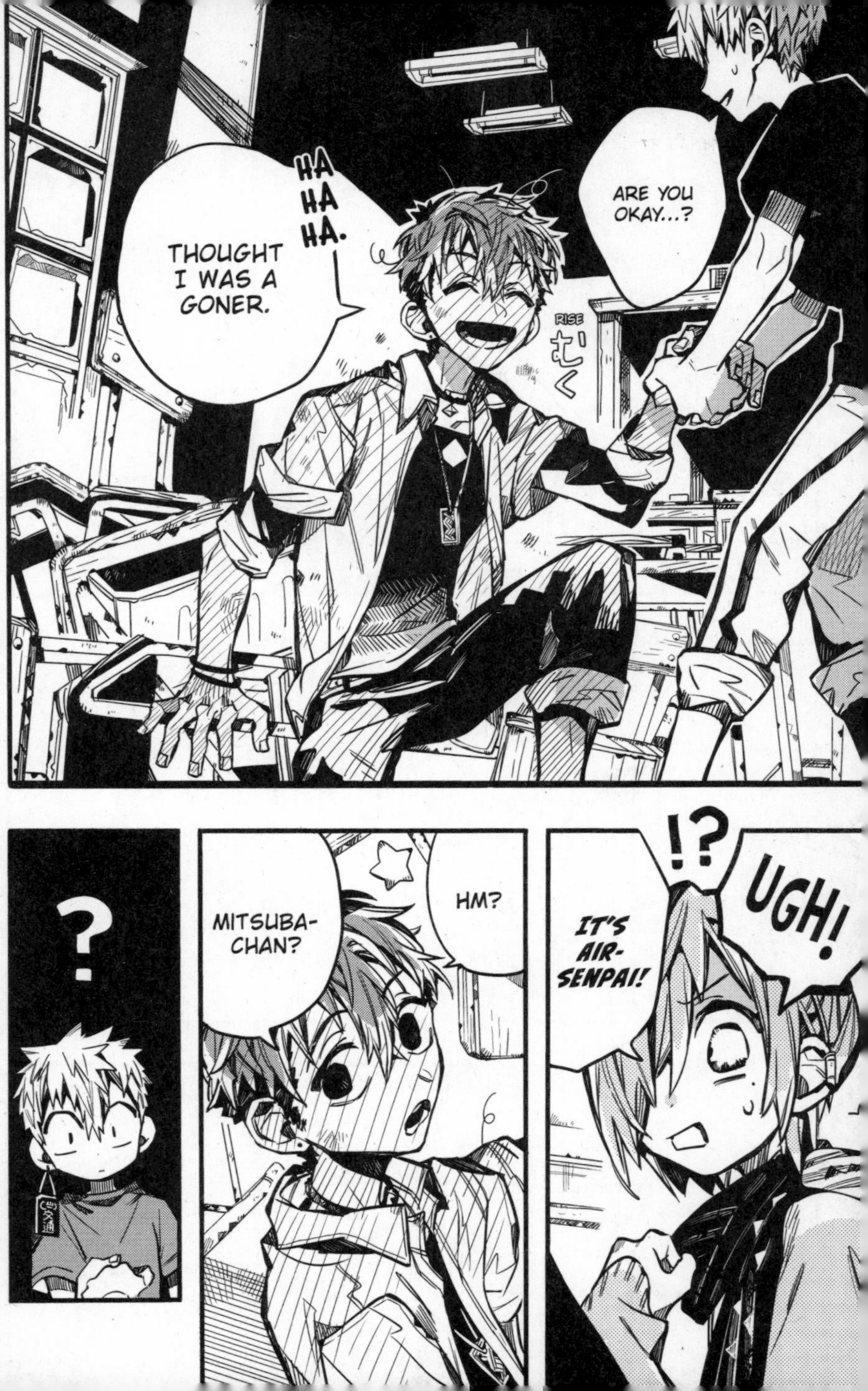
ARE YOU OKAY...?
HA HA HA.
THOUGHT I WAS A GONER.
RISE むく
!?
UGH!
IT'S AIR-SENPAI!
HM?
MITSUBA-CHAN?
?

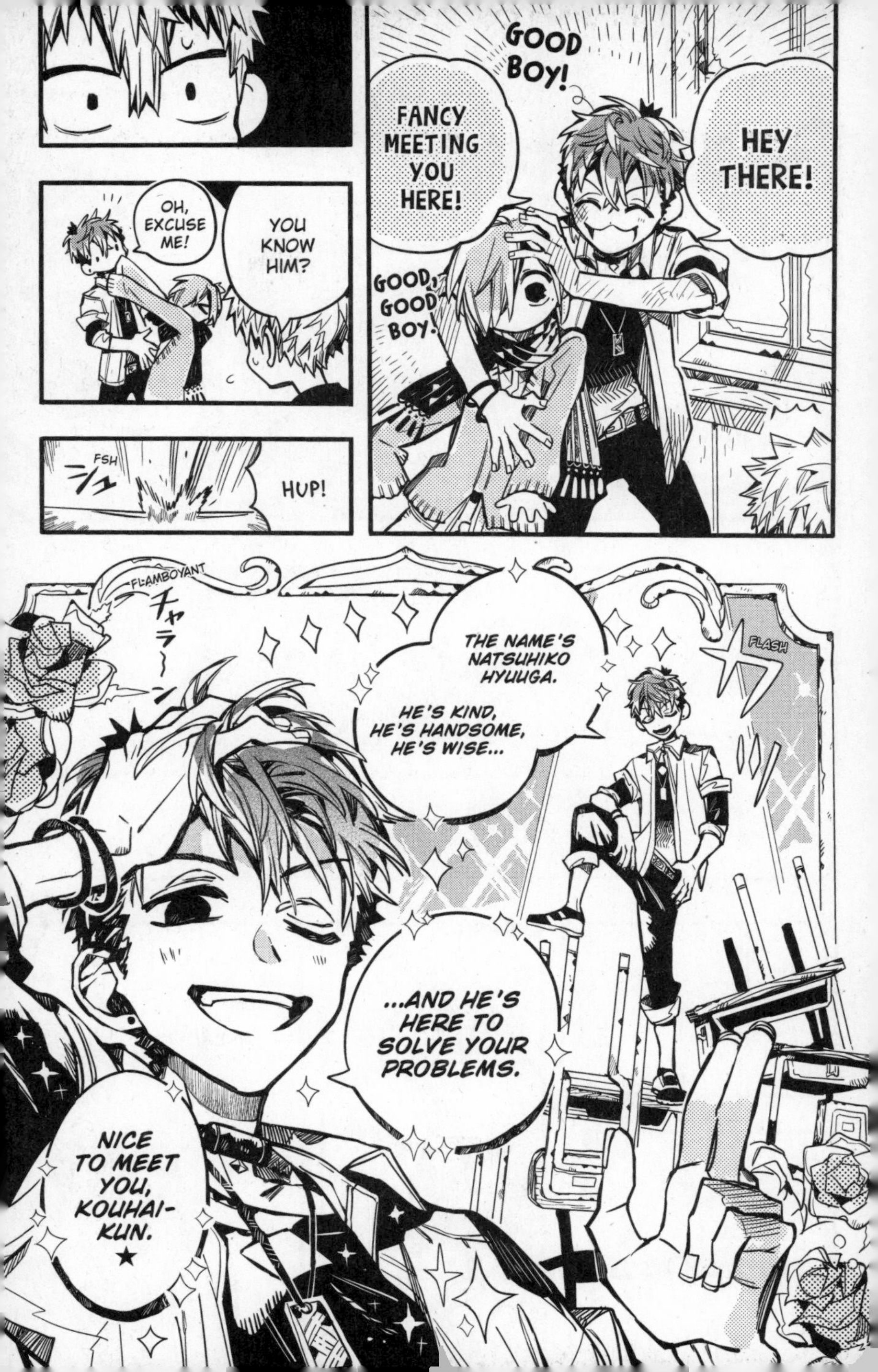
HEY THERE!
GOOD BOY!
FANCY MEETING YOU HERE!
GOOD, GOOD BOY.
YOU KNOW HIM?
OH, EXCUSE ME!
HUP!
FSH
FLASH
THE NAME'S NATSUHIKO HYUUGA.
FLAMBOYANT
チャラ〜ン
HE'S KIND, HE'S HANDSOME, HE'S WISE...
...AND HE'S HERE TO SOLVE YOUR PROBLEMS.
NICE TO MEET YOU, KOUHAI-KUN. ★

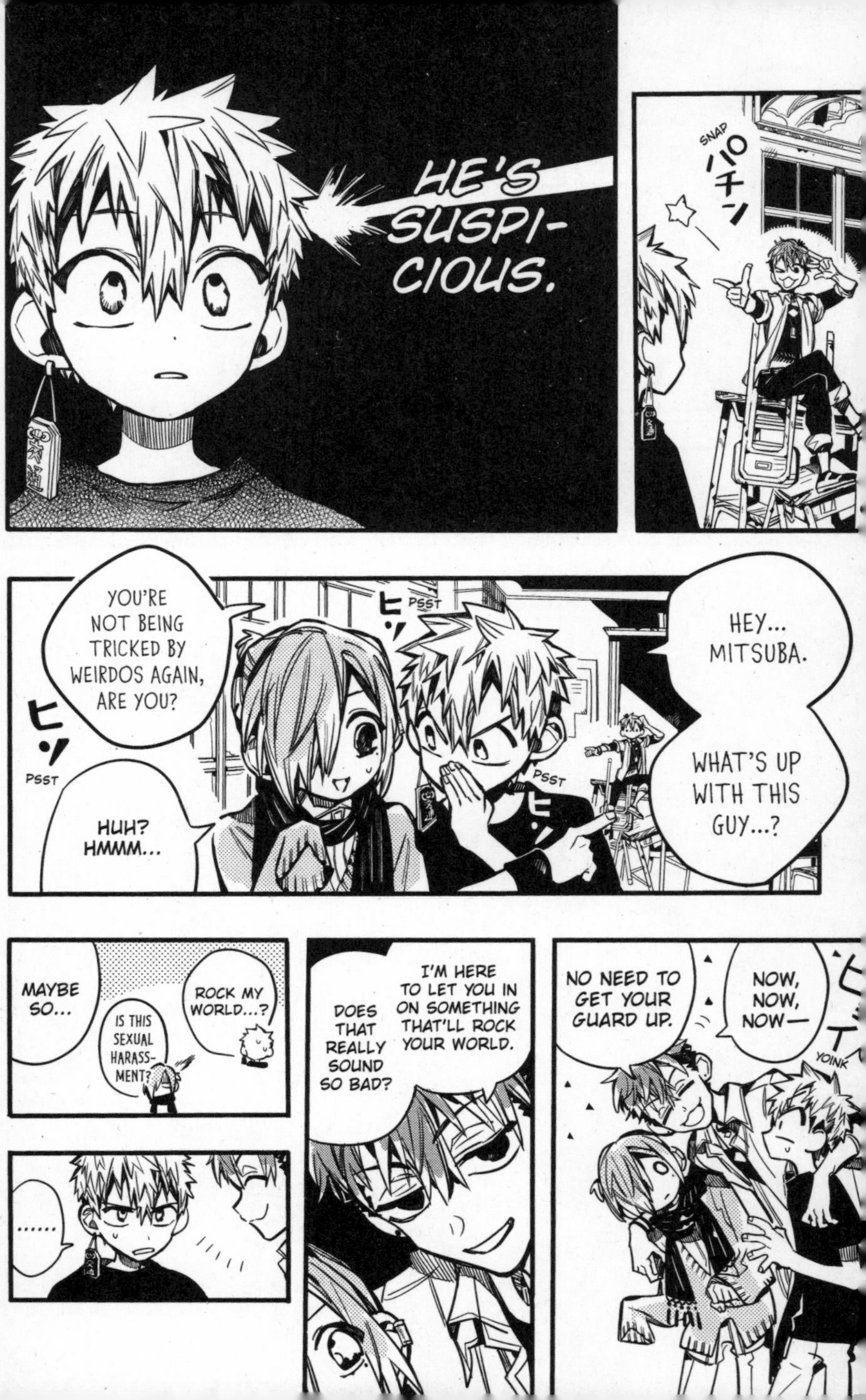
SNAP
パチン
HE'S SUSPICIOUS.
HEY... MITSUBA.
WHAT'S UP WITH THIS GUY...?
PSST
YOU'RE NOT BEING TRICKED BY WEIRDOS AGAIN, ARE YOU?
PSST
HUH? HMMM...
NOW, NOW, NOW—
NO NEED TO GET YOUR GUARD UP.
YOINK
I'M HERE TO LET YOU IN ON SOMETHING THAT'LL ROCK YOUR WORLD.
DOES THAT REALLY SOUND SO BAD?
ROCK MY WORLD...?
MAYBE SO...
IS THIS SEXUAL HARASSMENT?
......

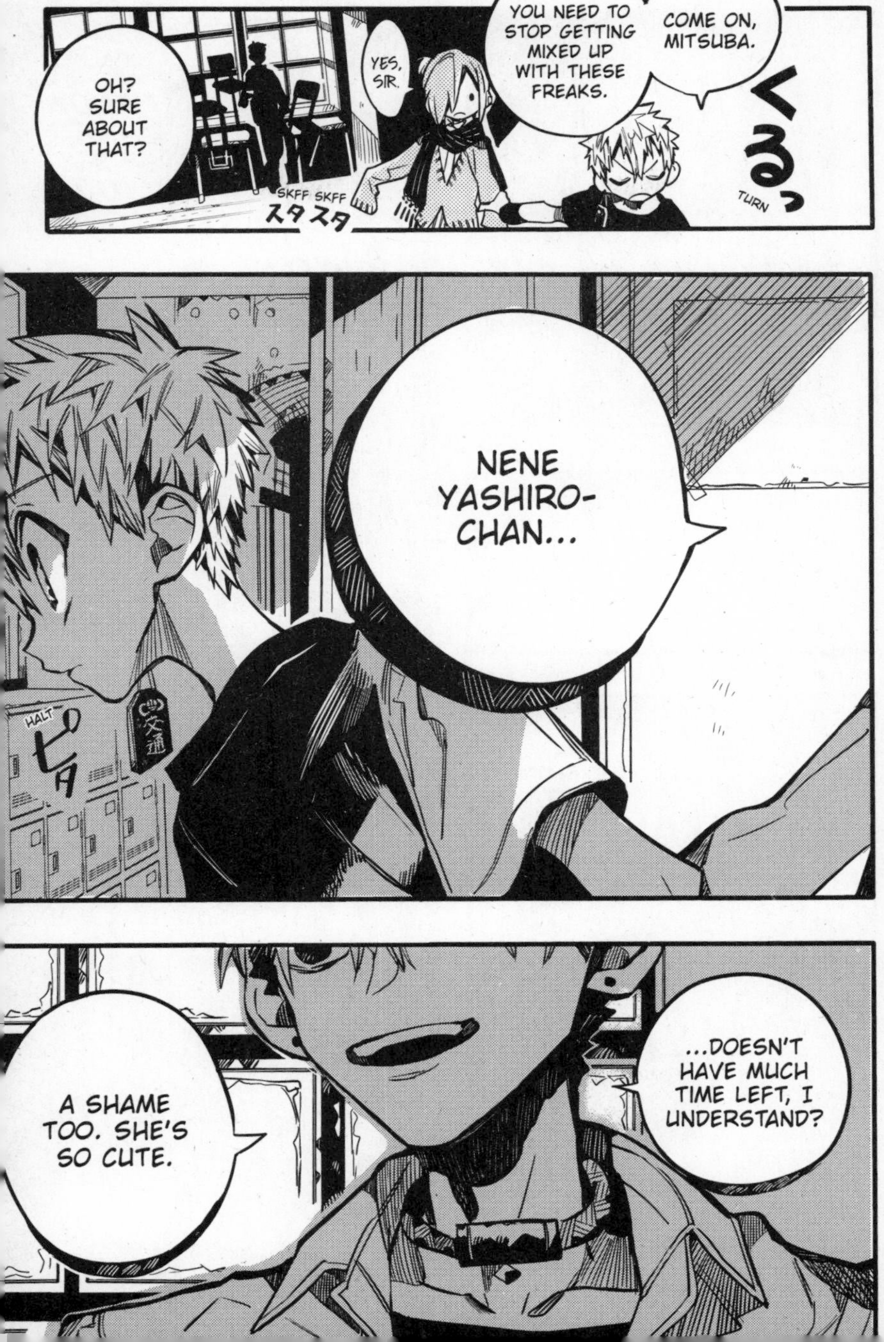
COME ON, MITSUBA.
YOU NEED TO STOP GETTING MIXED UP WITH THESE FREAKS.
くるっ
TURN
YES, SIR.
SKFF SKFF
スタスタ
OH? SURE ABOUT THAT?
NENE YASHIRO-CHAN...
交通
HALT
ピタ
...DOESN'T HAVE MUCH TIME LEFT, I UNDERSTAND?
A SHAME TOO. SHE'S SO CUTE.

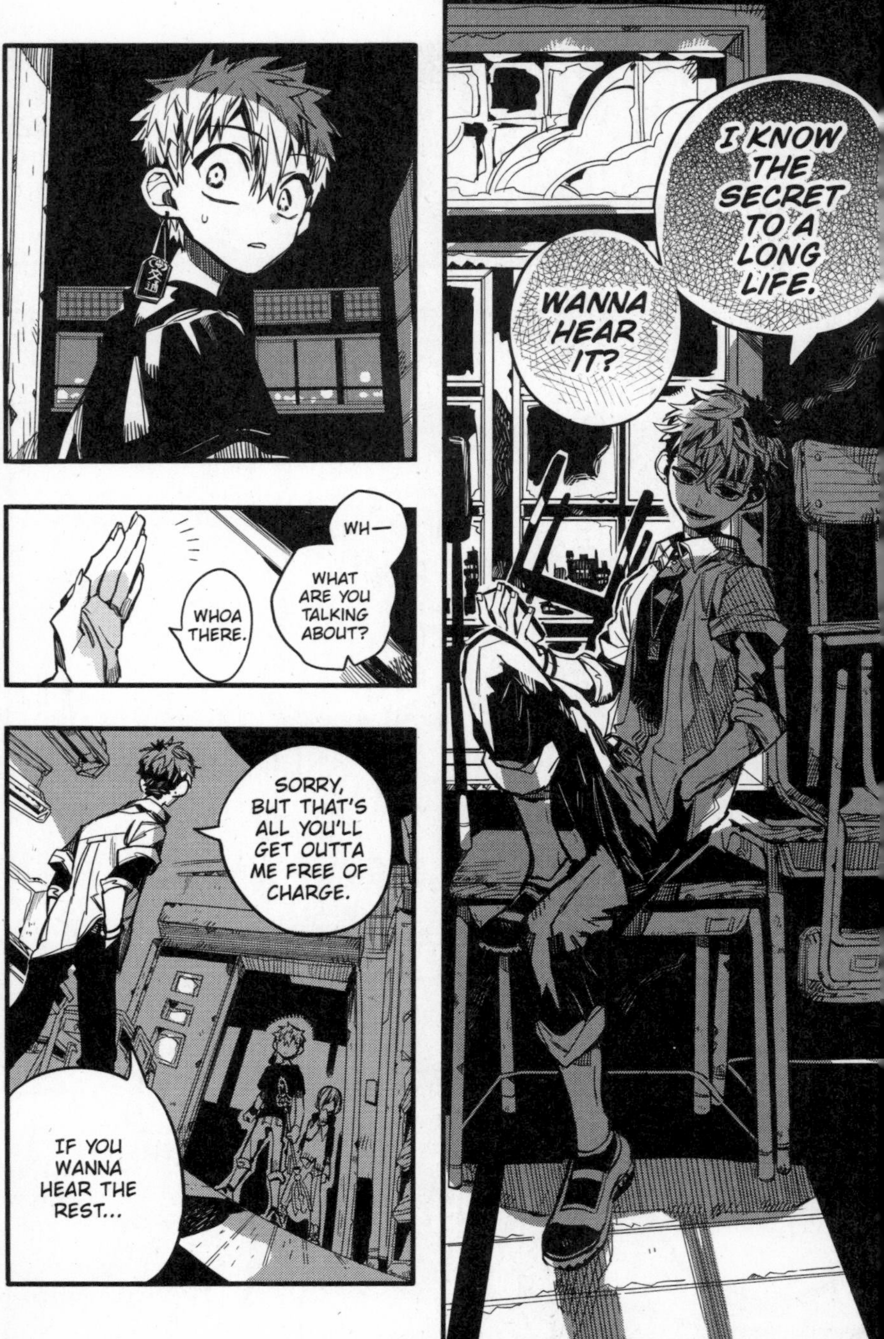
I KNOW THE SECRET TO A LONG LIFE.
WANNA HEAR IT?
WH— WHAT ARE YOU TALKING ABOUT?
WHOA THERE.
SORRY, BUT THAT'S ALL YOU'LL GET OUTTA ME FREE OF CHARGE.
IF YOU WANNA HEAR THE REST...

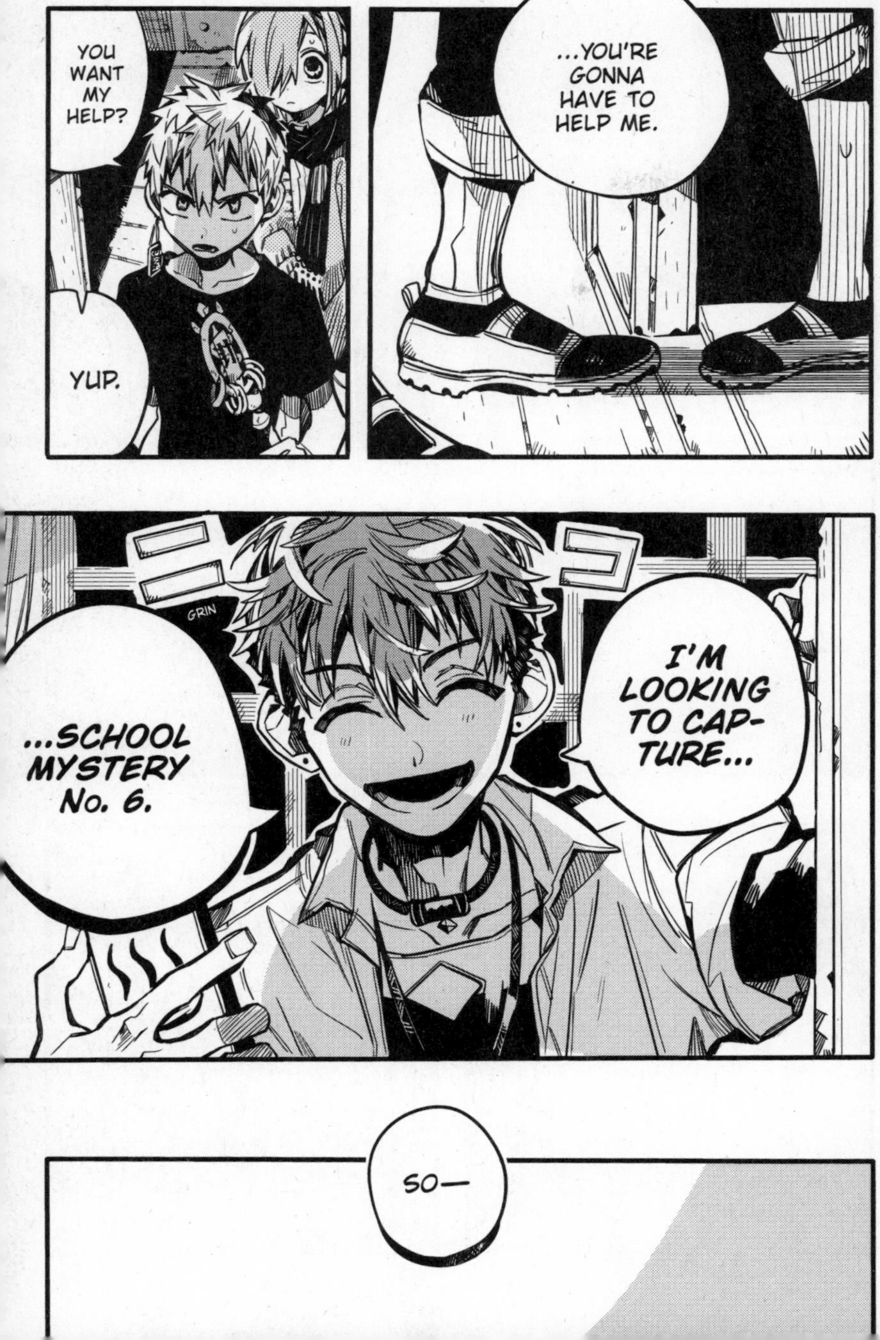
...YOU'RE GONNA HAVE TO HELP ME.
YOU WANT MY HELP?
YUP.
I'M LOOKING TO CAP-TURE...
GRIN
...SCHOOL MYSTERY No. 6.
SO—

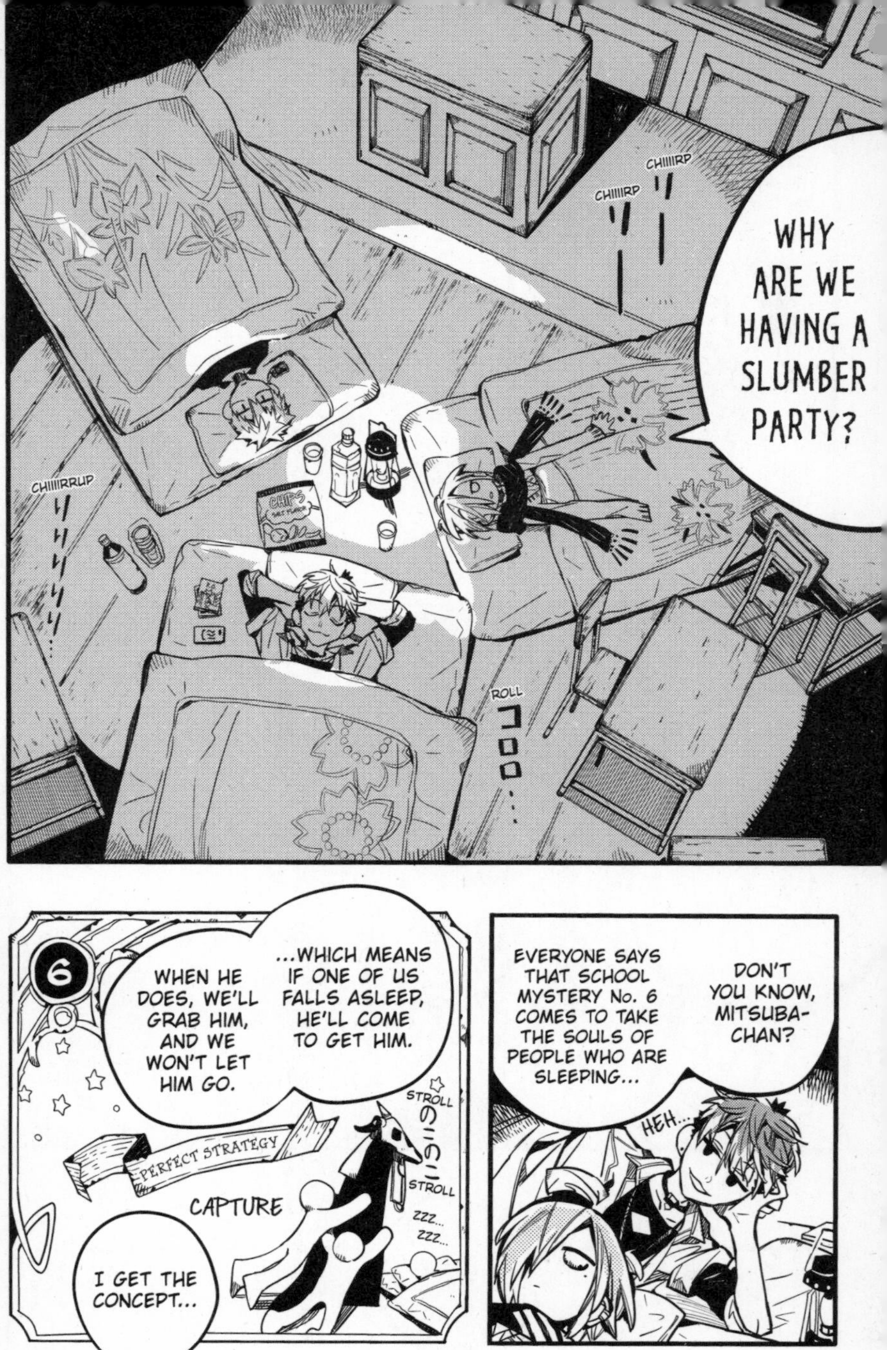
WHY ARE WE HAVING A SLUMBER PARTY?
CHIIIIRP
CHIIIIRP
CHIIIIRRUP
ROLL
DON'T YOU KNOW, MITSUBA-CHAN?
EVERYONE SAYS THAT SCHOOL MYSTERY No. 6 COMES TO TAKE THE SOULS OF PEOPLE WHO ARE SLEEPING...
HEH...
6
...WHICH MEANS IF ONE OF US FALLS ASLEEP, HE'LL COME TO GET HIM.
WHEN HE DOES, WE'LL GRAB HIM, AND WE WON'T LET HIM GO.
STROLL
STROLL
PERFECT STRATEGY
CAPTURE
ZZZ... ZZZ...
I GET THE CONCEPT...

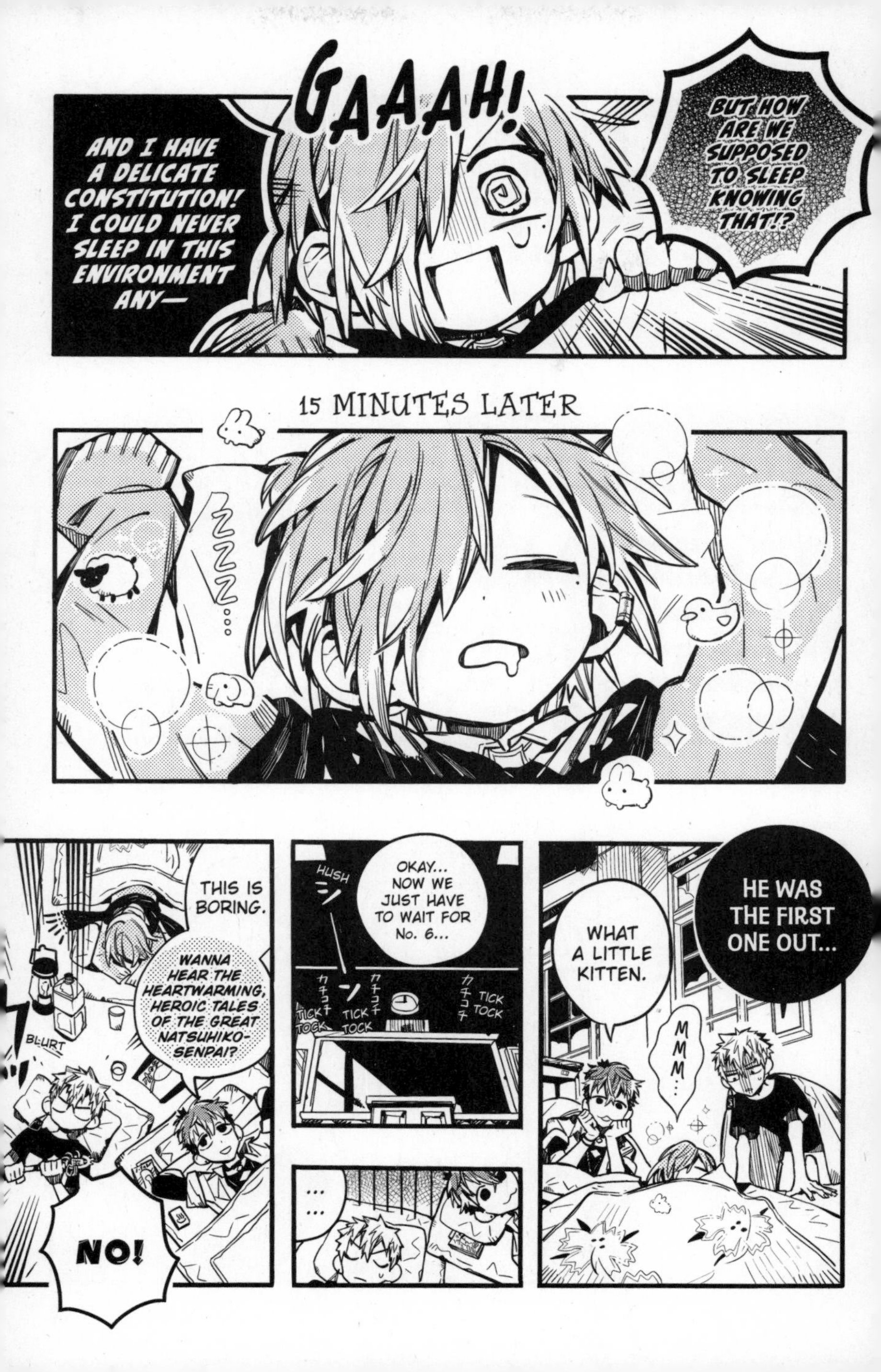
BUT HOW ARE WE SUPPOSED TO SLEEP KNOWING THAT!?
GAAAH!
AND I HAVE A DELICATE CONSTITUTION! I COULD NEVER SLEEP IN THIS ENVIRONMENT ANY—
15 MINUTES LATER
ZZZ...
HE WAS THE FIRST ONE OUT...
WHAT A LITTLE KITTEN.
MMM...
HUSH
OKAY... NOW WE JUST HAVE TO WAIT FOR No. 6...
カチコチ TICK TOCK
カチコチ TICK TOCK
カチコチ TICK TOCK
...
...
THIS IS BORING.
WANNA HEAR THE HEARTWARMING, HEROIC TALES OF THE GREAT NATSUHIKO-SENPAI?
BL-URT
NO!

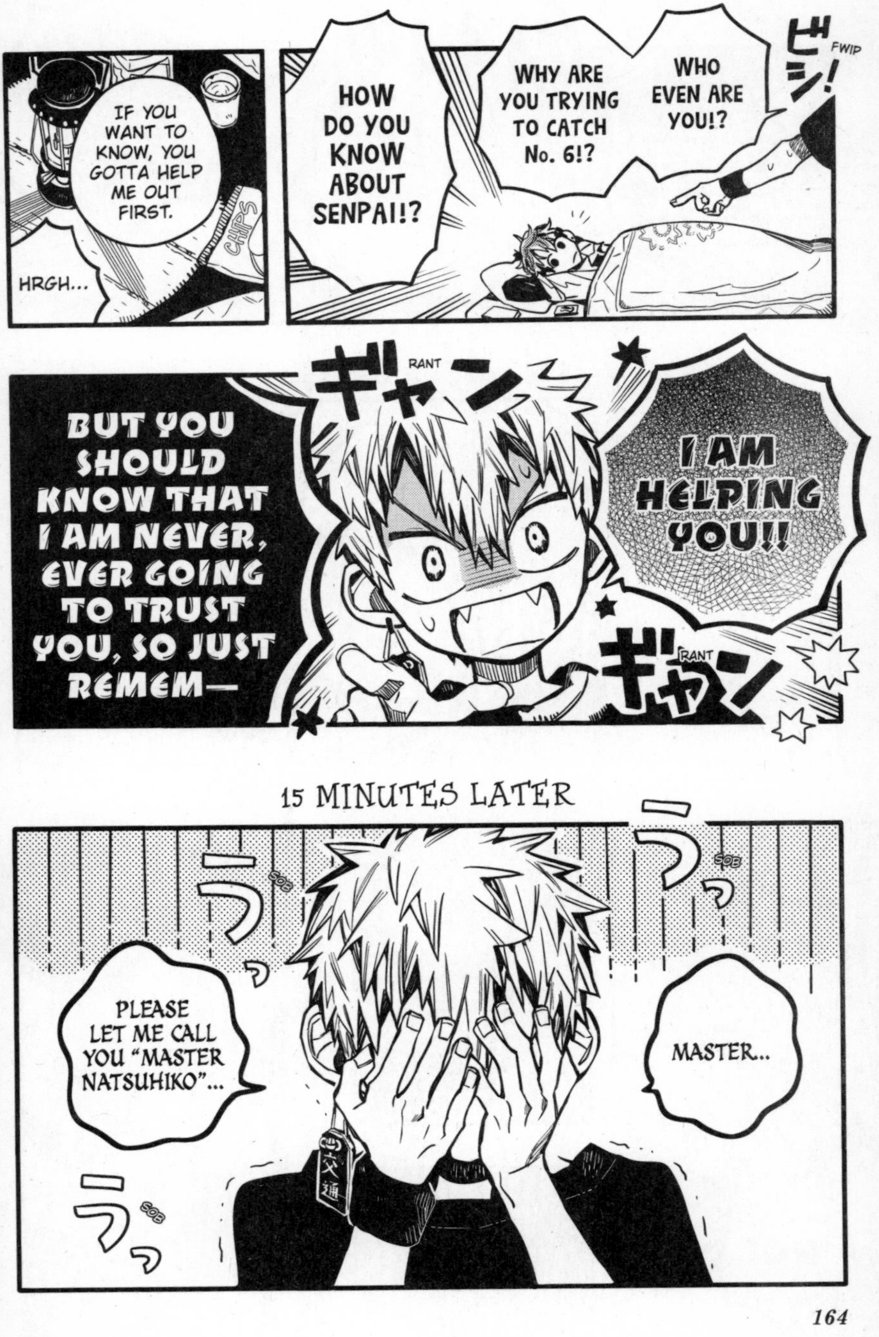
FWIP
WHO EVEN ARE YOU!?
WHY ARE YOU TRYING TO CATCH No. 6!?
HOW DO YOU KNOW ABOUT SENPAI!?
IF YOU WANT TO KNOW, YOU GOTTA HELP ME OUT FIRST.
HRGH...
RANT
I AM HELPING YOU!!
RANT
BUT YOU SHOULD KNOW THAT I AM NEVER, EVER GOING TO TRUST YOU, SO JUST REMEM—
15 MINUTES LATER
SOB
MASTER...
PLEASE LET ME CALL YOU "MASTER NATSUHIKO"...
SOB
SOB

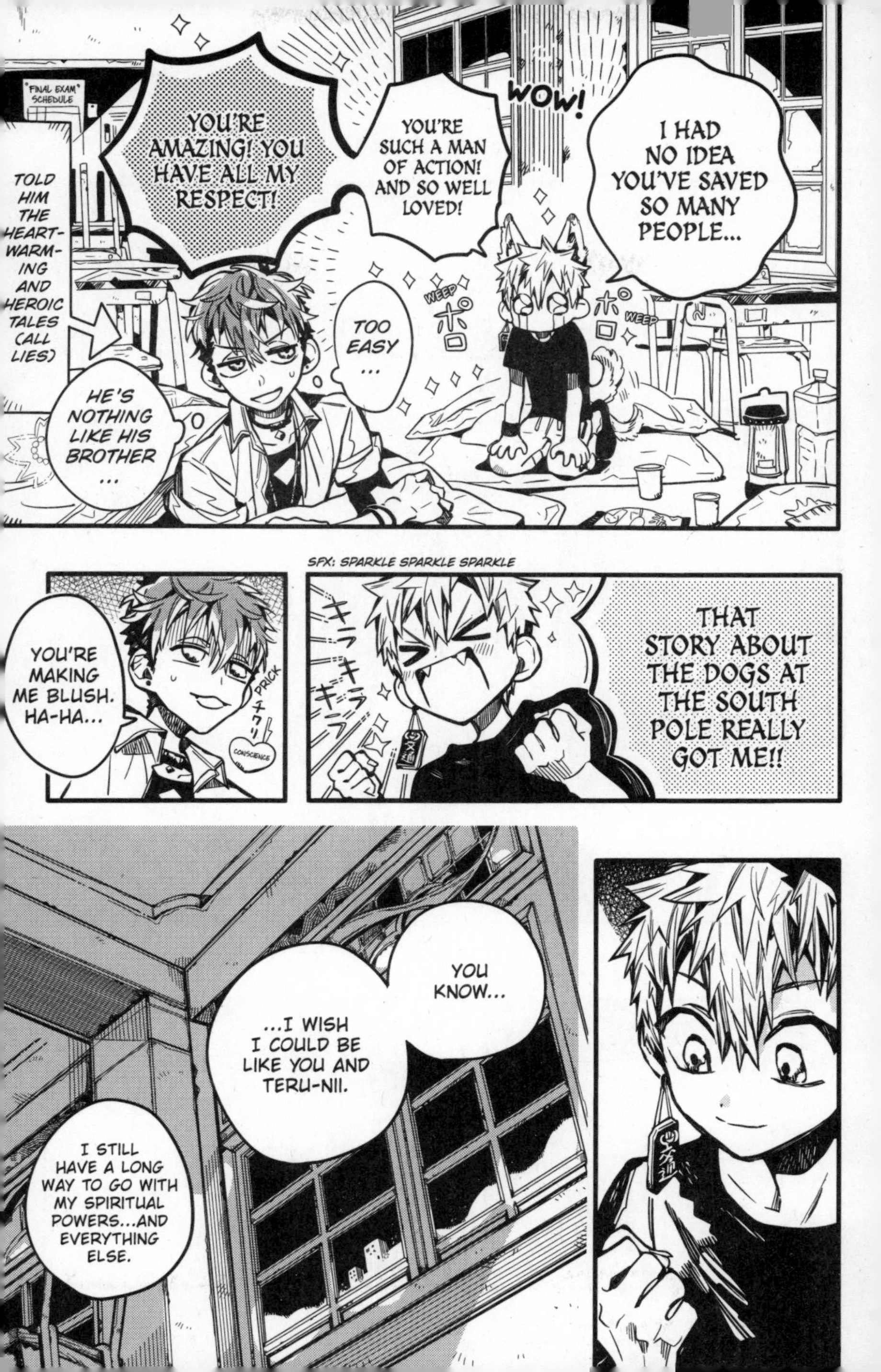
I HAD NO IDEA YOU'VE SAVED SO MANY PEOPLE...
WOW!
YOU'RE SUCH A MAN OF ACTION! AND SO WELL LOVED!
YOU'RE AMAZING! YOU HAVE ALL MY RESPECT!
"FINAL EXAM" SCHEDULE
WEEP
WEEP
TOO EASY...
TOLD HIM THE HEART-WARMING AND HEROIC TALES (ALL LIES)
HE'S NOTHING LIKE HIS BROTHER...
SFX: SPARKLE SPARKLE SPARKLE
THAT STORY ABOUT THE DOGS AT THE SOUTH POLE REALLY GOT ME!!
PRICK
CONSCIENCE
YOU'RE MAKING ME BLUSH. HA-HA...
YOU KNOW...
...I WISH I COULD BE LIKE YOU AND TERU-NII.
I STILL HAVE A LONG WAY TO GO WITH MY SPIRITUAL POWERS...AND EVERYTHING ELSE.

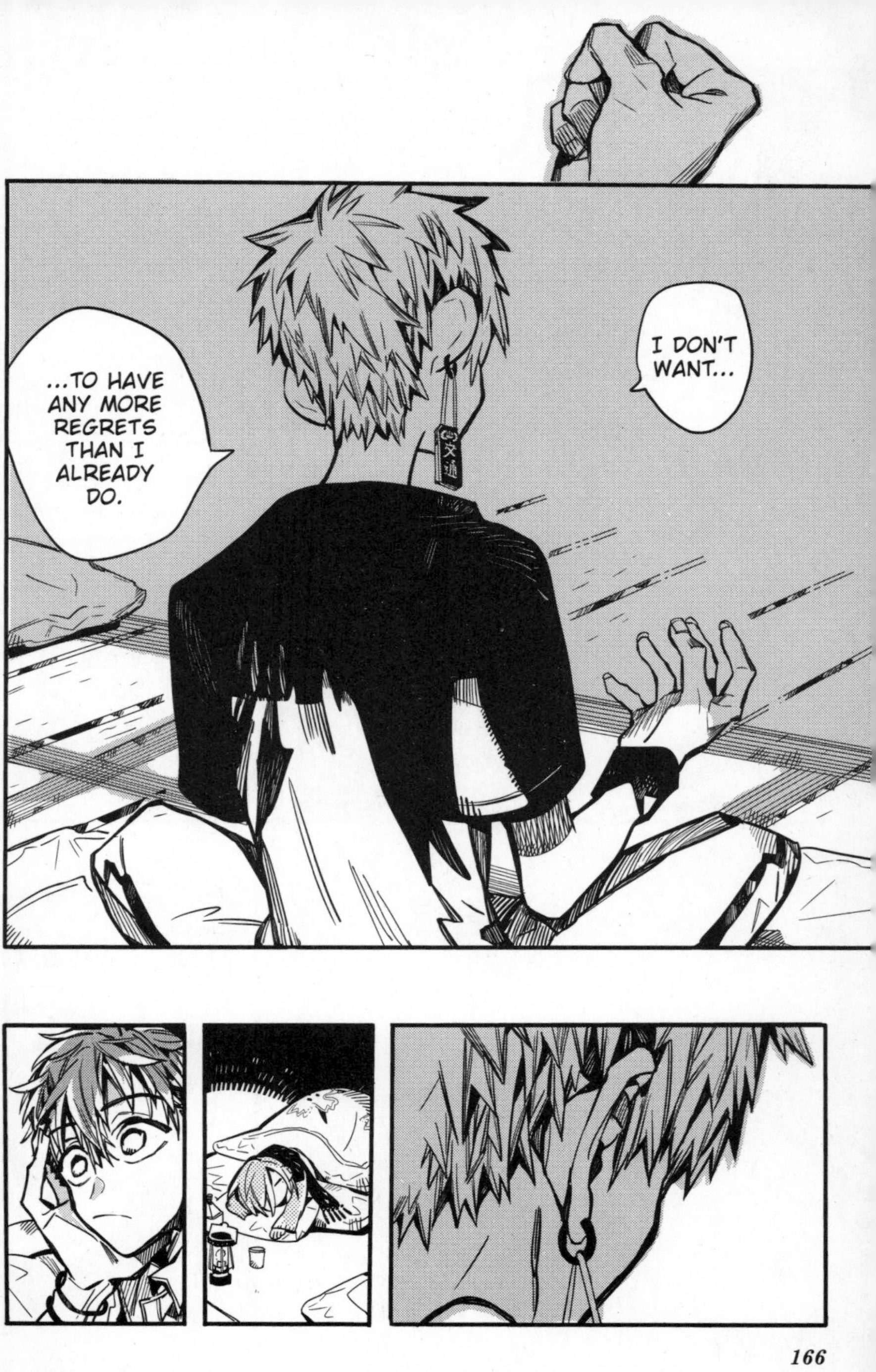
I DON'T WANT...
...TO HAVE ANY MORE REGRETS THAN I ALREADY DO.

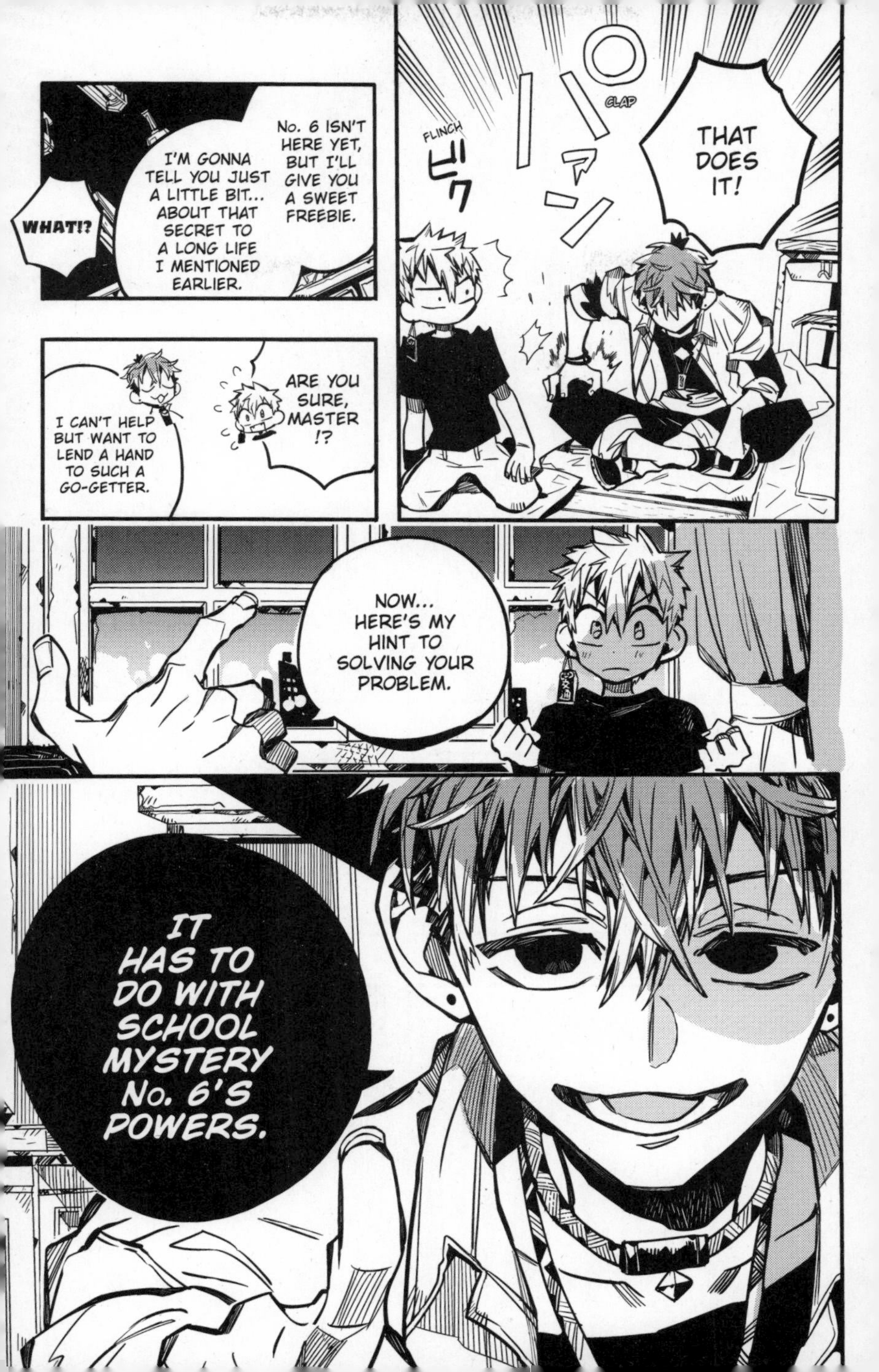
THAT DOES IT!
パァーン
CLAP
ビク
FLINCH
No. 6 ISN'T HERE YET, BUT I'LL GIVE YOU A SWEET FREEBIE.
I'M GONNA TELL YOU JUST A LITTLE BIT... ABOUT THAT SECRET TO A LONG LIFE I MENTIONED EARLIER.
WHAT!?
ARE YOU SURE, MASTER !?
I CAN'T HELP BUT WANT TO LEND A HAND TO SUCH A GO-GETTER.
NOW... HERE'S MY HINT TO SOLVING YOUR PROBLEM.
IT HAS TO DO WITH SCHOOL MYSTERY No. 6'S POWERS.

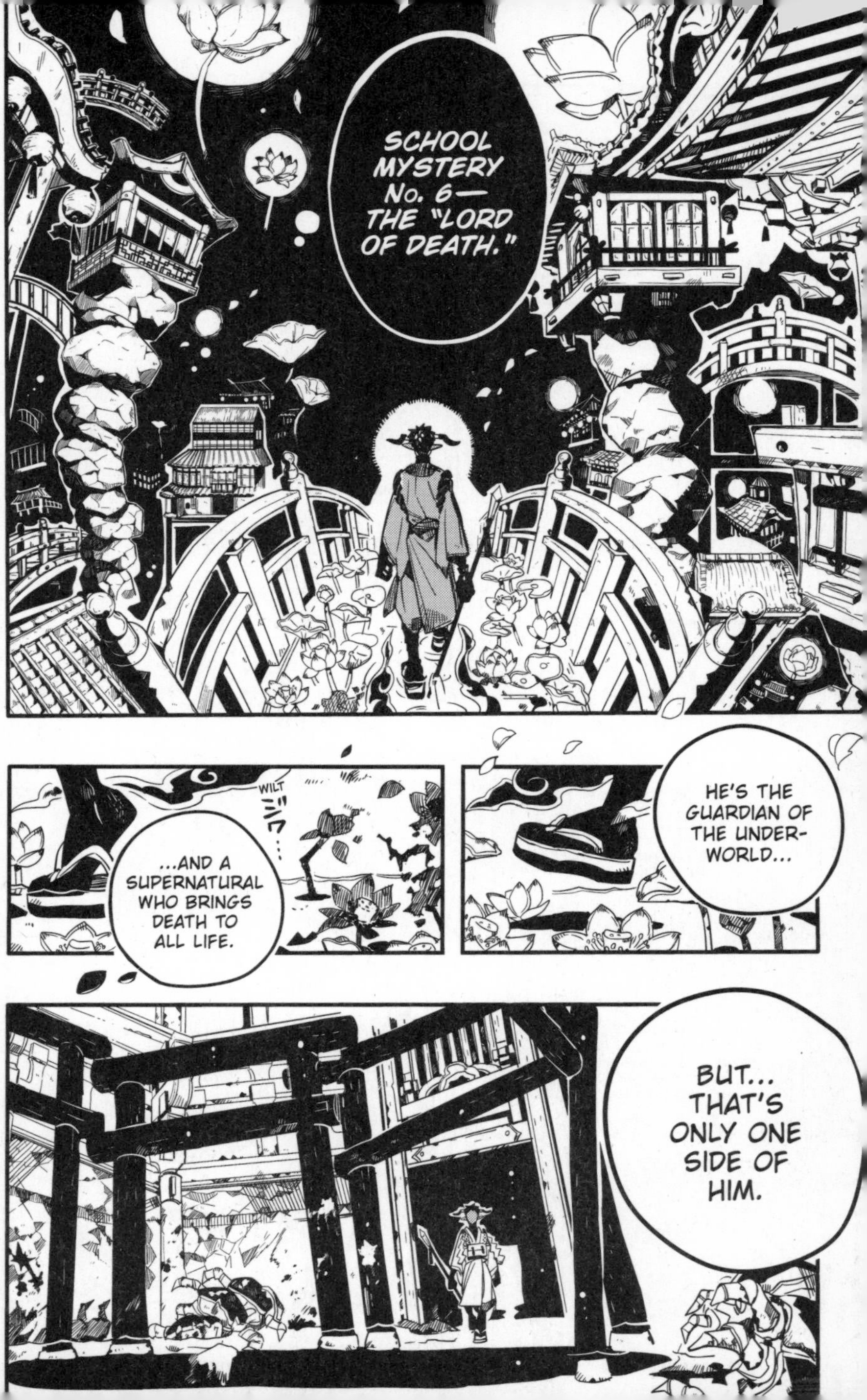
SCHOOL MYSTERY No. 6— THE "LORD OF DEATH."
HE'S THE GUARDIAN OF THE UNDER-WORLD...
WILT
...AND A SUPERNATURAL WHO BRINGS DEATH TO ALL LIFE.
BUT... THAT'S ONLY ONE SIDE OF HIM.

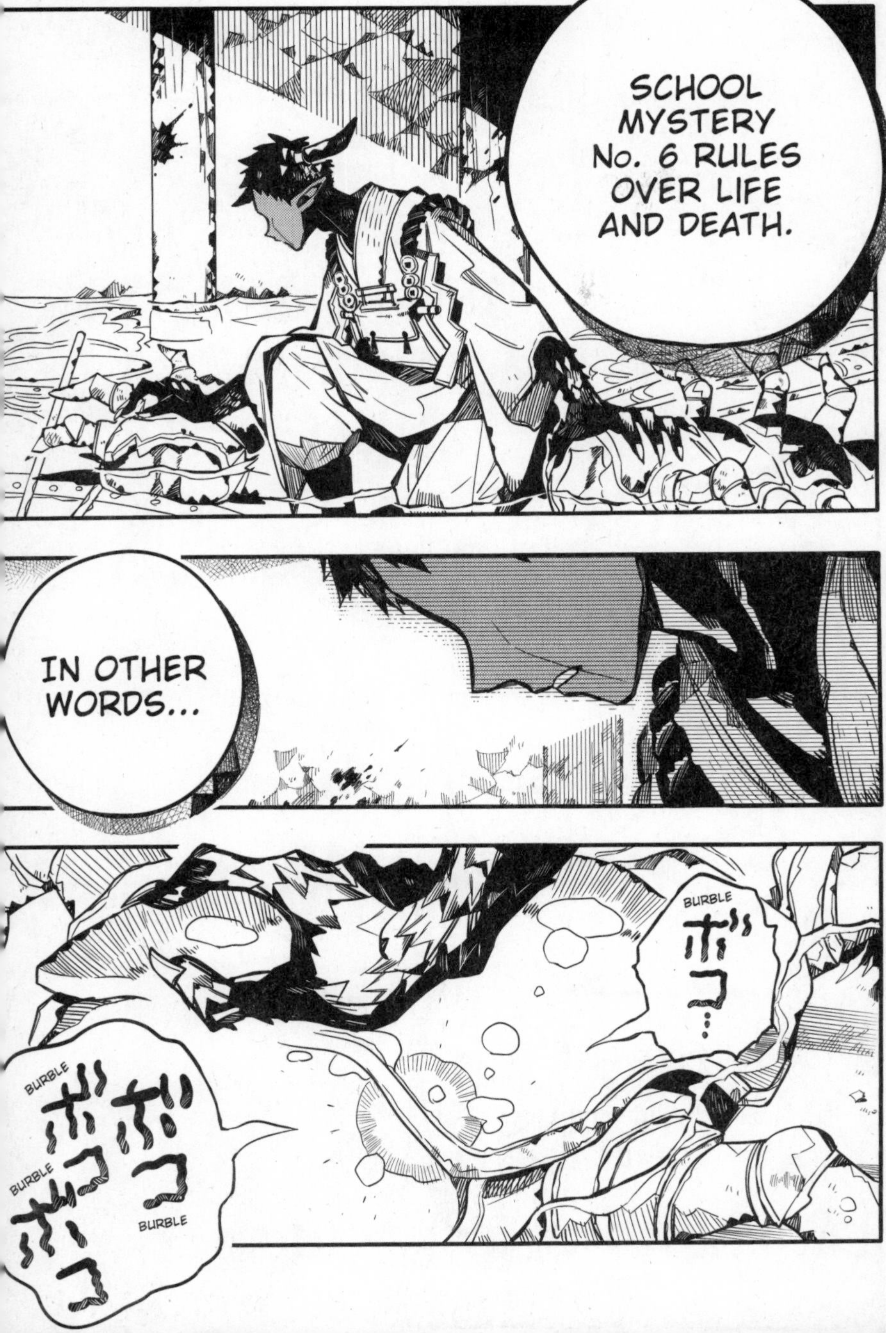
SCHOOL MYSTERY No. 6 RULES OVER LIFE AND DEATH.
IN OTHER WORDS...
BURBLE
ボコ…
BURBLE
BURBLE
BURBLE

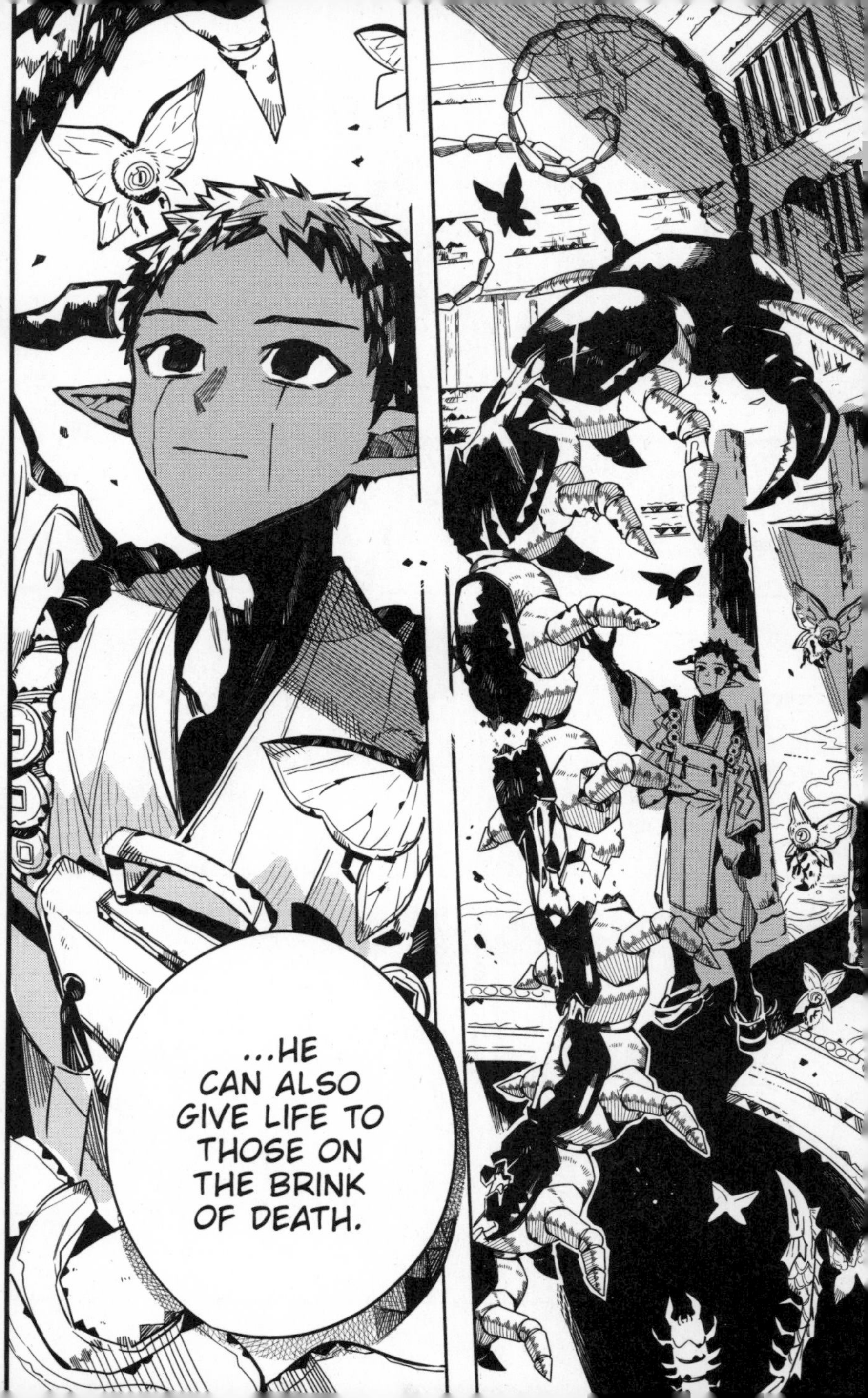
...HE CAN ALSO GIVE LIFE TO THOSE ON THE BRINK OF DEATH.

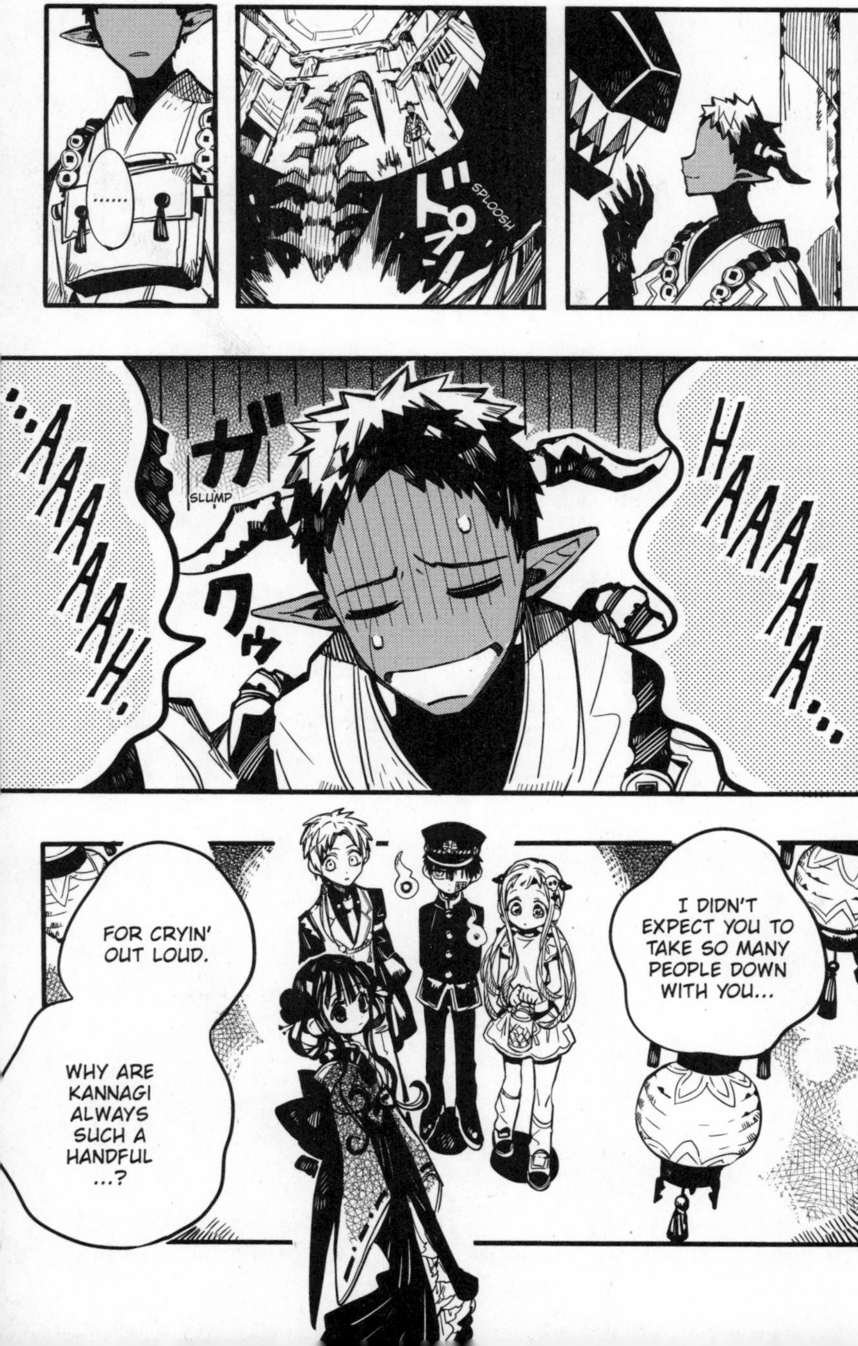
SPLOOSH
......
HAAAAAA...
...AAAAAAH.
SLUMP
I DIDN'T EXPECT YOU TO TAKE SO MANY PEOPLE DOWN WITH YOU...
FOR CRYIN' OUT LOUD.
WHY ARE KANNAGI ALWAYS SUCH A HANDFUL ...?

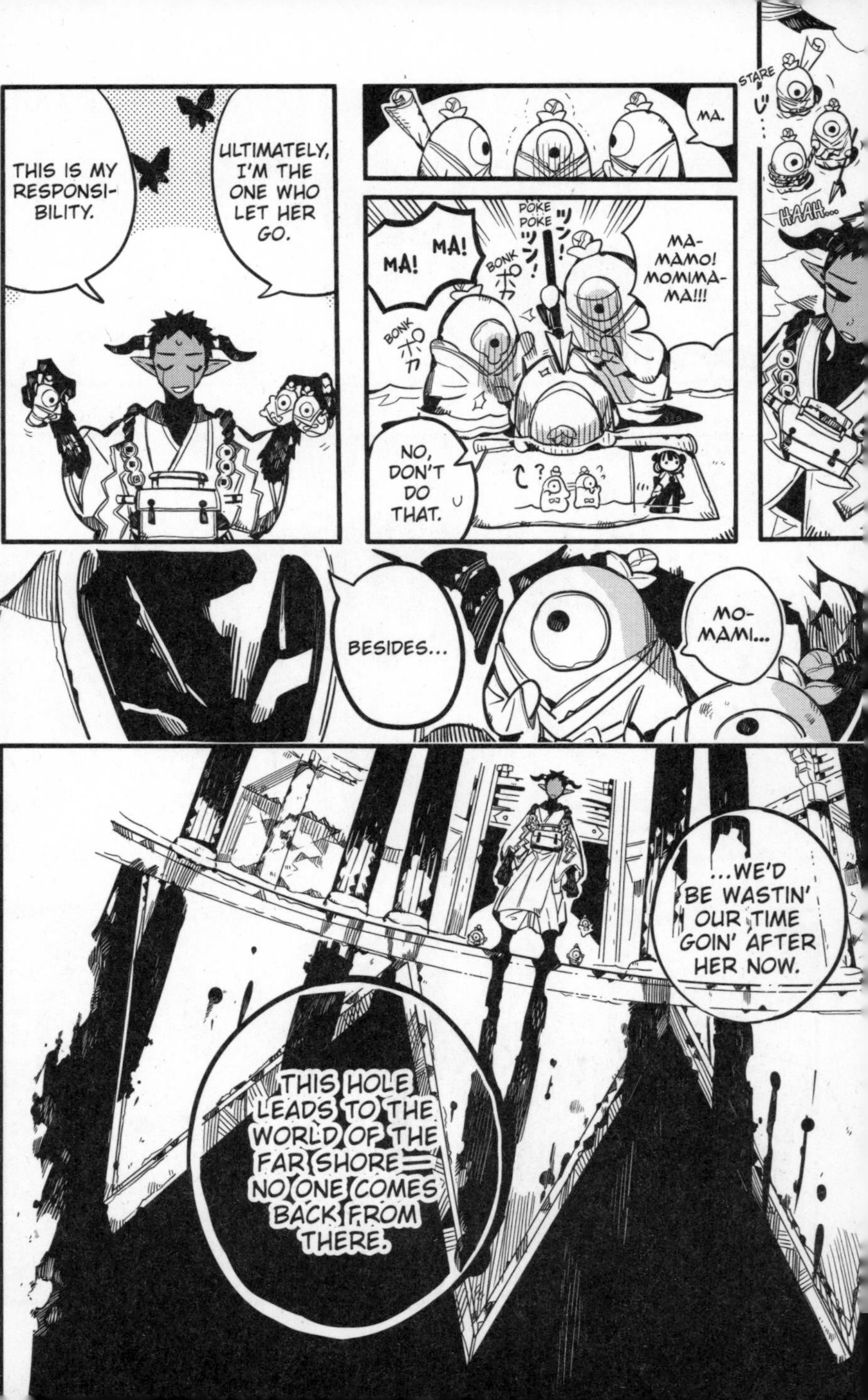
STARE
HAAH...
MA.
MA-MAMO! MOMIMAMA!!!
POKE POKE
ツン! ツン!
MA!
MA!
BONK
ポカ
BONK
ポカ
NO, DON'T DO THAT.
ULTIMATELY, I'M THE ONE WHO LET HER GO.
THIS IS MY RESPONSIBILITY.
MO-MAMI...
BESIDES...
...WE'D BE WASTIN' OUR TIME GOIN' AFTER HER NOW.
THIS HOLE LEADS TO THE WORLD OF THE FAR SHORE—NO ONE COMES BACK FROM THERE.

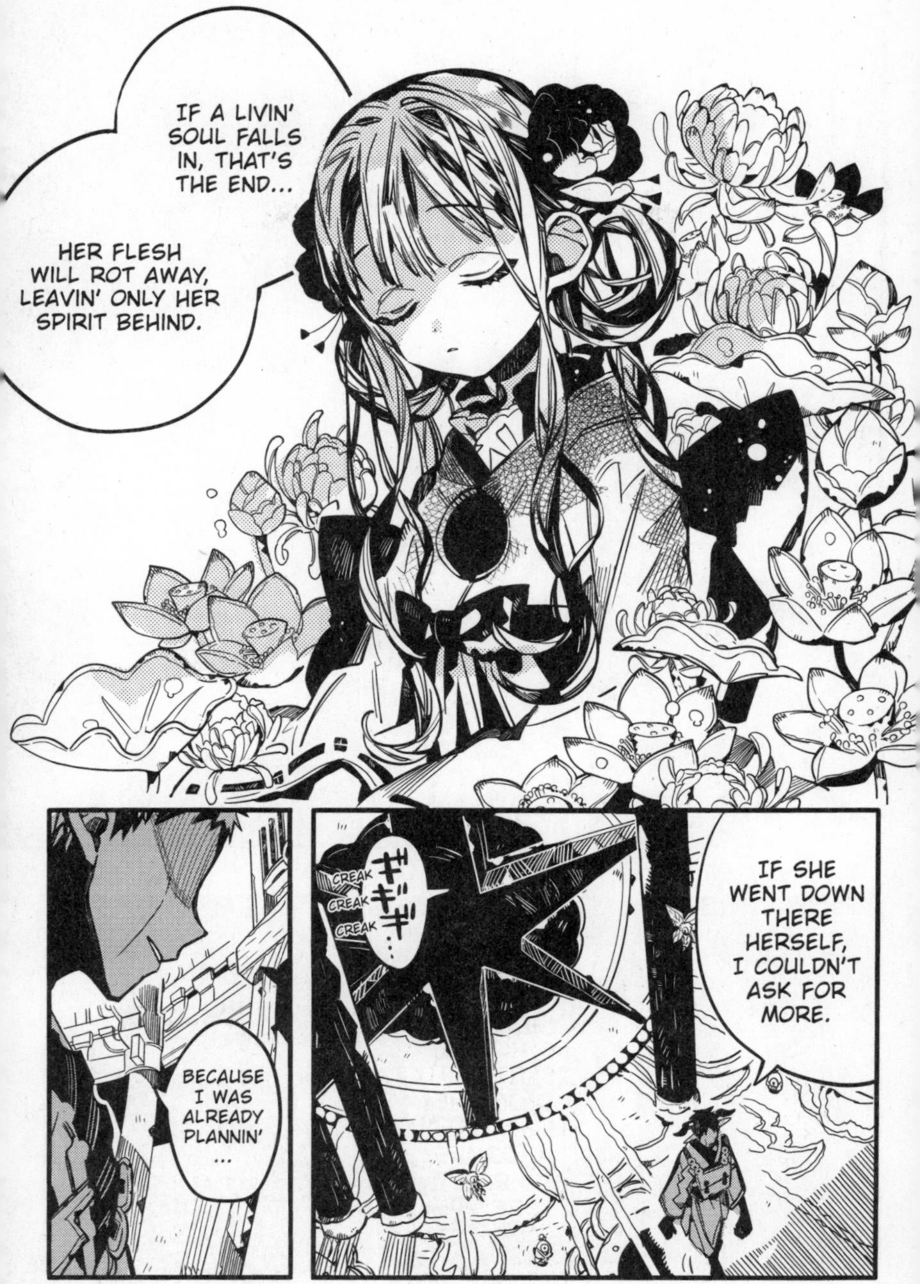
IF A LIVIN' SOUL FALLS IN, THAT'S THE END...
HER FLESH WILL ROT AWAY, LEAVIN' ONLY HER SPIRIT BEHIND.
IF SHE WENT DOWN THERE HERSELF, I COULDN'T ASK FOR MORE.
ギギギ…
CREAK CREAK CREAK
BECAUSE I WAS ALREADY PLANNIN' ...

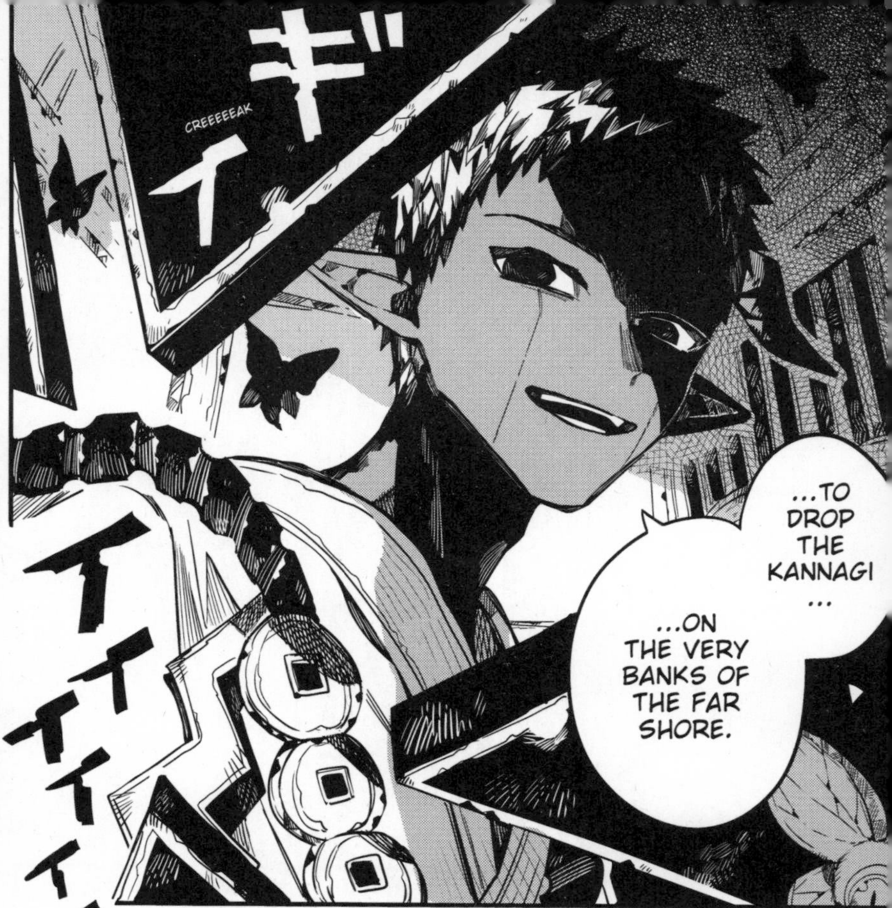
CREEEEEAK
...TO DROP THE KANNAGI ...
...ON THE VERY BANKS OF THE FAR SHORE.

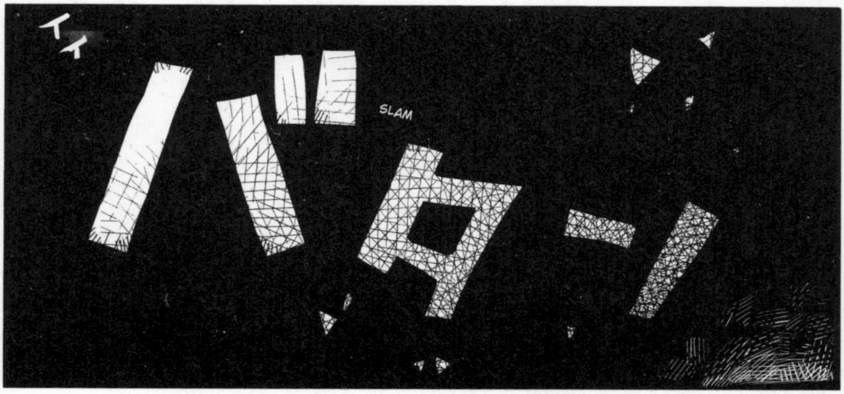
SLAM

TO BE CONTINUED IN TOILET-BOUND HANAKO-KUN 14!

TRANSLATION NOTES

Common Honorifics

no honorific: Indicates familiarity or closeness; if used without permission or reason, addressing someone in this manner would constitute an insult.

-san: The Japanese equivalent of Mr./Mrs./Miss. If a situation calls for politeness, this is the fail-safe honorific.

-sama: Conveys great respect; may also indicate that the social status of the speaker is lower than that of the addressee.

-kun: Used most often when referring to boys, this indicates affection or familiarity. Occasionally used by older men among their peers, but it may also be used by anyone referring to a person of lower standing.

-chan: An affectionate honorific indicating familiarity used mostly in reference to girls; also used in reference to cute persons or animals of either gender.

-senpai: A suffix used to address upperclassmen or more experienced coworkers.

-sensei: A respectful term for teachers, artists, or high-level professionals.

Page 9

As Tsuchigomori partly explains on page 33, Urabon is another, older name for Obon, the day when the spirits of the dead come to visit their graves, and the living throw giant festivals to welcome them. (Obon lasts for three days, but there is a regional variant known as "old Bon," specific to the same date as Urabon, so they seem to follow the same schedule.) *Ura* is also a homophone for "opposite" or "reverse," making this name well suited for a sort of "anti-Obon" for supernaturals.

Page 49–50

This is another counting song like the one in Volume 12. ("Four" is represented by the last three bubbles on page 49 all having four syllables in Japanese.) The song becomes even more ominous when the numbers are used to make homophonous words, translating roughly as "O mortal, open the box at the bottom of the sea. How long will we be trapped, together in this web...?"

Page 76

The sequence of button presses to reach No. 6's boundary, 4 2 6 2 10 5 1 6, contains a hidden message in Japanese. A few extra numbers have been added in to throw readers off the scent—6 and 10 are likely there to represent "60" (as the Japanese word for "sixty" is both written and read as "six-ten"), the elevator floor where No. Six's boundary is located, and the second 6 can be read as *mu*, a homophone for "nothing," implying that it is supposed to remain unsaid. The remaining digits, 4 2 2 5 1, can be read as *shi ni ni ko i*, which combines into the words *shini ni koi*, meaning "Come here to die," echoing No. 6's first question to Nene and Akane.

Page 85

"Whack-a-mole" is *itachigokko* (weasel game) in the original, an old children's game where one player pretends to be a weasel and pinches the back of the other player's hand, while the other player pretends to be a mouse and pinches them right back. Since this game is pointless and unwinnable, it came to be used as a metaphor for futile effort in the same way whack-a-mole has.

Page 144

Kou's tower reminds his friends of Sai-no-Kawara, the "Children's Limbo." In Japanese Buddhist tradition, children who cause their parents pain by dying before them must do penance by building stone altars on the bank of the Sanzu River (the border between this life and the next). Once a child completes their altar, they will have paid their debt, but before they can, demons knock down the tower, beat the child, and strip them naked. However, the bodhisattva Jizou can save the children by hiding them in the sleeves of his robe and giving them scraps of clothes, which is one of the reasons why you can find statues of Jizou covered in offerings of clothing all over Japan.

Page 165

Natsuhiko may have taken his inspiration for this story from the tale of Taro and Jiro, two sled dogs who miraculously survived an ill-fated Japanese expedition to the South Pole.

HANAKO-KUN MEETING

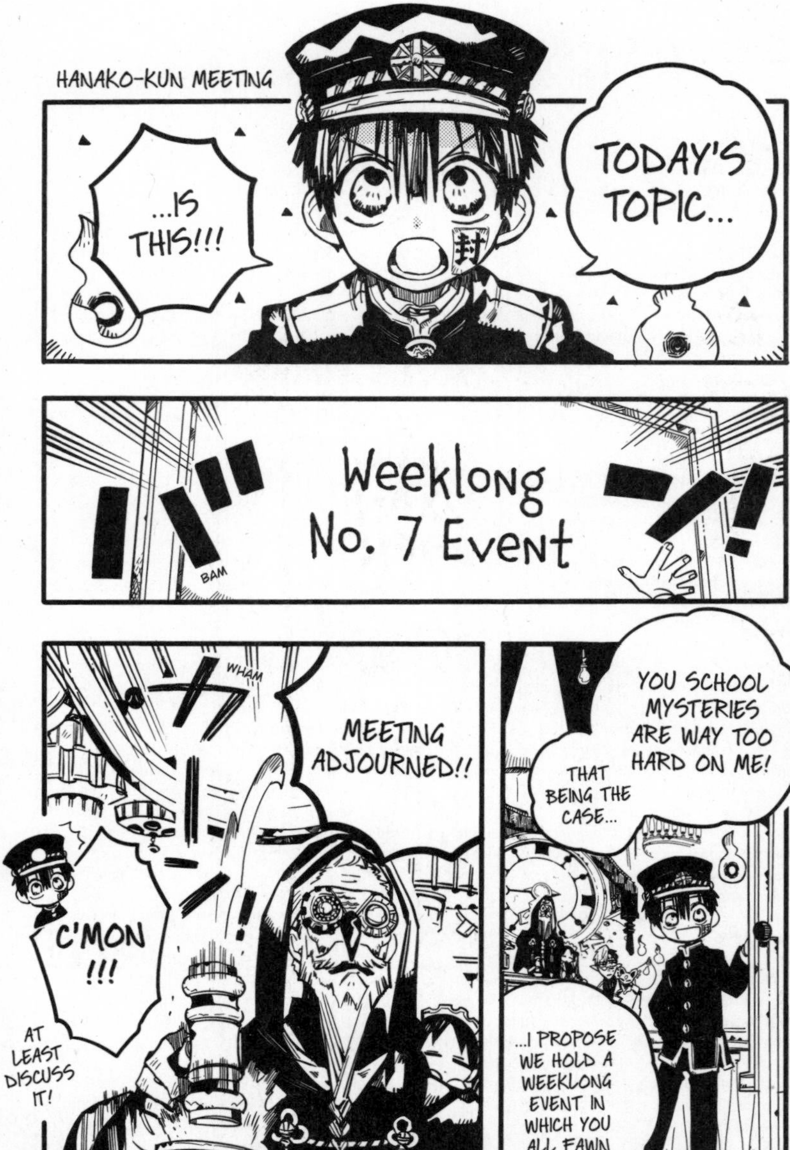
TODAY'S TOPIC...
...IS THIS!!!
BAM
Weeklong No. 7 Event
YOU SCHOOL MYSTERIES ARE WAY TOO HARD ON ME!
THAT BEING THE CASE...
...I PROPOSE WE HOLD A WEEKLONG EVENT IN WHICH YOU ALL FAWN OVER ME.
WHAM
MEETING ADJOURNED!!
C'MON !!!
AT LEAST DISCUSS IT!

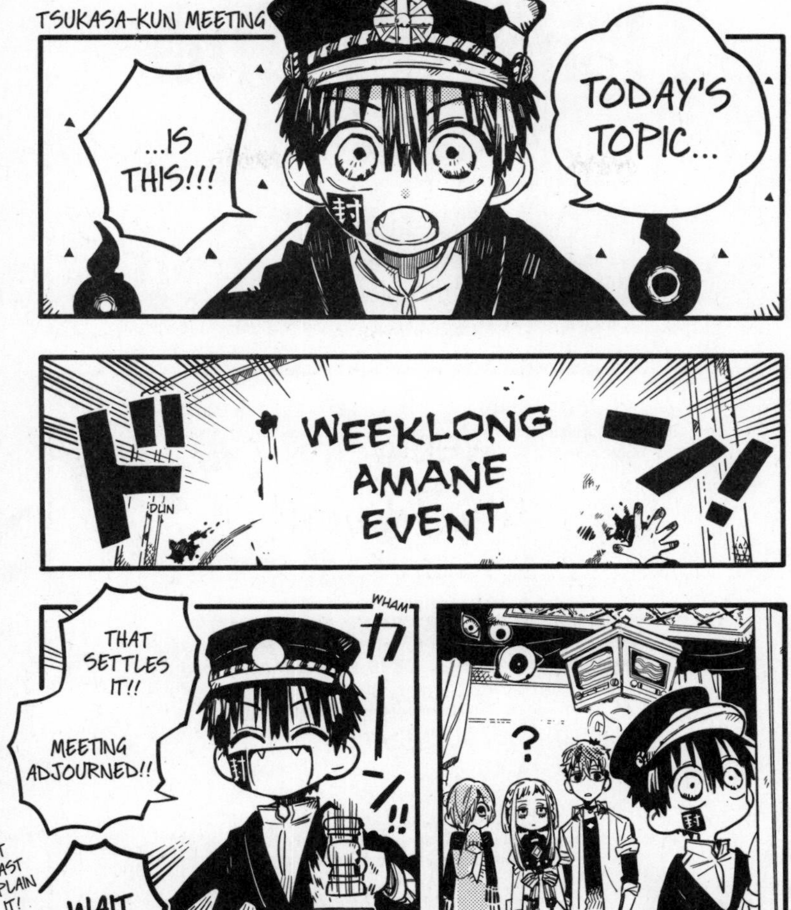
TSUKASA-KUN MEETING
TODAY'S TOPIC...
...IS THIS!!!
ドーン!
DUN
WEEKLONG AMANE EVENT
?
WHAM
THAT SETTLES IT!!
MEETING ADJOURNED!!
!!
WAIT!!!
AT LEAST EXPLAIN IT!

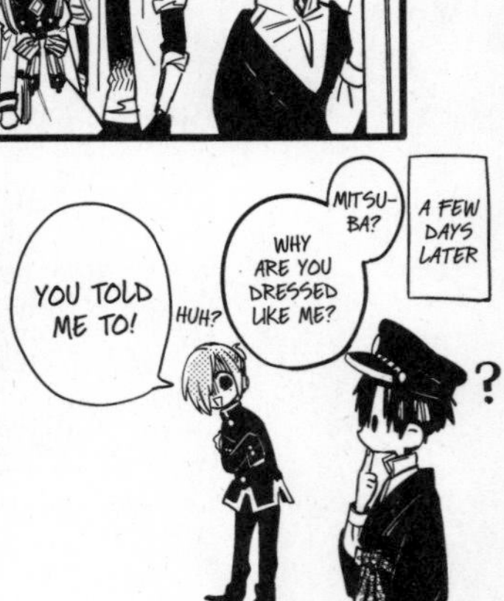
A FEW DAYS LATER
MITSU-BA?
WHY ARE YOU DRESSED LIKE ME?
HUH?
YOU TOLD ME TO!
?

SPECIAL THANKS

EKE-CHAN OMAYU-TAN YUUJI-CHAN

REYU-CHAN KURUMI-CHAN RUI-CHAN

MY EDITOR

IMANITY

AND YOU

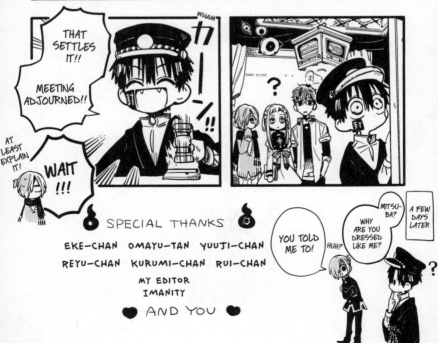

Toilet-bound Hanako-Kun 13

AidaIro

Translation: Alethea Nibley and Athena Nibley
Lettering: Kimberly Pham

JIBAKU SHONEN HANAKO-KUN Volume 13 ©2020 AidaIro / SQUARE ENIX CO., LTD.
First published in Japan in 2020 by SQUARE ENIX CO., LTD. English translation rights arranged with SQUARE ENIX CO., LTD. and Yen Press, LLC through Tuttle-Mori Agency, Inc.

English translation © 2022 by SQUARE ENIX CO., LTD.

Yen Press
150 West 30th Street, 19th Floor
New York, NY 10001

Visit us at yenpress.com • facebook.com/yenpress • twitter.com/yenpress • yenpress.tumblr.com • instagram.com/yenpress

First Yen Press Print Edition: March 2022
Originally published as an ebook in August 2020 by Yen Press.

Yen Press is an imprint of Yen Press, LLC.
The Yen Press name and logo are trademarks of Yen Press, LLC.

The publisher is not responsible for websites (or their content) that are not owned by the publisher.

Library of Congress Control Number: 2019953610

ISBN: 978-1-9753-1909-0 (paperback)

10 9 8 7 6 5 4 3 2 1

TPA

Printed in South Korea